JAN 2012

WHITE
TRUFFLES
IN WINTER

WHITE
TRUFFLES
IN WINTER

A NOVEL

N. M. KELBY

W. W. NORTON & COMPANY

New York · London

For information about permission to reproduce selections from this book,
write to Permissions, W. W. Norton & Company, Inc.,
500 Fifth Avenue, New York, NY 10110

For information about special discounts for bulk purchases, please contact
W. W. Norton Special Sales at specialsales@wwnorton.com or 800-233-4830

Manufacturing by Courier Westford
Book design by Chris Welch Design
Production manager: Julia Druskin

Library of Congress Cataloging-in-Publication Data

Kelby, N. M. (Nicole M.)
White truffles in winter : a novel / N. M. Kelby. — 1st ed.
p. cm.
ISBN 978-0-393-07999-9 (hardcover)
1. Escoffier, A. (Auguste), 1846–1935—Fiction. 2. Cooks—Fiction. 3. Monte-Carlo
(Monaco)—Fiction. 4. Cooking, French—Fiction. 5. Domestic fiction. I. Title.
PS3561.E382W48 2012
813'.54—dc22
2011029292

W. W. Norton & Company, Inc.
500 Fifth Avenue, New York, N.Y. 10110
www.wwnorton.com

W. W. Norton & Company Ltd.
Castle House, 75/76 Wells Street, London W1T 3QT

1 2 3 4 5 6 7 8 9 0

To Steven—always.

"The day is coming when a single carrot freshly observed
will set off a revolution."

—PAUL CÉZANNE

WHITE
TRUFFLES
IN WINTER

T HAT LAST SUMMER, THE KITCHEN REEKED OF PICKLING spice, anise seed and juniper berries. Watermelon jam, lavender jellies and crystalized fennel cooled on the pantry shelves. Jars with mango pickles and pickled onions, an old habit from his days in London, were set aside in the wine cellar to cure. Honeycombs were stacked in bowls on the sideboard, draining, waiting to be melted into candles or mixed with olive oil and pressed into soaps. Thunderstorms were canned along with plum jam. Memories seeped onto the pine floorboards. Tears turned to sweat.

Escoffier didn't notice. He was too busy writing his memoirs.

Lushness had returned to Monte Carlo and, surprisingly, to La Villa Fernand. Monte Carlo was an island of rock floating on the pristine blue waters of Côte d'Azur, leaning into Provence. Embroidered with bougainvillea-covered mansions and villas, it was a fortress, a magical confection, a surreal wedding cake topped with gilded casinos, hotels, and cafés that lit up the night, seemingly spun from sugar and wayward stars. La Villa Fernand, Escoffier's grand stone manor house, curved along its winding coast. Every evening, clouds crawled over the horizon and pushed the pink sun down into the blinding noise of blue that was the sea.

Quiet. Quiet, he would think, and keep writing.

At sunset, Madame Escoffier instructed the staff to pull back the curtains and throw open the windows to capture the night air. Black currant pies, tart and sweet, often warmed the cool evenings. The sound of crashing waves against the shore lulled the gaggles of grandchildren, great-grandchildren, grandnieces and grandnephews—their names now interchangeable to Madame and Monsieur Escoffier—to sleep in the evenings. And woke them in the mornings. The air swirled with the gales of laughter.

But it was all just noise to him. Made it difficult to think. Every morning Escoffier wished for evening to come again; the only time he could concentrate was when the house finally fell silent.

In that final year, every triumph was hard won. The first of May had brought an unseasonable heat; waterspouts spun like ballroom dancers across the brilliant sea but never touched ground. Fruit withered on the vine. When the rains finally came, the earth cracked open and drank them whole.

Madame Escoffier found herself dreaming of the first days of their marriage.

"Close your eyes," he had said to her. "Food demands complete submission." And then he placed a perfect scallop in her mouth. "Do you taste the sea?"

Delphine did. Not just the salt of the sea but the very air of the moment that the shell was pulled from the sand. "A storm, perhaps. There is a dark edge to the sweetness of the meat. What do you taste?"

"The hand of God."

That was not surprising. He was, after all, a devout Catholic.

Before Delphine married Escoffier, food was bothersome. A piece of toast, an egg, a handful of greens—it made no difference to her. All she wanted was to write her poetry and be exempt from the foolishness of the world. Love, motherhood, marriage—they all filled her with disdain. "A woman only needs herself to survive."

Her father, apparently, had other ideas. Or, at least, that was to be assumed. He used her hand in marriage as a stake during his weekly billiards game.

"You 'lost' me?"

"Escoffier played as a man possessed by love," Paul Daffis told his daughter.

It seemed impossible. Her father was a very good billiards player. For a moment, Delphine thought she'd misheard him. He rarely lost this weekly game and when he did, he always complained that Escoffier had an unfair advantage. "He never has to bend over to sight the cue!"

It was unkind, but accurate. Escoffier was an exceedingly small man.

"Is this some sort of a joke?" she asked.

"It is the perfect love story, is it not?" her father said, hoping for forgiveness.

It was not. Delphine had only met Escoffier a handful of times and always in the company of her father. They were nearly strangers.

"How could this happen?"

"It was quite simple. He said, 'Today I shall win.' And I said, 'What will you bet?' and he said, 'Anything you want for the hand of your daughter in marriage.' "

"I don't understand."

"I have to admit that I was very partial to the idea of Escoffier's bet. He's such a very talented chef. How could I refuse? A weekly dinner from him would have been heaven."

"I truly don't understand."

But she did. It was obvious. Delphine was not unattractive. She had a sturdy beauty with a straightforwardness that suggested an adventurous spirit—and yet her prospects for marriage had been slim. "Too independent," her father told her, even though he admired the spirit in her. She was, after all, a respected poet and writer. Her independence was what made her successful, fearless even, and yet in the nineteenth century fearlessness was not a desired trait in a wife.

And so Paul Daffis had no choice but to marry off his eldest daughter any way he could. A publisher of antiquities, he was in a business that lacked "vigor," as he often told Escoffier. Paul had no sons—just two little girls, who he called his "surprises," as both were less than three years of age, and Delphine. If something happened to him, his family would be left destitute. Delphine needed a successful husband and Escoffier was certainly that. He was thirty-four years old: older than Delphine, but not too much older. For many years, he'd served as the *chef de cuisine* at Le Petit Moulin Rouge—which, Escoffier was quick to point out, was not associated in any way with the risqué Moulin Rouge cabaret in Montmartre but was a very respectable post at an exquisitely famous restaurant.

It was, however, only open during the summer months, and so he also owned a small grocery store and restaurant in Cannes that he operated during the winter tourist season.

Industrious, hardworking and successful—Escoffier seemed to be everything a father could hope for for his daughter. The fact that he was slight and delicate-boned as a small child was unsettling to Paul, but he understood his friend to be driven to succeed. Escoffier was the kind of man who would provide well for his daughter and that was all Paul needed to know—at least that's what he told himself—and so he took Delphine into his arms and said, "You must trust me. He is an artist in the kitchen. And you are an artist with words. You will be happy."

She could hear the question in his voice.

He whispered, "He is my friend. I love him as if he were my own son."

She had no choice.

The next day Escoffier came to claim his bride. Delphine sat on the settee in the parlor, surrounded by trunks and hat boxes. When he came into the room, she did not speak or move but looked at him as if she'd never seen him before. He was pale and nervous, seemingly as uncomfortable as Delphine herself. But he was not unattractive and appeared well groomed for a cook—that was what he was to her at the time, a laborer. He was, however, impeccably dressed in a cuffed shirt that was stiffly pressed, an extremely expensive dress coat—a Louis-Philippe—and knife-pleated trousers. His dark mustache was manicured and well oiled. He smelled of lavender water and talc. If he were not a cook, he would have been nearly perfect. But he, unfortunately, was a cook.

Delphine could not imagine living the rest of her life with this man. *He is so small,* she thought, *more like a young boy.*

Escoffier seemed to hear her thoughts. His face reddened. He spoke without looking at her, focused on the array of belongings at her feet. "I cannot make you love me," he said. "Nor do I expect it. I am not unaware that I am a man who is compromised by nature but yet I think that you may find my heart to be most agreeable."

They sat for a moment, at a loss for words. Behind the parlor door, Delphine could hear her mother, father and baby sisters whispering. When her father cleared his throat, as if to prompt her into speech, Delphine closed her eyes and said, "I have been told that love eventually comes."

Behind the door, her father popped the cork on the champagne. The bottle overflowed. The effusive wine spilled onto the floor, slipped under the door and puddled at Delphine's feet. The sight of it made her weep.

The early days of their marriage were spent in the kitchen of Faisan

Doré, the Golden Pheasant, Escoffier's café in Cannes. There was no time for a honeymoon; winter season was less than a week away. "A menu must be created," he had told her as they boarded the overnight train.

The next morning, Escoffier made coffee and left the apartment before sunrise. "Join me," a note said. When Delphine finally woke, she dressed carefully and walked down the street to take her place at a long kitchen table that Escoffier had set for her alone. There were fine linens and silver, just as in the dining room, and a series of crystal glasses for both water and wine. He placed a fresh bouquet of red roses in a blue Chinese vase.

She had never been in a restaurant kitchen before. It was surprisingly clean and orderly with large windows to let in the light. It was not what she expected at all.

As soon as she sat down, Escoffier began to lecture her as if she were a student.

"Kitchens," he explained, "need organization, and so I have created a system, a concept that I am working on, a hierarchy, a ranking, a *brigade de cuisine*. Instead of making a cook frantically try to prepare each element on a plate, I have divided the kitchen into certain areas, each run by a *chef de partie*. A plate is moved from chef to chef and assembled as it goes. Someday all kitchens will be run this way."

Delphine did not really care about how kitchens were run, or would be run, and yet the way he spoke of it, the passion he brought to the work, made it all seem very interesting. Her father had told her that Escoffier had been a cook in the army, and then a prisoner of war. And it was clear. He seemed to have a love of rank and systems that was common for military men. His overwhelming need for order spoke to her of a time lived in chaos.

"I have given this system an extreme amount of consideration and hope someday to perfect it."

"Professor, will there be an examination later?"

"There will be," he said and kissed her hand. Delphine blushed for the first time that day, although she was not a woman given to blushing. They had not yet shared a bed.

One by one, Escoffier's staff arrived. After a warm embrace and a series of questions about each man's family, of which Escoffier seemed to have intimate knowledge, they took their stations and work began. Chopping. Peeling. A suckling pig was butchered. A basket of fish filleted. Ducks were plucked and scalded. Everyone had a task.

"Do you not see how brilliant and yet simple this is? Each man is in charge of one element of the dish. When the plate is brought to *poissonier*, he places the fish on it and the *entremetier* adds the vegetable. Each element is given the finest care."

It's only a kitchen, she thought. *You're just making something to eat. Fuel for the body and mind. It's not poetry.*

But it was. As soon as the cooking began, Delphine could see that. Escoffier would create each dish while the men watched. They in turn would replicate several servings of it. The *brigade de cuisine* allowed the cooks to move like dancers; an orderly rhythm was soon established. The plate traveled from one hand to another. The men moved as verses moved; they built upon each other until the final conclusion.

Slowly, Delphine began to understand that each dish was created, not merely cooked as one would cook a slice of toast. Each had its own beauty and depth: its own poetry.

Course after course, the finished plates were passed among the chefs and sampled with care: small briny oysters from Corsica were nestled into a bed of pink rock salt; white asparagus were trimmed and served alongside a smoked duck salad; cream-fed pork was braised with pears and apples, and new potatoes were browned in duck fat and dusted with late summer truffles. Each dish was more amazing than the last.

After each tasting, the discussion of the chefs was lively. Each chef, no matter what his station was, offered suggestions. There was little praise.

Escoffier sat across from his new wife and studied Delphine very carefully while she ate. He seemed to weigh her response to each dish. It unnerved her.

"And this?" he would ask. The other chefs fell silent and waited for the verdict.

She wasn't exactly sure what he wanted her to say. "It's delicious," she said time and time again until finally Escoffier could bear those words no longer.

"No. It is not delicious. It has what I call 'deliciousness.' The fifth taste. Bitter, salty, sour, sweet and deliciousness. I tell people this and they think it is all in my mind but it is on your tongue and so deliciousness is there by design. Veal stock imparts it. Someday everyone will recognize this. But that is not what I am asking of you. Think of each plate as you would a poem. It is not enough to say that food is edible or that the words are properly spelled. Where in this alchemy is beauty? Where in this is the nature of the divine?"

"But it is only food, Auguste."

"Perhaps when someone else is the chef. But when I give you this plate, I give you the nourishment that you need to continue to live and yet I also change how you see the world. I offer you a creation that allows you to see a single fresh carrot in a way that you have never seen it before, in a way that bespeaks not only its beauty but the unexpected possibilities of roots buried in the earth—I make them sing. I give this carrot a new life, which, because you eat it, will give you life. It becomes part of your very skin, hair and teeth. And so, when you address the plate, you must ask yourself where in this beauty is the knowledge that there is a God? Where is evidence of His love?"

From that moment on, Delphine never thought of food in the same way.

"We will begin again," he said, and another round of courses was created, served, critiqued and refined.

Despite Escoffier's best efforts to create an elegant setting for Delphine, it was still a kitchen and the heat soon became oppressive. Only coal and coke could achieve the high temperatures necessary for the roasting and rapid finishing of dishes, and so the room was an inferno. The young bride had arrived wearing a proper bonnet, jacket, gloves and boots—but eventually the heat made her feel as if she herself were aflame. First hat, then gloves, jacket and vest—little by little, parts of her propriety were neatly folded and set aside. Her hair slipped from its combs.

After a time, the heat made everything in the kitchen seem heightened. The staff, sweating, moved with the rumble of storm clouds. The aroma of lamb grilling on the coals or wild strawberries pureed with fresh mint nearly made Delphine swoon with pleasure.

At the center of it all, Escoffier in his Louis-Philippe dress coat and striped trousers seemed calm, unmoved. While the others spun around him in their kitchen whites and toques, he never stopped teaching, answering her questions before she asked them.

"The tradition of the caps began with the master Marie-Antoine Carême. They keep your hair from burning and also designate your rank. Sauce cooks and bakers wear little more than a cap; the supervising chef, a small pleated toque; and the head chef balances a towering toque of starched white, the number of its pleats dependent on the number of ways he knows how to cook an egg. Everyone knows that he is the man in charge. His toque is the tallest of them all."

"But why do you not wear one?"

"I do. But, to be quite frank, the wearing of a toque is a demeaning practice. Most men only know a hundred ways to cook an egg, which is why there is a hundred-pleat limit. However, I know six hundred eighty-five, and so when I wear a toque I am forced to compromise. And that is unacceptable."

In that sea of white, in his formal clothes, Escoffier was the sun that everything revolved around. Searing. Chopping. Silent. He was focused beyond the moment. In his own kitchen, in control, he was more handsome than any man she had ever known. As the day wore on, Delphine's heart raced at the sight of him. The wave of his hair, his dark quick eyes, his pale skin: he was luminous. He wore tall plat-form shoes that allowed him to reach the stove and made him tower over everything, and yet he had a gentleness that Delphine had never seen in a man before.

Everyone called him "Papa." No matter what happened, Escoffier never would shout or lose his temper. Any time he seemed at the edge of anger, he pulled at his earlobe with a fist of his thumb and finger and rubbed his cheek, as if he were a tired child. Any disagreement was taken outside and settled in whispers. "In my kitchen, you are expected to be polite," he said. "Any other behavior is contrary to our practice. Here we approach cuisine as an art and cooking as a gentle-man's profession."

And it was true. Delphine soon learned that in Escoffier's kitchen manners were valued above all else. No cursing. No fistfights. No smok-ing. No drinking. In his kitchen, the endless wine that most provided for their cooks to keep them hydrated and happy was replaced by a spe-cial wheat drink that Escoffier had commissioned a physician to create.

"In most kitchens, heat, wine, knives and temperament of the chefs lead to violence. Violence does not sell plates."

And even simple things were different. The man who always shouted back the waiter's orders was not called "the barker," as he was in other kitchens but "the announcer"—and was forbidden to shout. The staff worked in whispers.

"Rush hour in the kitchen is not the time for a rush of words. Cooking is the most sacred of the arts and should be approached with the required reverence."

At the end of that first day, Escoffier shook the hand of each of his staff members. "Thank you, chef," he said to everyone, even the dishwasher.

"It's a matter of respect," he told Delphine. "They must all have the desire to replace me someday." And then he poured her a glass of Moët. He was not a drinker—"Medicinal purposes only," he said. Nor did he smoke. This pleased her.

"One last dish," he said. The sun was now setting. He lit the beeswax tapers, placed them in the silver candelabra, and set it on her table.

The dish was simple. Six large brown eggs, an ounce of sweet cream butter, and a *poêle*—"Americans charmingly call this a 'fraying-pan,' but since it is not frayed, I have no idea why"—that was the heart of it. Escoffier beat the eggs, but not too much. He then added a bit of salt and pepper and placed the pan on the barest of heat. With one quick movement, he stabbed a peeled garlic clove with the tip of a knife, and held it up as if it were a prize.

"Madame Escoffier," he said as if testing the sound of her new name, trying it on.

He glistened with a thin sheen of sweat—as did she. Her cotton blouse was damp, as were her skirt and stockings. Her long dark hair was thick and unruly. All she really wanted was a bath and a glass of water. And yet, when he said her name, all that was forgotten.

"Madame Escoffier, come here."

Blue flames hummed beneath the poêle. It was so quiet she could hear herself breathe.

"Delphine Daffis Escoffier," he said again. "It has such a lovely sound, does it not?"

Delphine stood at the edge of the chopping block, an arm's length away. The butter was beginning to melt. He held up the knife topped with the garlic clove. "This is my secret. I tell everyone that the eggs are made in a special silver pan and that is what gives them their perfect taste."

"Why not tell them it's garlic?"

"Garlic is peasant food. If they knew, it would scandalize."

"But it smells like garlic. They believe you?"

"Of course. I am, after all, Escoffier."

"And now I am, too."

"Yes," he said, pleased. "That is delightfully true."

And then he kissed her hand, slowly, finger by finger. He never looked away. She felt the heat of him. "Now," he said softly, "we will stir the butter with our secret and then let the eggs set for a moment and then stir again. Gently."

Then he corrected. "Well. You will stir the butter gently. I have cooked all day for you. It is your time to cook for me."

Delphine took a step back as if she were about to bolt from the room. "I don't cook. Not well, at least."

"Stir," he said. It was not a command, but an invitation.

"I can't."

He shook his head. "You can. I wanted you as my bride from the first moment I saw your eyes—fearless." He handed her the knife and she took it. She leaned across the chopping block and began to stir but each stroke was awkward—tentative and elliptical. She barely touched the butter at all.

"That won't do," he whispered and took her arm and gently pulled her closer to the pan, then stood directly behind her. "What do you smell?"

"Butter."

"At this point you should only smell cream with a slight edge of

garlic. When it smells like butter, it's beginning to brown. The flavor cannot develop with too much heat. Turn it down. Slow it down.
Some things cannot be rushed. Some things need a gentle hand."

He then put one hand over hers and held the knife with her. With
the other hand, he reached around her thin waist and poured the
beaten eggs slowly, a golden ribbon, into the center of the warm butter.

He was standing so close that she could feel the quickness of his
breath. She leaned into the heat of him. "Only a moment in the pan to
set and then continue to stir," he said softly. "The eggs cannot cook too
quickly or that will cause lumps to form—this is a thing that should
be avoided above all. So again, slow. Slow. Do you understand?"
She did.

They stood together like that for a long time—stirring, not speaking, just leaning into each other. There was no need for words.

When he finally stepped away, he hollowed out two brioches with a
quick turn of a knife and then chopped a fist of butter into a fine dice.
Delphine continued to stir, not looking at him, still feeling the heat
of him, until the eggs were creamy and smooth—and yet, still moist.

"Finis," he whispered, pulled back her hair, kissed her neck, and
took the pan away from the heat. He sprinkled in the chopped butter,
added cream, and with two turns of a spoon he slid the eggs into the
brioche cases and then placed them on china plates.

One taste. One kiss. She was lost.

The thought of that moment still made her blush.

Now, fifty-five years later, she must remind Escoffier of that night,
and all the rest, when he cooked for her alone, made love to her alone.
When he was hers and no one else's.

It was, after all, her last chance. She was dying, that much was
quite clear. And in all those years, Escoffier had never created a dish
for her. Kings, queens, emperors, dukes, duchesses, opera singers,
cardinals, diplomats, clowns, hairstyles (the pompadour having at

least two), American presidents, actresses (including so many for that Sarah Bernhardt that Delphine had lost count), painters, musicians, a housekeeper, patrons, characters from books, foreign countries, and a girl who sold flowers—even the last voyagers on the *Titanic* had been graced with a meal especially designed for that momentous and yet ultimately unfortunate journey. But Delphine was forgotten.

She knew that Escoffier could, with just a bit of cream or a shaving of truffle, allow her to live forever. Not many could remember the great diva Nellie Melba anymore. But when she performed *Lohengrin*, her soaring operatic voice greatly moved those at Covent Garden, including Escoffier. And so while the details of her performance are forgotten, as is the opera itself, nearly everyone in the world has had a variation on Peach Melba. Perhaps, unlike the original, it was not covered in a lace of spun sugar or served in a silver bowl resting on a block of ice sculpted to look like the wings of the mythical swans that appear in the opera's first act, but it still contained ripe peaches, vanilla ice cream, and a puree of sugared raspberry, and was most certainly called "Melba."

Madame Escoffier had asked him many times for a dish but he always refused.

"One should never attempt to define the sublime."

"You are afraid?"

"Of course."

She didn't believe it.

And so Delphine needed to convince Escoffier to create a dish for her. And, although she wasn't sure how, she would make that kitchen girl, that Sabine, help her.

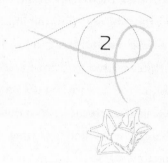

2

SABINE HAD NEVER SEEN A KITCHEN LIKE THE ONE AT La Villa Fernand. It was a nightmare. There was too much of everything everywhere. Forty wooden spoons stuffed into one drawer. Cake and butter molds in the shapes of rabbits, elephants, swans, crosses, trees, stars, moons, countless different variations of Saint Nicholas, several fleur-de-lis, and an assortment of lions and lambs. And there were molds for petit-fours, tarts, madeleine, brioche, *tartlett-croustade, dariole-baba,* parfait, charlotte, bombe, ice cream loaves, poundcake and *terrine à pate.* There were larding needles, salamanders, a cocotte and a conical, pyramid-shaped, of course. And there were so many multiples of potato ricers, mashers and whisks of every size and shape that they tumbled onto the countertop with the slightest provocation. Porcelain dishes and pottery bowls were stacked and stuffed into every available space along with boxes upon boxes of silver serving spoons, plates and bowls that Escoffier had bought at estate auctions for use at his restaurants. And—perfect or chipped, some matched and some not—there seemed to be enough dinnerware to feed several armies, and then some.

Each pot and pan, each tin, every spoon and plate—was part of the history of Escoffier's life and it was all gathering dust.

And to make matters worse, that last August, through some small miracle, tomatoes were abundant. Delphine directed Sabine to gather as many as she could find. "Pick them. Buy them. Steal them. I don't care," Delphine said. "We must be awash in tomatoes."

And they were. There were tomatoes in various shades and shapes from pink and squat to thin and red as chipped lacquer. They were piled in boxes on the floor, in the hallway, on the back stoop. Pearl or pear-shaped, green-tinged or overripe, they bled onto the white marble countertops where Sabine spent hours peeling, and cursing the eccentrics that she'd come to work for.

"What will you use them for?"

"Stories," Delphine said.

"Crazy people," Sabine said under her breath.

Sabine had only been with the Escoffier family for a week when Delphine's children had spoken to their mother about their concerns. She could understand their trepidation. Sabine was an insolent girl with wild red hair, willful eyes and a pronounced limp that Delphine decided was the reason that the father had forced the girl into service. He obviously thought that no one would marry such a defective young woman, no matter how beautiful she was—and she was beautiful— and so she would forever be passed from one housekeeping job to the next.

"My daughter is yours for however long she can be of service to you," the father said to Delphine. "And in turn, perhaps, Monsieur Escoffier could be so kind as to return a similar favor to me someday. Perhaps he could lend his expertise—and perhaps a bit of money. We could work arm in arm as he did with Monsieur Ritz. I am opening a new resort when the tides turn, have you heard?"

She had heard. Everyone in Monte Carlo had heard of this fool from Paris. He had no connections in town and knew no one. "When the tides turn"—it was ridiculous. The Great Depression of America had spread to every country in the world, even Monaco. The rich were no longer beautifully rich. They still flitted from New York to Paris to London to Cannes to Hollywood to Monte Carlo to Biarritz to Geneva—and back again. They still drank brandy milk punches for breakfast, martinis before lunch and dinner, and champagne with all meals. They still cheered at the Automobile Club de Monaco's Grand Prix; bet fortunes on Algerians, French and Americans in Bugattis, Ferraris and anything painted British Racing Green. But no one cared anymore. All talk was of war.

When the tides turn. The man was a fool. War seeped into every room, every dream.

Normally, Delphine would have refused such an offer. Forcing a girl into service was against everything that she believed in, and yet she took Sabine into her home. She felt a certain kinship with the girl. After all, Delphine's own father had also deemed her unsuitable for marriage. But the real truth of the matter was more complicated than that.

Sabine bore an uncanny resemblance to the actress Sarah Bernhardt.

"Tell me your name again?"

Even her voice had that silver tone, like the sound of a flute, for which Sarah was famous. For a moment, Delphine wondered if the morphine had finally taken hold of her brain. She felt anxious, euphoric. Sarah had been dead a long time, thirteen years or more, but there she was. Or at least, appeared to be. And there was that old ache, the jealousy, but oddly enough, there was comfort, too. To see this girl, so much like Sarah in her prime, so alive, it was as if Delphine and Escoffier were young again. And Sarah, of course, was Sarah.

Delphine could not help but feel an odd tenderness for her.

Unfortunately, as a cook, the girl was useless. Everything had to be explained over and over again. If Delphine had not been confined to a wheelchair, she would be cooking herself. Her daughter-in-law Rita, Daniel's widow, and all the nieces could not even properly roast a game hen among them. Germaine, her own daughter, was too intimidated to raise a spoon in any kitchen. And Jeanne, her son Paul's wife, was only interested in making preserves and pickles, and then only with Escoffier. Besides, they lived in Paris, near Place de l'Étoile, and only visited when Delphine or Escoffier took a turn for the worse.

And so the house needed a cook, but what they had was Sabine.

And now the girl was making a disaster of the tomatoes. Delphine was at the end of her patience.

"You know if you place the tomatoes in hot water, the skin will crack, making them easier to peel. The skin will just slip off."

"I know that."

"Then why aren't you doing it?"

"Hot water makes the kitchen hotter."

"Peeling them wastes the meat."

"A hot kitchen makes me dizzy."

Useless.

Sabine kicked a box of tomatoes with the toe of her boot.

"How can you cook stories with tomato sauce? It makes no sense."

When it came to Sabine, patience was required.

Delphine wanted to explain that stories engage the heart and mind and palate and make the simplest dish the most lavish of all because a well-told story, true or not, reminds you that, yes, the world is an exotic and magical place, and yes, it can be yours for a price. Enchantment always has a price—and sometimes the cost is love. But Sabine wiped tomato juice from her cheek and said,

"The children cannot eat stories."

It was true, of course. There were so many mouths to feed and so little money. Escoffier was famous, but broke. He'd lost every fortune he'd ever made. His pension was laughable, a dollar a day. The Great War had devastated his vast investment in Russian bonds, his house was mortgaged to the limit and his new book, *Ma Cuisine*, was not selling at all. But it didn't matter. All the canned goods, and now the tomatoes, were for him. They were Delphine's last gift.

And so what she wanted to say to Sabine was, "The story, and how you tell it, is life itself."

But what she said was, "Sabine, it is time to gather Monsieur Escoffier."

The sullen cook limped away like an ocean liner in high seas.

It was some time before Escoffier appeared in the kitchen. His heart was not well; it leaked a bit. His hands were shaking. He sometimes walked with an odd gait, a drag-and-slide movement that was difficult for Delphine to watch.

"The girl said we were packing tomatoes now?" he said, and made his way across the room. He was dressed as always, ready for company. His black Louis-Philippe dress coat had grown slightly shiny with age; the cravat was faded; his shirt was worn thin, the cuffs frayed.

Time worries us like a stone, Delphine thought.

The cook followed closely behind. "Escoffier is here," Sabine said, as if Delphine could not see her own husband in front of her.

Just one slap, Delphine thought. "Sabine. The bottles from the wine cellar. Please fetch them."

"All of them?"

Perhaps two slaps.

"Yes."

The girl stormed away. Lurching.

Delphine felt cruel and reckless. And helpless. *Too helpless.* There was a line of ants making its way toward the rotting fruit—*Slow and sure as vanity.*

"Ants," Escoffier said as he sat down next to Delphine's wheelchair. He was horribly winded. The mid-afternoon sun filled the room with heat and light. It made him seem more like a dream than flesh and blood.

He picked up a fat black ant and sniffed it. "We should dip these in chocolate."

"They're ants."

"They're black ants. You fold them right into the warm chocolate and it hardens around them and preserves them."

"Alive?"

"Yes. Entombed. They can live about three weeks."

"That's horrible."

"No. It's very good. They're very moist when you bite into them. Sometimes they still have a little fight in them, too." The ant was large and black, struggling in his hand. "Is there any chocolate in the house? You really only can use black ants, and this size is just right. The red ants are too spicy."

The sun was in his eyes. He was squinting to see her. His hands were stained with ink. His skin smelled of acid and sweat.

"That's barbaric."

"Not at all. Two egg yolks, vanilla, butter—it's a very civilized recipe."

"You are making this up."

Outside the kitchen window, the children were playing a raucous game of leap sheep. Delphine could see them. They formed a single line, squatting, child after child. It trailed down the walk. Then one leapt over the back of another and then another and then another—squealing and laughing—and then tumbled onto the ground.

"You would eat the grandchildren if no one was watching."

He looked out the window. "I don't know how you can say such a thing. After all, they look rather gamey, don't they?"

The children were so loud that it took a moment for her to realize that Escoffier was still speaking.

"*Excusez-moi?*"

"I said I have now come to think of the new memoir as an annotated cookbook. My life dish by dish. Every chef around the world will want it. It will be an instant success."

A publisher's daughter, Delphine knew that most chefs had no money. The book that they wrote together, *Les Fleurs en Ciré*, Flowers in Wax, was beautiful, espousing the elegance of wax floral arrangements, but very expensive to produce. With so many illustrations, including a halftone portrait of Escoffier, and forty photo-engraved drawings, its last reissue sold well but showed little profit. With war on the horizon, this new book, like the others, would not bring in enough to pay even a month's bills.

"Are you sure you don't want to make chocolate-covered ants?" he said. "We can tell the children what they are after they have eaten them. The looks on their parents' faces could be great fun."

Delphine took his ink-stained hand and held it in hers.

"No. No ants. And no cooking books, either. You need to write about your famous clients, tell their secrets. That would sell. Everyone wants to know how the famous really lived and you are one of the few left who can tell them. You've already written so much about cooking, so many articles, a magazine even, and all those recipe books. *La Riz* and *La Morue?* Who needs cookbooks about rice and cod? *Ma Cuisine*, for home cooking, was just published. And you revised *Le Guide*. What? Two years ago?"

"Fourteen years ago. And although as you say *Le Guide Culinaire* is merely a recipe book, it is my most profitable to date. Every kitchen needs several guides to the art of fine cookery."

"But no one has the money. To write another type of book like this would be a waste of time. People want to read about the beautiful lives of the rich now. They want to know the secrets of kings and queens and you could tell them."

"People who cook are still very interested in technique. They would buy dozens of books if I wrote them."

"But Germany—"

"Always Germany."

Delphine could not bear to hear any more. "Sabine!"

The girl was standing behind her with a box of empty champagne bottles.

"There's no need to shout, Madame," she said.

"And these tomatoes," Escoffier said. "They are everywhere. We are making sauce now?" He had that look in his eyes that was so familiar, the look of a chef addressing an unexpected bounty.

"They will be crushed and poured into the champagne bottles. Is that not how it's done? As it was done at Le Petit Moulin Rouge?"

"Could the factory not send us the Escoffier label?"

"It's August. Everyone is on holiday."

"And we could not wait?"

"Sabine. Bring Monsieur a tomato."

The cook put the dusty box down and wiped her dirty hands on her apron. She picked up a tomato from the sink. It was so large that it filled the palm of her hand, and so ripe that the juice of it ran down her arm onto the floor. She held it out to him. With the afternoon light streaming behind her, her wild hair and defiant eyes, he suddenly was struck by the resemblance he hadn't seen before.

"Sarah?"

His voice barely scratched the surface.

Although this was exactly the reaction Delphine had expected, the look on his face—confusion mixed with joy and love—pained her.

I have become an old and foolish woman.

"Her name is Sabine," she said. "Put the tomato down and leave us, Sabine."

Escoffier took the fruit from the girl. Sniffed it. He held it up into a shaft of sunlight that streamed into the kitchen. His hand shook. "The color is good," he said to Delphine. "Unafraid of its own boldness. Much like yourself." He took a bite and slowly chewed the flesh. Juice ran down his arm, staining his carefully pressed cuff.

"Is it lovely?" she asked.

"Oui," Escoffier said. "So very lovely."

He held the fruit out for Delphine to taste. She leaned into it. Closed her eyes and took a bite. "Summer. The taste of summer."

"Exactly. Makes one reckless, no?"

"No."

Sabine cleared her throat. "The ants should be sprayed with poison."

"Not in the kitchen," Delphine said.

Escoffier handed the fruit back to the girl. There was a stray ant running up her arm. He plucked it from her. "Sabine, do you like ants? They are very good covered in chocolate."

"Non."

"Tomatoes?"

"Non."

"Tomatoes are so sad a fruit, are they not? Bruised like a heart?"

"Non," Sabine said, grinding stray ants into the counter. "Hearts, bruised or otherwise, are muscles that are usually purple or pink. At least that is true of cows. This is a fruit that is rotting in my hand."

"She is a delight," Escoffier laughed. "Even the ants seem to like her."

"She is Sabine," Delphine said.

"I know that. Do you?"

"She is the cook, nothing more."

"But the cook is everything."

"The chef is everything. The cook is just a girl."

"Sabine. *Le Guide Culinaire*. Quickly. You must prove your worth to Madame."

Sabine placed the tomato back in the sink and washed her hands over it. The smell of olive oil soap filled the air.

"Sabine. Be careful. Now the tomatoes are covered with soap and will all have to be rewashed," Delphine said, but no one seemed to notice she was speaking. Escoffier slowly removed his dress coat; for a moment his arm was caught but he shook it off. He rolled up his shirtsleeves. He took a clean apron from the drawer. Sabine pulled the cookbook from the shelf.

"Page twenty-two," Escoffier said. "Salt pork. Carrots. Onions. Butter. And white stock, is that correct?"

Sabine read the recipe and nodded. There were thousands of recipes in the thick book. She was clearly amazed that he could remember the page number of even one.

"Is there white stock made?" Escoffier asked.

"Poultry, not veal."

"That will do."

The old man suddenly seemed ageless. He stood with relative ease and walked to the chopping board without a trace of ill health. Sabine handed him an onion and the vegetable cleaver. He sniffed the onion for freshness and then began to chop while she gathered ingredients and laid them out in front of him on the marble counter.

His small hands were a maze of bulging veins and liver spots, curled like claws, but once they held the knife they moved with the grace of a young man's.

"We will also make noodles," he said. "One pound of flour, one-half ounce of salt, three whole eggs and five egg yolks—then we'll say a short prayer: the making of noodles is a difficult thing. Saint Elizabeth will often intercede, but since she is actually the patron saint of bakers, noodles are not her responsibility. Still, she has such beautiful eyes and a heart of great kindness, so I always pray to her. She has never failed me. Pray to her and she will take mercy on you and your noodles will not be leaden."

Escoffier chopped the onion into uniform pieces and diced the carrots into equal cubes with startling efficiency.

"If anyone asks, Saint Laurent is who you should actually be speaking to in this matter; his responsibilities include restaurants, pasta, candy makers and dieters. But I prefer not to speak to him at all. How could he aid both candy makers and dieters? I fear he must be ineffectual at both tasks."

Escoffier made the girl laugh. Delphine suddenly felt uneasy and slow witted. The old anger rose in her, sharp and acidic, as if each of his indiscretions, each mistake, each inept investment, each moment of ill-placed trust, was new and fresh.

She tried to push through the dullness to form the words, a sentence, anything that made sense, but all she could think was, *All these tomatoes*—and was panicked by them. She knew she should have had the cannery simply send cases of tomato puree for the household—it was the Escoffier Ltd brand specialty, after all. They would have done so happily. More than likely they would have also included, as a kind gesture, the Escoffier Pickles, the Escoffier Sauce Melba, the Escoffier Diablo Sauce and maybe even some of the tinned meats. Even though the factory was no longer theirs—it had failed as everything else Escoffier invested in had failed—the new owners were kind enough and somewhat generous.

Her thoughts ran together, making her exhausted.

It was inevitable.

Even before the world changed, before the Germans rose again, everyone seemed to make money off Escoffier except for Escoffier—the hotels, his collaborators—and then that Philéas Gilbert suddenly claims to be the author of *Le Guide Culinaire* and co-writes *Larousse Gastronomique* with recipes stolen from *Le Guide*.

Betrayal after betrayal but no money.

Escoffier and Sabine chopped and peeled. Delphine couldn't stop thinking about the money.

Even the help Escoffier had given Mr. Maggi and his cubed soup paid nothing to them. *And now the world cans tomatoes!* No one even considered processing tomatoes in cans until Escoffier convinced a fruit cannery to produce two thousand cans for The Savoy. For years he begged them and then—*Voilà!*—the next year they produced sixty thousand. Now in Italy and America millions and millions of cans of tomatoes are sold.

Thought upon thought rolled tighter and tighter inside her head. Morphine always made her feel this way, like a whining engine burning itself out.

And where is the money?

The art collection: sold. The good silver: sold.

"I don't understand," she shouted, although no one was speaking to her. The sound of her own voice surprised her. It was too loud, too shrill.

Escoffier put down his knife.

"Madame Escoffier," he said. In his white apron, he was again the man she loved. The gentle man who only spoke in whispers.

"I am sorry," she said.

"I am not."

He leaned over and kissed her. His lips tasted of tomatoes, sharp and floral.

The moment, filled with the heat of a reckless summer, brought her back to the gardens they had grown together in Paris in a private courtyard behind Le Petit Moulin Rouge. Sweet Roma tomatoes, grassy licorice tarragon, thin purple eggplants and small crisp beans thrived in a series of old wine barrels that sat in the tiny square. There were also violets and roses that the *confiseur* would make into jellies or sugar to grace the top of the *petits-fours glacés*, which were baked every evening while the coal of the brick ovens cooled down for the night.

"No one grows vegetables in the city of Paris," she said, laughing, when Escoffier first showed her his hidden garden, "except for Escoffier."

He picked a ripe tomato, bit into it and then held it to her lips. "*Pomme d'amour*, perhaps this was fruit of Eden."

The tomato was so ripe and lush, so filled with heat it brought tears to her eyes and he kissed her.

"You are becoming very good at being a chef's wife."

"I love you," she said and finally meant it.

Pommes d'amour. The kitchen was now overflowing with them.

"I love you," she said again.

Escoffier nodded. "Should I get the nurse?"

"It was just a moment."

"Good. We are nearly finished."

He went back to his work and Delphine looked into the box that Sabine had brought up from the cellar. The champagne bottles were covered with cobwebs and layers of dust, but to Escoffier they were priceless. Every one had been part of a historic menu; that was why he'd saved them. Some dated back to his days at Le Petit Moulin Rouge. She had heard Escoffier tell visitors their stories over and over again. Even though many of the labels were gone for more than fifty years, the shape of each bottle, the color, held its history, and Escoffier never forgot a dinner or a menu.

Delphine held out a clear bottle in her good hand. It was obviously old, with flaws, bubbles of air lurking beneath the grain. It appeared to have been blown very quickly.

"Tell me, Georges," she said, "What is the story of this one?"

Escoffier was slicing salt pork; he didn't look up.

"The chop is important," he said to Sabine. "The carrots, onions and pork must all be cut into the same size cubes; it is more pleasing that way."

"Georges, you look tired."

Escoffier continued to cube the pork. "Make a note, Sabine. When you go to the butcher, ask that he give more fat on the salt pork. That is the entire purpose of it, is it not? The more fat, the more the flavor permeates."

"Georges," Delphine said loudly, "come sit with me."

Again, he didn't answer. *He may have forgotten,* she thought.

It had been a very long time. "Georges" was not Escoffier's name— although at one point in his life he embraced it so fully that he had it placed on a visiting card and even wrote it into early editions of *Le Guide Culinaire.* But it did not appear on his birth certificate nor would it appear on his grave. It was a name that Delphine had given him years before: the same day she had said that she would take the children back to their home in Monaco and leave her husband to live in London alone. She was pregnant with their third child and told everyone that she hated London and didn't want the baby to be born there.

"It is just a few months before the winter holiday season begins in Monte Carlo," she told Escoffier. "You will join us then."

"People will talk."

"People are already talking."

Escoffier could not deny it. He had been less than discreet.

"It is not as you think," he said, although he knew it was exactly what she thought—but even more complicated.

"I think that the distance may make us strangers," Delphine said as she loaded their children onto the train. "So I will call you 'Georges' so that you are reminded that I am not sure who you are anymore and you must win my hand over and over again."

"Don't go."

"Goodbye, Georges."

"I will become undone without you."

And they were gone.

Her threat did not work. Escoffier stayed in London—a city Delphine never returned to. He never came back to Monte Carlo for the winter season, or hardly any other season. Just a yearly post-Christmas visit, at least most years, and then back to work.

They had letters. He always signed "Much love, Georges, and sweet kisses" and often included a bit of professional news, such as a speech that he had given about the importance of suppressing poverty or a new menu he'd created for Prince Edward, his "Dear Bertie." But when Escoffier moved to Paris, to the Hôtel Ritz, Delphine would still not join him. Or maybe he didn't ask. Or maybe she didn't. It was so long ago, neither could remember. All in all, they lived apart for thirty years. Work, grandchildren and the luxury of freedom always got in the way.

After all those years, when Escoffier decided to retire, he appeared unannounced at Delphine's door with steamer trunks, boxes, crates, endless cases of used champagne bottles (and more than a few that were filled) and an assistant. He was her own Ulysses but smaller, stooped. The white of his hair made those fierce eyes seem even deeper. His elegant nose was more finely etched by time.

"I have told everyone that Madame Escoffier cooks better than I do," he said, and then removed his hat and bowed.

Her heart beat with the rattle of broken wings.

Yet less than a year after he arrived, Escoffier returned to work. The widow of his friend Jean Giroix, with whom he worked at Le Petit Moulin Rouge and whose place he had taken at the Grand Hôtel in Monaco, asked if he would help her develop two projects. He told Delphine he could not refuse.

"One more year."

And he was true to his word; he only stayed a year. However, there was still so much to do. The articles, the essays, the fourth edition of *Le Guide Culinaire* needed revising and so he went back to Paris alone, to work, and then on to London, and America, and back to Paris and continued to leave until his doctor forbade him to travel anymore.

"I am a better husband in retrospect," he told her.

But there was something more, something dark and unforgiven between them. She had no idea what it was; he wouldn't talk about it. And there was so much of his life she knew nothing about. And time was short.

She decided to give it one more try. *Maybe the secret is in the bottles.*

"Georges, is this not from a Veuve Clicquot rosé? Did you not tell me once that they blow these very quickly because it is difficult to keep up with demand?"

Escoffier turned to her.

"Enough," he said quietly. "Do not call me 'Georges' ever again."

Delphine was surprised to see that there were tears in his eyes. The bottle slipped out of her hand and shattered on the floor.

The Complete Escoffier: A Memoir in Meals

POTAGE SARAH BERNHARDT
Chicken Consommé with crayfish quenelles and a julienne of black truffles and asparagus tips

In case you have a question, this is not made from the famed actress herself, although the name could suggest that. But, yes, of course, that would be impossible. She barely has enough meat on her to make it worth the skinning.

This is a problem with all actresses.

This is a soup for Miss Bernhardt. It is simply as delightful as she was. I personally have served it to her on several occasions and it is one of the many dishes that she asked for repeatedly, although once it's served she will not eat it. She only requests it to make you happy.

To begin, you must add three tablespoons of tapioca to one quart of boiling chicken consommé. Simmer. For the pan—copper. I prefer the Mauviel for this, their Windsor pan is widely available. The narrow base quickly heats liquids while the wide top speeds evaporation.

Simmer, do not boil, this broth at a low heat for fifteen minutes. Or eighteen. Do whatever you feel is long enough to make the broth rich and the texture substantial and yet not lose its pristine clarity. Use your best judgment here, although she will not eat it in any case and so you cannot be in error no matter how long you choose to cook it.

Miss Bernhardt eats nothing. Well, that is untrue. She eats my scrambled eggs. Or appears to. But if you do not feed her as if she were a child, she will scoop the eggs onto the floor for that cheetah of hers. So you must always feed her. I find that the best technique is a bite of egg, then a sip of champagne to make sure that she swallows it. This is the only way that one can, with absolute certainly, know that Miss Bernhardt is taking nourishment.

Yes. There was, indeed, a cheetah. At 77 Chester Square. She actually wanted two small lions, but the man at Cross Zoo in Liverpool only had two very large ones. *Quand même*, as Miss Bernhardt is so very fond of saying—I'm not sure how you Americans or English would say it. "No matter," perhaps? All I know is that she would never allow a person or thing to stop her once her mind was set to a task. In any case, Miss Bernhardt took the cheetah instead.

She could be rather sensible at times.

For most, a cheetah as a domestic companion would have been a questionable choice. But "It is very droll," she said. Unfortunately, as we all know, the English have no sense of humor when it comes to wild things. Look at how they treat their Irish.

So when Miss Bernhardt arrived home with her cheetah in a cage, her wolf on a leash, six small lizards in a box and around her shoulders, tethered to a gold chain that one usually uses for pince-nez, a rather large chameleon that harrowingly resembled an ancient Chinese dragon—it created, let us say, an incident. A scandal, actually. Everyone was speaking of it everywhere and the talk became so intense that her employer Monsieur Got from the Comédie-Française begged her to take her brood back to Liverpool to their keeper at Cross Zoo.

When faced with logic, Miss Bernhardt did what she usually would do. She defied it. She set the cheetah on the wolf, sending them both into a howling frenzy, which made her monkey laugh and won the heart of the jolly round Got.

Or so she said. It is often difficult to tell what is a fabulous story and what is the truth. But then, why does that matter? Truth is often irrelevant. And whenever you speak of Miss Bernhardt, it is as if speaking of an angel or a demon, as either would be likely to appear at any moment and often at the same time.

Quand même.

When the broth is thick and pleasing to the tongue, form twenty small quenelles from the forcemeat of chicken and crayfish butter. She will not eat these, either. She once wore a pair of pet crayfish on her ears to a party. Miss Bernhardt makes it a practice not to eat her pets.

The quenelles—they must be exactly five-carat weight, and I do mean this in the jeweler's sense. When Miss Bernhardt raises her silver spoon, and it will be a silver spoon, she will be able to weigh the quenelle by sight alone. If it is six-carat weight, it will be tossed aside. Six is excessive. Four, of course, would be an insult. It must be five-carat weight, exactly, and formed in the marquise cut.

As soon as the quenelles are molded, poach and set them aside. Saw twelve small marrow rounds from a veal bone; they should be the size of a golden ring. Poach and set them aside also.

Once these steps are complete, place the quenelles and the marrow in a soup tureen. Add one tablespoon of a julienne of black spring truffles. The perfume of new grass is crucial to this dish. Add to it one tablespoon of new asparagus tips. Again, they must be the very first of the season. Pour the consommé over the garnish.

When you are finished, serve it quickly. Leave it on the table and walk away. Do not turn around. Heed this advice especially if you are serving this to a beautiful woman. Do not even think to glance over your shoulder. The very moment when the spoon is brought to her lips, when she embraces the deep rich aroma of the truffle and the whisper of spring asparagus, her face will soften with pleasure and she will think of her own childhood, not the stories she tells others but her real childhood.

It will be a simple moment that she can tell no one about and all the artifice that she has been burdened to create will slip away and her inner light will reveal itself to you. And you will never be the same.

There is no way to approach such divinity without offending it or being overwhelmed by it. So do not hesitate. Close the door gently behind you. Be thankful if you get out alive.

3

"AND SWEET KISSES—SWEETER THAN *FRAISES SARAH . . .* "
Escoffier had signed a letter like that once. Delphine
remembered that when Sabine knocked at her door.
Bernhardt. Always Bernhardt.

"Madame?"

The evening meal had been served long ago. Instead of crushing and canning the tomatoes, Escoffier and Sabine made gallons of
tomato sauce. Delphine was told by her nurse that he'd shown the girl
how to make noodles and then the two prayed to Saint Elizabeth over
them.

"Never marry a Catholic," Delphine told the woman.

There were eighteen at the table that night, so many mouths to
feed, but bread, noodles and sauce were all they had. Delphine stayed
in her room, exhausted. The nurse cleaned her, turned her, dressed
her in her white lace nightgown and lace bed cap, gave her a dose of
morphine and left.

Delphine could not sleep. She turned on the reading lamp by her
bed and tried to pick up a book with her one good hand, but the hand

went weak and the book tumbled onto the floor. The nurse had left the window open; the curtains were pulled back. Delphine lay for a very long time and watched the lights of the city flicker and spark.

When the house finally fell quiet, she heard Escoffier turn on his radio. He was hard of hearing. He turned the volume up loud. News filled the night air. The German president Paul von Hindenburg had died. Rather than hold new presidential elections, Hitler's cabinet passed a law combining the offices of president and chancellor with Adolf Hitler holding both. Germany was now under the control of a single man. The newsreader had said the leader had taken the title of *Führer*, or "guide."

The radio went off abruptly. Sabine knocked again.

"Madame, I was told that you wanted to see me."

"Come in."

Sabine opened the door gently. For a moment, she seemed apprehensive, more like a young girl than the cross young cook. She'd changed out of her kitchen whites and into a cream-colored blouse and long, pleated skirt. Her nails were freshly painted red. Her hair was set in Marcel waves and then curled into a net, as was the style. Her shoes were impossible, four-inch red heels with ankle straps. They looked like dancing shoes, which was surprising considering her limp. Delphine suspected that Sabine was going to meet someone, a man more than likely. She smelled of cigarettes and cheap perfume.

"Come closer," Delphine said.

The girl took one step. No more.

"Fine," Delphine said. "Do you know how to make spun sugar?"

"No. May I go?"

"No. That can be worked around. Have you seen many strawberries at the market? We will need hothouse fruit, about three to four pounds. And you'll need a pineapple; go to the Grand. Escoffier was their *directeur de cuisine* many years ago."

"The hotel?"

"Queen Victoria herself stayed there; that is how she came to know Escoffier. They will sell their fruit if you ask for the *directeur*. The man's name is Bobo. He is tall and tan. He looks indolent but is far from it. Pay him the least you can and listen to nothing he says. He fashions himself to be very good with the ladies."

"Is he?"

"No."

"Then he's odd?"

"Crazy. They all are. You know how long most chefs live? Forty years. Smoke. Heat. Pressure. It all makes them insane. Bobo needs to feel dangerous and so we humor him. It makes him happy. Now. After the pineapple is procured, the ice cream must be made—"

"Madame, I have spent all the household money on tomatoes."

"What?"

"There is no money for pineapple, strawberries or cream. You directed me to buy tomatoes, and I did. And tonight Monsieur Escoffier has directed me not to sauce them again. The children, apparently, do not like them that way."

Delphine had forgotten. "But what will we make with all the tomatoes, then?"

"Stories."

The girl was like a small nasty dog.

Delphine imagined the disaster the kitchen would soon be with cases of rotting tomatoes staining the marble, filling the air with flies. "So now are we to eat tomatoes every night until September or until they all rot?"

"Yes. May I go?"

"No. Sit."

The girl did not sit. Nor did she avert her eyes, as most servants would have done. Sabine reached into her skirt pocket and pulled out a pack of Gitanes. She took out a cigarette and put it in her mouth and waited for a response.

"I would like you to sit for a moment," Delphine said quietly. "Please. And you may smoke if you wish. It doesn't bother me."

That was clearly not the response Sabine had expected. The cigarette hung in her mouth unlit. Her red lipstick was beginning to smear. There was a thin bead of sweat above her upper lip. "You can tell me what you want while I am on my feet," she said. "I don't like sickrooms. It smells in here."

She's afraid of illness. Delphine wondered what it was like to be Sabine, so beautiful but with polio. Flawed and broken. How many hospital rooms had the girl seen?

"I agree," Delphine said. "I don't like them, either. But this will only take a moment."

"If you are planning to dismiss me . . . "

"And if I am?"

"Then there is no need to have me sit. I will go readily."

"Your father would be furious."

"I will tell him that you have no money and he will gladly have me back."

"And I would tell him that you are lying. And that the great Escoffier demands that you stay."

Sabine suddenly developed a slightly rabid look about her. She pulled a box of matches from her pocket, lit her cigarette and inhaled deeply. Smoke leaked from her mouth.

"Fine, then. We understand each other," Delphine said. "Stand if you want."

The girl blew smoke at Delphine, but it did not offend her. In fact, she liked Sabine better for it. The moment of independence reminded her of her own youth. "Do you like poetry?"

"No."

"What do you like?"

"American music. Big Band. That Créole Josephine Baker. "

"La Baker favors tomatoes."

Sabine nearly smiled.

"It is true," Delphine continued. "And she is unafraid of garlic. Escoffier once presented her with a blackbird cooked in forty cloves of garlic and she laughed out loud. It was a very witty gesture."

"I would think that she would have been gravely offended."

"Then you do not know her art. She became very rich because she is a black bird with a beautiful voice. She sang songs while dressed as an ignorant jungle girl, which all of Paris knew she was not. So they laughed. *Genre* Folies Bergères. Very chic."

The girl flicked an ash onto the oriental rug. "Is that all you need to know, Madame? My taste in music?"

"No."

Delphine had hoped for so much more from Sabine, like kindness or even cooperation, but it was not forthcoming, so she continued. "I need you to help Monsieur Escoffier create a dish for me. It will mean extra work for you. But if you do this, and tell no one that I asked you to do this, I will give you that coat and release you from service, if that is what you wish."

Delphine pointed to the full-length ermine coat that she had had her nurse drape over the trunk at the foot of her bed. Queen Victoria's furrier had designed it; his tag was in it. It was Victorian in style—floor-length with oversized sleeves and a high collar made from some sort of dyed mink—it was old but still beautiful. It arrived by post, years ago; the first of many gifts sent with a card signed "Mr. Boots."

Unfortunately, the coat was so small that she couldn't even fit her arms into it. She had wanted to give it away but Escoffier refused. He wouldn't even allow her to give it to his beloved Little Sisters of the

Poor so that they could resell it and feed the old age pensioners and the hungry.

"It was a gift," he told her, and the way he said it told Delphine it was a gift to him, not her. It was all very odd.

Sabine carefully crushed her cigarette out on the bottom of her shoe, placed the remains in her pocket for later. She picked up the coat and ran her hand along the champagne-colored silk lining. Held its soft collar to her face for a moment.

"Try it on," Delphine said.

The fit was perfect, as if made for her—which pained Delphine. The girl looked more like Sarah than ever before. The black fur set off her wild eyes. If her hair were in a topknot, as it usually was, it would have been like looking at a ghost.

"Take it off before Escoffier sees you."

Sabine reluctantly removed the coat. Folded it gently and placed it back over the trunk where she found it. "What kind of dish?" she said. "What sort of dish do I need to make to get a coat like this and my freedom?"

Delphine had no idea what she was looking for. Something. Anything. It didn't matter. "I thought perhaps if you made the *Fraises Sarah* it would inspire him. It was a very famous dish. After it was served, all the newspapers around the world wrote of it."

This was only partially true. The articles were about a worldwide event, the first *Dîners d'Epicure*, at which four thousand members of Escoffier's gastronomic club *La Ligue des Gourmands* sat down and ate the same meal at the same time in New York and thirty-seven European cities. It was the first global event ever—monumental in scope.

Of course, Escoffier had created a dish to honor Sarah Bernhardt—yet again. *Fraises Sarah* was, in fact, much to Delphine's chagrin, the centerpiece of the entire meal. He even had commissioned a poem written about the dish.

Always for her.

During the first course, predictably, a telegram arrived from Bernhardt. All the newspapers reported it. "My two hands stretch out to my dear friend Escoffier . . . and sensitive lovers of real life." *Real life.* Delphine no longer remembered the exact words of the rest of the message, but did remember that certain newspapers reported the telegram made Escoffier breathless.

Even their children felt a sense of shame. Yes, Escoffier and Bernhardt had been lovers long before he even met Delphine. And yes, they had remained close all those years—how close was something Delphine never cared to think about—but the thought of their names in the newspapers together, *so indiscreet*, still made her angry.

"And sweet kisses—sweeter than Fraises Sarah." How could he have written such a thing to me?

Sabine sat in a chair next to Delphine's bed.

"Does Monsieur Escoffier know he is creating a dish for you?"

"No. It is your job to suggest it and encourage him until he completes it," Delphine said. "Once it is complete, I will give you a list of newspapers that you will send the recipe to. You will say that it was Escoffier's dying wish to make this dish for me."

"Is it?"

"That is not important."

"Then I would be a liar."

"You have never lied for something or someone?"

Sabine looked out the window at the lights of Monte Carlo. She pushed a stray hair back into her netting. "Why should I do this?"

"Because I will give you the coat and your freedom."

Sabine shook her head. "No, Madame. My question is why do you want me to do such a foolish thing?"

"Because he loves me," she said. "And if we die without his ever creating a dish in my honor, no one will believe he loved me. They will think he loved them all better than me."

"Especially the actress? What was her name again?"

This girl clearly knew the power she could possess over Escoffier—that much was clear to Delphine. And her father knew, too. That's why she was sent to the house. *Perhaps they are not idiots after all.*

Sabine looked at her closely, studied her face. Delphine knew what she saw. Bedridden and enormously fat, she was no longer the famed poet Delphine Daffis Escoffier but a horrible creature rolled about on gurneys and in wheelchairs, paraded about for the grandchildren to see. A fool. A monster.

"Never mind," Delphine said. "Go."

Sabine didn't move. "Madame, it could be possible that if the great Escoffier does not create a dish in your honor, people may believe that he didn't love you. But it could be possible that they will think he loved you so very much that he didn't need to prove that to you."

"You are very insolent."

"I am the cook."

"Will you take the coat?"

"No, Madame. It sheds."

Delphine looked at the girl's cream blouse. Indeed, even in the dim light, she could see fur from the collar all over her shoulders. Delphine wanted to weep.

"May I go?"

Delphine looked out the window again. So many lights now searched the coastline. Perhaps *La Royale*—the French Navy. *Germans. They are coming,* she thought. *Soon, nothing will matter.*

"You know I saw La Baker in Paris. In *La Folie du Jour* at the Folies Bergères Theater. She had sixteen bananas strung into a skirt and a few beads for a blouse. Very charming. This beautiful naked creature was the only thing anyone could look at. She didn't sing as well back then, a very pale little voice. But no one remembers that. There was so much written about her, the newspapers immortalized her, so now everyone can only remember La Baker in all her glory.

"That's all we can ever hope for. To be remembered."

Delphine suddenly felt tired and closed her eyes. She continued on about fame and immortality and was still speaking when Sabine closed the door gently behind her.

After midnight, the door to Delphine's room opened again. Escoffier watched his sleeping wife for a moment, her small round face nearly lost in a sea of lace and sheets. The windows had been left open. The room was cold. Moonlight turned everything to steel.

When he crossed the room and closed the window, the fur at the foot of the bed caught his eye. He recognized it immediately. He picked it up and held it. It smelled of mildew and age. He closed his eyes. "I am sorry," he said, mostly to himself.

"Escoffier?"

"I didn't mean to wake you. The window . . . "

He was still dressed for company in his black Louise-Philippe dress coat and finely polished shoes. He put the fur back on top of the wooden chest.

"I'm cold," she said. "Drape it over me."

"I'll find you a blanket."

"Why? It can't be worn any longer," she said. "It sheds. I might as well have some use out of it."

He looked at his hands; they were covered in fur. "There must be something more suitable. The window is closed now. It will be too warm soon."

"No," she said, sharply. "The coat is what I want."

Escoffier gently placed the fur around her shoulders and then backed away. She felt dwarfed underneath the weight of fur and history. In the metallic light of the moon, her husband looked very frail.

It seemed as if there were a great many things that he wanted to say—so many in fact that he could not speak at all. He kissed her gently. He held her face in his hands, as if to memorize it.

"Good night, Madame Escoffier."

Escoffier stood outside the door of her room for a long time, waiting until he could hear the rhythm of her breath deep in sleep.

At his desk he began to write, reconstructing each line from memory.

"In this thin coat of skin / these silent hands / these clouded eyes / there is you. / Nothing that I am can be without you. / The timbre of my voice rises and falls with thoughts of you. / In dreams you come to me, as my true love, the one who completes. / And then I wake."

Escoffier read it several times and then tore it into tiny pieces. He opened the window and tossed them into the night air. White and fat, improbable as snow, his words floated on the sea breeze and then slowly tumbled onto the ground, littering the garden below.

And then he began to write again.

The Complete Escoffier: A Memoir in Meals

FRITÔT OU MARINADE DE VOLAILLE
Fried Chicken

October 23, 1844
The Eighth Wonder of the World,
the Divine Sarah Bernhardt, is born.

October 23, 1859
My professional career begins at the age of thirteen, when I become a
kitchen apprentice at my uncle's Restaurant Français in Nice.

October 23, 1870
Franco-Prussian War: the Siege of Metz, a decisive Prussian victory,
concludes with the surrender of France. I do not escape.

These are the three most defining events in my life and they all occur
on the same day. I have never written this down before. I am not sure
why I have now. Of course, the date of Miss Bernhardt's birthday often
shifts. Some agree with the 23rd. Some say it was the 22nd. Some say
the 25th. It matters not. We always celebrated on October 23rd and so I
will consider that official.

October 23rd may even be the day I met César Ritz. 1884. I am not sure what date exactly but I do remember it was October, sometime past mid-month. He died that day in October of 1918. Or was it the next? Midnight, I believe. I hadn't seen him for such a long time; he'd gone quite mad by then. He slipped away without notice.

But it was also on October 23 that I first tasted what is called "southern fried chicken." This, too, had a profound effect on my life.

I know no other food like it. In the American South, no Sunday is spent without it, but yet many do not realize that it is a dish of forgiveness.

The Scots, who as a culture have no cuisine of their own, first served chicken in this manner in the New World. They have a long tradition of deep-frying fowl, and, quite frankly, are a people who will fry anything. I have heard that a chef from Scotland's West Coast once served a fried peacock to Queen Mary at a royal banquet. He inserted the feathers where they had been in life and included a pint of malt vinegar.

This would not happen in France.

While it is possible that this story is not wholly accurate, perhaps a well-drawn fabrication on the part of Monsieur Echenard, my former maître d'hôtel at The Savoy, it is interesting to note that when Queen Mary of Scots did eventually arrive in Paris, she returned to her homeland with an entourage of French chefs.

To me, that is proof that the story is true enough.

Unfortunately, even with the exotic fruits and spices of a new world, the Scottish technique of frying chickens created an intensely plain dish. Chicken, fat and flour—that was all. No marinade to soften the old birds. No cream to finish. No cognac. No herb sauce. No lemon. No native honey. Nothing. Fry. *Fini*. Very sad.

However, when the slave trade began the Scots had their first contact with the Sudanic race, the only other people in the world who, at the time, also had a habit of deep-frying fowls. These enslaved Africans were purchased by the Scots to work on their plantations and those who were assigned to house duties were instructed in the "artistry" of Scottish cooking.

Luckily, they paid no attention.

When it came to the frying of chicken, they took pity on their captors and incorporated the seasonings and spices of Africa—garlic, melegueta pepper, cloves, black peppercorns, cardamom, nutmeg, turmeric and even curry powder. They forgave them their cruelty and presented them with what can only be described as a gift born in sorrow.

Food has the ability to move people in this manner. It can inspire bravery.

These kitchen slaves could have been beaten for this insolence, or perhaps even killed for such an act, but they served their fried fowl anyway. Not surprisingly, their captors were entranced by it. Soon southern fried chicken became a delicacy enjoyed by both cultures— it was the one point where both captors and captive found pleasure, although the Africans were only allowed to fry the discarded wings of the bird for their own meals. Despite the continued injustice, it was an inspired and blessed act of subversion.

Although born in slavery, this dish has not only brought together an entire region of people, it has transformed them. It is, as the Americans say, "democratic," and is now enjoyed by people of all walks of life and all parts of the country.

Even very famous international stars have fallen in love with this redemptive dish. While on tour and traveling in the opulent Pullman private cars, where crystal and china service is set for every meal including midday tea, the great opera singer Adelina Patti was introduced to it outside of New York City. She, in turn, introduced it to Miss Bernhardt, who became so enamored of it that she introduced it to me on her birthday. Well, actually, she arranged to have the famed

Negroid chef Rufus Estes re-create the dish for me so that I might learn
how to cook it myself for her.

I have met several Africans; however, I had never met a man like
Chef Estes before. Not tribal at all, he reminded me a great deal of
myself. He was impeccably dressed, soft-spoken and seemed well liked
by both his staff and patrons. Although his French was barely passable,
he told me that he'd worked for the railroads for many years, and had
cooked for many celebrities such as Henry Stanley, the famed African
explorer, and the presidents Grover Cleveland and Benjamin Harrison.

He was also quite well known for his cookbook, *Good Things to Eat
as Suggested by Rufus: A Collection of Practical Recipes for Preparing
Meats, Game, Fowl, Fish, Puddings, Pastries, Etc.*, and even inscribed
a copy to me. The book is extremely interesting; it includes nearly six
hundred recipes—although few are for eggs despite the fact that his
toque had at least sixty pleats, which would indicate that he knew sixty
ways to make eggs. But then, so many things are different in American
kitchens. It is, after all, a new world.

What I found the most amazing was that Monsieur Estes had been
born a slave. He had no father of record, but his surname, and that of
his nine brothers and sisters, was that of the man who had owned him.

The implication of this is horrendous. And yet, "Forgive and forget," is what he said to me. After living through Metz, I could not
agree. For some, it is human nature to be inhuman. "My people say
forgive, but never forget."

"Then I am sorry for your people."

At the time, I did not think he was being honest with me. I know
from my own life that there are some sorrows that run too deep. After
France fell in the Prussian War, those of us held at Metz were loaded
onto trains to be taken to Germany to be held in captivity. For how
long and for what reason, we did not know. We were treated very much
like slaves. We were the spoils of war. Labor camps, anything was pos-

sible. They packed us into the train cars so tightly that we could barely breathe. We could not sit, only stand. For three days, we had no food or water. Our own foul waste surrounded us. No one dared speak to complain.

While the trip from Metz, France, to Germany is usually quite quick, the conductor made sure that the train crawled along the tracks slowly; we were, after all, the victor's prize on display for all in France to see. We were a way for the Germans to keep order, to make sure my countrymen understood that they were no longer under the control of Napoleon III. The French no longer belonged to France. We were Germany's.

When our train arrived at Nancy, the conductor stopped so that everyone could get a good look at us. It seemed as if the entire town stood at the station. Some threw stones. Some screamed.

"Down with you cowards!"

I could not believe what I was hearing. Although not all of the voices sounded entirely French, I could not help but wonder. Cowards? I saw little of the battle itself, only the suffering, but my fellow passengers were different. They had fought bravely only to be delivered to the enemy through treason, through the act of one insane man, and not because of a loss of nerve. They had suffered so much, and lost so much. Cowards? These men surrendered in tears, they fought for their beloved France, and now were being sent into an unknown captivity— these men were cowards?

How could it be? When I looked out over the crowd, there was so much anger. I could only imagine that this is what it was like for the slaves when they stood on the auction block awaiting their fate.

"How can you forget?" I asked Monsieur Estes.

The elegant man straightened his waistcoat, leaned in and said, "The forgetting is all you have. My two brothers went north to fight and died in the Civil War for my freedom. My mother couldn't shake the sorrow and died of a broken heart. That's too much death to bear. You have to forget. You have to give sorrow wings. You have no choice."

And then he told me of the origins of this dish and I began to cook it with him. Two men, two cooks, completely different and yet something at the core of us was completely the same. We were kindred spirits.

That night I served his chicken to Miss Bernhardt for her birthday celebration and she was quite thankful. Although the dish did not contain a puree of either *foie gras* or truffles, and it was not her traditional birthday meal of scrambled eggs and champagne, she consumed it in its entirety, including a side of what the English call "chips."

"Magic," she said. "It is magic."

And it was. The crust was crispy and light with a floral hint from the spices. The meat of the young chicken was fragrant and juicy. I have never seen an actress, any actress, each so much in one sitting.

Upon my return home, I had written Monsieur Estes to thank him for his time and his exquisite recipe, but my letter was returned a month later unopened. The famed chef had disappeared, never to be heard from again. Some spoke of the Klan.

It pains me to think that this gracious man may have fallen victim to violence at the hands of such ignorant barbarians. How is it possible? How could someone so famous just disappear?

Miss Bernhardt said, "The forgetting killed him."

I believe she may be right.

As for the recipe for the fried chicken, it is simple. Cut some boiled fowl into slices and marinate them in very good olive oil, the juice of a lemon and a handful of herbs fresh from the garden. I enjoy tarragon, for a hint of licorice; lemon thyme, to bring forward the citrus note; and the slightest bit of lavender. The fowl should marinate for at least three hours. Flour. Fry. Garnish with fried parsley.

It should be noted that this is not Monsieur Estes's recipe. To recreate his exact dish, you will need a quarter of a pound of butter, a spoon-ful of flour, pepper, salt, a little vinegar, parsley, green onions, carrots, and turnips. Cook in a saucepan. Cool. Place cut chicken in this mari-nade for at least three hours. Dry the pieces, flour them and fry. Gar-nish with fried parsley.

While Monsieur Estes's is a memorable recipe, it is not mine. To make southern fried chicken properly, you must add a bit of your true self—the history of the dish demands it. You must bring your heart. Although very few dishes require such bravery, when cooking there is no room for cowardice.

Life, of course, is another matter entirely.

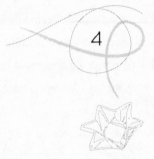

4

THE DIFFICULT THING ABOUT MEMORY IS THAT IT LEAVES a permanent stain. Even when details fade, there is a darkness that remains. The left foot will always be favored after the right is broken. The heart will always be reluctant once it understands how far it can bend.

It was the sound of Sarah's laughter—all bones and fury—that Escoffier could not forget.

They met in 1874, Paris, long before Delphine, marriage and children, at a time when the most scandalous city in the world was scandalized by the first exhibition of the *Société Anonyme Coopérative des Artistes*. "Impressions"—Claude Monet, Pierre Auguste Renoir, Camille Pissarro, Edgar Degas—was a show of outsiders, not sanctioned by jury or state nor salon, only themselves. Renegades.

Everyone had seen it. The critics were inflamed.

"Dirty three-quarters of a canvas with black and white, rub the rest with yellow, dot it with red and blue blobs at random, and you will have an impression of spring before which the initiates will swoon in ecstasy."

"One wonders whether one is seeing the fruit either of a process of mystification which is highly unsuitable for the public, or the result of mental derangement which one could not but regret."

"Impression!" the art critic Louis Leroy would later write. "Wallpaper in its embryonic state is more finished!" And so he named the group "Impressionists." Escoffier was intrigued. He had been studying sculpture with the artist Gustave Doré, who suggested that he attend the exhibit. He went without hesitation.

As a gesture to the working classes, the exhibit was open only in the evenings. Escoffier left the kitchen of Le Petit Moulin Rouge after nine. It had been a long day. The dining room was being renovated and the work was behind schedule. Summer season was just a month away. They had to be ready to open or the fickle fashionable set would find someplace else to behave badly in.

It was raining and unseasonably cool. The gas streetlamps were dim; some were out. The damp air made the city feel quiet. Mud stuck to the bottoms of his shoes, spattered his trouser cuffs. There was just the occasional clop of horse hooves on the cobblestone streets or the whispers of lovers in the darkness of doorways.

The exhibition was being held in Nadar's studio. Escoffier knew the photographer well. When he arrived, there was a great winding line of people—standing, pushing, seeing, being seen. The bourgeoisie, in their borrowed finery, huddled together and narrated the scene to one another in loud whispers. Some provided the names of the divetta and their cuckolded patrons whose faces they recognized from drawings in the newspapers; some just speculated on whose heart was lost and whose was won.

The second floor of the building where the exhibit was housed was brightly lit; laughter and anger drifted down to the street. Escoffier joined the crowd as they walked up the narrow flight of steep stairs, step by careful step. He was still wearing his platform shoes; slick from the mud, they pitched him forward and made each step tentative, made him feel even smaller. When he reached the landing, people were wildly arguing.

"Imbeciles!"

"Genius!"

A duel was challenged. Someone screamed but many laughed as guns were drawn and the men were escorted out into the night. Two shots. Applause. More laughter. Escoffier did not look.

There was a table with a tired man selling tickets. His eyes were bloodshot, his hair and beard unkempt. Admission was a single franc, and the catalogue, edited by the man, Renoir's brother Edmond, fifty centimes. Escoffier could barely afford admission. He studied the catalogue closely, and yet gently, so as not to break the book's spine.

"Would you consider an exchange?" he asked. "This fine book for a fine meal at Le Petit Moulin Rouge?"

Renoir's brother shook his head. "Fifty centimes is a small price for what I have gone through. Degas could not see his way to speak to me until the very last moment before we were to go to press. And Monet sent too many paintings and such horrible titles—*Entrance of a Village, Leaving the Village, Morning in a Village*—the man has no sense."

The brother opened to a page. The painting was Le Havre as seen from a window: the sun appeared to be damp and the sunrise was merely vapors. It was haunting in a way Escoffier could not explain.

"Thankfully, he let me rename them," the man said. "*Impression, Sunrise*—is that not the perfect name?"

It was. Escoffier gave the man fifty centimes.

"*Merci.*"

The brother entered the transaction neatly in a small ledger book. Escoffier could see that there were few entries on the income side. Notoriety had not brought profitability.

If this were a restaurant, the man would be rich.

Even though it was late, inside the studio the exhibit was crowded, although not many appeared to be from the "working class," as the organizers had hoped. The majority of the crowd was composed of artists, none particularly well known, along with courtesans and actors. They were the type of people Escoffier often allowed to eat as guests at Le Petit Moulin Rouge—the "decorative people," as he thought of them. Bohemians—gypsies of sorts—witty, attractive, charming and unconventional. They were amusing and essential to setting a tone in any dining room, especially the women. Without these women the restaurant would be filled with unhappy men. Respectable women were not willing to be seen dining publicly. At least, not yet. Escoffier was trying to convince the owners to add rose-colored lighting in the dining rooms. It would be flattering and soon all women would come to Le Petit Moulin Rouge. And come again. He knew that the civilizing presence of women, even Bohemian women, was key to success.

At the exhibit, however, they seemed slightly menacing. Most of them were drinking. All of them were loud and boisterous. The walls of the room were painted deep red, like a pomegranate. People were even arguing over that. "Blood," a man shouted. "The walls soaked in blood."

It all seemed rather ridiculous. *They are their own theater,* he thought.

Whatever the shade was called, however, it provided the perfect backdrop for the work. Each painting, and there were many, stood in sharp relief to the color of the walls. Each stroke, each illumination, each intent and every nuance seemed heightened, like the sun rising in an angry sky.

Escoffier, exhausted, made his way tentatively through the jumble of canvases and people. The rooms smelled of wet wool and sweat.

The work astonished him. There was a wall of oils and pastels all hung at eye level by Renoir; ten works by Degas; five by Pissarro; three by Cézanne and so many by Monet that he clearly understood Renior's brother's plight.

But he had never seen such beauty. Not even the most elegant woman cast in the rose-hued gaslight of a café could rival it. When he arrived at *Impression: Sunrise,* it was infinitely more breathtaking in real life than it was in the catalogue. He thought for a moment that he had fallen into a dream, a lonely dreamscape in orange and gray. It was everything Doré had told him Impressionist paintings would be. It was not like reality at all but more real somehow. It did not have a distinguishable line or form. And the color was not true to any color in life but its vibrant sun set against the dawn seemed to pulsate like the real sun in a universe yet to be discovered.

The work took Escoffier back to those moments when he first came to Paris as a young man and sat along the river and waited for the morning to come. The painting made him feel as if the world was still filled with promise, as if he was at the exact moment when everything would change.

It was as if Monet had harnessed the power of the sun itself.

Impossible, he thought, but the more Escoffier looked at the painting, the more it seemed alive. After a time, a voice behind him, a woman's voice, silvered and shining, said, "The secret is that there is no contrast in colors. The sun has nearly the same luminance as the grayish clouds. If Monet had painted the sun brighter than the clouds, as one finds in real life, the painting would bore."

Escoffier turned around. The milk cream skin, the elegant long neck set in relief against a Belgian lace collar and black velvet waistcoat. Monet's sun paled in comparison to her. Sarah Bernhardt. Her perfume, a musky rose, enveloped him. And yet a moment later, the crowd swelled around her and she was gone as if she never came. Even the scent of her had vanished.

Idiot.

He should have said something, anything. Escoffier had hoped for this moment for such a long time. When Sarah came into Le Petit Moulin Rouge, he stood behind the velvet curtains of the dining room and watched as she ate. Hers was the only ladies' hand in the dining room that he could not bring himself to kiss. Nor could he meet her eye. *One cannot approach a goddess.*

And so he sat in the darkened theater at all her performances, memorized the lines, and relived them in his dreams.

For so very long he wanted to meet her alone and thought of standing outside of the stage door or somehow leading her away from her dinner companions, but all of that seemed offensive, reckless—the type of behavior that lovesick fools engaged in.

And yet the goddess had come and gone and he was silent. *Fool.*

Or maybe it was just a dream.

He told no one of this meeting. To a man like Escoffier—a small man who worked in whispers, whose fleeting miracles were made one plate at a time—Bernhardt seemed well beyond his grasp. But there she was, whispering in his ear. He could still feel the warmth of her lips; could still hear her words, and that voice, weeks later. It made him sleepless.

And yet, he was just as famous as she was.

At the time they met, Escoffier was thirty years old and had already revolutionized fine dining in Paris. Not satisfied with the overly rich and elaborate classics Marie-Antoine Carême had set forth, *faites simple* was Escoffier's mantra. He served only the finest of ingredients and only in season. Excessively complicated sauces became elegant reductions. The gesture replaced excessive gilding. Food was pared down to its essence and so became a mystery to be eaten, not just admired.

Before Escoffier, all fine meals served were *à la française* with several dozen dishes served at the same time. Elaborately garnished soups, pâtés, desserts, fish, crèmes, meats, stews, and cheese were stacked high on shelves as a centerpiece to give the impression of great wealth. By the time the guests arrived at the table, most of the dishes were cold and spoiled. Some were several days old and rancid. Food was something to admire, not eat.

But Escoffier's food was served very hot, so that the diner could embrace the aroma, and *à la russe* with dishes being eaten one at a time in a series of courses, fourteen in all.

Elegance and, in turn, eroticism were the underlying principles. "Let the food speak where words cannot."

He was a quiet storm that swept over the tables of Paris.

She must have known who I was, he later thought. But the next time Escoffier saw Sarah in the dining room, her eyes seemed to look through him. Sarah was the darling of the Comédie-Française, after all. She was, by her own design, unforgettable. She slept in a silk-lined coffin and once attempted to have a tiger's tail grafted to the base of her spine. She was born "Rosine Bernardt," and later added the "h." Her mother was a Jewish courtesan and her father was unknown—at least, that was one story from the press.

It was also reported that Sarah was an American of French-Canadian descent who, as a girl, worked in a hat shop in Muscatine, Iowa. At the age of fifteen, she fell in love with the theater and made her way to Paris by taking on a series of lovers.

There were other stories, of course, most of which she created herself.

When it came to the Divine Miss Sarah, as Oscar Wilde had called her, confusion was understandable. She claimed not to speak any English but her French had an American accent, and so was always suspect. She said her father was "Edouard Bernardt" from the Le Havre of Monet's painting, a magical place, and he was a man who, depending on the moment, was a law student, accountant, naval cadet or naval officer. But "Bernardt" was her grandfather's name. He was Moritz Baruch Bernardt, a petty criminal.

When it came to Sarah, the truth was difficult to ascertain. Alexandre Dumas, *fils*, whose *La Dame aux Camélias* Sarah performed thousands of times, called her a notorious liar. She took famous lovers, including Victor Hugo, of both sexes.

She was thunder and lightning. She was Heaven and Hell. She was unforgettable.

After their meeting at the exhibition, Escoffier barely slept. He threw himself into work and his studies with Doré. Busy, always busy.

Two months had passed when Doré stopped by Le Petit Moulin Rouge to see Escoffier. The artist's studio was around the corner from the café and so he often ordered supper to be delivered, especially when he was working late with students.

"It's for Mademoiselle Bernhardt," he told Escoffier. "You know what she likes. Make whatever will suit her."

Escoffier could not believe what he was hearing. "She's taking lessons?"

"She's very good. It's surprising. Exhibition quality," Doré said. "And don't forget. Several bottles of champagne, of course."

Escoffier knew exactly what Sarah liked; he knew what everyone liked. He kept extensive notes about all of his favored diners. This was his second chance. He sent the champagne ahead and planned to cook and deliver the food himself.

Escoffier knew if he could win Sarah's heart it would be with a dish made of truffles and pureed *foie gras*, the one she often doted over. The subtle aroma of truffle, according to the great Brillat-Savarin, was an aphrodisiac. And so, "Let the food speak where words cannot," Escoffier said, making the sign of the cross, and cooking as if his life depended on it, because on some level it did.

When the chef finally knocked on the studio door, his small hands shook under the weight of the silver tray and its domed cover.

Escoffier had changed into clean clothes and now looked more like a banker than a chef. But he was, most certainly, a chef. Beneath the dome, caramelized sweetbreads, covered with truffles, lay on a bed of golden noodles that were napped in a sauce made from the *foie gras* of ducks fed on wild raspberries, the *framboise*, of the countryside.

It was a dish of profound simplicity, and yet luxury.

When Doré opened the studio door, Escoffier was surprised to see that Sarah was dressed as a young boy, which was, of course, illegal. She wore a black vest, gypsy shirt, riding pants tucked into tall boots with her wild copper river of hair twisted into a knot on the top of her head. Her eyes were dusty, tornadic. Her skin seemed more like marble than flesh. She held a chisel in one hand—the bust she was working on was rough, just a few cuts—and a glass of champagne in the other. The thing he would always remember about that moment was that she was covered with a fine white dust, like powdered sugar.

She could have dismissed him. After all, she clearly didn't remember that they had already met. "Put the tray on the table and go," is what he expected her to say. But she did not.

She looked at him as if he were someone whom she had loved and lost. She would later say that it was at that moment that she noticed that he had her father's eyes—eyes filled with a glorious burning. She had, indeed, remembered him.

As was the custom, she kissed him on both cheeks. "Le Havre," she whispered and Escoffier lifted the silver dome off the heavy platter.

The room was filled with a hint of raspberries, warmed by the summer sun, and truffles, dark as memory.

Sarah leaned over the dish and closed her eyes. "It is as if the very air is made of velvet."

And then she laughed: all bones and fury.

And he was forever hers. No matter whom he loved, or was loved by, the shadow of her always remained.

5

A T LE PETIT MOULIN ROUGE, THERE WERE ROOMS TO BE
seen in, rooms to be lost in, and rooms never to leave. The
restaurant, only open during the summer months, featured
a series of outdoor gardens with arbors of roses and lilacs trellised to
form fragrant walls. Inside there were two formal dining rooms on the
main level, two large private rooms on the second, and several smaller
rooms for more intimate dining on the third and fourth floors. There
were thirty rooms in all and a private entrance at 3 rue Jean Goujon
that was hidden by a roadside lilac grove.

Every night, every dining-room drama was scored by music from
Napoleon Musad's orchestra, who played in the band shell across the
street at the Champs Elysées gardens. That night was no different.

Escoffier usually worked the dining room, kissing the hands of the
ladies who were discreetly ushered in through the side entrance. But
that night, he waited in the kitchen so that he might catch a glimpse of
Sarah leaving Doré's studio, or maybe even find her standing outside
the back door waiting to thank him for such an elegant supper.

It is impossible that she is not moved, he thought and watched the couples in the park, under the gaslights. The ladies in their elegant bustled dresses and peacock-plumed hats. Men in their frock coats and silver handled canes. They strolled along dimly lit walks or sat drinking wine under the darkness of the trees. Musad and the orchestra were playing an evening of the work of Vincent d'Indy, mostly his chamber pieces; a charming backdrop for an evening in the park.

At eight p.m., when the last dinner service ended at Le Petit Moulin Rouge and the waiting horse-drawn hansom cabs began to leave one by one, the orchestra began the *Quartet for Piano and Strings in A Minor, Op. 7*. It was one of Escoffier's favorite works. The joy of it, the coyness, and then the bold dance of the keys and strings always reminded him of his grandmother, the warmth of her kitchen and the kindness that she showed a young boy who wanted to learn the art of cookery.

Tonight, however, the *Quartet* made him furious. All he could think of was Sarah and Doré listening, too, their bodies entwined. Some said Doré was handsome, but to Escoffier his mentor was not an attractive man at all. He looked like an educated ape with his wild hair and unsuitable clothes—he was quite fond of wearing checkered pants and an unmatched checkered scarf in all seasons. *What could Sarah see in him besides his talent?*

But as soon as Escoffier thought this, he understood that it was precisely what attracted her to Doré. He had, after all, illustrated the works of Milton, Dante, Lord Byron and that Spaniard Cervantes and his *Don Quixote*. Not a week passed without a new book illustrated by Doré. He was rich and successful, but it was more than that and Escoffier knew it. Doré was the heart of Paris. His etchings of the Prussian Siege showed a city at its knees—a mother watching in horror as a soldier killed her infant and market stalls selling rats, cats and dogs. Doré had been there, as they all had been there. He remembered for them all and so they would not forget.

And I am nothing but a cook.

And yet Escoffier could not bear to leave the window. *Just one last look.* When the staff left for the evening, Escoffier remained.

Hours later, the *boulanger* found him asleep in a chair facing the street. He shook him gently. "Papa, I have come to start today's bread."

"I was just . . ."

Escoffier could see by the look on the baker's face that there was no need to explain. He knew. *Everyone must know.*

"Yes. Well." Escoffier stood. Straightened his vest. "Please tell the staff that today's menu is in honor of my own personal triumph, the success of the meal that I made for our Miss Bernhardt and the esteemed Gustave Doré, my now former teacher.

"It will be *Noisettes d'Agneau Cora Dressés dans les Coeurs d'Artichauts* and *Pigeonneaux Cocotte.*"

The *boulanger* looked confused. "Artichoke hearts and pigeons?"

"It seems appropriate, does it not? A pigeon is a sucker and the *Coeur d'Artichaut* is a man who falls in love with every girl he meets."

The man laughed and hugged Escoffier as if he were his own son. *"C'est la vie,"* he said. "Enjoy your heartbreak now, while you can. One day soon a woman will come along and you will become an old married man like me with too many children and too little sleep."

"You have bread to make."

The *boulanger* winked, tapped the side of his nose. "Our secret," he said and then went back to his work.

Escoffier washed his face, gathered his topcoat and hat. "I will return before the luncheon service," he said. The light was still on in Doré's studio and so he walked up the stairs and leaned against the door. He could hear the chipping of chisel on marble. The muffled sounds of laughter.

He stood for a long time, listening. When a champagne bottle popped and then all grew quiet, Escoffier knew it was time to go home.

Later that morning, two notes arrived for him. The first was from former French Minister Léon Gambetta requesting a private salon for a meal that night. The menu was to include a saddle of Béhague lamb and the utmost secrecy.

The second was from Sarah.

Both eventually would come to haunt him.

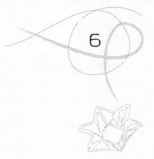

6

SARAH'S STUDIO WAS NOT AT ALL WHAT ESCOFFIER HAD expected. It was not a hot square box of a place like Gustave Doré's. It was a top floor flat in a small odd building that sat in a courtyard just beyond the Boulevard de Courcelles. It looked more like a greenhouse, with several rows of windows and a glass-paned roof. And it was filled with people—all of whom, oddly enough, had striking yellow hair.

Yellow as pineapples, Escoffier thought. He was not expecting this familial scene and felt foolish standing there with a large hamper of food and a chilled bottle of Moët.

"It is as if I am drowning in a sea of butter, is it not, my dear Escoffier?" Sarah laughed. She wore white trousers, a jacket, and a white silk foulard tied around her head like a washerwoman. A cigarette hung from her mouth. She looked beautiful, careless and cunning.

"Drowning in butter. I cannot think of a better way to die," he said, and she leaned into him and kissed him on both cheeks as was the custom, and yet his face went hot.

"Well, I can," she whispered. "But there are children present."

At the center of the room there was indeed a child, a small girl whose golden curly hair formed a halo around her angelic face. She was dressed as cupid wearing only a diaper and holding a small bow and arrow, a quiver on her back. She was obviously posing for Sarah. She had her head tilted to the right and her eyes toward the heavens. Escoffier had never seen such a beautiful child before. It would be difficult to do this creature justice in marble, but he had to admit that Sarah was well on her way. The sculpture she was working on captured the girl's innocence and also her mischievous air.

"This is young Nina," Sarah said. "She was sitting in the balcony last week. I was on stage and could not keep my eyes off her—which is a dangerous thing for an actress. I could have fallen into the orchestra."

An older woman with a straw-colored rope of hair—Escoffier assumed it was Nina's mother—smiled at the thought of the beguiling Sarah tumbling into the timpani. But the man next to her—his lemon-colored mustache made him obviously the child's father—fawned, "And we would have all run to your rescue and swooped you up into our collective adoring arms."

Sarah looked at the man as if he were a speck of dirt on her jacket. "Yes, well, I didn't fall. Lucky us," she said, and turned back to Escoffier. "I've seen your work at Doré's. The floral. You're very good. The poppy was so lifelike; how you crafted the leaf to appear as if it were folded, as if the wind had creased it, was quite remarkable. You *must* understand what I mean. The moment I saw her, I knew I must make a bust of her. A child this charming *must* have the soul of cupid within her. Don't you think?"

Escoffier was not sure what he thought. He had expected a private luncheon. And perhaps an indiscreet moment or two after lunch—Doré had obviously failed her—and then back to the kitchen to oversee Léon Gambetta's special dinner. A luncheon with a yellow-haired family was a possibility that he had not thought about.

"I must get back soon," he said.

Sarah smiled as if she could feel his disappointment, expected it, and yet was irritated by it. "We're almost done here," she said. "But if you are much too busy to wait, you could just leave the basket and put it on Doré's account."

Escoffier thought of the dozens of small plucked pigeons at the restaurant that were, at that very moment, being scalded, roasted and sauced—and felt a certain kinship.

"Mademoiselle, perhaps another time."

"Surely you can wait half of an hour for me."

"I could wait a lifetime."

"So could everyone else, but I only need a half hour from you."

Escoffier smiled and bowed. How could he not? "Shall I set that table?"

The only suitable table in the studio was a long rough wooden one filled with paints and old painting cloths. "Do you have anything clean to cover it with?"

"There are some clothes and things in those suitcases by the door. There might be something there."

The child began to fidget. "When will I get my special book?" she said. "My head is tired. I'm cold."

"Even angels can be ill-tempered," she whispered to Escoffier. "You should keep that in mind for the future."

In person, Sarah was nothing like he imagined. She was more human and somehow more real—and yet still magical. Everyone in the room was watching her. You couldn't look away.

She re-posed the fussy Nina with her head down and eyes up again. *"Mon enfant,"* Sarah said in her most silvery voice. "You have never seen an album like the one I am having made for you for being such a very good model." Sarah stubbed her cigarette out with the heel of her boot and began to chip at the marble again. "Every artist I know I have told of your beauty, and they are working on an offering to honor you. Meissonier, for instance, the painter, is doing a watercolor scene of the war: a Prussian regiment attacking a French inn being defended by French soldiers. It is as bold and brave as you are. Gounod, the composer, is working on a new song, *'La Charmante Modèle,'* because, of course, I have told him what a delightful model you are."

It seemed to Escoffier that the child and her parents were transfixed by the princely sum such a book would bring on the open market.

Escoffier set the table. He'd found a Japanese kimono, an obvious prop from some theater production, to use as a tablecloth. Paris had recently fallen in love with all things oriental. It was red silk brocade, covered with a flock of white flying cranes, and made from a single bolt of fabric. The neckline and cuffs were thickly stained with stage makeup but the kimono itself was quite beautiful. It ran the length of the thin table. The arms overhung one end.

Outside the building he'd seen a garden with a sign that read "Please do not pick." But it was, after all, for a beautiful woman. Who would deny him? And so Escoffier cut a bouquet of white flowers: roses, peonies and a spray of lilies, with rosemary stalks to provide the greenery. He placed them in a tall water glass and then opened the basket of food he'd brought. He laid out the china plates so that they rested between the cranes, and then the silver knives, forks and spoons, and a single crystal glass for her champagne. Even though it was early afternoon, he'd brought two dozen candles.

The food had to be served *à la française*; there were no waiters to bring course after course. So he kept it simple. Tartlets filled with sweet oysters from Arcachon and Persian caviar, chicken roasted with truffles, a warm baguette, *pâté de foie gras,* and small sweet strawberries served on a bed of sugared rose petals and candied violets.

There was a lovely domestic rhythm to the moment. On one side of the studio, Escoffier was transforming a corner into an elegant dining room. He pulled the red velvet curtains, lit dozens of candles to set the stage. On the other side, Sarah was sculpting the petulant cherub and weaving the tale of the magic book—a promise she would clearly not keep.

Half an hour elapsed. As promised, Sarah bid Nina and her star-struck parents goodbye.

"Such beautiful idiots," Sarah said after them.

"And the book is fantasy?"

She laughed, "But of course. I am fantasy."

A thundercloud passed overhead. A hard rain began to fall on the glass roof. The room filled with the scent of the flowers and wet earth, humus and peat.

Sarah washed her hands and face in the sink as if she were an ordinary groundskeeper. She scrubbed her elbows and arms with harsh lye soap and then wiped them dry with a torn cotton towel. Escoffier was mesmerized by the humility of the moment—this was after all the great Sarah Bernhardt. Then she shook off her scarf and her wild tumble of hair cascaded down her back. She took off her boots and rolled her stockings into a ball. She took off her jacket. And then her vest. Her trousers. She folded her silk blouse, unhooked her corset, and continued on until she was completely naked. She never paused once. It was as if Escoffier wasn't even there.

And then she rubbed her skin with a spiced oil that reminded him of walking down the street in the Moroccan section of Paris late at night, when the lingering fragrance of so many evening meals filled the air with cumin and ginger, cinnamon, cardamom and pepper.

She was Venus, that much was clear, standing naked in a darkened room, unashamed as a child. But the darkness that the rain brought made her skin seem so white that she could have been made of marble. She was as untouchable as any museum statue.

The rain fell hard against the glass roof. Escoffier could feel it in his veins.

Sarah turned to him and seemed bemused that he was still sitting there. "Most men would have either run or thrown themselves on me."

"I am not most men."

They both listened to the rain for a moment. It seemed to be letting up a bit. Dozens of flickering candles set across the long red table warmed the moment.

"Do you see this?" Sarah pointed to a half-moon scar on the side of her belly. "It is my one imperfection. Odéon. During the siege."

Four years earlier, during the Prussian War, Sarah had converted the Odéon Theatre into a hospital. She and the other actors had served as nurses. She hired doctors. She'd bartered sex for government rations for the injured and raised a flock of chickens and ducks in her dressing room to slaughter for those who only had a few days to live. Jules, Escoffier's pastry chef, had worked there with her. He stood alongside her as they collected the dead and dying from the streets. "Ambulance! Ambulance!" they would murmur as they walked along in the stunned darkness.

"The dead," Jules told Escoffier. "You never get over the sight of them. Nor that smell."

Escoffier understood. He'd traveled as a cook with Napoleon III's army, was a prisoner of war at Metz, and arrived in Paris in time for the uprisings in which Catholics like himself were slain in the street. *Too much death.*

"I am seeing Léon Gambetta this evening," he told Sarah and as soon as he did, he couldn't believe he'd said it. Something about her made him want to tell her everything. "But it is a secret. He is setting up some sort of meeting."

Sarah's face went pale at the mention of Gambetta's name. The rain clouds shifted and shafts of strained sunlight poured down through the glass roof. Her skin turned from marble to paper and she turned slight and frail. Escoffier found himself sweating hard.

During the siege, Léon Gambetta, the former Minister of Interior and of War, ordered that the French fight to the death. "Never surrender," he told the people. And so they didn't. They didn't feel that they needed to. The French had ingenuity and invention on their side— every man in the army was equipped with a new breech-loading Chassepot rifle and several had the *mitrailleuse,* an early machine gun. National pride was never stronger. Unfortunately, they were no match against the Prussian army, whose sheer numbers alone were overwhelming. Paris was soon surrounded.

Gambetta was undaunted. Like most born handsome, he never entertained the possibility of failure. He was emotional and unruly, given to equal parts of eloquence and heroics. He had only one eye and the empty socket reminded everyone that he understood loss and could overcome it.

For that moment in time, he was Paris and all of Paris knew it. He had a plan. He would pilot a balloon, the *Armand-Barbès,* to Tours, where he would organize an army to recapture the city.

It was an act of holy rage.

At the appointed time, everyone gathered where the Sacré-Coeur now stands. There were people as far as the eye could see. Shoulder to shoulder, in the valleys and along the hillsides, the city watched as Gambetta, theatrically heroic in his floor-length fur, was carried through the crowd. Saintlike and wild-eyed, he climbed into the ragged gondola basket. He looked up into the large gas-filled balloon, the burners flaming, and then nodded. A dozen men on the ground guided the balloon into the air, one by one they let the rope slip from their fingers while Gambetta unfurled a tricolor flag.

"Vive la France! Vive la République!"

The crowd joined in—shouting, weeping. Fear and joy intertwined.

Unfortunately, the *Armand-Barbès* did not ascend quickly. It spun, jerked and groaned its way forward low along the ground, taking the hopes of Paris with it. And then, suddenly, for no reason at all, the balloon took flight. An ambling ghost, it began its journey to Tours on the winds of hope.

But Gambetta arrived too late. Before he could mobilize his army, Napoleon III was captured and France, bloody and beaten, had surrendered.

"We would have followed him into Hell," Sarah said to Escoffier and ran her finger along the scar's jagged edge. "The army continued to store explosives in the theater's basement. It is universally known as a barbaric act to bomb the wounded, Gambetta told me this, but he should have told the Prussians, too.

"Toto was just a young boy; his grandmother left him in my care. He was like Nina, beautiful: round cheeks, lazy and charming. He was standing just a few feet from me, in the courtyard, when they bombed us and he was cut in two by a shell."

There was a flatness to her voice that was unexpected. Escoffier had seen all her performances on stage. If this were a speech written by Victor Hugo, Sarah would have made the windows rattle with the depth of her sorrow. But she stood before him, small and naked, and whispered.

"And then, of course, came the Peace Treaty and now the Prussians are Germans and parts of France are now not French. And all is to be forgiven, they tell us. But Toto. Beautiful Toto. There was no peace for him. It was as though a tiger had torn open the body with its claws and emptied it with a fury and a refinement of cruelty."

Sarah had a look in her eyes that reminded Escoffier of the horses of their regiment. One by one, he was forced to slaughter the elegant beasts; the men were starving. He'd say a prayer, slice each throat quickly, and then braise, sauce, stew and tell himself that each life taken saved dozens more. Lentils, peas, beans and macaroni—whatever he could find to make the meat go further and postpone the next death a little longer he would use.

Three days after the army's surrender a few skeletal horses remained dying in the waters of Ban-Saint-Martin. These beasts who'd carried their riders into battle, whom Escoffier himself fed whatever scraps of food he could spare, turned their dull eyes to him—as did Sarah at that moment.

"It was a brave thing you did for France," he said.

She shook her head. "It was my duty. I could afford to send my mother, sister and my little boy to The Hague and so I could afford bravery. Most had no choice."

She pulled a robe out of the suitcase and put it on. It was white satin with white feathers at the throat, wrists and the hem of its opulent train. It made her red hair seem as if it were on fire. Her skin was even more translucent. But her eyes were dark with sorrow.

Sarah sat down across from Escoffier.

"Why are you telling me this?"

"Because I want there to be no illusions between us."

Escoffier had to smile. "You are an actress. How is that even possible?"

"What you see on stage is a distillation of the history of my heart. What you see across this table is the person."

He poured her a glass of Moët. She took a long sip. The silence between them was awkward. They were strangers, after all.

"Very well," he said. "What else should I know?"

"I was raised in a convent and I not only wanted to be a nun,

I wanted to be a saint. I wanted to love God with a love that was boundless."

Escoffier sat back in his chair. "Now, I believe that you are making sport of me."

"It's true."

"Are you still a Catholic?"

"*Non.* I am actually a Jew by birth but I know many Catholics; many of them are brave radicals. I am sympathetic to them and appalled by their persecution here in France, but for me, God cannot exist. It is not possible. If he did why did He forsake Paris?"

Escoffier felt her sorrow as deeply as he felt his own. He'd asked himself the same question many times.

He picked up a small fragrant strawberry. "This is not a gift from God?"

"It is summer made manifest, that is all."

He brushed the strawberry against her lips. "And the scent?"

"A promise of beauty that cannot be kept."

Escoffier gently kissed her lips, nothing more than just a graze. "And the taste?"

He placed the fruit in her mouth and he could see on her face what he knew in his heart. The sweetness of the berry was intense. "How is there not a God?" he asked.

She laughed and took his small hands in hers. "You are a surprising man, my dear Escoffier. Promise me we will always be friends."

Friends? The word pained him. He had hoped for so much more.

Escoffier gently pulled away. Stood. "I'll have the boy come around and pick up these things when you're finished."

And then he left without another word.

7

SCOFFIER TOOK THE LONG THIN BONING KNIFE AND RAN
it quickly along the flesh of the pink baby lamb. He usually
had his *rôtisseur*, Xavier, do this as the man was from Alsace
and the meat and sausages of the Rhine River valley were legend-
ary. However, Léon Gambetta specified that Escoffier cook the entire
meal himself—for anyone else this request would be impossible but
the Minister had never reserved a private room for a meeting before,
and had certainly never dictated its preparation. Escoffier assumed
that the evening was very important and, as everyone else was
thinking, probably involved the Germans. Certainly, Prince Edward,
at the very least. The request for the lamb made that obvious. And so
Xavier could not be trusted.

Xavier, the *rôtisseur*, was a red-haired dour-looking man, one of
the many Catholics who believed that France lost the war because she
had lost her faith in God. Escoffier was not as radical in his beliefs.
The two men became colleagues when Xavier served with Escoffier's
regiment, starved alongside him during the Siege of Metz, and came
to Le Petite Moulin Rouge because he had no place else to go. His

wife and child had been murdered when the Prussians came across the border. The lush vineyards and rolling hills of Xavier's homeland were now in German hands. The river's abundant trout, carp, perch and crayfish now belonged to them. The seemingly endless flocks of pheasants, ducks and wild geese were now theirs, too. Even Xavier's own home had fallen into the hands of a Prussian officer; its century-old vineyard still produced a Gewurztraminer, which was filled with a ripe mouth of fruit and perfumed with a flowery bouquet, but now a German flag graced each bottle.

As Escoffier butchered the lamb, Xavier hovered nearby holding the small end of a tenderloin, green and dried from hanging in the cellar to age, and looking like a banished child.

"My friend, I want you to be beyond reproach. We must respect the Minister's request," Escoffier said and went back to his work. He was careful not to score the lamb's skin. He followed the line of the bone, quickly, again and again. Once the meat was trimmed, he pounded it flat.

"Come now. Work. Work heals the heart," he said and stuffed the lamb roll with truffle-studded *foie gras* that he had marinated in Marsala wine, then wrapped the lamb in muslin and placed it in a pâté pan, long and rectangular. He covered it with the remaining marinade and veal stock.

Xavier just stood there. Watching. Demanding in his silence, but Escoffier wouldn't look at him. The chef continued on, placed the lamb in another pan, a bain-marie, and filled it halfway with water. "Please," Escoffier said gently, not looking at Xavier. "The dining room will be open soon and there is so much to do. Xavier. For me. Work."

For a moment, the man seemed as if he was going to speak but decided against it. He slapped the beef loin he was holding onto the butcher block next to Escoffier and began to scrape away the mold, trim the hardened fat, shape and cut it until he had a perfectly mar-bled Châteaubriand, as large as his hand.

Escoffier put an arm around him, to comfort, to encourage. "There. It is beautiful, is it not?"

Xavier pulled away. "For those who can afford it."

The words made Escoffier's face go hot. Civility must be main-tained—that was the first rule of the kitchen. Xavier knew that. Escoffier tugged at his earlobe, a reminder to keep his own anger in check. "Lucky for you there are some who can," he said and immedi-ately regretted the tone and the implication that this man who had lost so much and suffered so much was somehow ungrateful. It was not the case, but there was no time for self-pity. Léon Gambetta would be arriving soon.

"I am sorry," Escoffier said and it felt as if he were whispering. Xavier said nothing.

All around them the others prepared for the night's rush. Like a cotillion, dozens of cooks, immaculate in their whites, swirled around and around each other locked in the dance of kitchen miracles. Fish were beheaded and scaled; ducks were plucked; dough was shaped into rows of baguettes, and blackberries were dusted with sugar. Har-mony and perfection happened at every turn, but Xavier and Escoffier were oblivious to it all. They stood as if on an island: shipwrecked.

Escoffier could feel the man's sorrow, the dark edge of it, but the lamb needed to poach for nearly an hour and then be thoroughly chilled. He had no time. "I consider this matter finished," he said and covered the lamb with a sheet of roasted pork skin, pushed past Xavier, and placed it in the oven.

"Ana Elizabeth was only six years old," Xavier said quietly.

The daughter.

Escoffier had seen a photo of Xavier's family. His wife was tall and dour, as he was, but the girl had the kind of smile that reminded

Escoffier of the first apples of fall, crisp and sweet. He could keenly imagine the pain of such a loss, and what he couldn't imagine he could see in Xavier's face. It was heartbreaking, but there was so much work to be done. Escoffier just couldn't bring himself to speak of it.

Unfortunately, he later understood that what goes unsaid is often the one thing that can never be forgiven nor forgotten.

Escoffier stepped past Xavier and began to wash the fat of the lamb off his hands in the large porcelain sink. The water was hot, steaming. The scent of the olive oil soap made his stomach growl. He'd forgotten to eat all day. He suddenly felt dizzy, tired. The restaurant was overbooked for the evening and Gambetta, Prince Edward and possibly the Kaiser would soon arrive. *No time. No time.*

"Papa," Xavier said, and put a hand on his shoulder but before he could say anything more Escoffier gestured him away. He would not look at the man. *This has to end.* He continued to wash his hands.

"No. No excuses," Escoffier said. "The kitchen must be your home, your church, your mistress, your family, your country—there is no room for any other love here. If you do not understand that, then you have no place here."

Escoffier's hands were scalded but he couldn't stop washing them. He suddenly felt unclean.

When he finally turned back to Xavier. "Work," he said. "Or go."

He knew the man had no place else to go. The family of chefs, the home of this kitchen, this sacred place, was all the man had left in the world.

Xavier's face was unreadable. He gently placed the Châteaubriand on a rack and went back downstairs to the meat locker, knife in hand.

Good, Escoffier thought.

"He's here," someone shouted. Escoffier quickly dried his hands. Minister Gambetta was not the sort of man who liked to be kept waiting.

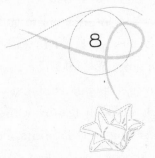

8

ESCOFFIER HAD HEARD ABOUT THE CHRISTMAS MEAL, OF course. When one serves kangaroo and elephant it does not go unnoticed, even during a siege.

Zoo animals—it was a practical last resort for cafés such as Voisin's. Before the siege, the restaurant's manager had stocked the cellars with tanks of fish, live rabbits, suckling pigs and wild hens but by December even the horse meat had run out. And, as Gustav Doré had immortalized in his work, the markets were selling dressed and trussed rats at a franc each; one franc fifty for the larger ones, which neared two pounds.

Christmas Day was the ninety-ninth day of the Paris siege. And so a holiday fête of this nature was inevitable. The zoo in the Jardin des Plantes could no longer feed these exotic beasts. Even the famed Castor and Pollux, the only pair of elephants in Paris, were not spared. The meal was a tribute to their exquisite beauty and a celebration of salvation—at least for those who could afford it. Who were very few. Most in Paris were dying of starvation, food poisoning or pneumonia. And yet, café life went on. It was, after all, the soul of the city.

When Escoffier saw the wine list for Gambetta's secret dinner, he knew that it was no mistake that he had demanded the same wines that were offered for that famed Christmas meal—Latour Blanche 1861, Château Palmer 1864, Mouton Rothschild 1846, Romanée-Conti 1858, and even the Gran Porto 1827.

"A Bollinger, too?" Escoffier asked, which made Gambetta smile.

"Of course you know," he said. "I knew it would be impossible to hide this from you."

"I never forget a menu. It is both my gift and my curse. Unfortunately, the only wine we have in our cellar is the Rothschild but it is a beautiful, yet melancholy, wine and should evoke the proper memory."

Voisin's Christmas celebration began with stuffed donkey's head and then moved onward to roast camel, elephant consommé, kangaroo stew, leg of wolf cooked venison style and *le chat flanqué de rats*—cat surrounded by rats. There was also *La Terrine d'Anteloupe aux Truffles*, a terrine of boned rack of antelope studded with *foie gras* and truffles—a dish that bore a striking resemblance to the lamb that Gambetta had requested.

Escoffier had a sinking feeling, which was made worse by the fact that Gambetta suddenly demanded that all the waiters be dismissed for the evening and that Escoffier not only cook the entire meal, but also serve it himself.

"You were in Metz, is that not correct?" Gambetta said. Escoffier had never hidden the fact, but was surprised that the Minister knew.

"That was a long time ago."

"For a great chef, a culinary magician such as yourself, the starvation must have been unbearable. Tell me, did you not dream of pastry and champagne every night?"

Escoffier pulled the selected bottles from the racks, hoping the conversation would take a different turn. He never spoke of the war, never allowed talk of it in his kitchen. It was over. Done.

Gambetta put an arm around Escoffier's shoulder. "Not many understand the beauty and passion of food as you do. The dreams must have driven a man like you to madness."

The Minister's breath was hot and stale. The dampness of the wine cellar chilled Escoffier. He pulled away slightly. "I dreamt of France and her children."

There are some things that one does not speak of. Even a man like Escoffier, the son of a blacksmith, knew that. But Gambetta seemed unwilling to end the conversation. "Of course," he said and then leaned in even closer. "Still. You must have longed for all this." He pointed to the wines that surrounded them, each bottle a part of the history of France: dark and complex.

"One makes do."

Gambetta seemed so pale in the candlelight, more like the memory of the man and not the man himself. Escoffier carefully took the Mouton Rothschild from the shelf, lifted the bottle to the flame to examine it. The wine was heavy with sediment, in need of a good airing before drinking.

Gambetta took the bottle from his hands. "May I?" He examined the cork, obviously looking to see if it had been removed previously, if the wine had been diluted or tampered with in any way. It was clear that he trusted Escoffier only to a certain point. It was outrageous to be treated that way, but Escoffier knew that to speak of such things would have been insolent—and the consequences of such an act would have been far worse.

And so he said, "The Rothschild is very lovely. You will be quite pleased. It reminds me of brown sugar, chocolate and dried plum—very powerful and elegant. Let me show you. The color is remarkable."

Escoffier uncorked the wine and slowly began to decant it in the candlelight, carefully leaving the sediment behind. "Amazing, isn't it?

Rubies—those are the only other things on this earth that are as beautiful as this is, are they not? No?"

Gambetta watched as Escoffier deftly poured the ruby river of wine, gently, slowly and carefully. The musty air was filled with the particular lushness of late summer with its ripe cherries and tart apples.

"Lovely," the chef said under his breath. "So very lovely."

Gambetta laughed. "My friend, you are a liar," he said somewhat charmingly, somewhat ruefully. "You pour that wine as one lowers his lover down upon silken sheets. You cannot tell me that you no longer hold the pain of hunger in your heart."

"We tracked prey and foraged just as the Indians did," Escoffier said, still pouring. "And so every meal, no matter how simple, was a feast to us—that was key. *Saucisson*, sardines—it did not matter. When eaten with the proper spirit, food nourishes both body and spirit."

Gambetta took the bottle from Escoffier's hand. "You nearly starved to death. How can you not feel anger?"

The conversation was exhausting. It was now quite clear that the Germans were coming, and Xavier would most definitely have to be sent home. And on such a night! They were short handed and every table for both the early and late dinner seatings was reserved. There was no one in the brigade, except Escoffier, who could adequately serve as *rôtisseur*. But of course, he had to also serve this meal. It was impossible. And now his own loyalty to France was in question.

Escoffier took a deep breath before he answered. "It was war. But even in war, there can be great gifts. The eve of the battle of Gravelotte was on the day of Assumption, the day of Our Lady, Patroness of France. We had a lovely *lapin à la soubise*. The rabbit was sautéed in a puree of caramelized onions and finished with cognac. It was really quite stunning."

At the mention of Gravelotte, Gambetta became enraged. "You speak as if you are a fool," he said and threw the bottle of Rothschild onto the floor. "The day of Assumption, the day of Our Lady, Patroness of France, as you say—this is the very root of France's problem."

"I am sorry. It was not my intention to offend," Escoffier said. It was all that he could think to say. He had no idea why Gambetta was suddenly livid.

"I assumed that you were a worldly man. Sophisticated. I see that I was wrong."

Gambetta was pacing in and out of the light. He was furious enough to walk out, leaving Escoffier with fine wines oxidizing and a lavish meal with no one to eat it. "I am extremely sorry," Escoffier said again, knelt, and began to pick up shards of glass with his bare hands. Wine seeped into the wool of his dove gray pants.

"Don't understand, do you?"

"I sincerely wish that I did."

Gambetta yanked him up by his collar. Escoffier's platform shoes made him unsteady. He nearly fell over backwards. The shards of glass dug deeply into his palms. His hands began to bleed. Gambetta did not notice.

"Look at me when I speak to you. How do you not see the danger that is all around us?"

"I am just a chef. My world is as vast as an egg."

"Which everyone knows that you can cook over six hundred ways. This sudden false humility is not becoming."

"It is not my intention—"

"You and I both know that we can no longer live in a country directed by religious superstition and unpredictable devotions. Catholics control everything and their passion makes them easily manipulated. The day of Assumption, the day of Our Lady, Patroness of France—it's obscene how they prey on the simple-minded."

Escoffier suddenly found it difficult to breathe. "This is about Catholics?" Blood and wine were running down his arm, staining his pants, the cuff of his white shirt. He hid them behind his back. The sight of his wounds would only make matters worse.

"These idiot Catholics think if they offer a fatted lamb to the heavens it will bring them luck. You cannot run an army or a country on luck and nonsense."

Escoffier knew where talk like this could lead. After the fall of France, the new ruling body, the radical Paris Commune, took possession of the city and began to arrest priests and prominent members of their congregations. A few days later, the Martyrs of Paris, as they had come to be known, were executed within the prison of La Roquette, shot down at the Barriere d'Italie and massacred at Belleville. Escoffier himself barely escaped.

Publicly Gambetta opposed these actions and ordered members of the Commune executed for their actions. And yet here he was.

"The Catholics must be dealt with," he said.

Obviously, this was some sort of a political chess game. Escoffier looked at the cuts on his hands, the stain of the wine.

"It was grace," Escoffier said. His voice sounded small, unsteady. His hands were throbbing. "We had been told that the day of Our Lady was chosen as a way to appeal to her mercy. We had hoped for grace."

Escoffier felt trapped like a small kitchen mouse.

Gambetta smiled. "And what you received was stupidity," he said. "Twenty thousand Prussians died—but no one secured the win. That fool, Marshal Bazaine, believed God was on his side and granted him grace, as you say, and so assumed victory and retreated. It was an act of treason."

"I have often said that he was a traitor to his country."

"Because he was a Catholic."

"Because he was a fool."

"Which is the same. He held God above France. That should never be. You of all people know that. How many days at Metz were you without food?"

"It is not important, I served my France."

"How many?"

"I ate better than most."

"How many days?" Gambetta shouted. The two men were standing face to face under the gaslight. Escoffier knew how he looked to Gambetta, who was after all a great man, a hero. To him, the chef was insignificant. Not brave, not bold, just a small man, an ungrown simple child.

Gambetta stepped back into the darkness. Unreadable.

"I am a patriot," Escoffier said. "If you need my secrecy for France, it is yours."

The Minister began walking deeper and deeper into the wine cellar, deeper into the darkness. His footsteps echoed on the cobblestone floor. He started raving. "This is not another uprising against the Catholics—do not be mistaken."

His voice boomed as if he were giving an address to a crowd of thousands. Practice, perhaps.

"We as a government no longer desire to share our influence with the Church. We desire simply to have liberty—true, lawful and noble liberty—both for the Church and for ourselves."

"I am here to serve my France," Escoffier said and felt as if he were shouting prayers into storm clouds.

From deep in the dark cellar, Gambetta laughed. "And your God? You see, I had been told that you are a Catholic. I am now trying to determine what kind of a Catholic you are.

"Who was the apostle who betrayed Jesus? Judas? Are you a Catholic like that? Or are you Thomas the Doubter? Or Paul the Loyalist?"

The words echoed. Escoffier felt his face go hot. If Gambetta could not trust him, all he'd worked for and suffered for would be gone. He'd be like Xavier—adrift.

"There is no place for God in my kitchen," Escoffier shouted and as soon as he did he felt ashamed. He turned away, raised his bloodied hands to his face. Tears burned his wounds.

For a moment, everything was silent. Then there was the sound of heavy footsteps on the cobblestones; this time they were coming toward Escoffier. Exhaustion overwhelmed him. Suddenly, Gambetta, still in the shadows, stopped. He was so close, Escoffier could smell him: tobacco and wet leather.

"The Prince of Wales claims that you can be trusted with matters of the heart."

"France is my heart."

"Why should I believe you?"

"Because cooking is a science, an art, and most important, a passion. The man who puts all his heart into satisfying his fellow men deserves consideration."

Gambetta stepped back into the light.

"Very well. You are Judas, then. Very good." He laughed. "Tonight, for France, you will do a great service. With this meal we will honor the suffering of the past and look ahead to a brave new future, a future in which France will become the glorious maiden we know her to be."

There was a tap at the wine cellar door.

Escoffier opened it painfully, his hands so scored he knew the dinner would not be his best effort. He was surprised to see a young boy standing there. "Vincent? Why are you not peeling potatoes for this evening's meal?"

The boy whispered in his ear, "Miss Bernhardt is in the kitchen with the body." And then ran.

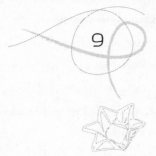

9

*n egg yolk needs one cup of oil to emulsify—less and it will
not bind.*

Salting meat before cooking prevents browning.

Green vegetables lose their color when cooked in a lidded pot.

*Fish is fully cooked only when specks of white albumen dot the surface of
the skin.*

Mushrooms must never be washed.

Flour must always be sieved.

Searing meat does not preserve the juices—quite the opposite.

These were the things that Escoffier knew for certain. He reviewed
them over and over in his head all evening long. They were unquestionable. Unchanging. They made sense. Xavier's suicide didn't. He
was a Catholic, after all.

"Stop thinking," Sarah said.

She was lying on top of the long wooden table where they had sat
hours earlier. "You're still thinking about it," she said. "Stop. Some
things never make sense."

The studio was filled with candles. Some Escoffier had brought earlier for their luncheon—they were made from beeswax and filled the air with a sweet caramel scent. The rest were Sarah's. There were exotics such as blood orange oil, frankincense and myrrh. The flowers he had picked—roses, peonies and a spray of lilies—opened into full blossom under the heat of so many flames and joined the heady mix.

Like dozens of tiny flickering stars, the candles and their scents made the dark night seem even darker, made the cream of her skin seem incandescent. She had washed Xavier's blood from her feet—there was so much of it that her silk slippers had been ruined. She had washed the smell of food and sweat from her hair and her skin—she had never served a meal before. She had no idea that once she put on the waiter's black frock coat and striped trousers, how much work it was to serve. The plates were heavy, the wine needed to be poured just so.

But someone had to serve the meal and Gambetta trusted no one else.

Once Sarah saw Escoffier's damaged hands, she insisted that she was the only one who Gambetta would consider an acceptable replacement. "At the very least," she said, "the Minister will find the substitution an amusing surprise and excuse any misstep that I might make."

He did not. Gambetta was so alarmed when Sarah walked into the private room to begin the service that he stormed down into the kitchen in a rage, pulled Escoffier off his feet and was about to strike the small man when the chef raised his shredded hands and said, "The Rothschild."

"There was to be secrecy."

"Surely your lover can be trusted with her silence."

It was an assumption on Escoffier's part but obviously correct.

Gambetta put him down and returned to his table. Of course, there was no choice. Edward VII, the Prince of Wales, Escoffier's own "Dear Bertie," Chancellor Otto von Bismarck, and young Wilhelm II, the future Kaiser and the Prince of Wales' cousin, were all seated at Gambetta's table in the private salon at the top of the stairs. Waiting.

Wilhelm II, with his withered hand and odd piercing eyes, seemed to Escoffier to be just a frightened boy; he fidgeted in his chair.

At the sight of the great actress Sarah Bernhardt dressed as a waiter, the men laughed, uncomfortable. Each one was not quite sure how many of the group Sarah had taken for her lover at one time or another, but each assumed that it was more than one. But they were not there to speak of such things.

The Germans, led by Bismarck, had been trying to isolate the French after the war, but Resistance efforts led by the Catholics plagued them. The Germans were his avowed enemy but Gambetta, always the politician, was more than willing to help them with their Catholic problem, their *Kulturkampf*, or "culture struggle" as Bismarck was fond of calling it, in exchange for more power. Dear Bertie was more than willing to help broker the deal, in exchange for more power for himself, of course.

And so, after the first wine was poured, Escoffier saw that they ignored the Divine Miss Sarah completely, and he returned to his kitchen for the evening. There was cantaloupe to start. And then a consommé garnished with gold leaf and the most delicate custard. A fried fillet of sole, in the style of the miller's wife, rolled in flour, fried and garnished with fish roe. A terrine of boned rack of baby lamb studded with *foie gras* and truffles. Chicken in aspic. Crayfish soufflé. And sweets, so many sweets. The final menu was daunting.

Melon Cantalop	*Soufflé d'Ecrevisses*
Porto Blanc	*Rothschild*
...	...
Consommé Royal	*Biscuit glacé Tortoni*
Paillettes Diablées	*Gaufrettes Normandes*
...	...
Fillets de sole aux laitances à	*Les Plus Belles Pêches de*
la Meunière	*Montreuil*
...	*Amandes vertes*
Selle d'Agneau de Behague	...
poêlée	*Café Moka à la Française*
Haricots verts à l'Anglaise	*Grande Fine Champagne*
Pommes noisettes à la crème	*Liqueur des Chartreux*
...	...
Poularde en gelée	*Vins Choisis: Chablis*
Salade d'asperges	*Col d'Éstournel, étampe 1864*
...	*Veuve Clicquot 1874*

The meal took hours to prepare and serve. Several times Escoffier bled through his gauze bandages and was forced to stop and change the dressing. But he considered himself lucky. His palms suffered the most damage and he could easily work around that problem with Sarah providing service.

For the most part, it went smoothly although Escoffier did not have Sarah present the terrine of baby lamb. That would have been Xavier's dish, the one he would have created. Escoffier brought it up himself. When he plated young Wilhelm II's serving, the boy quickly took a bite, and asked for more.

"Amazing," he said. "You must send the recipe to our palace chef. It is so German. Royal in nature."

The young have no sense of history, he thought.

It was now nearly midnight. The meal seemed so long ago. Sarah again was naked.

"You promised me that I would taste moonlight," she said.

"Then close your eyes."

Her skin smelled like butter. Her hair fell in soft waves off her delicate shoulders; it reminded him of autumn, the copper hills of the countryside. The half-moon scar on her belly was indeed her only imperfection, and yet he could not bear even to kiss her.

"I have misplaced my heart," he said.

"Stop thinking."

But he couldn't. The first time he'd seen Sarah that evening, she was on her knees holding Xavier's head in her lap like the Virgin with her holy Son, fresh from the cross. The *rôtisseur* was bleeding onto the floorboards of the meat locker. To Escoffier, it seemed like the loneliest place on earth to die. All around the man, rows and rows of beef had been left to dry on wooden shelves. The locker was filled with them, from top to bottom. The air was cold. It reeked of rotting flesh and mold. The pastry chef Jules, the former nurse from Sarah's Odéon hospital, stood behind her. He was angry and red-eyed as a spider.

"A blade to the heart."

Jules answered the question that had not been asked. It was clear he blamed Escoffier.

Sarah made the sign of the cross with cooking oil on Xavier's head and prayed, "Through this holy anointing may the Lord in his love and mercy help you with the grace of the Holy Spirit," and then onto his hands and said, "May the Lord who frees you from sin save you and raise you up."

The Last Rites, Escoffier thought. It was something she obviously learned from the convent or perhaps Odéon.

"Amen," Jules said.

"The police have been sent for, and paid for," Sarah said. "I arrived to tell you that I was sorry you left this afternoon. You seemed upset. And then this. Jules found him."

Escoffier could hear the shuffle of the kitchen brigade overhead. Imagined the men and their red sweating faces; the heat of the coke and coal fires, their own private Hell. *I ask so very much of them.* He looked at his bleeding hands.

Jules picked up Xavier's body from the floor as if it were one of his flour sacks and carried him out.

Sarah and Escoffier did not follow. They stood together in the cramped humid locker. She took his bleeding hands into hers, examined them closely.

"Gambetta?"

He nodded. "Le Petit Moulin Rouge was all Xavier had left and I threatened to send him away."

"Don't think about it anymore. You were angry."

"I never allow anger in my kitchen."

Then she did what she had done earlier that day—kissed the tips of his fingers one by one. He pulled away. His blood was on her lips.

"The Germans," he said. "They were Gambetta's honored guests and so they are my honored guests. Besides, Wilhelm is just a boy. He asked for second helpings, like any child would."

Escoffier wanted to say, "I had no choice but to welcome them," but that was not true and they both knew it.

"Don't think about it anymore."

The world felt small and dangerous, but she kissed his now bandaged hands so gently, he felt himself warm to her.

"You promised me that I would taste the moon, did you not?" she whispered.

"And so you shall," he said, even though he could hear the echo of sorrow in his voice.

Escoffier slowly folded his dress coat, removed his cravat and rolled up the wine-stained cuffs of his shirt. He washed his hands carefully in cool water and rewrapped them in fresh gauze. When he removed the cork from a tall thin bottle of white truffle oil, the dark deep scent of wet earth grounded the wildly fragrant air.

Sarah laughed with pleasure. "The scent alone makes me feel as if I am naked in a jungle at night."

"The air is warm?"

"Yes."

"And you find you cannot sleep."

"Yes."

"Good."

Then drop by drop—so very slowly—Escoffier poured a long thin line of white truffle oil between her breasts and all the way to the mound of her belly. With two fingers, he gently rubbed it into her skin.

Her breath was quick and uneven. As was his. With a small iridescent spoon, made from the shells of wild rock oysters, Escoffier slowly began to place tiny mounds of caviar, each a perfect circle, along the platter of her bone. Each shimmered with its own light—dark gold to pale amber and then light gray to blue black.

She was a feast before him. A fallen angel surrounded by stars and perfumed by the heavens. With the mother of pearl spoon he scooped the tiny blue-black eggs from the first pile and placed them gently against her lips.

"The moon," he said.

She did not open her eyes but let the caviar slip onto her tongue. He knew that once the fine skin of it melted, the flavor would be delicate and fleeting. And it was. He could tell by the look of pure pleasure on her face.

From the darkest beluga to the golden almas, creamy and subtle, to the osetra, with its hint of walnuts and cream, to the small gray eggs of the sevruga, with its overwhelming flavor of the sea, Escoffier fed Sarah a universe of moons. And she, in turn, met each with a kiss that was deeper than the last. But when she finally pulled him down on top of her, he stepped away. Breathing hard.

"Perfection," he said, "should not be so easily won."

When this evening was later recalled, Escoffier would not speak of Sarah. Nor Xavier. He would, however, speak of the private meal of important men. He would say that the supper, prepared by his own hands, was the beginning of a great friendship between France and England. He would often claim that the famous Entente Cordiale, a series of agreements between the two countries, which became official in 1907, was actually conceived that night at Le Petite Moulin Rouge.

The details of the evening were never given. All he would say was that Gambetta had requested a private salon for a special dinner for the Prince of Wales, Dear Bertie, and "another important foreign diplomat," whose name was seemingly forgotten despite the fact that the menu was recounted in great detail.

"The meal had a serious *raison d'être*," Escoffier was fond of saying.

It was an event that he was particularly proud of despite the fact that a few days after the dinner, on July 13 in the town of Bad Kissingen, a devout Catholic named Eduard Kullmann attempted to assassinate Bismarck. He said he was driven to the act to protect Catholic Law.

It was rumored that the man was also a devotee of French theater and Mademoiselle Sarah Bernhardt.

The Complete Escoffier: A Memoir in Meals

MOUSSE D'ECREVISSES
Crayfish Mousse

You must first select forty rather large and boisterous crayfish. They must be filled with life, able to snap your small finger with ease. If you need to test this, ask an assistant; that is what they are there for.

Once they are chosen, open a bottle of Moët. Pour it into a bowl. Add the crayfish. Stand back. They will put up a fight but rest assured that this is a merciful death, one that you would wish upon yourself.

History has recorded that I first served the dish to the Emperor of Germany Wilhelm II. The meal was presented on June 18, 1906, on the *Amerika*, a luxury liner. We will leave it at that. Discretion is an important virtue in a sophisticated world.

After you have removed the crayfish from the bowl, cook them quickly in a traditional *mirepoix*. This should be a fine dice—not to be confused with a mince for if this mixture is minced, then this would be a *matignon* and not a *mirepoix* and would result in an entirely different dish altogether. The *mirepoix* should consist of two carrots, two onions, two stalks of celery taken from the heart, one tablespoon of salt pork cut *paysanne*-style (for American chefs, this would mean that the pork should be 1/4 inch by 1/4 inch by 1/8 inch exactly), a sprig of thyme and a half bay leaf crumbled. Simple.

Moisten the cooked crayfish in a half-bottle of Moët. What you do
with the other half of the bottle will depend on if there are any young
ladies present.

Shell. Trim. Cool. Pound the shells together with three ounces of
red butter (Variation 142 in *Le Guide Culinaire*), one-quarter pint of
cold fish velouté (make sure that this sauce has been simmered with the
blandest fish possible, as it is to merely provide a back note that says
"fish" and not the entire orchestra of King Neptune) and six tablespoons of melted fish jelly. (This should be made with the finest Persian
caviar and a dry white champagne of unquestionable quality, such
as the Moët, but do not use the same Moët that you have used to take
the life of the crayfish, as their tears add too much salt.) Strain. Rub
through a fine sieve. Set in ice.

Now add cream. When one cooks for the Royals, there must
always be cream. They demand it. I believe it is because they have no
idea how inexpensive it is. Pour a pint of thick cream into a bowl and
whip. It is important that when whipping your mind is calm. If you
are angry or afraid, you will whip the cream into butter and that is not
desirable.

Perhaps this is why people today no longer care for good food. They
are worried that the Germans will come again. But they should not be
distracted by politics. Food is not political.

I knew the Emperor as a young man. Prince Edward, his cousin,
frequently brought him to Le Petit Moulin Rouge for *courir les filles*,
chasing of girls, which he took little interest in. I think it was because
of his arm. It was withered. No one was allowed to touch him. And no
one did. He was said to have a violent temper, but it was not my place
to notice.

However, I can tell you that I know personally that Emperor
Wilhelm II spoke highly of and respected his grandmother Queen
Victoria—his mother was her daughter after all—although, after a

time, he did not like Prince Edward and his wanton ways. He eventually came to call him "Satan."

Unfortunately when Royals bicker, people die.

It is interesting to note that when I placed this dish, *Mousse d' Ecrevisses*, on the menu of the *Amerika*, the Emperor's translator was confused by the word "mousse." He looked it up in a French dictionary and came to the mistaken belief that it meant "young sailor" and asked if I truly believed that the German people could be cannibals.

People should not ask questions that they do not wish to know the answer to.

And so I said, "Would not a very young sailor be more appetizing than that old Bavarian cream that has been on your menus for the last two centuries?"

I would like to think that they all laughed, but I'm not sure that they did.

At 7 p.m. when dinner was served one of the officers told this story to the Emperor and said, "Your Majesty brought Escoffier here especially from London. Did you know that he was a prisoner during the Franco-Prussian War and might well decide to poison us?"

Of course, I reassured them. "You may dine in peace. If, one day, your country once again seeks war with France, and I am still able, I will do my duty. But for the time being, you may relax and not let anything trouble your digestion!"

And then His Majesty and I shook hands, as gentlemen do.

You may ask how I remember the exact thing that I said all those many years ago. A memoir is reminiscence. This is how I remember the moment and the greatness of a man is always defined by how he sees his own life. Truth is not a consideration. In fact, it is often not welcome. What one looks for is a sense of the profound. Can the teller of the tale understand the meaning of his own life? Can he grasp his place in history?

It does not matter if the story is true or not. What fool calls for truth in a memoir? Nothing is more uninteresting. The only truth you need to know is that this is what I would have wanted to say at that time and that should tell you who I am. I would have wanted him to come into my kitchen to say he was sorry for my suffering; sorry that I was not treated well as his grandfather's prisoner of war. I would have wanted to say, "All I saw around me was the inhuman consequences of fratricidal wars. We can be German, French, English or Italian—but why make war? When one thinks of the crimes that are committed, of the widows, of the orphans, of the crippled and the maimed, of the poor women abused by invading forces, one cannot help but tremble with indignation."

I would have wanted to say all of that because it was indeed how I felt. And so you should imagine that I did.

When the crayfish mousse is set, decorate with the cooked tails, shaved truffle, and a perfect sprig of chervil. Cover it with a sheet of translucent amber fish jelly and serve on a silver dish encrusted with ice.

It is because of this dish, *Mousse d' Ecrevisses*, and a rather uneventful strawberry pudding, which I named *Fraises Imperator*, that the Emperor Wilhelm II had been widely reported in newspapers all over the world to have granted me the title *"Le Roi des Cuisiniers et le Cuisinier des Roi,"* King of Chefs and Chef of Kings.

This is not entirely accurate.

You must understand that this event happened at a time when every chef was called a "king." Even Ritz had been referred to as "king of hôteliers and hôtelier to kings." And gout, which seemed to be a plague for many of my clients, was known as "the disease of kings and the king of diseases." This was, apparently, a turn of phrase that people delighted in.

And so if the Emperor said it, it would have meant nothing.

But what he actually said was, "I am the Emperor of Germany, but you are the Emperor of Chefs." And this is entirely different.

It is also important to understand exactly how he said it. There was a sense of humility in his voice. He even gave a slight bow. It was remarkable. The year was 1913. Talk of war was everywhere. The Emperor had decided to take a short cruise on the SS *Imperator* before it was to set sail on its maiden voyage. Named in his honor, the ship was the newest and largest vessel at the time, as the *Titanic* had sunk just a month before, and unfortunately, horribly, sadly, taking my kitchen crew with it. They were great and glorious men.

Hearing of my work with the *Titanic*, The Ritz Hotel Development Company was hired to build and manage the *Imperator*'s kitchen. It was our charge to painstakingly re-create the dining room of the German ship to be a replica of the Carlton in London. The replica was so exact that it felt to me as if Ritz himself would walk into the room at any moment, looking fit and happy, to greet the diners. Of course, by that time, he had gone quite mad. Still, I imagined him on this beautiful ship.

When you reach a certain age, all you see are ghosts.

Because of our great friendship, the Emperor Wilhelm II himself had arranged for me to travel to Germany to design the restaurant for his magnificent ship. And then, later, he requested my return to manage this event. He had no fear of me, although there was talk that I might be the only person who could poison him. And yes, the last time we met I did say, "If, one day, your country once again seeks war with France, and I am still able, I will do my duty," but when asked to serve His Majesty again I did not hesitate. I went joyfully, proudly.

He was not our enemy at the time.

The challenge of feeding the Emperor and his court on such short notice was an enormous task, nearly impossible. I boarded the ship on July 7 to begin preparations. Two days later, 110 guests, many of them the most famous names of German aristocracy, arrived. The next day at 10 a.m., the Emperor and his court boarded and we served 146 guests a formal luncheon, followed that evening by a monumental dinner. The following morning, after an English breakfast of tea with cream, fried eggs, kidney, chops, steak, grilled fish and fruit, His Majesty entered the Palm Room to receive me. He shook my hand warmly, like an old friend, thanked me for coming all the way from London, and then spoke at great length about the strawberry pudding.

I knew that he had had a nervous breakdown a few years earlier. You could sense the hairline crack. And yet, in his eyes, I could still see the grave young man from his days dining at Le Petit Moulin Rouge and so as a father with two young sons of my own I said, "Your Majesty, I pray that before the end of your reign, we will see the time when the greatest of all humanitarian acts will be accomplished: the reconciliation of Germany and France."

This brought tears to his eyes. He assured me that reconciliation was indeed his greatest desire, something he had worked for and had been working for, but that he was misunderstood, misrepresented.

Indeed. The journalists in newspapers around the world had painted him a villain. And then he said, "I have the greatest hopes of seeing my desires realized, and I pray for it with all my heart, for the greater welfare of mankind. Reconciliation is my greatest desire."

I wrote his words down as soon as he said them and for many years have read and re-read them. In German, the word for reconciliation is *Versöhnung*. In French, *réconciliation*. They are completely different words, although I did not recognize it at the time.

Shortly after our meeting, on August 3, 1914, the Emperor declared war on France.

On November 1, 1914, my dear son Daniel, a lieutenant in the 363rd Alpine Regiment, was hit by German fire. A single bullet shattered his face, killing him instantly, and leaving his four children for me to bring up.

Brillat-Savarin once said, "Tell me what you eat and I will tell you who you are."

Thanks to the Germans, I have consumed a great many things that I would like to have forgotten—horses, rats, spaniels—and this has made me hungry in unimaginable ways.

10

OVERED IN SOOT AND COBWEBS, SABINE CARRIED TWO
cases of the empty champagne bottles up from the basement,
her stray foot dragging behind her. The summer heat had
bloated and bruised the tomatoes overnight—all of them—filling the
house with clouds of fruit flies, which followed her everywhere. She
placed the boxes at Escoffier's feet and swatted at the buzzing mass
that encircled her head.

"The flies have also appeared to have taken a great liking to you,"
he said.

Sabine did not find this amusing. "Can you not select six champagne bottles that you can part with?"

Escoffier shook his white head. "Each one is important. Each one is
history." Since dawn, the old man had been sitting in the kitchen in his
Louis-Philippe dress coat and striped trousers—not cooking, eating
or speaking—just polishing his copper pans. He had laid them out on
the table according to size. And then, slowly, gently, he dipped a lemon
into salt, rubbed the tiny butter warmer, and lovingly polished it with
a clean cloth. He then moved on to the next. And the next.

There were fifty or more. At this rate, it would take him a week.

Sabine asked him several times to stop but he refused. "Pick more lemons," he'd say. "Get more salt." And he just kept cleaning.

Just before sunrise, the nurses discovered that Delphine's paralysis was complete. She could no longer use her hands or any other part of her body. Her room was filled with children, grandchildren and great-grandchildren.

But Escoffier sat in the kitchen, amidst the rotting tomatoes, cleaning.

Sabine sat down in the chair next to him and wiped her hands on her apron, which made him frown. He tapped the side of his nose.

"Professional standards," he said. "Use a clean cloth."

She ignored him. A dirty apron was the least of her worries. The sticky sweet juice of the fruit stained her skin, and was starting to make the entire house smell of rot.

"I only need six bottles, not even a case. I have spoken to the butcher and he will trade me two of his own stewing chickens for six bottles of the sauce. These are birds that he has reserved for his own family. Fat. Juicy. But I need the bottles. Do you understand?"

If he did, he did not seem to care. Escoffier methodically wiped his hands on a clean towel, picked up an empty champagne bottle, sniffed it as if it still held wine.

"The Red Dinner: a celebration of winning a fortune, playing red at the roulette here in Monte Carlo," he said. "Everything was to be red and labeled with the number nine—the final winning number. The waiters wore red shirts and gloves. Tables were draped in scarlet linen and red rose petals strewn over it all. Candlelight streaming through the cut crystal of Baccarat glasses revealed the number nine discreetly etched in gold at the base of each stem."

"A fine setting for chicken," she said. "So, these can be used?"

"The Red Dinner was very famous."

"Most certainly it was, but everyone who attended is probably dead now and we will all die from hunger, too, if you cannot choose just six bottles for me to put sauce in."

All this talk of champagne made her thirsty. She fingered the box of cigarettes in her skirt pocket.

"Six bottles is all I ask."

"Are there not new bottles that can be used?"

"Madame said to use these, said we must use these, but if you need me to, I can empty six bottles of Moët myself."

"I am sure you can."

The door to the kitchen opened and Escoffier's son and daughter, Paul and Germaine, peered in.

"We were wondering where you were," Paul said.

In contrast to his father, who always appeared well dressed and elegant at any time of the day, Paul looked like a tourist in a city that did not welcome tourists. Despite Monaco's tropical disposition, he was pale. He wore a white shirt with short sleeves, white belt and open-toed sandals that accentuated his white feet. He was jowly and round but had his father's regal eyes and the same drooping mustache.

"Papa, are you listening?"

"I am cleaning."

Germaine, looking very much like her mother, her willful hair twisted in place, took Sabine by the arm. "Why isn't the girl cleaning?"

"The girl, her name is Sabine, is making tomato sauce."

The flies seemed to be getting worse. One crawled up Sabine's nose and triggered a sneezing fit.

"She's ill."

"She's fine."

"She's ill. And there are flies everywhere."

Sabine couldn't stop sneezing. She rubbed her face frantically. The small flies were slowly driving her mad.

Escoffier shooed imaginary flies away from his own face. "She is making tomato sauce."

Like a yawn, the shooing became contagious. Paul and Germaine joined in.

"She appears deranged," Germaine said.

"Willful, perhaps. But what chef isn't?"

"She is making tomato sauce?" Paul said. "This kitchen is filthy. Why are there so many tomatoes?" The strain in his voice seemed to attract the flies to him. They spun around his head. "This is absurd. And these flies!"

Sabine finally stopped sneezing, finally caught her breath. "Madame Escoffier ordered them," she said. "The tomatoes. Not the flies. She asked that we become awash in them. And we are."

"I don't believe it," Germaine said. "Why would she do that? This is a ridiculous amount of fruit even for a family of our size."

"Stories."

The children did not know what to make of this. Escoffier, however, seemed to understand.

"Pommes d'Amour."

Sabine stood and wiped her hands on her apron again. Escoffier did not notice. He picked up a tomato and held it gently as if it were a lush red rose.

"If it was Madame Escoffier's desire to fill the house with stories and tomatoes," he said, "we will have tomatoes. Everywhere. Sabine, there were no stories at the market?"

"But everywhere?" Germaine said. "This is too much."

Escoffier offered the tomato to her. The sweet sticky juice ran down her arm. She licked it and took a bite of the fruit.

"Pommes d'Amour."

Paul picked up a champagne bottle. "I must know the story of every one of these."

"Please, then," Escoffier said. "Begin."

Paul looked at his father. "But mother?"

Sabine took six bottles from the box. "I am using these for the sauce. The children cannot eat stories."

Paul studied Sabine and then his father. It was quite clear that while Sabine had never really seen the children, they, too, had never looked at her closely before.

Sarah.

"I'm sure Mother is wondering where we all are," Paul said; the coldness in his voice confirmed it. He, too, saw Sarah's ghost in the girl.

Escoffier slowly stood. "Come to me." He opened his arms and Germaine embraced him. He held his daughter closely to his chest and kissed her dearly.

"But Papa, all these tomatoes," she said.

Escoffier nodded and held his arms out to his son. "Paul?"

The man looked at Sabine and she looked away, out the window into the vast expanse of the Côte d'Azur. The water was so blue, she couldn't remember ever seeing anything that blue before. *Blue as truth*, she thought.

"Paul?"

The son kissed his father on both checks, as was the custom, but nothing more. And left the room.

"I'm sorry," Germaine said.

Escoffier closed his eyes for a moment. "We all are."

As soon as Germaine left the kitchen, Sabine picked up the box of bottles again. Escoffier took them out of her hands, placed them on the floor and sat down next to them. "Where were we?" he asked.

Sabine, resigned, sat next to the old man. Handed him the bottle he had been holding. Escoffier held it to the light as a jeweler holds a perfect stone. "Can you guess what was served at a red dinner?"

She sighed. "Tomato sauce?"

He shook his head. "A jam perhaps could have been fitting. *Confiture de Tomates*. But no. Try again."

The man was exasperating. The tiny flies remained persistent. She tried to ignore them but they kept landing on her face, making it itch. She took a deep breath and, unfortunately, swallowed one. Coughed.

The old man put the bottle down. Poured her a glass of the lemonade she had made for lunch. She drank, greedily.

"*Merci.*"

"The Red Dinner. Do you give up?"

"Yes."

"But you haven't even ventured a guess. Here, I will help. Imagine the Savoy."

"London?"

"Don't think about its being in London. Think of the Savoy as if it were a continent of civility where anything was possible."

"But we are speaking of London?"

"We are speaking of the Savoy. Consider a table set as if there had been a great windstorm of white and pink roses: they were everywhere. Upon the plates, there was a meal of blushing pinks. To begin, a chilled Alsatian borscht. And then I deepened the rouge palette with *Poulet au paprika*, the paprika and its brick-red foundation made the pink quite vivid. Finally, we ended with the magnificent *Agneau de lait des Pyrénées*—a beautiful tender softly pink lamb, very little fat, that is born and raised in the Pyrénées-Atlantiques of France. The mother sheep must spend at least eight months a year at pasture. The lamb, only fed by its mother, is slaughtered when it is very young. Not more that a fortnight."

"That sounds very sad."

"It was a palette for the palate."

"The poor lamb."

"The happy diner. Now. You see how it is done. And so, for the Red Dinner?"

She rubbed her face with her hands. The tiny flies were inescapable, as was the question. "Would this have been a meal of lobster, beets and strawberries?"

Above them, in Madame's room, there suddenly was the soft sound of crying. For a moment, a cloud passed over Escoffier's face.

"Wrong again. Nothing so simple! The real challenge was not merely to replicate color, the mood and texture of it, but the emotion behind the winning. The entire meal must build course upon course to the exact moment when one pushes the winnings back onto the roulette table, being ready to lose it all, and then watches the silver ball land on the Red Nine.

"So the question became how does one capture the moment that changed everything?"

"By making tomato sauce?"

"Can you not imagine it? How does one create such a meal?"

She could imagine it. Quite clearly. Escoffier's staff in their pressed white uniforms, those witches of nowhere else, correcting sauces, arranging meats, sculpting ice into the forms of swans; their magic lay in the fleeting perfection of the moment. But still, there was sauce to be made.

"Are you going to do this with every bottle?"

"Do you not want to know how to capture the moment when wealth overwhelms?"

"*Non.*"

"Well, I will still tell you."

He was, indeed, planning to do this with every bottle.

"The brilliance of the meal lay in the Golden Rain, a gilded whimsy. It was pure fantasy: a dwarf mandarin orange tree gilded in a 'rain' of gold leaf and spun sugar. It seemed to be growing from a pile of chocolate francs each with a tiny slice of orange glacée wrapped in a spangle of gold leaf. It was gold upon gold and unbearably sweet—exactly how one would feel after winning three hundred fifty thousand francs."

"Thank you. I would not have been able to sleep tonight without knowing that."

Sabine took the bottle from his hand and placed it with the rest. "We will use this box," she said. "After I sauce the tomatoes for the butcher, I will sauce all the rest. And I will use all these bottles. We will have a month of red dinners, so it is a fitting choice."

"The children do not like tomato sauce."

Sabine sank back down into the kitchen chair. "Fine. You are the great chef. What should I do, then? What do children like to eat?"

"Chicken," he said and then began to walk out of the kitchen but stopped at the door. "Seventy-five point six grams of the Demerara, if we have any left. If not, light brown sugar will do. Seventy-eight milliliters of malt vinegar. Boil together. Reduce. Cool."

"For the chicken?"

"*Non.* The tomato sauce. It's spicing essence. It heightens deliciousness, the fifth taste. Add a few drops and it will brighten the taste of the sauce. It will brighten any sauce, or mask the flavor of any meat that has gone bad. The tomatoes are past their prime. You can smell the rot. There are flies everywhere."

Exasperating. She picked up his cookbook. "And what page would that be on? This spicing essence?"

"None. A chef without mystery is merely a cook."

11

ELPHINE HAD NOT SEEN ESCOFFIER FOR THREE DAYS, ever since she'd taken a turn for the worse, but she could hear her husband in his room: the shuffle of his feet on the wooden floors, the snap and hum of his radio playing late into the night, all that talk about that man, Hitler, and even the scratch of pen nib on paper. Now that she was completely immobile it was amazing what could be heard. The world around her suddenly was loud and glaring. And garishly fragrant—the sweet scent of tuberose that lingered after her great-grandchildren's kisses brought her to tears.

The lives of stones, she thought. *How rich they must be.*

Outside her window, the vagueness of night obscured everything, heightened everything. In the narrow winding streets below she could hear the small betrayals of lovers who sat in the cafés along the famous square Place d'Armes. She could smell the food set before them on the domino rows of tables. Most of it was *Monégasque,* Monaco's peasant food, a food that she'd come to love so well.

And so, the time between 4 p.m. and 9 p.m. was marked not by minutes but by course after course: *oignons à la Monégasque,* the deeply spiced sweet and sour salad of onions and raisins, butter-rich pastries stuffed with pumpkin and rice, and the small hot *socca* pancakes made from chickpea flour. And grilled prawns, olive oil, thin-skinned lemons, orange water, anise seed, garlic, small black olives—the scent of them twined with the sea breeze, became memory. Delphine was a young wife again, leaning into a soft kiss at the moment of daybreak; a young mother with three small children at her feet, her youngest son, Daniel, was still alive, had not been to war, and Victoria was still Queen. Every Christmas, every New Year, every Easter, and every birthday came back to her. Every moment the sun warmed her skin she relived dish after dish.

Her nurses claimed they could not smell a thing.

"And it is impossible to hear anything at Place d'Armes from here; it is too far away," one said.

"You are only dreaming," said the other.

Delphine knew they were wrong. Even sleep had a dark lavender scent.

But that night she could not sleep. Indian mangos, the peach-sweet air of them, would not let her rest. When Escoffier was at The Savoy, six cases were delivered to her. The card was, of course, signed "Mr. Boots."

"Why would the mysterious Mr. Boots feel I need so many mangos and a side of Scottish beef, the rare Aberdeen-Angus breed, two cases of vintage champagne, and fifty pounds of small yellow butter potatoes from Sweden?"

"Perhaps he is smitten."

"Perhaps he is."

The food was always so lush, so extravagant, and somehow so intimate—erotic in its excess—her face went hot with the memory.

And then Escoffier coughed. And even though he was not in the room she could hear him as clearly as if he were standing beside her.

"Do you remember the mangos?" she asked. She thought she was whispering but the scratching of the pen nib stopped. "You must remember them."

She could hear him push the chair away from his desk, slowly stand and then lean against the wall. The floorboards creaked.

"The mangos?" she said again.

She could hear him breathing. He cleared his throat and then, quietly, said, "They were sweet, were they not?"

"It was a sweetness more intense than anything I have ever known."

And then the room fell quiet. The two sat listening to the familiar sound of each other's breath. Without words, there was comfort: a sonata, tone poem of silence and knowing.

After a time, Escoffier said, "The Hindus believe that mangos are a true sign that perfection is attainable."

She thought of the mangos with their smooth marbled skin, the carmine and field grass green of them, and then the flesh itself, that vivid orange, and then, each bite, the juice sliding down her arm.

"Perfection," she said. "And yet, after a few days they slowly began to shrivel and turn black. Just one spot, then two, then soon the fragrance shifted from sweet to rancid and the fruits themselves became smaller and smaller with each passing day. It was as if the rain within them was returned back to the heavens, bit by bit, until all the sweetness was gone."

"Perhaps," he said, "the rain slowly abandons all of us."

She could hear Escoffier lower himself down onto his chair, that familiar creak of the springs. She waited for him to begin writing again, but he did not. She sat listening for him to say something else. Anything. But he remained silent. Eventually, she closed her eyes and just before she tumbled into the darkness of sleep he said, "Nothing is real except for dreams and love."

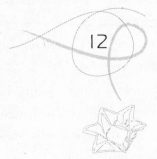

12

THE NEXT DAY, LANGOUSTINES WERE THE FIRST TO BE delivered. There was an entire bushel of them—dozens of tiny beasts industriously crawling over and under each other until they made their way out of the basket and onto the kitchen floor. Each slim lobster was the color of hibiscus, an orange pink, with long slender claws and black peppercorn eyes. They snapped at whatever they could, mostly Sabine. It was, after all, her fault that they were there.

"The old man has not a single *sou* and dozens to feed," Sabine told the butcher when she brought him the tomato sauce in exchange for the chickens. The butcher then told the greengrocer who told the dry grocer who told his cousins who worked at the Grand Hôtel and the cousins told the *directeur* Bobo.

"That will not do," Bobo said and paid the fishmonger from his own pocket and the langoustines arrived. Pinching.

"Devil bugs," Sabine called them as they pinched at her hands, her red ankle-strapped shoes, and grabbed onto the hem of her starched white apron.

The fishmonger had once worked for Escoffier at The Savoy in

London. It was his job to wrap the leftover food for Papa to give to the Petites Soeurs des Pauvres, the Little Sisters of the Poor, so that they could feed the destitute. And so, he pulled the langoustines from the boat himself and delivered them to Sabine along with several bottles of chilled champagne, the national drink of Monaco.

"The rich are no longer hungry. Papa is."

As is Sabine, she thought.

After the fishmonger left, Sabine popped open a bottle of champagne; it overflowed onto the floor and onto the langoustines and their snapping pink claws. She poured a teacup full, pulled *Le Guide Culinaire* from the shelf and sat. Lit a cigarette. The insidious creatures crawled over her shoes.

"Go ahead. Enjoy yourself," she said. "In a moment, I am going to kill you all."

Sabine felt only a slight tug of remorse. She had had enough with this household. First there were tomatoes everywhere and then the insistent flies and now this. She wished she had never heard the name Escoffier.

Sabine took a long drink of champagne. The house was quiet in a way that made it feel abandoned or perhaps merely exhausted. Madame Escoffier had been ill for so long, more than four years. Death had lost its exotic sheen. It was no longer a stranger who arrives unexpectedly speaking a new language, changing schedules, and shifting plans. It had overstayed. Sorrow had become routine. The family was bored by it. After all, there are only so many times a person can say goodbye, and so many tears that can be shed with sincerity. Now no one knew what to say.

"*Au revoir!*"

"*À bientôt!*"

"*Adieu!*"

"*Salut!*"

"Ciao, arrière-grand-mère!"

It was embarrassing.

And so slowly the family had taken their leave. Sabine hadn't even noticed. That morning, as usual, she'd set the dining room table for breakfast. She'd filled the sideboard with what little they had—a few soft-poached eggs sprinkled with chives, stacks of toasted oat bread, a squat jar of wild plum jam, and a pot of chicory coffee—but no one came to eat. Even the tray that was delivered to Madame Escoffier was brought back untouched. At midday, Sabine warmed the poached eggs in butter until they were hardboiled and then pounded them into a smooth paste seasoned with anchovies and mustard and spread them on the leftover toast. Again, no one came.

By the time the langoustines arrived that day, it was clear to Sabine that everyone had left except for Escoffier, Delphine, and the two nurses—she could hear them all moving on the floor above her. Everyone else was gone. For how long was uncertain. No one bothered to tell her anything. No matter. Sabine topped off her teacup with more champagne and opened Escoffier's cookbook to the "Fish and Seafood" section while the langoustines snapped.

"Are you crayfish or lobsters?" she asked. The shellfish were silent on that matter. Sabine decided that they could be lobsters for her purposes. They looked just like them. After taking the size difference into account, with just a few adjustments to the recipe, dinner would be, finally, a decent meal. It would be the type of meal one would expect in the house of Escoffier.

"I must advise all of you to take a moment to consider your eternal soul," she said to the assembled crustaceans and her stomach growled.

The first recipe in the lobster section was for *Homard à l'Américaine*. Since Sabine was wearing her red high heels that looked like the dancing shoes of that American Ginger Rogers, she decided that American-style devil bugs were fitting. It began:

"The first essential condition is that the lobster should be alive. Sever and slightly crush claws, cut the tail into sections, split the shell lengthwise. Put aside the intestines and the coral."

Alive?

Even for Sabine that seemed a bit cruel. Yes, the langoustines were both annoying and delicious but tearing them apart was unseemly. Her grandmother usually made a *Monégasque* dish of them. It was peasant food, and not suitable for the likes of Escoffier, but it was so delicious it was known to bring tears to her father's eyes. Sabine could not remember how the shellfish were disposed of, probably with a prayer or two, but was sure that her frail grandmother did not hack devil bugs apart with a cleaver. Sabine took a hard drag from her cigarette and blew the smoke into tiny rings. The champagne made her feel exotic.

The next recipe began, "Section the live lobster as directed above."

It was disheartening. Over and over again, each dish began with the chopping apart of live lobsters. Crayfish met with only a slightly better fate, often being boiled alive.

Sabine poured herself another teacup of champagne. Escoffier stepped into the kitchen and stopped. With her wild hair twisted upon her head, the champagne bottle in one hand and the langoustines at her feet, the sight of her took his breath away. She stood quickly, jostled the champagne.

"I thought there would be no harm . . . "

"Life is not worth living if one cannot break rules. True?"

Her father told her that Escoffier was notorious, and it wasn't difficult to believe.

"Now, tell me, you are wearing the shoes of a fashionable young woman and yet with your hair done in this manner you seem to be from another generation. This was your father's idea, was it not? He believes that I am in the throes of dementia?"

"Of course."

"What did he tell you about Miss Bernhardt?"

"That every year for decades you created private dinners for her birthday and you were the only guest in attendance. You were quite obviously lovers."

"And how does he know this?"

"He says that everyone knows this."

"And do you believe this gossip?"

"Of course."

Escoffier leaned over and put out her cigarette. "Your father has told you a great many things but, apparently, nothing about the humility of servants."

"No. He mentioned it. Demanded it, in fact. But it is not an idea that I am willing to embrace."

"Understandable. What else do you know of Miss Bernhardt?"

"She was famous for being famous."

That was all Sabine knew. She was ten years old when Sarah died. Like many, her family traveled to Paris to mourn her. She could still remember the crowded streets, the smell of sweat and tobacco pressed in on her, and the line of horse-drawn carriages draped in velvet and roses. She remembered waiting for hours squeezed between rough wool and quick hearts and when the doors of Sarah's house were finally thrown open the cheer of the crowd shook her bones. She remembered the crush of bodies as thousands poured in through the front doors and into the darkened parlor filled with flowers and lit by hundreds of candles. And Sarah. She remembered Sarah lying in state in the coffin that she claimed to have slept in most of her life. Her long hair dyed bright copper. Her lips and cheeks painted pink. In the dim light, she looked more like a child than a woman of nearly eighty.

She looked like Sabine and it frightened the girl.

Around Sarah's neck was the cross and ribbon of the Legion of

Honor, which Sabine's father explained was the highest honor France had to bestow.

"And she was rich, too," he said.

Money. Always money.

Escoffier poured Sabine a bit more champagne.

"So if I call you Sarah when no one is around?"

"Sabine."

He patted her on the hand and smiled. "You must hate your father so."

She took a drink. "It has been said. Yes."

Escoffier picked up a langoustine that had crawled onto the chair, placed it gently on the table, straightened the crease in his pants and sat across from her. "I must tell you that I knew the very moment I saw you in the kitchen with the tomatoes why you were sent here but that does not mean that I do not enjoy the deception."

"Still. Sabine."

"Very well."

Above their heads the voices grew louder. Escoffier picked up the tiny lobster. "Your new friends are?"

"A gift from Adrien, the fishmonger. At least, that is what he said. It seems to me, however, that he was not the type of man to give a gift like this. I think someone else paid for it. But, he claimed it was from him. A gift."

"A gift?"

The irony did not escape him. After spending his life giving to, defending, and raising money for the poor he was penniless himself.

Escoffier looked out the window. He couldn't see the cobalt sea; fog veiled the sun. All he could see were crows: oil black and screeching as they fought over the scraps of the uneaten sandwiches that Sabine had left out for the cats.

"Did you know that in English a group of crows is called a 'murder'?

I believe that is the only bit of poetry in the entire language although I cannot be sure. I only know a few words and never learned to speak it. To speak English would be to think in English and thereby to cook in English. I would have been ruined forever.

"French. Always French."

He held his hand over his heart, as if saluting the flag.

Sabine took a champagne glass from the pantry and poured him a drink.

Escoffier watched the perfect bubbles rise in the glass and then picked up a langoustine and placed it headfirst into the wine. He did this without malice. It was a simple natural movement, like a wave of a hand or a kiss. The small lobster struggled, slapping its tail against the sides of the crystal. Sabine made the sign of the cross.

"The champagne is for them," he said. "It is the most humane way. The alcohol slows them."

"That is not in *Le Guide Culinaire*."

"The editor removed it. 'Who would waste good champagne?' he said. "But he is dead now, so it will appear in my new book. There are some benefits to longevity."

Overhead, the floorboards in the hallway outside of Madame Escoffier's room creaked. And then, quite clearly, the old woman began crying. The sound seemed to catch in Escoffier's throat. He coughed until there were tears in his eyes. He wiped them away quickly. He seemed smaller, diminished. The langoustine stopped struggling.

Sabine poured him a glass of water. His hand shook while he drank.

"They are not like us, these creatures," he said. "They have no brain. No vocal cords with which to scream. They have no sensitivity to pain. They live. They die. For them it is that simple."

He took the creature out of the glass. "A bowl."

Sabine took two large glass bowls from the sideboard and placed them on the table in front of Escoffier. She filled them both with champagne, and then langoustines. They watched as the small lobsters frantically struggled and then, one by one, began to slow down. Quiet.

"Is it true that when you name a dish for someone they become immortal?"

"If the dish is very good and can be made by an unskilled chef it will live on."

"So even I could make it?"

"If only I can make it, it will die with me."

"But if I—"

"If you could make it, it would be a miracle."

"True."

Above them Madame Escoffier's sobs settled into a rhythm. Sabine picked up the cookbook again. "Are they lobsters or crayfish?"

Escoffier closed the book. "Put the Windsor pan on the front burner and add to it equal parts of butter and olive oil, just enough to sauté."

He took a large chef's knife from the rack above the kitchen sink and began to pierce and then chop the drunken langoustines into small pieces with a singular focus. The blade moved quickly through the head, then shells. He had no remorse. Sabine could see that her devil bugs did not cry out or even react. They were severed cleanly. The claws and tail moved a bit, and then nothing.

She filled the bottom of the pan with oil and butter.

"Too much," he said. "It should just be the tip of your fingernail's worth." She poured the excess fat into a glass jar.

"Good. Now just a small blue flame. Very low."

Sabine adjusted the gas. The ring of blue flame sputtered a bit, threatened extinction, but then caught.

Escoffier handed Sabine the knife. "Now you. Don't think. Cut."

She chopped blindly.

"*Non. Non.*"

He took the knife from her hand. "One quick movement beginning at the head," he said. "To die painlessly, the brain must be silenced. Anything else is cruel."

It was clear that he was not speaking of the langoustines.

Sabine held the tiny lobster to the chopping block. Its tail slapped her palm. A long pink claw caught her thumb. She could hear one of the nurses speaking loudly over Madame's cries.

"Chop," Escoffier said.

She did. Sabine pulled the point of the blade through the head and right between the eyes. The body went limp. It went more easily than she imagined.

"Good. But you need to work quickly. The meat is sweeter when cooked shortly after death."

Escoffier slid the pan off the flame and took another knife from the block. Langoustine after langoustine, they chopped and diced. They were silent as they worked. The only sound was that of their knives against the wooden cutting boards, sweet kitchen music. Through the door, they could hear a nurse making a phone call. "Morphine," she said. "We've run out of morphine."

Sabine knew there was no money to pay for it.

Escoffier slid the pan back onto the fire. The butter and the oil bubbled. They tossed in the langoustines by the handful.

He stepped into the pantry to gather an armful of spices. "Two minutes. Just until they begin to pink. Then arrange them on a platter. And then into a warm oven."

A nurse opened the kitchen door. "Monsieur Escoffier?" she said. She was thin and dry as a leaf.

"We are cooking."

"The doctor is coming."

"There is enough food."

"Monsieur Escoffier, he is coming to speak to you. He requests that you return to your bed and wait for him there."

"I am busy."

Sabine piled cooked langoustines on a platter, put it in the oven. Escoffier tossed dried herbs into the used pan—savory, fennel, basil, lavender, a sprig of thyme and a bay leaf. He ignored the nurse but spoke to Sabine in the hushed voice of a child up long past his bedtime. "When this reheats, it will fill the room with the air of summer. You'll see."

And then he chopped a fistful of purple garlic.

"The Parisians would not eat garlic until I told them it was an aphrodisiac. Then they were crazy for it."

"Is it?"

"It is an aphrodisiac if I say it is."

The nurse cleared her throat. "Monsieur Escoffier? The doctor insists—"

"Go away."

The nurse slammed the kitchen door behind her.

Escoffier added the rinds from both lemons and oranges. "See how they release the oil when they hit the heat?"

"I can finish this."

"Our work here is more important than a doctor telling us what we already know. You will see. I am right."

The hot pan made the oil seep from the rinds. The scent did, indeed, remind Sabine of a summer's day in Provence.

"Words are clumsy and limited by nature," he said. "Only food can speak what the heart feels.

"Now. How many tomatoes and how many carrots should I add? And onion. There were onions. How many?"

"I don't know."

"Sabine. Think. The langoustines are sweet. The herbs are fragrant. Tomatoes are sweet, also but acidic. The ragout will be served alongside the crustacean, not on top of it. You should be able to move from the ragout to the langoustines and taste the perfect melody of earth and sea.

"Now. Peel and chop the right amount of vegetables."

"I can't."

"Try. Close your eyes and imagine a finished dish. Think about the right balance—what do you need to achieve the perfect pitch?"

Sabine closed her eyes. He held the fragrant pan underneath her nose. "This is what we have already, the foundation. Now add the rest of the ingredients in your mind. Think of how they would taste as you add each one. Always remember that we want to bring the sweetness and the brininess of the langoustine forward. Now adjust. Imagine adding more onion, and then less onion. More carrot. Then less. Be careful not to add too much celery, it can be a very loud vegetable, very aggressive on the palate. It should always be an undertone. That's where it shines.

"Now can you imagine how the dish should be?"

Sabine could not. Still, she diced carrots, celery and onions. Escoffier adjusted the amounts and she added them to the pan to soften.

"You'll learn," he said. "Now remove the bay leaf and sprig of thyme. Add salt and pepper for seasoning."

Escoffier retrieved the large white platter of langoustines that she had placed in the oven. They were still moist. The kitchen was filled with a briny sweet scent. He took a handful of wilted endive from the pantry and ran cold water over it to refresh it. "Now, tell me, how many cocoa beans?"

"I love cocoa so I will use two cups of beans."

"*Non*. A perfect dish is a harmony of flavors working together to create something new." He ground a small amount of cocoa beans with a mortar and pestle. "Cocoa is used as a spice in this; it needs a gentle hand. Now taste. See if it has balance."

Sabine took a wooden spoon from the drawer and tasted the ragout, first by itself and then with a langoustine. She ate it shell and all.

It was overwhelming—the tight briny taste, the crunch of the soft shell and the floral sweetness of the ragout—it was like her grandmother's dish but not.

"It's very good."

Escoffier scowled. "That isn't the question. Imagine what it would be like with a bit more salt. Or does it need lemon? Anything that is too flat or too acidic can be rebalanced with salt. Anything that is too salty can be rebalanced with acid, like lemon."

Sabine took another taste. "More salt," she said.

It was her best guess. Escoffier knew that. He took a spoon from the drawer and dipped it in the sauce very quickly. Tasted a small amount. Added salt. Tasted it again. "This is just how I remember it."

"How can you remember a taste in such detail?"

"How can you not? Food is transformational. It engages the senses and emotions."

"But to remember a taste so specifically?"

The question pained him. The damp sea air gusted, rattled the kitchen window. Cold air leaked through the rotting frame. There seemed to be no room for words but finally he said, "It was the saddest and yet most romantic meal I ever had in my life. It is impossible to forget."

He plated a small amount for himself.

"What is this called?"

"It has no name. It was made for me the first night I came back to this house after living alone in London at The Savoy. I'd been gone a very long time. A lifetime. Madame set a table along the hillside. Where the garden is now. Made this dish."

Above them, Madame Escoffier was suddenly silent.

"Perhaps you should name it after her."

"It is not complicated enough, or passionate enough, or sensible enough. Nothing is."

The doctor arrived; the cherry tobacco from his pipe announced his coming, the chatter of the nurses trailed behind him. He opened the kitchen door. Escoffier grabbed Sabine by the arm. "Take the platter to Madame. Hurry."

The large platter was heavy and hot. Sabine ran up the back stairway carrying it precariously, two tea towels wrapped around her hands, a napkin across her arm, and a fork in her pocket. With her red dancing shoes and her weak leg she found it difficult to keep her balance. At the top of the stairs, she placed the platter on the hall table so that she could readjust the tea towels and strengthen her grip, but the dish was beautiful, too beautiful. She suddenly began to eat it by the fistful. The hot sauce ran down her arm. Some splattered onto her shoes. Her white apron was stained. She didn't care. She chewed the heads, tails, and claws. She licked her fingers clean after each.

She could hear the doctor's voice below her in the kitchen, then the nurses, then Escoffier. They were arguing. The old man said something, pounded the table, and then slid into a coughing fit. It made her eat faster.

I will only eat three. No one will notice three gone.

She ate four. *That's all.* But she was still very hungry and they were still very wonderful. Each bite was more wonderful than the last. *One more will not be noticed.* Two more were eaten.

When Sabine ate the seventh langoustine, even though it was a very small one, her stomach began to hurt. She rearranged the remaining food to fill the gaping holes. She wiped her hands on one tea towel and cleaned her face with the other. She adjusted her apron. There was still a smudge of ragout on her face.

Madame Escoffier's door was open. Sabine had not been in the room since the night they had spoken about the fur coat. She was shocked to see how pale Delphine was, how crooked with pain. And she was quite mad, speaking as if performing a dramatic reading to a crowd of people assembled before her.

"Cité à l'ordre de l'armée pour son superbe courage."

Her words slid into each other, veered off course, piled up, toppled into ruts of silence. Her dull eyes were focused on a heaven somewhere beyond Sabine. The poem was something about her son fighting in the war. The girl felt the keen urge to run but knew she had nowhere else to go.

"Madame?"

The old woman did not seem to notice her standing there. The hot, heavy plate was beginning to slip from her hands again.

"It is Sabine."

Madame Escoffier had become another sort of creature, not quite human. *Or maybe,* Sabine thought, *maybe more human. Maybe this is what children are like when they are born—straddling this life and that.*

The platter was heavy. She couldn't stand there much longer. "I have brought a dish for you that Monsieur cooked himself. Langoustines with ragout."

Madame Escoffier's eyes suddenly cleared.

"Closer."

Sabine placed the large platter on the bedside table and sat on the side of the bed. She peeled each langoustine tail and fed the old woman as one would a child.

Delphine closed her eyes and chewed slowly. She was radiant.

"Another."

"Quick, quick," she said over and over again, and laughed, although Sabine was not sure why. Still, Delphine's happiness was so pure that she felt it herself. She fed her fork after fork until they could hear the doctor's grave basso tones in the hallway. Then the old woman whispered, "Tell Escoffier I still want my dish."

Sabine did not want the coat but did, indeed, want more meals such as this one.

"Oui, *Madame.* I will tell him."

"Good. Now clean your face."

At that moment, she sounded so like Sabine's grandmother that, out of reflex, the girl took the corner of her apron and wiped her cheeks quickly. "Clean?"

"Clean."

The cherry smoke of the doctor filled the room.

"Bland food only. How many times do I tell you this? Why does no one in this household listen to me?"

Sabine picked up the platter but a nurse shooed her away. "Put it down and leave. We'll take care of it."

Sabine gave her a shattering smile. "How very kind, but *non,*" she said. The doctor looked stricken, which pleased Sabine greatly.

At the foot of the steep servant's stairway, Sabine ate several more langoustines, wiped her mouth repeatedly and then removed her red dancer's shoes. They threw her off balance, made her limp even more pronounced. She placed one in each pocket of her stained white apron. She wanted to be very careful. The langoustines were, after all, the only thing left in the house worth eating.

In the kitchen, Escoffier was still sitting at the table where she had left him. The small plate of langoustines that he had made for himself sat uneaten. His handkerchief was bloodied. He coughed again.

"You should rest now. The doctor—"

"Is an idiot."

"But he is paid well for it, so perhaps you should follow his advice."

"Did she ask where the langoustines came from?"

"*Non.*"

"If she does, tell her Mr. Boots of Southsea."

"She will not ask."

"But if she does. Mr. Boots . . . of Southsea."

"Yes. Southsea."

"Good. England."

"Yes."

Escoffier slowly stood. With the meal cooked, he was no longer the great chef but a small broken man. Sabine wondered how much time he had left.

That night, the fog cleared and the full moon rose icy red over the wild cobalt sea. Delphine fell in and out of the haze of life: one moment letting go of things she no longer needed like language, and then the next moment, grasping onto it tightly, a frayed rope by which she would try to pull herself back into the world.

"*Cité à l'ordre de l'armée pour son superbe courage.*"

Escoffier knew that line. It was from "Invocation," Delphine's poem for their son.

Bloody bodies. Valorous soldiers. Daniel.

He leaned against the other side of the wall, listening. "I am sorry," he said. "So very sorry." He knew she could not hear him. The ruby moon turned his tears into small dark jewels. With the taste of salt in his mouth, he could not bring himself to go into her room. He did not want to remember her that way, frail and dying—drowning in loss. He turned on the radio. There was news from Berlin.

"The results given out by the Propaganda Ministry early this morning show that 89.9 percent of German voters agreed that the offices of President and Chancellor should be joined into one. This endorsement gives Chancellor Hitler, who became a German citizen just four years ago, power unequaled since the days of Genghis Khan. It is interesting to note that the Ministry also reported 871,056 defective ballots, which they attribute to protestors attempting to sabotage 'Germany's Golden Age.' "

Escoffier turned off the radio, touched the wall. "Soon."

By morning, Delphine had let go of dreaming. She had decided that all she required was the deep cool darkness of sleep. Dreams were too untrustworthy. They could turn quickly, without warning. She was no longer willing to accept their mercurial ways. There was no need. Her stillness allowed her to live between time. She was no longer a slave to it. She could be young or old. She could pass into the next world or stay in this one. With the taste of the langoustines still on her tongue, she could feel her husband's soft hand against her thigh and the tangle of their bodies, the heat of it. *Quick. Quick.* Dreams had become unnecessary.

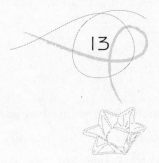

13

THE *FOIE GRAS* AND THE JOLLY ROUND FIGURE OF M. Heursel of the Maison Bruck, whose calling card announced that they were the makers of the finest *pâtés de foie gras de Strasbourg* in the world, arrived by motor car early the next morning along with a slab of larded pork and two geese that were, thankfully, quite dead. M. Heursel was also kind enough to bring six black truffles wrapped in brown paper that to Sabine were unimpressive as rocks.

"Le grand mystère!"

The stylish round man picked up a truffle and held it in his dough-like hands, offered it to Sabine as if it were a rare diamond. *"Voilà!"*

Sabine took the truffle in her hand gingerly. Sniffed. Squinted. It had a strange piquant odor and looked like a dirty walnut. She held it away from herself as if it were a small dead mouse.

"What should I do with these?"

"Whatever you want."

"These are a type of mushroom?"

M. Heursel was crestfallen. He puffed his chest again and said,

"Mademoiselle, truffles are the great ancient mystery of the vegetable kingdom. They are said to be the children of thunder."

Sabine frowned. "And so what does one cook thunderous children in? Butter?"

A look of panic passed over M. Heursel's well-fed face. "You are the cook?"

"I am the cook."

"Is Monsieur Escoffier here?"

"*Non.*"

Sabine could see that the man wanted to pack the food back into his perfect wicker baskets and run back to Paris, back to the famed Maison Bruck where people understood how to enjoy the finest *pâtés de foie gras de Strasbourg* in the world, but it was too late. There was no graceful way to leave now and save face. He offered Sabine the truffles again, hopeful that she misunderstood what he was saying.

"These are from Périgord."

"And I am from Paris."

Sabine did not misunderstand. She just did not care. *How can I feed an entire household with six dirty mushrooms?*

"Perhaps his son, Paul? We have dined together on many occasions. His lovely wife . . . "

"Everyone is gone," she said and yet the house was filled again with the voices of children and adults.

"I see."

M. Heursel wiped a thin sheet of sweat from his shiny head with a white silk handkerchief, looked at his pocket watch. "Will Monsieur Escoffier return soon?"

"*Non.*"

Above their heads, the old man coughed. It was clearly Escoffier. Unmistakable. They both knew it. Sabine smiled.

"When Monsieur Escoffier arrives home, I will give him your card."

"Is Madame in?"

Sabine held up the man's calling card. Waved it in the air. "I will tell them both that you called. They will be sorry to have missed you," she said, hands on her hips.

"His assistant?"

"Dismissed."

"The butler?"

"Gone."

"The head housekeeper, then?"

"Only on Tuesdays now."

"A nurse, perhaps?"

Sabine picked up a half-plucked chicken from the sink and shook it. "I am very busy, but I will tell everyone that you have left a bounty of gifts," she said and handed him the empty wicker baskets and held open the back door so that he could easily take his leave. There was not even the offer of a single glass of wine.

"I see," he said again.

Sabine didn't want another mouth to feed, not even for one meal, and if he stayed one more minute, lunch would have been expected. And that was impossible. The family—all the children, grandchildren, grandnieces and grandnephews—had returned to the house. She had been baking bread and cleaning chickens since dawn.

"I'm sure Monsieur Escoffier sends his profound gratitude," she told the Frenchman whose wrinkled linen suit smelled of duck fat and garlic, and then locked the door behind him.

"Au revoir," she shouted out the window. *"Ciao!"*

Monsieur Heursel turned back for a moment. He looked confused, and so she waved. It was a dismissive wave—more like a shooing away—but it was the best she could do. She didn't want to encourage the man. He did not wave back, but huffed rather loudly and then made his way through the garden and then out into the street, weaving back and forth, walking from one shaded area to another.

He must be from Provence, she thought. *They hate the sun so much there that they all walk sideways, like crabs.*

His motorcar started with a bang. He drove away in a cloud of exhaust.

Finally.

And yet, when Sabine turned back to the table, she regretted sending the man away so quickly. *What is to be done with all of this?* Geese, she understood. Rub with salt, cover with lard, and roast with potatoes. At what temperature she would roast the birds was a mystery, but she was quite sure that an hour would be long enough. An hour seemed like an eternity to wait for anything.

But to roast geese in the spring was unheard of. *Maybe in Provence,* she thought. *They do many odd things in the countryside.* But Monaco was the playground of the rich, of royalty, and with the warmth of February most began taking *la sieste* in the afternoon again. To eat roast goose with the promise of summer on everyone's mind would be absurd.

And truffles. She had never eaten them nor could she understand why anyone would want to. They were so black it seemed as if you'd have to scrub forever to get them clean. She sliced one in half. It was black inside, too. It had a fine grain, like marble. *The provinces are filled with fools.* And while she had indeed heard of *foie gras,* and knew it was a delicacy, it looked disgusting. Huge. Pale. These particular lobes of fatted liver were as big as her foot, at least two pounds. And Sabine was supposed to touch them. *Ridiculous.*

She knocked on Escoffier's door. Silence. Then knocked again.

"I can hear you breathing."

"I am working."

"I will feed it to the cats."

Sabine could hear the old man's chair slide away from the desk, hear the floorboards of his room creak. Escoffier slowly opened the door. He looked as if he hadn't slept all night. His eyes were red-rimmed and dull.

"You are an impossible woman."

"It is true."

Soon, under Escoffier's watchful eye, Sabine was chilling her hands in ice water, so she could handle the liver. It made her wish she'd fed it to the cats after all.

"*Foie gras* is sensitive to heat," he told her. "It must be kept at a constant temperature of about three degrees Celsius."

Her fingers were certainly 3°. They were white, numb and shriveled. "I hope this is worth the suffering of the cook."

"As a chef, it is your job to suffer."

Escoffier leaned against the counter as if trying to keep his balance. He coughed into his handkerchief. *More blood,* she thought and looked at him closely. His skin was gray. His hands shook. He was obviously unwell. He quickly stuffed the handkerchief into his coat pocket. He washed his hands in scalding hot water, then cold.

"Ready?" he said.

"*Non.*"

"Good."

The lobes were packed in ice. Escoffier ran his fingers over the surface with a series of quick taps. And then gently pressed the liver, holding it with his thumb underneath and four fingers on top.

"Now, see how I touch? If it is firm, it has too high a fat content and it will shrink when you cook it. If it is spongy, it has too little fat and it will burn. It must have the appropriate amount of give when you touch the flesh." He tapped it quickly again. "This is perfect. See how there is a slight imprint of my thumb? Now you."

Sabine's fingers were so cold that she could barely feel anything. She tapped the liver once, with her thumb. "Perfect."

Escoffier frowned. It was clear why people called him "Papa," he had her father's look, a disappointed look that Sabine knew well. He took her hand in his and tapped her fingers against the liver repeatedly.

"Now. Do you now understand what texture we are looking for?"

"No."

"Then you are not trying."

"That is true."

"Sabine . . . "

"Why did you not soak your own hands in ice?"

"I am Escoffier."

Apparently, that was all the explanation that was needed.

Sabine washed her hands repeatedly in hot water, rubbed them until the circulation returned to her fingertips, until any trace of the liver was gone. And then she washed them some more.

"If you are quite through—"

She wiped them on her starched white apron. Escoffier cocked an eyebrow and said, "That is unsanitary. You are a professional. Act like one. Clean towel always. Now wash again."

And so she did. The old man joined her, filling the kitchen again with the scent of olive oil soap and lavender. When they were finished, "Let me see," he said and inspected her hands closely.

"What are you looking for?"

"Some suggestion that you work for a living. Your hands are perfect. Your nails are meticulously manicured. No one trusts a cook with beautiful hands.

"Now, what do we do next?" he said.

"I boil the liver, as you have attempted to boil my hands, to make certain that it is cooked?"

Escoffier closed his eyes. Tapped the side of his nose. He seemed to be trying to compose himself.

"*Foie gras d'oie* is the liver of the goose and very fatty, more so than the duck. I have even made ice cream from it. You do not boil it. That would render the fat and make it tough."

"Ice cream?"

"It was not green as you are right now and thereby appetizing to all."

Escoffier lifted the large liver from the ice and placed it on the cutting board. Examined it closely. Sniffed it.

"Very good. This has very few veins. Most will be kept so that it retains its shape. A small knife, Sabine?"

Sabine pulled a paring knife from the block. It was the only sharp one left.

"Now," he said. "Which way do veins run through the liver? Look closely. Can you tell? It is important that large veins be removed or the remaining blood will discolor the *foie gras* when it's cooked."

He gently tapped the lobes of liver. "Think of this as if it were your own organ."

"I'd rather not."

"Then think of it as mine. Now, which way do the veins run?"

Escoffier blotted the liver with a clean towel. There were a few bits of white membrane clinging to the outside. He peeled them away gently and then trimmed a few green spots. He pulled the lobes apart with his hands and offered them to Sabine.

"See? A vein connects the two. Take the knife and cut it."

Sabine held her breath and sliced the vein quickly.

"Good. Now pull it out. Slowly, gently, an even motion."

"Out?"

"Out."

"I am sure you could do this much better than me."

"Pull."

Sabine, squeamish, pulled the vein very slowly.

"Does it help to imagine that it is my liver you are dismantling?"

"It does, yes."

"Good."

He laughed for the first time that she could remember. The house was so quiet that his laughter rang through the room, slid under the door, pealed. She imagined the nurses thought it scandalous to laugh at such a sad time, with Madame so gravely ill, and so she laughed, too.

Escoffier opened his cookbook to *foie gras* cooked in brioche. "Read," he said. "Then cook." He was suddenly sweating but the room was cold. His hands began to shake again.

"And the geese?" she said.

"Confit. First, cure with one-quarter cup of sea salt for each pound of meat." He took a pen from his pocket and began to write on the inside cover of the cookbook. Suddenly he coughed, long and hard. Sabine poured him a glass of rose hip tea that she had set out in the windowsill to steep. He drank, cleared his throat, and started to write again.

"To cure the goose, you must add salt, cumin, coriander, cinnamon, allspice, clove, ginger, nutmeg, bay leaf—make sure it's Turkish—thyme, and garlic. After two days, take it to the Grand and ask for—"

"Bobo?"

"How do you know Bobo?"

"Madame told me—"

"That he thinks he is a rogue?"

"Yes."

"Of course she did," he laughed. "Madame cannot keep a secret, that is why she is a poet. The truth is, Bobo never leaves his kitchen. He does not even come out to greet the ladies. Let us not hold that against him. Tell him to simmer this in duck fat."

"I can boil a bird."

"You can barely boil water. Bobo is a good man. He will take the care needed to make sure the geese do not go tough. When done correctly, the meat will flake away when poked with a knitting needle."

"But I can boil a bird."

"No. You can pick the meat from the bones, cover them with the duck fat and a layer of salt, and pack it into jars for the cellar. You can also convince Bobo to give you the rendered goose fat to brown potatoes. He will do anything for a beautiful woman, he meets so few of them."

"What of Madame?"

"She need not know you did not cook the bird. We won't mention it."

"No. I meant should we not make a dish for her with the goose? Something special?"

"She enjoys confit."

While that might be true, Sabine was not sure that she did. It sounded horrible. She was hoping for something more—something, perhaps, with veal. "Confit is so common. Perhaps you could create something for Madame that includes champagne?"

"A dish in her honor?"

"Yes. Maybe not with the goose, but, perhaps, with champagne. And maybe oysters."

"No."

"We still have several cases of champagne. And it would be simple to get oysters. The fishmonger willingly brought langoustines . . . "

"No."

"Caviar?"

"No."

"Veal? Veal can be so lovely."

"Yes. Veal is lovely. But no."

"Madame so wants a dish: something with her name on it. Something rich, expensive and complicated so that we must make it many times and taste it to be sure that it is correct."

Escoffier looked at Sabine closely. "She has told you this herself?"

Sabine nodded.

"Well, it is impossible," he said and then walked out of the kitchen.

Hours later, Sabine had packed the geese away in the spiced salt mixture and baked the *foie gras d'oie*. Despite its rather tough and burnt brioche crust, she sold half of it to the first café she saw in Place d'Armes. It was only worth a couple of francs to them.

"No one has money for such things anymore."

"But Escoffier himself baked this."

"I didn't know he was still alive."

Heathens.

The shops were closing but Sabine reached the tobacconist just in time. "Lucky Strikes," she said. "For the house of Escoffier."

Being American, the cigarettes were more money than she had, more money than most had, but Sabine suspected that wouldn't matter.

"I have heard Escoffier is dying?"

Sabine conjured up the spirit of Sarah and nodded with such sadness she felt it in her bones. "And Madame also."

The small thin man pushed the francs back across the counter. "Tell him his money is no good here."

This could be easier than I thought.

That evening Sabine set the sideboard with three roast chickens, cold stewed tomatoes and what remained of the *foie gras* with bread. She had cut away the burnt crust and sliced it so cleanly that the truffles retained their shape. In the pantry, she'd found a bottle of oil marked "Olio di Tartufo" and drizzled some over the slices and tasted a bit. It had a complexity that she had never tasted before—darkness with a hint of chocolate. The richness of the *foie gras*, so like butter, and the earthy perfume of the truffle oil made her laugh with pleasure but it needed wine. In the cellar, there were four bottles marked 1932 Bordeaux "Grand Cru Classé." Sabine had no idea what that meant or what it would taste like, but could see it was red and she liked red wine, so that was all that mattered.

She uncorked the wine and tasted it. It seemed bitter and weak. *Good enough for them,* she thought and poured two bottles into carafes, and set them on the sideboard, rang the dinner bell, and waited.

The dining room was still warm from the day. The *foie gras* quickly began to melt. She rang the dinner bell again. By twos and threes the family arrived, ignored the tomatoes, sniffed at the *foie gras*, and ate the chicken. While they were still eating, Sabine removed the liver and placed it in the icebox.

Idiots. How can the children of Escoffier not know fine food when they see it?

She opened another bottle of the Bordeaux and poured a glass. The doctor had given her strict orders not to enter Madame's room under any circumstances and so she sneaked up the backstairs with a plate and a glass of red wine. She opened Delphine's door slowly so that she would not be caught. The nurses were bathing her.

"Go away."

Sabine took the tray to Escoffier's room. Knocked. "Supper."

"Leave it by the door."

"But it is wonderful."

He opened the door. "Truffle oil?"

She nodded.

He picked up the plate and sniffed it. "Very nice element."

"Perhaps you could name this for Madame."

He took another sniff. "You burnt the crust, no?"

"I removed it. No one knew."

"Did they eat it?"

"No."

"Then they knew. And do not serve red wine with *foie gras*. Sauternes or Monbazillac. Something sweet."

"I like red wine."

"Unless you are Queen Victoria, no one cares. This is the Saint-Émilion?"

"Grand Cru Classé."

"You have no idea what that means, do you?"

"None whatsoever."

"Then learn. Taste the wine. Study it. But do not drink it with the *foie gras*. Go. I am working."

And then he closed the door.

By the time Sabine cleaned the kitchen and washed all the dishes, most in the grand house were either asleep or taking a late night walk around the square. La Villa Fernand was once again quiet.

Burnt crust or not, Sabine ate the remaining *foie gras* at the dining room table on the Canton blue plates and wondered what it would be like to travel to places like China where people spoke different languages and ate different things. The *foie gras* did not taste burned to her and she enjoyed the red wine with it. In fact, she drank the last bottle herself, the bottle that, surprisingly, was no longer harsh and thin but felt full and ripe in her mouth.

At 2 a.m., Sabine was still dressed, lying across the small bed in her room, dreaming of a China where all the houses and people were as blue as porcelain, when the service buzzer went off, just as it did every night. It was Escoffier wanting his nightcap, his "youth elixir," as he called it.

The yolk of one fresh egg beaten with several spoonfuls of sugar, mixed with a pony of champagne and a glass of hot milk. Sabine could barely stomach it. She was dry-mouthed and dizzy from the wine. A few minutes later, she held the tray in her shaking hand and knocked softly. "Monsieur Escoffier?"

He opened the door in a panic. "She's crying again."

The house was quiet. All Sabine could hear was the sound of the sea, the waves crashing along the shore.

"Madame?"

"Yes. Can't you hear it?"

Sabine could not. "We'll call the nurse."

"She is sleeping. You can hear her snoring."

Sabine listened for a moment. "I hear nothing."

Escoffier took her by the arm and roughly pulled her into his room. Tapped the wall. "Listen here."

She put her ear to the wall.

"I hear nothing, Monsieur. Perhaps you fell asleep at your desk. Perhaps you were dreaming."

Escoffier sank back into his desk chair, held his head in his hands. Sabine placed the tray on the desk next to him, glancing around the room. She had never been inside of his room before. It was worse than the kitchen, a jumble of things.

On top of the bookshelf was a reproduction of a passenger train sculpted in sugar. Over the desk was a picture of a tiger created with tiny kernels of rice pasted on canvas. There were menus everywhere, too, richly painted as if greeting cards. Some with geishas bearing Moët, some were obviously for royalty painted with jeweled crowns, ermine and red velvet, and some were funny— one had a group of monkey chefs cooking atop a camel in the desert sun.

There were stacks of newspaper clippings in several languages and hundreds of photographs piled on the floor, under the windowsills and on the top of every surface. At her feet was a photo of the Australian opera star Nellie Melba signed: *"À Monsieur Escoffier avec mes*

remerciements pour la création Pêche Melba," and dated 1914, the year
of the Great War. Next to it was another war photo, this one of a very
young Escoffier tasting a Christmas pudding with a group of soldiers.
There was also a picture of Escoffier in the midst of a kitchen brigade
of a hundred men, all dressed in white, standing in front of the luxury
liner the RMS *Titanic*.

Sabine had heard all the stories but never imagined them to really
be true. But here was the proof.

She looked at the small shaking man. Still holding the tray, she
patted his back awkwardly, like one who is childless trying to comfort
a lost boy. Tears fell into his lap. He put his hand to the wall, as if to
reach beyond it into Delphine's room.

Sabine set the tray down, popped the champagne and poured it
into a glass. "Monsieur, you must sleep."

"What did she say to you about the dish that she wants?"

Sabine fingered the box of Lucky Strikes in her pocket. "You have
named a dish for everyone except her. She does not wish to be forgotten by history."

He picked up the photo of his lost brigade in front of the *Titanic*.
He stared at it, touching each face as if remembering each name, each
family that the loss of their lives left behind.

Sabine poured the beaten egg mixture into the champagne and
handed the glass to him. He drank the warm milk instead.

"Sleep well, Monsieur."

"Goodnight, Sarah."

Sabine did not correct him.

∽

IN THE MOMENTS before dawn, Delphine was sure that she heard
his voice quite clearly. She wasn't sure where it was coming from. It

seemed to rattle around inside her head. But it was Escoffier. There was no doubt.

"Which contains potatoes, apples, gherkins and herring fillets? German Potato Salad? Muscovite Apples? Herrings à la Russe? Or Herrings *à la Livonienne?*"

"German Potato Salad. Equal parts of all four."

"Correct. Which contains onion, powdered curry, white consommé and cream? Indian Curry? Mutton Pudding? Salt Cod in the Style of India? Coulis of Rabbit?

"Indian Curry."

"*Non.* Couils of Rabbit. There is no cream in Indian curry."

It was their game. And so she said, "Which contains King Edward potatoes, garlic, butter, Cantal cheese and pepper?"

"That is too simple. *Aligot.*"

"It could have been gnocchi. The King Edward is well known as the finest potato for gnocchi."

"Madame Escoffier. If it were anyone else, it could be gnocchi."

"Yes, well. *Aligot* is wondrous."

"True. But it is still just mashed potatoes, garlic and cheese."

"Is it? But what if you add white truffles? What did Brillat-Savarin say? 'Truffle awakens erotic and gastronomic ideas . . . '"

"Madame. There are children about."

"And that is thanks to my *aligot.*"

"Fine cuisine, only."

When they were first married, Escoffier and Delphine would each lie in the dark, each in their own tiny bed, and tally their scores. They were too tired to sleep. Too worried to make love.

Two months after the wedding, Delphine's father suddenly died. Four months later, her baby sisters contracted diphtheria. The publishing house failed. Faisan Doré was a distant memory. The newlyweds moved back to Paris to be close to Delphine's mother, who would not eat or speak or sleep but spent her days silently wandering the house, walking from room to room, looking. Just looking. As if she were waiting her turn.

Delphine and Escoffier's lives had unraveled around them and so the game was born. That was back at a time when food wasn't about balance sheets and bottom lines, the dance of profit and loss, but when a *meule* of vintage Comté with that distinctive Gruyère taste of nuts, small ripe pears, and a perfect glass of Pomerol would be enough to bring them both to tears.

And now the game had begun again. It was still Delphine's turn.

"Which contains currant, apricot jam, custard and Grand Marnier? A Cabinet Pudding? Trifle? Apricot Mousse? Rice Pudding?"

"Cabinet Pudding. Very clever," Escoffier laughed. "A trifle could contain Grand Marnier but usually it is either port, sweet sherry or Madeira wine. Sometimes there is fruit juice. But a Cabinet Pudding always contains ladyfingers soaked in liqueur."

"Correct. One hundred points."

They went on like this until dawn, when the moon paled and the sun began to push its way through the surface of the azure sea, staining the sky red.

"But what kind of red?"

"Strawberry?"

"Beet?"

"Theater curtain. They are always red, are they not?"

"Food only. Currant. It is that particular tone of red."

"Then why not cherry?"

"Ripe?"

"Of course. The sky turned as ripe as cherries."

"*Non.* Overripe. On the page, it would read—'The sky is stained, overripe.' The cherry need not be mentioned; it is implied."

"Better."

"Of course. You forget that I, too, am Escoffier."

And then they laughed as if they were young again, lying in the dark, holding each other's hands and wanting so much more from a world that seemed to have forgotten them. And then he said, "Which contains egg, butter, truffle and cream?"

"Everything should, but what are my choices?"

"It is something you have not made me in a very long time."

And then there was silence. The game was over.

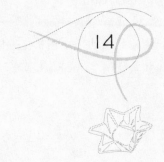

14

"**T**ODAY WE SHALL COOK," DELPHINE SAID.

Sabine did not like the sound of that at all. In just a night, the old woman seemed to have become transparent. Her voice was a mere whisper, rough and raw as open water. She was fading away. The nurses had carried her into the kitchen and placed her on her hospital gurney and left her there as if she were a plate that needed washing.

This would not do. Sabine was wearing her red dancing shoes again. Cooking was not what she had in mind.

"Madame, should you be—"

"Dead?"

"—in your room."

"I should be dead and in my room but I am neither and so we will cook."

Sabine could hear children crying in the house and the ineffectual whispers of their parents. In the garden, gray rabbits were chewing at the new shoots of carrots, chicory and the young roquette. "Madame, there must be twenty or more for the midday meal today."

"Do we have eggs?"

Sabine had hoped to lay a plate of warm bread, almond butter and fig jam in the dining room, ring the dinner bell, and, before anyone arrived, slip out the back door and down to the docks where most of Monte Carlo spent their days watching the sailors of the French navy on their battleships polishing the endless rows of guns, and waiting. Every one was waiting: the sailors on shore leave, the young men who fled to neutral Monaco to avoid conscription, the priests hoarding sacramental wine, and the doctors quietly tearing bedsheets for bandages.

Führer und Reichskanzler. Every newspaper, every radio carried news of him.

Prince Louis II, who in his younger days had enlisted in the French Foreign Legion, often joined them on the docks. Dressed in his old uniform, black patent boots and saber, he would listen to the stories of those who, like him, had fought in the first war, but shared none of his own. After a time he would address the crowd.

"The French navy is here to protect you. I am here to protect you. Go back to your homes. You are safe."

And yet he would linger, watching the coastline, waiting.

There was a reckless air about the world. Anything could happen. Anything was possible. On the docks there were hearts to be won or broken. And so Sabine wore her shoes. It was oddly thrilling.

But the old woman wanted to cook. Sabine could not understand why. She was obviously too ill. When she spoke Sabine could barely hear her.

"Eggs?"

"Yes."

"We have a bucketful."

"Bread?"

Dough had been rising in long thin baguette tins on the counter. "Soon."

Sabine turned on the gas to warm the oven. There was the familiar whoosh. She lit the gas; the flame shot up and spread out like a blue wave.

"Now. Knock on every door," Delphine said. "Tell them I am cooking. Tell everyone in the house. The children, the grandchildren— knock on everyone's door, but do not tell Escoffier. There is no need to bother him. When the meal is ready, he will come."

"He did not eat last night."

"He will eat today. Set the table. Then we shall cook."

The rasp and ragged edge of the old woman's voice unnerved her. "Go."

She did. Sabine placed the bread in the oven and then knocked on every door in the house. The response was quizzical. Madame did not have the use of her hands or legs. How could she cook?

"Where are the nurses?"

"Whose idea was this?"

"Does Papa know?"

But no one offered to help.

When the bread turned golden brown, Sabine set the table with the full service of Canton plates, from soup bowls to bread plates to the larger dinner plates. She took out the good silver and lace tablecloths. In the garden, she picked a bouquet of lavender and gathered the thin red limbs of apple blossoms from a neighboring tree. She placed them in a heavy cut glass vase and set it in the center of the table.

In the kitchen, Delphine lay watching a bevy of swans in a nearby pond.

"Finished, Madame."

"Swan makes a fine meal."

"Swan?"

"If you marinate them in vinegar and ginger, you can bake them into pies or *pâté*."

"But they are so beautiful."

"They are also temperamental. Listen to the hissing. Sounds like a bevy of chefs, does it not?"

"The children are quite clear that they would rather eat chicken."

"If you are to feed this family when I am gone, you have to learn how to take what is offered. Rabbits are everywhere, why should they eat and my grandchildren starve?"

"No one is starving."

"The war is not here yet."

"Yet."

"Show me the eggs."

Sabine held the basket out in front of her. Delphine looked at it closely. Leaned her head in for a sniff. "This morning?"

"Yesterday."

"Truffle?"

"There are still two left."

"Good. Butter must be melted."

Sabine scooped pale butter from the crock. It sizzled as it hit the deep copper pan. She turned down the heat to simmer. Began to whisk.

"Good. You're learning," Delphine said. "Very nice. Now pay attention. There is a hierarchy to eggs—you must always remember this. The scrambled egg is the most difficult and so it is the most perfect of all gifts. If not worked with a masterful hand, they will be tough. The soufflé is next. It takes some skill but there is much room for error. All one needs to do is to whip egg whites and carefully fold them into the batter, it is quite simple. Any chef can coax air into eggs if he pays attention. The same is true of an omelet—again the air into the eggs is key, but it is not the work of an artist. The poached egg is about mechanics; there is no poetry.

"Today we shall make fried eggs."

"What is the skill in fried eggs?"

"None. That is why I believe that if you follow instructions closely you will be able to make them correctly."

"Monsieur will not allow me to make eggs at all. He mentioned specifically that the frying of eggs was prohibited."

"This is my kitchen."

"He says fried eggs are an insult."

"And it is my kitchen."

"He will be angry."

"If you make them. If I make them they are something altogether different. You are merely my hands. Get out the earthenware bakers, three, the large ones."

"To fry eggs?"

"How do you make fried eggs?"

"You place butter in a hot pan and crack eggs into it."

"*Non.* That is the American way. And Escoffier served them with bacon and toast for a princely sum, but they are no good. You will learn the proper way—*Oeufs sur-le-Plat.* Place melted butter in the bottom of three dishes, enough to cover, and then crack the eggs into a bowl and gently, very gently, pour them in. Do not break the yolk."

Sabine took an egg, cracked it along the edge of the bowl and broke the yolk.

"This is too difficult."

"Cooking is the marriage of science and poetry. Has Escoffier not told you that? He says that all the time, perhaps you have not listened carefully enough. Crack the egg gently on the counter first. The laws of science prevent clean break if you use the side of the bowl."

"I always crack the egg on the bowl."

"And you are a very bad cook. Since I am cooking, we will do this my way."

Sabine cracked an egg on the surface of the counter and poured it gently into the bowl. The yolk remained intact.

"Science and poetry."

"Or luck."

"Luck has no place in the kitchen. Science. It is always science."

One by one, Sabine cracked the brown eggs on the surface of the counter, opened them into a bowl and then gently, carefully, poured them into the earthenware dishes. Each yolk remained perfect—firm and fat.

As Sabine worked, the voices of the family gathering at the table could be heard. The heat of the day and that of the oven made the house feel oppressive. The adults were sniping at each other. The children were fussy.

"I wonder where that stupid girl is," someone said.

"The crippled one?"

"Who else is left?"

"Probably at the docks. She looks like the kind who sells herself to sailors."

"She certainly can't cook."

Delphine was quite surprised that Sabine's face colored. Perhaps the girl was not as much like Sarah as she thought.

"The eggs are ready to be cooked, Madame."

Sabine presented the three dishes to the old woman. The uncooked yolks sat high, were the perfect shade of marigold. They were obviously fresh.

"Pour a tablespoon of cream over each and cook. Then shave the truffles over them."

"What about cheese?"

"The dish has no cheese."

"But we have Gruyère. Enough to cover. It would impart a nutty taste that would work quite well."

"Fine. Good. You're learning. Spoken like a chef. Bravo. Cheese. Bake until warm. Then truffle."

Sabine poured the cream and grated the cheese, then gently placed the dishes in the oven to brown.

Eggs, cream, butter, cheese—the aroma quickly made its way into the dining room. The family became quiet.

Above their heads, the old man pushed his chair away from the writing table. The floorboards in the hallway creaked. When Escoffier's foot hit the top stair of the back stairwell, "Sabine!" he said. "How many times must I tell you it is an insult to fry eggs? I can smell the butter all over the house. Fried eggs are for a family meal from one member to the other. Food has etiquette—"

"I should get some wine from the cellar," Sabine said. "Champagne? Or maybe a red."

"Beaujolais," Delphine said but the girl was already halfway down the stairs.

"Champagne is better," she shouted.

"Of course."

When Escoffier entered the room he stopped at the sight of Delphine lying there.

"The eggs are your doing?"

"They are my gift to you."

"You should be in bed."

"I should be immortal."

"Madame, how many times must we discuss this?"

That odd alchemy of married love—passion, betrayal, fury, kindness, and companionship—lay there exposed between them. Sabine stood at the doorway watching.

The eggs would take a minute or two, any more and they would be ruined.

"It is impossible," he said.

"It was never impossible to name something for the Emperor."

"Madame Escoffier, that was different."

"Dish after dish for him, for Germany, and now war again. You should have poisoned him when you had the chance."

It was time to shave the truffles over the eggs. Sabine could smell that they were being overcooked.

"Beaujolais *and* champagne!"

Her arms were full, a small cask of wine and two bottles of champagne. She limped her way across the room. The two did not look at her. She washed her hands quickly, wiped them on her apron, and then opened the oven. The eggs were just set and the cheese nicely browning. She shaved the truffles over it all and placed them back in the warm oven until the bread finished baking. Just a minute or two.

"I am serving now."

"Very good," Escoffier said.

Escoffier tugged at his ear; took a deep breath. There was a sorrow in his eyes: a look of profound loss, the weight of it was remarkable.

Sabine could not bear to watch any longer and the eggs were just starting to turn from golden brown to the color of old wood. "The eggs, Monsieur."

"Sabine. Serve," Escoffier said.

She quickly placed the hot bread and the earthenware dishes onto a heavy silver tray and carried them into the dining room.

"From Madame," she said. Germaine and Jeanne burst into tears and held each other as if they were sisters, not sisters-in-law. Sabine arranged the food on the sideboard quickly.

The door to the kitchen opened.

"Papa!"

"There is wine, also," Escoffier said. He was holding the small cask that he quickly tapped and poured into a carafe, a white linen napkin draped over his arm as if he were the *sommelier*. "Please. Eat. Food must be served piping hot, that is the way the nose prefers it. If cold, then all is left up to the tongue and that is a very dull instrument indeed. Eat while you can still smell that it is delicious."

"I'll get Madame," Sabine said.

He caught her by the arm. "I called for the nurse to take her back to her room."

"But she—"

"The eggs, Sabine. The eggs are growing cold. Serve."

Sabine served the eggs, spooning them gently onto the plates. Escoffier poured the wine, as if he were again at The Savoy. Wiped the rim of each glass. "A fine vintage," he said, lifting the glass to the light. "Last week, I believe." And everyone laughed. "It is a very old joke, but I am a very old man."

When he came to a grandchild's glass, "Sabine, we'll need water for the children. Half wine and half water always," he said and winked at the round-faced child.

Sabine was surprised to find Delphine still in the kitchen.

"Take me in."

"Madame?"

"Sabine. Please."

Sabine rolled the woman into the dining room and everyone stopped talking. Escoffier put the carafe on the table. Delphine's voice was nearly a whisper.

"He was the Emperor," she said. "There was nothing you could do."

"He may have been the Emperor but I was Escoffier."

The air itself seemed to become dead weight. They all looked at their plates, their hands, their feet. Anywhere but at Madame and Monsieur.

"Old man, you are such trouble."

"And you are unbearably difficult to love: a trial that would tempt Job."

And then Escoffier kissed his wife as a young man would, all passion and promise. He kissed her until the gaggle of grandchildren, great-grandchildren, grandnieces and grandnephews began to squirm again, then giggle.

"And you, the great Escoffier, cannot put that on a plate?"

"That is the core of the issue."

And so he kissed her again. And the children laughed out loud.

"I miss Daniel so very much," she whispered in his ear.

"Soon," he said.

"Soon," she said.

15

ATER THAT AFTERNOON, ESCOFFIER REMOVED THE COPY OF *LE Guide Culinaire* from the kitchen and replaced it with *Ma Cuisine*.

"It is for housewives."

"Perhaps you should hire one."

"Try, Sabine. Try. That is all I ask. Memorize the rules and the rest will come naturally. The *sauciers* are the enlightened chemists of the kitchen and at the foundation of all great sauces is stock. Begin with stock. Stock ennobles the ordinary sauté. It adds amazing depth to any stew. Make stock and then we will create magic."

Sabine did not make stock. Nor did she even open the book. Supper that evening was simple. With the large mortar and pestle, Sabine mashed handfuls of almonds together with anchovy fillets, garlic and fennel until it became a paste. She served it as a spread with warm crusty bread and fried ravioli made with goat cheese. There were bâtons of raw vegetables and tomatoes broiled with fresh herbs. While she had other cheese to bring the meal to a proper end, she also made a milk gratin with cognac topped with warm caramel and ripe pears that she had "borrowed" from the neighbor's tree.

It was well received by all except Escoffier.

"This is not from *Ma Cuisine*."

"But it is what a housewife would make."

He opened the book to page twenty. "Read. Then cook." When Sabine delivered his nightcap at 2 a.m., he seemed more tired than usual.

"How is the stock? I could not smell it."

"It is complicated."

"It is simple. First make the white stock and then use it to make the veal. The carrots, and bacon, combine to create a taste on the palate that makes the diner think 'veal' because together these elements bring out what is the best in the meat. It is pure."

"It is soup."

"It is the foundation of civilization."

"It is a vehicle for noodles."

"Read the book, Sabine."

And so she did.

While her favorite rule was, "Monotony jades the appetite," that night she'd fallen asleep with the book in her hand dreaming of the line "One must not forget that good sound cooking, even the very simplest, makes a contented home."

The next morning she awoke wanting a cigarette and a sailor. Unfortunately, neither was readily available and Escoffier was waiting for her in the kitchen determined that she'd make the veal stock. His way. Page twenty. Simple.

It wasn't even sunrise.

"White stock first—ten pounds of veal, shins and shoulder, carrots, cloves. Five hours. Then use that stock as the base and add more veal, six to eight pounds, bacon, onions and all the rest. Three more hours."

"Eight hours for soup?"

"Stock."

"Stock is soup."

"Stock is revolution."

"And if you put noodles in revolution, it is soup."

Escoffier rubbed his forehead. Closed his eyes. "What have you learned from *Ma Cuisine?*"

"That you have no idea what the word *simple* means."

She poured him a glass of lemonade. "This was not in *Ma Cuisine*, either. But it is very good." Strawberry honey, fat lemons and just a touch of lavender—he drank it all. It was, indeed, very good.

"You are not hopeless, obviously. But you cannot get discouraged. Music is always difficult for one who has never been taught how to play an instrument."

"Or the tone deaf."

"Madame made the same claim when we met. Perhaps you need a teacher."

"Perhaps."

She brought him a small jam tart that she'd made for the children. "You need to eat more."

He took a bite. "This shows promise."

"I can cook. I am not you, however."

"The geese. Bobo at the Grand will boil them. Do not forget."

She promptly forgot.

And so later that morning, Sabine stood in the pantry with *Ma Cuisine* in hand, hoping for inspiration. She had no idea how to make stock without veal or the money to buy veal. In the pantry, there were the usual staples—flours, salt, sugar, spices, jellies, chutneys and condiments of all kinds. There was golden quince paste to be spread on fresh bread. Crocks filled with persimmons cured in brown sugar and dark rum. Dozens of paraffin-sealed jars of watermelon jam made from the pale-skinned *meraviho*. There were still champagne bottles filled with tomato sauce, of course, which the children would still not eat. But there was not much else. Only two eggs remained after she'd made the milk gratin. Butter. *Crème fraîche.* There was some goat's milk yogurt that could be made into cheese again, as she had done for the ravioli, and some leftover chicken, roasted, but just a small amount.

And the geese, of course, the geese, which were salted and stuffed into crocks ready to be simmered in duck fat by Bobo and preserved for a later time.

But none of it would be enough to make a day's worth of proper meals for the house. And none of it would make veal stock. And she was out of cigarettes again. A trip into town was in order.

Someone must want to give Papa a side of veal.

Outside the kitchen window, Sabine could see that the swans had returned, hissing, and the rabbits resumed their insistent chewing of the remaining greens. The red oak, chicory and *roquette* were all bitten down to the quick.

Swan stock. Rabbit stock. Sabine thumbed through the pages of *Ma Cuisine* without luck. *If only there were a stock made of grass.*

"Stock is everything in cooking, at least in French cooking," Escoffier wrote. "Without it, nothing can be done. If one's stock is good, what remains of the work is easy; if, on the other hand, it is bad or mediocre, it is quite hopeless to expect anything approaching a satisfactory result. The cook mindful of success, therefore, will naturally direct his attention to the faultless preparation of his stock, and, in order to achieve this result, he will find it necessary not merely to make use of the freshest and finest products, but also to exercise the most scrupulous care in their preparation, for, in cooking, care is half the battle."

"Care?" Sabine mumbled. "If I have to care about cooking then we shall all starve to death, Monsieur Escoffier." She continued on, skimming the pages.

"Meats are more nourishing than vegetables, but to make the best of both of them they should be eaten together."

"A good dinner and a fine dinner should preferably end with fruit . . . "

"Coffee, carefully prepared and taken some time after the meal, in the drawing room, helps the digestion."

The cookbook was no help at all and so Sabine decided to take the cured geese to the Grand to be simmered instead. *To Bobo*—she laughed at the thought of his name. *He may be handsome.* And so she dressed for the occasion, replaced her white cotton apron and black uniform with a lace cotton dress that was soft as silk and the color of ripe blackberries. And of course, her red dancing shoes.

The hotel was unquestionably grand. So grand that a woman carrying two large baskets bearing salted geese could not walk into the elegant lobby and simply ask the bellboy where the kitchen was—even if she were wearing red dancing shoes—which she was, in addition to a splash of vanilla extract behind each ear and in the crooks of her arms.

And so, once she saw the seemingly endless rows of Rolls Royces idling, it was clear to Sabine that she had not thought of the logistics of the situation when she walked down the hill. Nor had she thought of the time. It was nearly noon.

There must be a delivery entrance.

She walked around the hotel's grounds carrying the geese, her hands growing numb with the weight of them, until she found an unmarked door, which luckily was open. The stairs led into the basement where the kitchen was. When she pushed her way in past the waiters it was if she'd walked into Hell itself.

The chefs were in the middle of luncheon service. The room was as hot as an oven. The ventilation had obviously been turned off to keep the finished plates warm until they could be served. The windows and doors were closed tight. Woodsmoke from the ovens bellowed. It was so thick she could hardly see. The air felt toxic. Coal fires seared the steaks and then flamed two, three feet high.

The smell of the kitchen was intense—the food, yes, but also sweat, the pungent notes of garlic, rosemary and then that sweet sticky smell of fresh blood from the fish still flapping when slapped on the table and sliced open without a second thought.

It was chaos but the *brigade de cuisine* pushed on. Plates were passed from one station to the other. Everyone was red-faced and sweating, shouting and running from place to place, in and out of this fog of soot and cinders. There were fifty or sixty men. Maybe less. Maybe more. Some were speaking French, but there were other languages, too.

Sabine could hardly breathe. *Forty years. How can they even live that long in a place like this?*

"Who's the doll?" someone yelled and the entire room came to a halt.

There were a few rude comments made in assorted languages; a handful of wolf whistles. And then, in the center of the smoke, she heard a voice. "Jean Paul, get Papa's geese from the girl. Everyone else back to work."

She assumed the voice belonged to Bobo but he never stepped forward. The wearing of the red shoes had gone to waste. She checked her watch. *Back to work,* she thought. Supper would have to be started soon. And so she left. Sabine slowly made her way back up the hill, leaning one way and then the other—the shoes were unmerciful—wondering what a man named Bobo would be like.

When Sabine returned from the Grand, she discovered that Escoffier had disappeared. She knocked on his door and received no answer. The bed was neatly made, as if he hadn't slept in it.

If his son Paul was worried, it was difficult to tell. He and the rest of the family were getting ready to go back to Paris on the early evening train. Everyone was leaving. The grandchildren were squirming. The suitcases were packed. The train would be leaving soon. Paul checked his watch.

"Does my mother know?"

"*Non.*"

"He could be at church."

Mass had been over for hours. No one remembered him at break-fast. Or lunch. In fact, no one could remember the last time they had seen Escoffier but they didn't mention that to Sabine. She was the help after all.

"Did you pack our supper?" Paul asked.

She had indeed. For the trip, Sabine put *Ma Cuisine* aside and filled the food hampers with luck and industry. She made little green pies of wild leeks that she'd found growing alongside the road on the way back from the hotel. A Joséphine salad was thrown together using leftovers and bits from the garden and pantry—chicken from the night before, curry powder, preserved lemons, and dried coconut. And for something sweet, she made curd tarts of lavender honey and lemon jam.

They were the recipes of her *grand-mère*, not of Escoffier. And as she made them they felt like a gift—not for the children and the inter-changeable grandchildren and great-grandchildren—but for herself. She also placed a small cask of wine in the hamper, some soft cheese that she had made from goat's milk, and several bottles of lemonade.

When she delivered the food to Paul he thanked her warmly, which surprised Sabine. "This is quite lovely," he said. "It all looks very good."

"What should I do if Monsieur does not return?" she asked.

"He will," Paul said, but didn't sound convinced. "He may have gone to Paris ahead of us. He knew we were leaving. Last time he stayed at Hôtel Garnier on the rue de l'Isly. We will check there when we arrive."

"Has anyone looked at the casino? He could be at a table," Ger-maine said.

Paul put on his overcoat. "Law is still law. Citizens still cannot gamble and he would not be there just to watch. It would make his hands itch."

"Maybe a kitchen somewhere. He has always been quite fond of that chef from the Grand. The one with the stupid name."

"Bobo?"

Sabine considered this a moment. Escoffier had indeed reminded her about the geese.

"If Monsieur Escoffier does not return in an hour," she said, "I will call the police and tell them to check the hotel."

"Check yourself. If you call the police, they will want to speak to Mother and that will upset her. She doesn't know Papa is gone."

Paul looked at his watch again. "The train. We must leave."

And then the children, grandchildren and great-grandchildren ran up the stairs to Delphine's room to say goodbye. Sabine retreated to the kitchen, ran up the back staircase and slipped unnoticed into Escoffier's room. She could hear the daughter's voice.

"We will be back soon," Germaine said.

"I will be waiting," the old woman said.

Sabine hoped that was true. She didn't want to be left alone with the dying.

In Delphine's room, she could hear kisses upon kisses. No one mentioned Escoffier. And then they were gone. She watched from his window as the gaggle of relatives made their way down the steep slope in a single line; everyone following Paul who from a distance moved very much like Escoffier, and looked very much like him but, sadly, wasn't.

The house went quiet. Sabine heard Madame say, "He is gone, isn't he?"

At first she thought Delphine was speaking to a nurse, but the evening nurse had yet to arrive.

"Was he not at the hotel?"

Sabine leaned into the wall. Listened. "Madame?" she whispered. No answer. She returned to the kitchen, where she'd been making sugared flowers. Mint leaves, tiny violets and old-fashioned rose petals, heavy with perfume, lay on the counter. Very gently she dipped each one into the stiff egg whites, then in confectioners' sugar, and then placed them on the baking sheet, which she put in the warm oven, the door ajar. It gave the room the scent of a garden, heady and sweet.

Sabine had planned to store the sweets in canning jars—there were still a few gaskets and lids left—and save them for cake. When she was a child, her *grand-mère* had once made her a *Saint-Honoré* for her birthday. It was the most wondrous cake in the world. Not a cake at all but a composition of tiny puffs of choux pastry filled with vanilla cream, very much like *profiteroles*, but molded together with caramel and covered with whipped chantilly cream fresh from the dairy. Her *grand-mère* decorated it with candied flowers and mint leaves.

Sabine never had anything like it before or since and suddenly wanted to make that cake again. She packed the flowers gently into jars and placed them in the pantry. The house was so quiet, the silence settled under her skin. Made her itch. It soon would be dark. Escoffier could be anywhere.

She took off her shoes, walked quietly back up the stairs and opened Delphine's door without knocking. The curtains had been pulled back. The plum sky of early evening seemed to bleed into the deep azure seas.

"He is at the hotel?" Sabine asked.

"Take the car."

"There is no gas."

"Put gas in it."

"Money, Madame."

"Open my dresser. The pearl inlay."

Sabine opened the carved mahogany dresser with its lions' heads and leaping fish. In the top drawer was a gold cigarette case with pearl inlay squares.

"Sell it."

The gold case was monogrammed DDE. It wouldn't bring less than a franc, if anything at all. Sabine removed the Gitanes and sniffed them. They were stale but they were still cigarettes. She put them in her pocket and put the case back into the drawer.

"The sun will set soon. I'll check the outdoor markets first."

"He's at the Grand."

"Marché de la Condamine on Place d'Armes. Those cafés, I'll look there. Marché de Monte-Carlo on St-Charles, he has a friend there, the fishmonger."

"He is at the hotel."

"How do you know?"

"I know. I always know."

The night nurse opened the door to the room; Sabine pushed past her and into the hallway. Rain began to pelt the roof, the windows: a quick shower. She knew she would need an umbrella, her raincoat. And if she was going to the Grand, her red shoes again. She stopped by her room. Slid underneath the door was a thick envelope from the Carlton. It was addressed to her. The familiar handwriting, shaky and yet still elegant, was unmistakable. The stationery was so old it was yellowing. He'd obviously taken boxes of it when he'd retired from the hotel.

"The Grand. 19:00 Hours. Formal dress."

He hadn't even bothered to sign it. Sabine looked at her watch. She had just enough time to change.

16

S HE BARELY MADE IT. AS SOON AS SABINE ENTERED THE
hotel, the rain showers burst into a storm. The doorman
welcomed her. The bellman took her coat and umbrella.
"You can refresh there," he said and pointed to a door marked
"Lounge" where she found soft towels to dry herself and perfumes
from many countries. When she was finally presentable, she walked
back to the lobby and stopped. The hotel was indeed, grand. Unlike its
hellish kitchen, the dining room was opulent and of another time—
Victorian, to be exact. That fact did not escape Sabine. Every wall was
gilded. The curtains were red velvet. The ceiling was painted with
frescos. The carpeting was brocaded in deep red and gold. Thousands
of candles cast warm light on the faces of the diners and the crystal
chandeliers shone like the tears of a widowed queen.

It was the kind of room that demanded formal dress but Sabine
had none. Her cream blouse and black linen skirt were plain, and
still a bit damp, but she wore her unruly red hair as Sarah would
have, swept into place. After all, that was obviously what Escoffier
wanted—supper with Miss Bernhardt.

But Bobo was waiting for her.

"The likeness is remarkable," he said.

Sarah, again.

The *directeur de cuisine* was not at all what Sabine had expected. Madame Escoffier said he was tan, and that was true, but he had the bearing of someone well born. He was not in chef's whites, but was wearing a double-breasted suit, obviously hand tailored. He had alarming eyes; they were too blue and were wild as the storm itself.

He offered his arm to her. "I am to show you to your table, Mademoiselle."

Sabine hesitated, imagined herself limping across the elegant room and everyone turning to look at the crippled girl.

"Lean on me a bit," he whispered, as if entering into a waltz.

He knew. Of course he knew. Escoffier obviously told him about the polio. She wondered what else had been said but she took his arm anyway. Leaned into him. His skin smelled of woodsmoke. *They only live forty years.* Madame had told her this. If that were true, ten years and he'd be gone. *Pity,* she thought as if it didn't matter but she could feel her heart break, just a little.

They walked together across the vast dining room; it was nearly empty. The few couples that were there seemed to have fallen out of time. The men were old, mostly white-haired; most wore white dinner jackets, many of them covered with medals from wars that could never be remembered or forgotten exactly.

The women all seemed to be wives, not mistresses, and each couple resembled each other in that way that couples often do, the same grinding of life leaving similar scars. Some wore tiaras and gloves that buttoned up to the elbows. Their gowns were long and tarnished. Some of them wore feathers and pearls wrapped over and over again around their necks, making them look like overdressed ostriches. Earrings pulled their lobes down low.

Sabine was staring. He could see that. "They are dusty," he said underneath his breath. "The rich have become dusty."

They reminded Sabine of that picture of Escoffier's staff about to board the *Titanic*. She wasn't sure why.

And while she was staring at the diners, they were staring back. Every head turned when the *directeur de cuisine* escorted her to her table, not because she was the crippled girl—but because she was beautiful and he was handsome and on such a stormy night, there was not much to talk about. The Germans were momentarily forgotten; the world had not yet burst into flames.

"Have you known Monsieur Escoffier long?" she asked.

"All my life."

"I am told you are not to be trusted, as you are very fond of the ladies."

"Have you also been told that I am a madman?"

"*Non.*"

"Very good. Something should be saved for the wedding day."

The table was a two-top overlooking the sea. It was lush with silver and white linens and a row of crystal wine glasses but it was only set for one. He pulled out the chair for her. Sabine sat and looked out over the stormy waters. The rain that had followed her to the hotel was beginning to slow. Low gray clouds hung over the cliffs uncertain; lightning did not strike the ground but spun a web inside of them. The air felt close. Everyone around her spoke in whispers as if waiting for the thunder that did not come.

"Champagne?"

Before she could answer, he raised his hand and a white-gloved waiter appeared with a bottle of Moët and a glass. Another brought a silver-domed plate. When he lifted the lid, she could see a mound of small gray eggs, glistening.

"Escoffier says that all meals worth eating begin with caviar."

"Of course."

The third waiter had brought a menu for her. It was handwritten by Escoffier himself with a drawing of a peacock in the corner.

"Sweetbreads with fresh noodles served on a puree of *foie gras* and truffles? Will I like this?"

"Papa made it."

"I assumed he'd be dining . . . "

"Madame Escoffier's illness prevents . . . "

Sabine nodded.

"He asked if I would keep you company while you dined. Is this agreeable?"

Sabine looked around the vast elegant room, expecting to see Escoffier, in his black Louise-Philippe dress coat and striped pants, his white mustache freshly waxed, his thin white hair swept into place, standing behind a column watching. He was not.

"Do you know how to make stock?"

"But of course. Papa taught me himself."

"Then I apparently have no choice."

WHEN ESCOFFIER ENTERED his wife's room she was asleep. He took off his shoes and lay down in the bed next to her and kissed her forehead.

"Chef?"

"Hen bones, carrots, shin and shoulder of veal, onions, cloves, celery."

"Stock?"

"Stock."

17

THE NEXT DAY A NOTE FOR SABINE ARRIVED IN THE
midday post. The handwriting was unmistakable. She didn't
need to go to Escoffier's room to know he was not there.

"The car will arrive at 19:00 hours."

There was a return address that she did not recognize. It was near
the Grand, a residential district. This did not surprise her at all.

On the other hand, Bobo was keenly surprised to see his mentor
sitting in the kitchen of the Grand when he arrived that morning.

"I need to see your house," Escoffier said.

"Is there something wrong?"

"How old are you now?"

"Thirty."

"Then there is something very wrong."

Outside, the day was cool. There was a crispness that made the sky
seem even more brilliant. The two men slowly made their way down
the street, mostly in silence. The old man seemed unsteady on his feet,
but determined.

Bobo lived alone in a tall thin house that overlooked the hotel. As *directeur de cuisine* he made a respectable living. The house was plain, tidy, but since he spent most of his time at the hotel, a thick layer of dust covered everything. The kitchen was the largest room; the walls were the color of sunflowers, which gave it a cheerful feeling but the room itself was cramped. Against one wall there was a large black stove that was discarded from the Grand; it took up most of the room. It had several burners and a grill. Copper pots and pans hung from a ceiling rack alongside cords of braided garlic and dusty lavender that was set to dry too many years ago. There was a marble-topped sideboard and a small round table with a checkered cloth and two chairs. Except for the outsized stove, it looked like every other household kitchen on the French Riviera.

"Mundane," Escoffier said. "Dining room?"

"If you would tell me what we are looking for?"

"When I see it I will know. Dining room?"

In the dining room, the red walls were the color of ripe peppers. Escoffier ran a hand along the wall. "Better," he said.

In the center of the room there was a wide walnut table and twelve delicate chairs painted white. "From the neighbors. They moved to Spain."

"What does your attic look like?"

"Empty."

"And yet romantic, would it not be? Romantic and exotic."

"You want to see my attic?"

"Of course."

The spiral staircase leading up to the second floor concerned Bobo. The rosewood railings were beautifully curled and turned and the stairs themselves were wide, but so steep, it would be difficult for Escoffier to manage. And it was dark. The walls were the same shade of crimson that the dining room was. The floors were made of terracotta tiles. The only respite from red was the bright

green tile baseboard and a long tall window on the second floor landing. Escoffier stood at the bottom of the stairway for a moment and
looked up.

"That window. What can you see from it?"

"If you lean just right, you can see the sea."

"If you open it, can you hear the orchestra from the Grand?"

"Of course."

He considered this for a moment. "The landing appears round?"

"It is."

"And big enough for a table? The one in the kitchen?"

"*La potée d'amour?*"

The old man smiled. "But of course. What did you think this was
about? Cover the table with fine linen. You will also need china, silver
and candles; they should be the same tone of gray, the color is very
important. And, of course, several perfect cabbages."

"Cabbages?"

"Several. Four or five at the very least to place in terracotta pots."

"And the *potée d'amour?*"

"More cabbage."

"Cabbage? Are you sure?"

"About romance, I am never wrong."

The two men returned to the kitchen. Escoffier sat at the table and
wrote out the recipe. "Begin with a pot, deep and mysterious, and
add to it veal shank, beef ribs, brisket. Cover with cold water and salt.
Simmer one hour. Skim. Add spice bag with thyme, parsley, bay and
peppercorns and a clove-studded onion, garlic. Simmer two hours.
Skim. Add marrowbones, a supple young chicken, very supple, a half
bottle of white wine, and of course cabbage, potatoes, leek and turnip.
Simmer another hour."

Bobo read the recipe over closely.

"*Pot-au-feu?*"

"The foundation of the Empire."

"It is farm food."

"I once served *pot-au-feu* to Adelina Patti, the great diva, at her request. Right here at the Grand. She asked for a family meal—something not too rich. And so I served *pot-au-feu* with horseradish sauce. It matched the dish perfectly. Of course, I did give into a small sin. I included an excellent chicken *de la Bresse* that was larded with bacon, roasted on an open spit, and served with a mixed salad of chicory and beets. And then, of course, a magnificent *parfait de foie gras*, which I called *Sainte-Alliance* because it was made up of Alsatian *foie gras* and Périgord truffle. Remarkable! I had served that also at Armistice Day— the French and German together in one dish—very naive, very poetic. I ended Patti's feast with an orange mousse surrounded by strawberries macerated in curaçao. We could not have La Patti walk away hungry. Still, it was the most simple family meal found on any table in France."

"But that is my point exactly. *Pot-au-feu* is a family meal."

Escoffier tapped the side of his nose. "My son, have you learned nothing from me? Yes. A family meal. Romance is always about the promise, is it not?"

And then the two men smiled.

"You really are not good with the ladies, my dear Bobo. You will not become a great chef until you are."

After the luncheon service at the Grand, Bobo returned home and moved his small round kitchen table to the landing at the top of the stairs. Once covered in a gray linen, silver and crystal it looked as romantic as any table in the Grand's dining room. As directed, he placed several vibrant green cabbages in red clay pots on the landing. The colors were intense, intimate.

He bathed, even though it was not Tuesday, trimmed his mustache and carefully pressed his best linen shirt with lilac water and starch. He couldn't stop thinking about her.

The night before, Sabine had left him confused. She was the most aggravating woman, opinionated about food in a way that he had never seen before.

"Eggplant? It has no taste."

"It tastes like eggplant."

"Eggplant is nothing."

"If you fry it—"

"It tastes like oil. It has nothing to commend it on its own. Garlic. Olives. Tomatoes. They give it taste. Eggplant is a needy fruit."

They had shared just one glass of champagne and yet he felt intoxicated by her. Or maybe just enraged.

"Green beans?"

"Green string."

He hadn't noticed when the waiter cleared their table completely. Or when the last couple left. At 11:30 p.m. the dining room, by law, was to be closed.

"Sea urchin?"

"Dirty sponge."

"No."

"Yes."

"It's sweet, briny and creamy."

"It's ocean spit."

His maître d'hôtel brought fresh candles to the table, lit them, and then turned the hotel dining room lights off and locked the door behind him. They continued on.

"Lamb?"

"Too helpless to eat."

Bobo looked at his watch. It was nearly one o'clock in the morning. The kitchen had been closed for hours.

"It's very late," Sabine said, without asking the time, and stood. "Monsieur expects his nightcap at two a.m. Promptly."

She thanked him with a handshake—and that left him sleepless.

"How did you know?" he asked Escoffier the next day.

"I always know."

At the appointed time, the Grand Hôtel's discreet black Citroën made its way down the winding road and stopped at his door. He looked out the window. The driver tipped his hat.

Sabine saw him watching and smiled. Bobo's hands began to sweat.

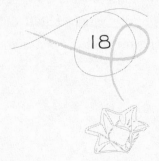

18

THE INGREDIENTS WERE LAID OUT ON THE COBALT-TILED countertop. Set in relief against the sunflower yellow walls, the tableau was an odd kitchen still life—a Vermeer, perhaps—the pink-skinned veal shin bones, skeletons from laying hens still bearing their heads, tiny peeled carrots, young pearl leeks, a soft stalk of old celery, white onions studded with fat cloves, a sprig of thyme, a rather attentive handful of parsley and a single fresh bay leaf.

"We are making stock?"

"*Oui.* Of course. Papa mentioned there was none at the house."

The kitchen was empty except for a single chair. Sabine sat. Took off her red shoes. Obviously, there was no need for them now.

"I thought we were having supper."

The *pot-au-feu* gently simmered on the stovetop. Rich roasted meats, the sweet air of caramelized cabbage, the dark note of garlic—she was so hungry, it made her ache. The horseradish sauce was plated in a silver bowl—she put her finger in it, tasted it and proclaimed, "More horseradish and a pinch more salt."

Bobo frowned, but tasted it. She was, unfortunately, correct. She grated the root and added the salt.

Upstairs on the landing the windows were open slightly. The night air was cool and fragrant—the salt of the ocean mixed with the perfume of lavender growing in the crooks and crevices of the cliff below. In the distance, music from the Grand Hôtel could be heard. The orchestra was playing waltz after waltz while the lonely moon shone on the small round table elegantly set with crystal and silver. The candles were lit. Wax dripped onto the gray linen. The potted purple and green cabbages were gathering dust.

It was all gathering dust.

"Soon," Bobo said and handed Sabine a clean chef's coat. "You may need to roll up the sleeves."

She did, but it didn't help. The coat itself hung down to her knees. Barefoot, she looked like a lost child.

"Your hair," he said and made a winding motion, which Sabine took to mean that he wanted her to wind it into a bun on the top of her head.

"No pins."

"May I?"

"No" was the answer, she had spent a very long time curling it so that it looked just so.

"I won't hurt you," he said and gathered Sabine's long red hair and twisted it gently as if it were a bit of frayed rope and then tied it in a knot on the top of her head. "It will stay." The knot tipped to one side.

"I look even more lopsided."

"That is true. But you cannot cook with that hair everywhere."

That is true? Cook?

Things were not going the way Sabine had hoped. "Madame said that you were quite odd but I now have decided that you are not odd at all, but fearless in your stupidity."

He handed her a large chef's knife.

"Amazingly fearless in your stupidity," she said.

"Clean the veal from the shins and then break the bones into small pieces, as small as possible."

Sabine put the knife down and began to undo the knot of her hair.

"Your hair," he said.

"I look ridiculous."

"That is because you are not working. A chef must always work."

He re-tied the hair knot, and then removed his best suit coat, rolled up his sleeves and took another chef's coat from its hook. He filled a large pot with cold water.

"What are you waiting for?" he said gently, "Wash your hands. Then hurry with that bone."

"We really are cooking?"

"Not until you wash your hands."

He had that same look that Escoffier always had when it came to cooking—a "mad-eyed twinge" is how Sabine thought of it. She knew that if she wanted to eat it was clear that stock had to be made first. Sabine suddenly thought of Madame Escoffier. *Papa must have driven her insane.* She washed her hands and sliced the tender pink meat away from the bone. It was soft. It didn't smell like flesh at all but grass and cream.

"It's very good veal, no?" he asked.

"It will be overwhelmed."

"What do you mean?"

"It's too mild for stock."

"It is veal," he said. "It is fine."

"Too mild."

"It is veal stock."

"It is brown veal stock. The type of veal used is important."

"I am a student of Escoffier and *directeur de cuisine—*"

"I am very pleased for you but a stock this light can have no soul."

"It is meant to be quite neutral in taste."

"Then why are we making it?"

"You cannot poach quail without it."

"Are we planning to poach quail?"

"That is not the point. No kitchen is complete without veal stock."

"Do you have veal stock in this kitchen? Does your neighbor?"

"It is the foundation of all sauces. It adds a complexity. Deliciousness. Has Escoffier not told you of this theory of five tastes? A Japanese chemist proved it, and called it 'umami,' which means deliciousness."

"If the stock is neutral, then it is a good deal of work for nothing because something neutral does not taste delicious. It merely tastes neutral."

"But the stock brings out the savoriness in food."

"Unless it is magic that makes no sense."

"It is based on Brillat-Savarin's concept of *osmazome*, but Escoffier took that idea and refined it. It is a great discovery."

"It makes no sense."

"Escoffier says it is so."

"I did not take you for a sheep, following blindly, but I obviously was mistaken."

Still, Sabine began to chop the bones, splintering them, not cutting. Shards flew.

Bobo took the knife from her. "Do you not know how to use a knife?"

"It is not sharp enough."

"Pay attention."

He held the knife firmly and chopped the bones into small pieces. The knife was indeed dull, his knuckles were white from leaning on them, but he had the strength and skill to overcome it. "We are looking to make the stock as gelatinous as possible, so the marrow must be exposed but the bones cannot be splintered."

"I sincerely thought we were having dinner."

"Please tie the celery around the leeks."

She looked at the celery and then at Bobo. *"Non."*

"The age of the celery won't harm the broth. Veal stock is never as clear as beef stock, so don't worry if this is not as pristine as other stocks you have made."

"Please listen. I will not tie the celery around the leeks, nor will I chop it, nor will I put it into a pan."

"There is absolutely nothing to worry about. We will remove the celery later. It will just infuse the stock with a subtle undertone."

"Good night," she said and unbuttoned the chef's coat.

"You are taking the freshness of this celery to an extreme degree, which I admire but—"

She handed him the coat. "I am leaving."

"Why? The celery—"

"Does not matter to anyone except you. I have had only three hours sleep a night every day this week. And tomorrow, despite the fact that it is Monday and the only day I am to have to myself all week, I will only have three more because both Madame and Monsieur are dying and I am the only person, except for an insolent nurse and an ignorant housekeeper, who is keeping the household running. And, by the end of the week, La Villa Fernand will once again be filled with hungry, screaming, arguing, confused members of an enormous heartbroken family who will expect me to be everywhere at once. I do not want to cook. I came to eat."

The two stood in the kitchen, not knowing what to say, watching each other, wary, surprised that they were quietly exposed in ways they did not plan for. The sound of the orchestra at the Grand, a waltz, someone else's waltz, filled the silence.

"Why do you stay at La Villa Fernand?"

The question surprised her. She could leave; it was true. She had thought of leaving. Her father would be angry, but he was always angry so it mattered not. But somehow, she couldn't. "I don't know. No place else to go, perhaps."

"Or you are fond of them."

"They do not pay me very well."

"Then you are fond of them. As you are of me."

"You are very arrogant."

"Yes. And the kitchen of La Villa Fernand needs veal broth, so what will you do?"

Sabine, too weary to stand any longer, sat down on the chair and began to put her shoes back on.

"You can't leave now," he said.

"I can. I am," she said but did not move.

"Why?"

"Why? You have no idea, do you? Perhaps this is the reason why you are not unattractive, and yet old and not married."

"I am old?"

"Yes."

"I didn't notice."

"That's because you are always cooking. Let me see your hands."

He held out his hands for her as a young child would. Sabine examined them. "Look how red and raw they are." She held them to her lips. For a moment he thought she would kiss them, and she knew that, but she merely gave them a sniff. "Onions, garlic, leeks."

"And yours?"

She offered them to him. "The same."

He took her hands in his and smiled. Then kissed them—slowly, gently—they were not chef's hands at all. He kissed them for so long, she began to think that he hoped to make her shy, but he could not. She was merely bemused.

"Frankly, I am not very surprised that you have no wife."

"Perhaps I had a wife and she ran away."

"That would be likely. All you speak of is food."

She slipped her hands away from him and went to undo the knot of her hair, but he caught her wrist. "And you? Do you not dream of food?"

"Non," she said and it was true but suddenly felt like a lie.

"Then I have overstepped," he said. "Forgive me."

He kissed her hand once more, this time as one would a maiden aunt's, and then let it fall.

She could see that he was tired, too. She imagined his feet hurt; hers did. All that standing. The crook of her back was always sore. Her short leg throbbed so she often couldn't sleep, even when she had the time to. She noticed that Madame Escoffier was right; he had the eyes of a gypsy. There were gypsies everywhere in Monte Carlo these days. Refugees. *If the Germans had their way, they'd all be dead. Or soon will be.*

"There is an entire world outside of this kitchen."

"And it is an awful place. When we cook, we know perfection: we can touch it; we can create it. We are like gods. How can you not dream of your own personal heaven?"

The orchestra at the Grand was playing a waltz from Chopin; it made her feel as if they were in an American movie; the world went black and white around them. A slight smile crossed his face like a bit of smoke. She imagined that he wanted to be back at the Grand Hôtel, in that kitchen filled with all that is perfect, and in perfect order, that heaven. Not here with her in the dust. She suddenly felt very sorry for Madame Escoffier.

"Is it lonely in your heaven?" she asked.

"Escoffier says it lacks a certain respectability."

"And what do you say?"

"There are women, but . . . "

"But."

The distant orchestra went silent.

"I should go."

The simmering *pot-au-feu*, the fresh baked bread with olives and rosemary, the salt air of the ocean tinged with the scent of lavender from the garden—all spoke of such promise. They searched each other's faces for lies, for truth, for some glimmer, a spark.

"Stay."

"You will break my heart."

"And you will break mine. That is the human condition, as is forgiveness."

And then he kissed her, gently, quietly.

Sabine put the chef's coat back on and wrapped the limp celery around the young leeks. Bobo placed the veal bones in a deep pot to boil.

"Roast them first," she said.

"But Escoffier—"

"Is not here. If you roast them they will bring out a caramelized flavor. Do not be a sheep."

Sabine took the pot from his hands; turned up the oven and patted the bones dry.

"I thought you didn't know how to make stock."

"I know how to make it the way my grandmother did. Housewife cooking is very good."

She rubbed olive oil on the bones, meat, carrots, leeks and onions. Put them in a large roasting pan. Placed it in the oven.

"They will burn."

"They will brown."

"It will be too forward a taste."

"It will have taste. Once they're roasted, we cover with cold water and then simmer. It will be fine. Escoffier will have his stock."

"He's working on a new dish, isn't he? I saw him today; he had that look he gets. That distracted faraway look."

Sabine had no idea if this was true or not, but the thought pleased her greatly and her answer would have been the same in any case.

"Yes. He is working on a dish for Madame. And you can help. He will need lobster. And Russian caviar. And truffles from Italy—they are very good; I had no idea. I'm sure you can get this all from the hotel."

"And why do I believe that you are suddenly crafting this fiction?"

"It was your suggestion, not mine."

"Very true. Well, then. What do you think of *foie gras*? It is his Holy Trinity, after all. Truffles, caviar and *foie gras*."

"I am very unsure about it. He has made ice cream of *foie gras*. Did you know that?"

"If one could escape the color, the fat would provide an interesting—"

"What is wrong with you men? No. It would not. Goose liver is the liver of the goose. It is not ice cream."

"But with wild black currant to flavor. The tartness, that nearly lemon-like edge to the fruit could provide a balance to the richness of the *foie gras*. I think it would be wonderful."

"Wild strawberries or Belgian chocolate for a sweet after a meal. Not liver. Never liver. Please, do not encourage the making of liver ice cream."

"Very well, mademoiselle. And what else is on your shopping list for Papa?"

"Plenty of champagne. And Lucky Strikes."

"Lucky Strikes? Papa does not smoke."

"They are needed."

"He is trying to make a stew of Lucky Strikes?"

"I cannot say for sure. These artists are secretive. However, it is safe to assume that if one can make ice cream from liver, tobacco could go very well with a saddle of venison. Or, perhaps, they could be added to the grapevines to smoke sturgeon. In any case, we will need plenty of cartons of Lucky Strike. As you know, Papa is a great experimenter."

"Lucky Strike is the brand you smoke?"

"*Oui.* It is a happy coincidence."

She moved away from him, took the lid off the casserole that held the *pot-au-feu*. *Marrow, ribs, bread and wine.* "It is time to eat. How long does the veal stock need to simmer once the bones have been browned?"

"Seven to eight hours."

She checked her wristwatch. "About two a.m. Just in time for Papa's nightcap."

"It is, as you say, a happy coincidence."

And then he kissed her and she him.

"You are very beautiful."

"I know."

And so as the veal bones turned from pale to deep caramel brown, the wax from the candles on the table at the top of the stairs melted completely, covering the bases of the silver candlesticks and solidifying into the gray linen tablecloth. They snapped and spit alone, and finally extinguished themselves. The cabbages wilted. Bobo laid out an old lamb's wool blanket on the kitchen floor. It was cream, not gray, but it was soft to sit on. After all, the bones in the oven had to be watched so they did not burn. Instead of the fine china, crystal and silver that he had borrowed from the hotel, he set the blanket with forks and knives that did not match, two coffee cups for wine and the least-chipped plates that he could find.

"I'll plate."

For her, he placed a thin slice of both the brisket and the chicken breast next to a slight strip of cabbage, a single potato and the smallest turnip Sabine had ever seen. On his plate, there were several ribs, sausage, chicken legs and thighs and a heaping mound of cabbage and potatoes. She took both plates from him and emptied them back into the casserole and did not plate the *pot-au-feu* again. Instead, she set the entire dish on an iron trivet and placed it in the center of the blanket. He poured the wine. She turned off the lights. The flames in the oven cast the room in blue; it was like dining in the clear azure sky of a lonely heaven. They were still wearing the starched white chef coats. She picked up a marrowbone with her fingers. He ripped the heel from the bread.

"Brillat-Savarin said tell me what you eat and I will tell you who you are."

Bobo took the bone from her and spread the marrow onto the warm bread. The weight of its fat, the earth of it, its rich unctuous mushroom earth, melted slightly and mixed with the rosemary and olives that he'd baked into the baguette.

He held it out to her, that first taste, although he knew what it would exactly taste like just by looking at it.

When she put it in her mouth, the richness of the marrow made her laugh with pleasure. She undid the knot of her red hair; it unraveled slowly. To Bobo the blue of her eyes was as blue as the sky to birds. It was all he could see, and all he needed to see. She then fed the marrow to him and kissed the crumbs from his lips.

Chicken legs, beef ribs—they ate the food with their fingers, dipping into the horseradish sauce, feeding each other greedily. Laughing. They rolled leaves of cabbages and chewed on them like monkeys. They ate the golden potatoes as if they were apples. By the time they returned to the making of stock, and took the roasted veal bones from the stove and put them into the pot and filled it with enough cold water so that it could slowly simmer, their own legs no longer ached, their feet felt as if they could stand the weight of their bones for yet another day and they tasted of garlic and wine.

"Thank you, chef," he said.

"Thank you, chef."

She opened his cheese larder and took out a wedge of runny Camembert, which she covered with a handful of white raspberries that he had draining in a colander by the sink. He opened a bottle of port.

The dishes could wait. They sat on the back stairs of the tall thin house and looked over the lights of the steep city of Monte Carlo and out into the endless sea. The air was cool, the cheese and raspberries were rich and tart; the port was unfathomably complex with wave and wave of spiced cherries, burnt caramel and wild honey.

"The darkness feels so blue, it is as if I am flying," he said and put his arm around her.

"You talk too much," she said and kissed him.

The next day, shipments from Mr. Boots began to arrive again at La Villa Fernand. Inside the boxes there were wild strawberries, chocolate, oysters, champagne and a package of Lucky Strikes.

"How do you know Bobo?" she asked Escoffier.

"He was left on my doorstep when he was a boy. I put him to work, of course."

"What an interesting doorstep you must have had."

The Complete Escoffier: A Memoir in Meals

FILETS DE SOLES RACHEL

It is not a simple task to name a dish for someone. It is an art that combines the telling of impossible truths and the chemistry of memory that only cuisine can provide. Some dishes expose the chef's inner feelings for the recipient and that is not always desirable. Some dishes fall short of the profound love that a chef feels and that is insulting. Some dishes are merely named after people because a chef once made it for them—if they liked it or not it is no matter. Some are named as a way to make money, and that is all. This can be a very sound business practice. And some are purely born of convenience—this often is the best dish of all.

For example, if your brother-in-law is an expert fisherman and gives you more sole than you can sell each week, then you should create a dish such as *Filets de Soles Rachel*. Named after the well-known Swiss-born tragedienne, this dish has been a remarkable success, a dish that will stand the test of time. It is the most simple of preparations. Place one tablespoon of fish forcemeat—a combination of raw chopped fish, herbs and stale bread mixed with cream and egg—and four slices of truffles on a fillet. Fold. Poach. Drape with white wine sauce. Garnish with one tablespoon each of finely chopped truffles and asparagus tips. Serve.

Mademoiselle Rachel has such a triumphant story. She came from

being a child singing in the streets of Paris to being the Divine Sarah of
her day. She was heroic and so a waiter can expound upon her story so
elegantly, plates will fly out the kitchen.

This is crucial. No matter how a plate came to be named, the end
result is that it must sell.

This is why there are hundreds of dishes named after Sarah Bernhardt. In fact, if you add pureed *foie gras* to the *Rachel* then you
have *Filets de Soles Sarah Bernhardt*, a convenience which, on a slow
night, allows the waiter to paint a long and poetic story about the two
actresses and their mutual love of sole and how that created a bond
between them. This, of course, is not true. It is unclear if they ever
met. No matter. You must do what you need to do. Sole is not a fish
that keeps well.

Impossible stories—they are the key to all good restaurants.

"How is the sole tonight?"

"Glorious as Mademoiselle Rachel herself was. Divine as Bernhardt.
Just taken from the last boat moments ago."

It could be frozen; it makes no difference. The diner will think it
fresh, glorious. He pays for the story. If the story is told well, with
imagination and conviction and the right amount of ego and embroi-
dery, then it is true enough. And something that is true enough is all
anyone can ever ask for.

When naming a dish after someone your goal should be to create an
opportunity for a story that would fill the American showman Phineas
Barnum with professional envy. He was an unparalleled promoter,
unrepentant liar and public dreamer—a man with a chef's heart.

However, one must understand that there are serious considerations
in this grave undertaking.

First, not everyone is pleased by having a dish named after them.
Carpaccio was given the name after the painter Vittore Carpaccio,
because of a striking similarity of the color of the thinly sliced raw beef

to the red paint he was known for. By the time the dish was named he was dead, so it made no difference.

On the other hand, *Crêpes Suzette* was actually an accident, and then an international incident. Its creation is claimed by a then-fourteen-year-old assistant waiter, Henri Charpentier, who was preparing a dessert for King Edward, who at the time was the Prince of Wales, and his companion *du jour*, Suzette. The waiter wrote in his memoir, *Life à la Henri*, "It was quite by accident as I worked in front of a chafing dish that the cordials caught fire. I thought it was ruined. The Prince and his friends were waiting. How could I begin all over? I tasted it. It was, I thought, the most delicious melody of sweet flavors I had ever tasted . . . "

Nonsense.

He then claims that he at that very moment decided to name the dish after the Prince, which given the feminine nature of crêpes would have been indiscreet, at best. The boy would have been fired on the spot. But he goes on to turn the story in his favor.

" 'Will you,' said His Majesty, 'change it to *Crêpes Suzette*'? Thus was born and baptized this confection, one taste of which, I really believe, would reform a cannibal into a civilized gentleman. The next day I received a present from the Prince, a jeweled ring, a panama hat and a cane."

It is a very nice story, is it not? I especially like the promise that it will "reform a cannibal into a civilized gentleman." Such flourish. Can you not hear this story being told and retold by waiters all across the world? Still, I doubt it is true. The incident happened in 1895 at Café de Paris, right here in Monte Carlo. I know from experience that it is not the type of establishment where an assistant waiter serves a prince.

It makes no matter. This dish will probably not outlive Suzette or me.

Ingredients are always crucial. While Dear Bertie loved the crêpes, his association with such a feminine creation would have been inappropriate. You can also go wrong if your ingredients are too humble. For example, King George V loved the American Philadelphia brand cream cheese, but you cannot create a dish of cream cheese in honor of a king. It would be rude. So change the name. Say the cheese came from a remote island off the coast of Iceland—no one travels there or cares to. It will make it seem quite exotic.

You would be surprised at how many names you can give such a lowly ingredient and when properly named how much you can charge for it.

The basis of our profession is two parts skill, one part ingredient and one part legerdemain, the "lightness of hand." The English call it "sleight of hand." If you do not understand that, you have no place in the kitchen.

I was once asked what I thought of the suicide of François Vatel, who impaled himself on his sword because a shipment of sole did not arrive in time for a banquet in honor of Louis XIV at Château de Chantilly. There were reported to be two thousand hungry guests. It was a problem. Yes. And yet, the moment of his defeat was also the moment of his greatest triumph. It was on that very same night that he created *crème chantilly*, which is now used in éclairs, cream puffs and pastry all over the world. Defeat, and yet triumph. And yet he killed himself.

And so what can a reasonable person think about such a sinful and untidy act?

One can only come to the conclusion that Vatel was not such a great chef. He had no understanding of the lightness of hand. I, however, am a master of legerdemain. No fish? That is not a problem. I have taken the tender white meat of chickens—very young chickens—and made fillet of sole with it on numerous occasions.

It is simple. You crush their flesh with a pestle, add breadcrumbs, fresh cream, egg white and salt. Pass it through a fine sieve, shape into convincing fillets, dip in beaten egg, coat with breadcrumbs, sauté until brown in clarified butter, serve with anchovy butter spiced with paprika and a garnish of a single truffle slice, more butter and chicken fat. *Filets de Soles Monseigneur.* No one ever knew the difference.

And so, if you can take the Philadelphia cream cheese and call it something else, let us say, for example, *"fromage frais," "spécialité fromagère," "fromage à la crème"* and say that it comes from a French patriot on a tiny family farm off the coast of Iceland who sings "La Marseillaise" every morning to his cows as he milks them—"Ye sons of France, awake to glory!"—how can they resist?

Another very good example is "Jésus de Lyon" (or "de Morteau" in Franche-Comté), a sausage cured in a beef bung cap that gives it a pear shape that is alleged to resemble baby Jesus. Out of respect for the name of Christ, Jésus de Morteau is spelled Jésu by Mortuaciens and generally smoked. Jesus is quite a popular fellow with my people and has many small sausages named after him in the Basque and Savoy regions. However, since Christ was born a Jew in a pig-less culinary culture, I doubt very much if he would approve this bounty of *sau-cissons* and yet, it matters not. They fly off the shelves, especially at Easter.

Guilt does wonders for the appetite.

19

WHEN THEY WERE FIRST MARRIED, DELPHINE HAD taken to telling strangers that her sons were actually princes. It was understandable. She, Escoffier, and their boys, Paul and Daniel, traveled to Switzerland in the summer and back to Monte Carlo for winter season. She met the same mothers and their children every year, but they were families of rank and privilege. When they asked, she had to tell them something. "My husband's the cook," would not do.

In the summer, at the Hôtel National in Lucerne, a castle set against the lush and ancient lake, the young boys and their mother would spend the day swimming or hiking in the wildflower mountains, or shopping in the marketplace alongside movie stars and kings. They were tan and fat.

At night, when the boys were asleep, Escoffier would bring her "gifts," which they would eat together on the tiny balcony overlooking the moonlit lake. Each plate was an intricate jewel—*Filets de soles cardinal*, sole and whiting mousse stuffed into crayfish shells and sauced with cream, cognac and crayfish tails, or *Noisettes d'Agneau*, tournedos of lamb on artichoke bottoms napped with a Madeira-scented bécha-mel. They would eat and plan books they never had time to write together and vacations they never seemed to be able to take.

In the winter, back in Monte Carlo, in the early morning, Escoffier would kiss his sleeping family, make a pot of strong coffee, and walk from La Villa Fernand to his offices at the Grand Hôtel to decide what Queen Victoria would have for dinner, and later, after the boys were in bed and the hotel dining room was closed, he would meet Delphine for drinks in the casino, and sometimes in a private room with Prince Edward himself.

It was not the life of a cook.

And so London was unexpected.

"Why can't you just go for the summer season?"

"Ritz says we shall be ambassadors for France."

"We shall be miserable."

"Ritz is brilliant."

"Ritz is deranged; an obsessive perfectionist. He will be miserable, too. London is filled with the English."

"But you love the Queen. And the Prince."

"Those two are the least English of the lot."

"Echenard has agreed to join us."

"He's leaving Monte Carlo, and the Grand, with you?"

"He will be maître d'hôtel for us. He knows London."

"Then he cannot be happy."

"If you love me, you will come."

"If you love me, you will not go."

But Escoffier had no choice. There had never been a hotel like The Savoy before. Owned by producer Richard D'Oyly Carte, and built though the success of the Gilbert and Sullivan partnership, particu-larly *The Mikado*, it was the most modern building in the world.

The previous top hotel in London was entirely lit by gaslight and offered only four communal bathrooms for five hundred guestrooms and none for their restaurant at all. The Savoy, however, offered electric lights, telephones and private bathrooms lavishly appointed in marble with hot and cold running water.

The food, however, was horrible, and so no one cared. The Savoy was on the brink of bankruptcy when Ritz was given full control. His first act was to fire most of the staff—a detail he forgot to share with Escoffier.

The chef arrived in London on a Sunday. "Drive to the Strand entrance, but do not venture to travel into the courtyard, the hill alongside is very steep," he told the cabman the directions that Ritz had given him, but unfortunately the man did not speak French and was traveling too fast. His horse slid the last ten yards. Escoffier hit his head. His bags tumbled into the courtyard. The driver demanded a sizeable tip.

It was not an auspicious start.

The day was dark and very damp. The cold made Escoffier's bones ache. The bump on his head was throbbing. He had brought too many bags with him. There were no doormen waiting as one would expect. The hotel seemed deserted. Ritz knew when he was to arrive, had promised to meet him, but was nowhere to be found. However, Monsieur Echenard was sitting in the lobby looking pale.

"A rather unpleasant situation has unfolded," he said.

When Escoffier entered his new kitchen, the most modern kitchen in the world—it had electricity, its own ice room, windows to let in fresh air and light and hot and cold running water—it was in ruins. The previous manager and his staff were not pleased with their firing. Every window was shattered; crows picked their way through quail's eggs and duck liver; black starlings hissed and hummed, drunk on rotted cherries and overripe plums. Dogs ran wild as wolves chewing their way through the chicken cages, the long-dead birds uncaring.

Every glass, plate and bowl had been broken. The stoves had been dismantled and piled in a heap. The doors of the ovens were missing. Milk and cream covered the floors. Lobsters and langoustines were left to die in heaps of decaying fish. Sides of beef and racks of veal were charred, left in the ashes of coke fires, but no wood or coal was anywhere to be found. Not even a grain of salt remained.

"It's Sunday," Echenard said. "All the stores in England are closed. Impossible to buy a thing."

They were scheduled to open for breakfast the next morning.

"And Ritz?"

"He says he has all the confidence in the world in you. He and his wife are upstairs settling in."

Escoffier and Echenard and the handful of staff who had remained worked through the night. Louis Peyre, an old friend who ran kitchens for the Charing Cross Hotel, was roused from his sickbed and cheerfully supplied enough basic food and cookware so The Savoy could reopen the next day.

"The English are a very good people," Escoffier later wrote Delphine. "Welcoming."

She did not respond.

The next morning, a traditional English breakfast, miraculously, was served. It was the full "fry-up" with poached eggs, crisp browned potatoes, blood pudding, sausage, pink bacon, baked beans, mushrooms and broiled tomatoes. There was fried bread served with lemon curd and blackberry preserves. The juice was freshly squeezed from Spanish blood oranges.

It was lovely, though not exactly the breakfast that Escoffier had in mind. There were no croissants or brioches. No cheese. The only fruit was juice. *Café au lait* was not offered, but tea and milk were served. Still, it was a solid success although he knew that if The Savoy was to win over the elite of English society, he couldn't give them what they could eat in Charing Cross.

That first morning, Escoffier walked through the dining room stopping at the tables that Echenard said he needed to, kissing hands and nodding. He spoke no English, although people often spoke to him, and so he replied in French and even though they did not understand a word he said they found him to be witty.

Prix-fixe, he thought.

At the Grand Hôtel, he and Echenard had realized that their English clients didn't speak French well enough to order without assistance. Some were even intimidated. But walking through the dining room that first morning, Escoffier knew that if he offered a fixed price menu that contained most of the items *à la carte*, he could feel free to create dining experiences that the English would embrace. And didn't need to pronounce.

"Each menu will be a new adventure," he told Echenard—and it was.

With wall panels painted by Whistler, rose silk–shaded chandeliers and diners starched and scented, elegant in their formal clothes, Escoffier found himself profoundly inspired. He spent hours crafting dish after dish, polishing them like jewels: *Filets de sole Coquelin, Homard aux feux eternels, Volaille à la Derby, Chaud-Froid Jeannette,* named after the North Pole expedition ship *Jeannette,* and for the Prince of Wales, Dear Bertie, *Cuisses de Nymphe Aurore,* less poetically known as frogs' legs (although *cuisses* is, in fact, the word for thighs. Escoffier was often quick to point out that *Nymphe Aurore* did not mean frog, either).

When a white-tied waiter bearing a silver-domed plate presented *Tournedos Rossini,* a perfect filet mignon topped with a slice of *pâté de foie gras* draped with Périgueux sauce made from Maderia and truffles, to Rossini, its namesake, the famed Italian composer, it made every newspaper in the world. Elegant and corpulent, guided by the love of food, not music, Rossini was quoted as saying, "I know of no more admirable occupation than eating. Appetite is for the stomach what love is for the heart," and then made his way through twenty plates of the dish. Suddenly there were barely enough cattle in Scotland to fill the public's need.

"Fantasy certainly sells," Escoffier said.

Nothing proved to be impossible at The Savoy. A patron's desire for dinner in a Japanese garden was made possible by completely transplanting the courtyard. For a green and white banquet, fruit trees, still bearing fruit, were trimmed to become tables with glass tops and each chair was a softly sculpted bush. And when a millionaire decided that he wanted to dine in Venice, the gardens were flooded, and diners were set along an improvised canal so that the maestro Caruso could serenade from a gondola.

The kitchen was massive with a brigade of fifty men. Although Escoffier refused to learn English, most spoke no French, and so together they built a language on gesture, intuition and culinary skill with bits of French, English, Polish, Italian and Chinese thrown into the mix.

The Savoy quickly became a rousing success and yet every night Escoffier found himself alone.

"Please," he wrote Delphine. At first he tried to visit Monte Carlo at least once a month, but it was difficult to get away.

"She will come around," Ritz told him. But she did not. They began to argue every visit.

"The very thought of London makes me ill," she said. "Every morning I rise and cannot eat, or drink."

"How can a city make a person ill?"

"There is no sea. The people are pasty."

"The people are kind. The city is exciting."

"There are no taxes in Monte Carlo. You cannot lose your residency."

"Two houses are too expensive to maintain."

After a time, Escoffier began to wonder if his wife didn't join him because of Sarah. The actress spent a great deal of time in London. It would be awkward for the two to meet. Delphine knew that he and Sarah had been lovers and did not seem pleased that they had remained close through the years. In fact, when he defended Sarah against accusations of immorality, it truly seemed to annoy his wife.

"She has had a child without a father."

"She is a devoted mother and cares for her own mother and sister, too."

"She wears men's clothes."

" 'I am so original,' she once said, 'that I prefer to be at peace with my conscience and with God.' "

"If you must tell people you are original, how original can you be?"

Even before he went to The Savoy, Sarah had been a problem between them. When the international press accused Bernhardt of orgies while on tour in America, one of which was at an all-male supper party hosted at Delmonico's by the editor of the *New York Herald*, Delphine called it a "publicity stunt" to sell tickets. Escoffier found this very confusing.

"All the society women returned their theater tickets. She wouldn't jeopardize her art with a 'stunt,' as you say."

"Outrage is her art."

"Is that not also the poet's art form?"

Delphine would not speak to him for a week.

However, when Sarah married Aristide Damala, Delphine seemed to warm to her. Pictures of the couple were everywhere. "They look happy," she said. "Don't they?"

Escoffier had to agree. Damala was as beautiful as an angel, twelve years younger than Sarah. A diplomat turned actor. "This ancient Greek god is the man of my dreams," the actress was quoted as saying.

"Perhaps being Madame Damala suits her."

Unfortunately, Damala was also a morphine addict. Soon the press began to pick away at them; one review featured a cartoon of Bernhardt holding Damala like a puppet, manipulating his limbs.

"I made him a monster," she later told Escoffier. "He wanted me to take his name, to become Madame Damala. I could not and he could not bear it."

Three weeks after their wedding, Damala went missing for days and later surfaced with a girl in Brussels. She was the first of the many girls, prostitutes and mistresses that Sarah would be forced to share her husband with—and the press covered every indiscretion. When he had a child with another actress, an extra whose primary job was to shoot him with heroin during intermissions, Sarah threatened to have the infant drowned in the Seine.

With each headline, Delphine grew more and more quiet on the subject of Sarah. It was difficult to criticize the actress as a wife. Time and time again, even after they were legally separated, Sarah took her husband back. She'd had plays commissioned for him, bought him a theater and even canceled her own performances to attempt to nurse him back to health.

In the end, nothing could save him.

A few months before Escoffier moved to London, Damala was found dead from an overdose of morphine and cocaine.

When asked for a quote, "Well, so much the better," Sarah said. Her husband was finally out of his misery. That was her public response. Privately, she changed her legal name to Damala, as he had wanted, and wore mourning dress for more than a year.

"Perhaps love is the worst addiction of all," Escoffier told his wife.

And that was precisely what Delphine was afraid of—complete surrender. That was why she could not join him in London. She tried to explain that to him but he didn't seem to understand. In Monte Carlo she had a house filled with her family. Not just her own children, but also her sisters and their families, her mother and her aunts. She was a part of something larger—La Villa Fernand. Everyone depended on her. Everything revolved around her. She had her own world.

"I know no one in London. Only you."

"What more do you need?"

"Myself."

After a time, Escoffier found himself not eating. A plate of sweet pink shrimp or veal chops in a blackberry sage sauce or a simple roasted wild duck made him think, "I'll wait until Delphine comes." Even at Sunday dinner with Ritz, Marie and their children, Escoffier would find himself eating very little and thinking how lovely it would be when Delphine and his sons arrived and the two families could spend sunny afternoons feasting under the chestnut trees.

Later that first year, still in mourning, Sarah came to London to oversee the English translation of a new play by Victorien Sardou, *Fédora*.

She and Escoffier sat at a table in back of The Savoy's American Bar. It was between lunch and dinner service. She drank champagne. He looked at his watch.

"It's about a princess who wears a particular kind of hat. A man's hat. It's a perfect role for me, is it not? As soon I place this new hat on my head, the fedora will be famous."

"Of course," he said.

" 'Of course?' That's all you can say?"

"You look very nice in hats."

"And I am, of course, a princess."

"Of course."

Escoffier was too thin, gray and tired.

Sarah leaned across the table, lifted her black veil, and kissed his hand.

"I'm not losing you, too. Am I? I could not bear it."

A single tear rolled down her face and into his palm; slipped down his lifeline.

And so he told her of Delphine's hesitation. "I have never felt so alone."

The next day, Sarah moved her entire entourage into The Savoy; it became her London home.

"After all, we are friends, are we not?"

"Yes, we are friends," he said and that statement both surprised and comforted Escoffier. At first, friendship was not what he wanted at all but through the years he had come to find refuge in it. Sarah never seemed to be far from him. And now she was a part of his every-day life. Every night when she returned from the theater, Escoffier would bring her something exotic, savory or sweet, and they would sit together in her rooms and look out over the city of London and some-times talk and sometimes make love. But mostly just sit. Together. Peacefully. It calmed him. It calmed them both.

And so Rosa Lewis was an unexpected development.

Even before they met, Escoffier knew everything about her; every-one in London did. She was the competition. When Lady Randolph Churchill acquired Rosa's services, the Prince of Wales spied her drinking champagne and, mistaking her for a partygoer, kissed her. When informed that he had just kissed the cook, he was not surprised. After that lovely dinner she was deserving of a kiss, he explained.

"She takes more pains with a cabbage than with a chicken."

The future king had English tastes, after all.

Of course, as was always the case with Dear Bertie, one kiss alone would not do. Rumors were rampant. Escoffier was intrigued. It was difficult not to be. Every day at exactly the same time, he passed through the park on his way back from church and there she was. Rosa was unmistakable. Her hair often seemed aflame; her laughter crackled and popped. She would cross the park dressed in her chef's whites—her tall white toque, starched white dress and high laced "cooking boots" made of soft black kid leather—with a gaggle of identically dressed assistants trailing behind her like a mother duck with her ducklings. And at the very end of the line would always be someone who Escoffier imagined to be her junior chef, an assistant of some sort, a very young woman dragging a feisty black Scottish terrier behind her.

"Afternoon, Mr. Escoffier," Rosa would say, although sometimes she'd speak to him in French—at least, he assumed it was French—her Cockney accent was so strong he could barely understand her.

"Do you have women in your kitchen?" she asked.

"I have them everywhere," he replied.

He enjoyed the confusion greatly.

Early one morning, Rosa appeared in the kitchen of The Savoy. She was wearing her famous black cooking boots but was not dressed for cooking. She wore a gown of white silk with a large black hat covered in white silk lilies and a black-and-white ribbon. Against the backdrop of her red hair, it was striking. From her towering hat to her black cooking boots she was very tall, a Victorian version of Marie Antoinette.

But no one noticed her.

The kitchen was hot and bustling. A family of Russian men arrived carrying sides of beef thrown over their shoulders; they nearly ran her down. Fishmongers with bushels of lobsters, the mahogany claws snapping aimlessly, shouted, "Clear off!" as they pushed by her. Men were everywhere: their arms filled with screeching songbirds in bamboo cages or dried sausages hung like so many rosaries. Her carefully rolled hair began to unravel under the heat of it.

The kitchen was divided into several rooms on two floors. On the top level, there were vast spaces; one obviously was the staging area. It had a long tiled archway over a seemingly endless steel counter. On the wall, block letters designated several cooking stations, *"Entrées, Légumes, Grillades, Poisson."* A small army of waiters with immaculate long white aprons on top of their tuxedoes leaned over the counter questioning each *chef de partie* about the day's offerings, making copious notes.

Behind the chefs, in the bowels of the kitchen, hundreds of silver pots and copper pans were suspended on racks over dozens of stoves and griddles and cooking pits and more gleaming counters. Coke and wood stoked the fires; the flames spat. In the great white-tiled room freshly plucked wild turkeys, geese, pheasant and ducks were slowly spinning before a roaring fire. Sides of mutton were being slid onto spits. There were men making stocks with beef and hare. Some were just peeling, continuously peeling carrots, potatoes, the fat knobs of rutabagas and small pink beets. Some were brushing the dirt off bushels of wild mushrooms with a wire brush or washing the truffles in brandy and patting them dry. Escoffier was nowhere to be seen.

One floor down, the air was cold; that part of the kitchen was filled with ice. Rosa had never seen that much ice before. In the center of the room, there was an entire table stacked with dressed partridge, woodcocks and quail set on trays of ice. Boxes of ice held fresh fish—gray sole, Scottish salmon and skate—and fish that had been poached, studded with truffles and embedded in amber jelly. There was even a table filled with iced trays of *petits-fours* and *pâté de fruits.* And in the corner of the room there were three men dressed as if it were the dead of winter, carving harps, birds, and some sort of life-sized Grecian woman out of solid blocks of ice and next to them, two men making pink roses and baskets out of spun sugar.

I want this, Rosa thought. *This is what my kitchen should be.*

"He's in the alley," a young boy said. He was carrying a tray of *pâtés* as he ran past her. She opened the back door and stepped into the bright street, the thick soup of London. In the alley, there was a line of delivery carts carrying even more meat: racks of lambs, birds of all sizes and shapes and fishes that were still flapping. There was a wide and deep wagon filled with small and larges casks, some marked "vinegar" and some marked "wine." The nervous horses bucked as she walked past.

At the very end of the line was Escoffier in his immaculate chef whites. He stood on the back of a rotting wooden wagon helping two nuns load boxes of food. The driver was too ancient to help. The horse looked even older. He stopped when he saw Rosa.

"I had no idea that the only women in your kitchen were nuns," she said.

"We are just here for Gala Nights," they said.

"How very provocative."

Escoffier jumped down off the cart. "That's what the pensioners call them. Gala Nights."

"We can't afford meat at the Home. If it wasn't for Monsieur Escoffier, we would not have money to feed the horse, either."

"He's put us on the menu," said the novitiate. "Quail Pilaf à la Little Sisters of the Poor. We're famous."

Mother Superior did not look pleased. "Fame is not a virtue, Sister."

"It is in the restaurant business," Rosa laughed. "But what is a Gala Night?"

"When we get to finally eat meat, of course."

Escoffier opened up a box. It was filled with tiny quail carcasses that had been cleaned away except for two perfectly uneaten legs.

Rosa picked up a carcass and laughed. "And because proper society won't grab the bird and give it a gnaw, the good sisters can feed pensioners?" she said in her Cockney brand of French. "And the recipe?"

"Stolen from the Russians."

"Only fitting."

"The bird is coated with spices and wood-smoked and then placed on the pilaf."

"I had no idea you were noble."

"No one should go hungry."

The two nuns kissed both his cheeks and his hands. "You are too kind," Mother Superior said.

"Wait." Escoffier took a small cask of wine from the next cart. "For all the sisters. Medicinal purposes, of course."

As the cart pulled away, Rosa linked her arm in his. She towered over him but he didn't seem to mind.

"I could learn from you," she said.

"In the kitchen?"

"Wherever you like."

"Let us begin in the kitchen, then."

"I'm not dressed to cook."

"Then we must undress you."

⁘

ROSA WORE ESCOFFIER's chef's whites; they fit her well enough. The head housekeeper of The Savoy removed her dress from his rooms and had it pressed and hung in his closet. The request was not out of the ordinary. Rosa was, after all, one of the Duke's women. All of the Duke's women took up much of the staff's time.

"How many plates?"

"Eighteen hundred for lunch and supper."

"Blimey."

"*Oui.*"

And so, at lunch, Rosa stood with Escoffier as he inspected each dish before it left the kitchen. Each rib of lamb, each fillet of fish, every mousse and aspic—everything from sauce to soup to garnish was placed just so.

Shortly before lunch was over, Ritz entered the kitchen with a plate in his hand. Escoffier inspected it.

"It is perfect."

"Yes, it is," Ritz said. "But somehow our guest understood that *Poulets de grains à la Polonaise*—even though our dear Monsieur Echenard said that he had described the method of cooking, and how the juices of the liver soaked into the bird, and how important the essence of the chicken which permeated the liver was—meant something fried with chips."

"And so what does he want now?"

"Fried tripe, onions, sausage and mashed potatoes. I assured him it was a brilliant combination, a splendid choice. He's very rich. And so how do we make it?"

"We don't," Escoffier said.

"I know of a stall," Rosa said. "It's near a cab stand, not far from here."

Ritz kissed her hand. "Send a boy, then," he said. "The customer is never wrong. They are ignorant. They are foolish. They are often embarrassing. But never incorrect."

Later that night, upstairs in Escoffier's rooms, he ran a hot bath for Rosa. Steam filled the small room. She took off her clothes slowly, without modesty. Slipped into the water. He handed her a glass of Moët.

"Will you teach me the art of French cooking?"

"Of course."

"I'm a woman."

"You are also clever, unafraid of work and skilled in your own right."

"People would talk."

"That is true."

It was very true and they both knew it. But, at that moment, the possibility of scandal seemed to be worth the risk to Escoffier. There was something about Rosa that reminded him of Sarah. A much younger Sarah, of course, and Sarah was more beautiful, more regal in bearing, more like a queen, but Rosa had that same red hair and elegant neck, the pale butter skin.

Dear Bertie was so predictable.

Naked, against the white marble walls, in the pure porcelain tub, Rosa's skin was like moonlight, cloudless and distant, and yet shining.

So white, he thought. *Such a particular shade of white.*

An idea was suddenly taking shape. *A notion. A taste. A small delicate gift.*

Earlier that morning, Escoffier had brought up a large bucket of white rose petals, white violets and vanilla orchids that he'd been thinking of creating a dish with. The *pâtissier* had crystalized some of the flowers, and left him a plate of meringue shells, a handful of vanilla beans and fresh cream. He wanted to create a new dish for Sarah, a sweet, something surprising, something to engage her. She'd been playing Joan of Arc, the virgin saint, a seventeen-year-old girl. It was a role she made famous, difficult at any age, but for a woman in her mid-forties, it was nearly impossible.

Escoffier tossed a handful of white rose petals into Rosa's bathwater.

The white skin. The white roses. *The essence of Saint Joan is in shades of white, like shades of innocence.*

Spun sugar, he thought. *Vanilla cream, of course.*

Escoffier was thinking about the possibility of incorporating a small amount of rose water into the whipped cream when Rosa said, "No man has ever given me roses. Jewelry, yes. Furs. Money. But roses are different: each one is a unique miracle. You don't give miracles to the cook."

He took a petal from her knee and tasted it. *Crisp and floral, a perfect note for the richness of cream.* And then ran it along her lips. She closed her eyes.

"Can you imagine the taste of it?" he asked.

"Too green. It needs vanilla to develop the flavor."

"Very good."

"Of course. I am a cook, after all."

"*Non.* A chef. An artist."

"A cook. We are elegant savages, ducks," she said. "But savages nonetheless."

Escoffier felt something beating in his chest like wings, something wild, something that would soon fly away from him. Rosa stepped out of the warm water and wrapped herself in a thick Turkish bath towel. Rose petals clung to her shoulders.

"What should we do now?"

She was naked, young, but it was all too complicated. Sarah, Delphine: they already tangled in his thoughts. *Rosa.* He brushed her cheek with his hand.

"I will teach you," he said. "That is what we can do."

To his surprise, she seemed disappointed.

"Then teach me," she said in perfect French, her Cockney accent suddenly gone. It was obviously an act. She let the towel drop to the floor. She was persistent, after all.

Venus, he thought and spread a handful of the flowers on the thick bed of goosedown and silk. He arranged them to look as if a spring wind had caught them by surprise and then laid her down in the center of it. Her long red hair made him miss the Sarah of his youth even more. He took the small violets and wove them through the undertow of her hair, arranged the orchids across her breasts.

Each petal, each flower was placed just so. When he was finished, she was indeed Venus rising, not on a half-shell from the sea, but Sarah as Venus rising from the gardens of his youth.

The sight of her made him want to weep.

"Don't move," he whispered. "Close your eyes. Rest."

Rosa soon tumbled into a deep sleep, dreaming of pure color and scent. At first, it was like sleeping in a garden of roses and violets, a deep, sweet sleep. But then it shifted, the scent of cream and vanilla cooking woke her.

Escoffier was standing in the small kitchen, still dressed in his striped pants and white-cuffed shirt, pulling sugar into lace.

"*Baisers de Vierge.*"

"*Vierge?* Virgin?"

"Kisses of a Virgin."

Underneath the veil of spun sugar, twin meringues from the *pâtissier* held cream perfumed with Tahitian vanilla. They were like two perfect breasts strewn with crystalized petals from white roses and wild violets.

"It's for Sarah, isn't it?"

His face colored.

Rosa put her arm around him. "That's just fine. Right as rain. I won't love you any less, ducks. Don't worry. This isn't the first time that's happened, you know."

ESCOFFIER DID NOT see Rosa in the park the next day as he made his way to mass. He lingered for a time, pretending to watch nannies pushing prams under the golden, autumnal sky. He waited for so long that he missed the sacrament of confession that was always offered before the service. He missed the welcome, the reading from the Old Testament, the New Testament and the Gospel. He even missed the presentation of the Holy Eucharist. The interventions had already been asked for. The water had turned to wine and the bread, His body. When Escoffier finally arrived at the Cathedral of Saint Paul, the congregation was on its knees.

Lead us not into temptation.

The words were like thunder running through him.

"And deliver us from evil," he said, as he genuflected and took his place near the marble altar. The dark stained windows made it difficult to see Jesus on the cross, and all the saints, but he knew they were there. Their unseeing eyes, their gaping wounds.

Above him, on the gilded ceiling, there were demons and angels, fools and saints. Soaring marble pillars kept the heavens at bay.

"Amen."

It was time to take the sacrament of communion. Row by row the congregation filled the aisles. Queen Victoria. Prince Edward. Lady Randolph Churchill and her odd stuttering son, Winston. When Escoffier's pew began to empty, he could not stay behind; people would notice and speculate about what mortal sin had tarnished his soul. And they would talk, and implicate, and ruin.

Rosa. Sarah. Delphine.

He could not afford a scandal. Escoffier stood, took his place in line, and prayed for forgiveness, but knew there could be no absolution. The church was quite clear. Adultery is a mortal sin and profanes the divinity of Christ. He was late for penance and now unclean.

"Body and blood," the priest said and placed the wafer on his tongue.

"Father, forgive me," he said but his voice could not be heard over the organ pipes, thunderous as the rustling of angels' wings, and the pale choir of white-robed boys leading the hundreds of congregants in song, in praise, for the glory of a gilded God who lived in vast halls of cool marble, not in the tiny miracles that a man like Escoffier performed every day.

The wafer melted on his tongue. Tasteless.

20

Escoffier smiled and handed sarah another fruit from the plate of small sweet apricots. They had been halved, sprinkled with cognac, sugar, and butter, one pat for each, baked and then broiled until caramelized and set upon a golden plate. They were warm, not hot, and topped with a small piping of *crème chantilly*, whipped heavy cream infused with vanilla, and a tiny thin leaf of twenty-four-carat gold.

They were lovely but Sarah had actually hoped for a bowl of chicken soup with noodles. Something warm and soothing. She called down to his office and requested something simple but it was Escoffier, after all.

"I have a new sweet I've been working on for you. A study in white with rose-scented cream. In honor of Saint Joan."

"Joan loved soup," she said. "That is a known fact. Her last meal was soup. It's a very saintly dish."

"But you are not a saint."

Escoffier did have a point.

It was difficult to argue with him. White truffles, spiny African lobsters, ice cream made from African honey, a perfect, speckled quail egg—he gave her these things as other men gave her jewels.

But the day had been difficult, too long.

Sarah closed her eyes and chewed slowly, afraid to choke. Her throat felt as if it were on fire. Tonight, for some reason, the tragedy of Joan stuck to her. She was sleepless, uneasy. The rusting moonlight seemed to have turned her skin to the color of embers. She couldn't stop smelling smoke. Her dyed red hair, cut as short as a boy's, just a mop of curls, reeked from it. She'd washed it over and over again, but could not clean away that singed smell. It only grew worse and spread to her hands, her feet, her belly. Sleep was impossible. Joan would not let her rest. She tried to think of her grandchildren asleep in the next suite of rooms, but couldn't. She was leaving for a holiday in Brittany in a few days' time; she tried to think of that but it was impossible.

There was only fire.

And so when Escoffier had knocked, Sarah opened the door, naked, and held out her hands to him.

"They feel as if they are burning," she said.

"Have you eaten?"

He knew the answer before he asked. He covered Sarah's reedy body with sheets from her bed and fed her the golden fruit as one would a dying child—taking in every moment, every sound, every scent and committing it all to memory. The darkened caramel, the cardamom oil she rubbed on her skin, the rose water she bathed in— he lingered on each moment knowing it would probably be their last together.

Delphine had finally agreed to join him.

Escoffier kissed away the tears from Sarah's cheeks while London slept around them. She took off his jacket, his vest. He let her. He would miss the every day of her presence. Sarah at high tea with her pet chameleon lounging on her shoulder like a bejeweled broach set against the embroidered silks of her gown. The doting ageless grandmother watching her golden-haired Simone and Lysiane and Ritz's son Charles stuff themselves full of jam tarts and chocolate but eating nothing herself until chastised.

He did not know how to tell her.

"You must eat when I am not with you," he said.

"Be with me, then. Come to Brittany."

Escoffier slowly kissed her cheeks, the back of her neck. *Sixteen years.* It was a long time to love such a person. It was like loving the morning sky or the ocean before a storm.

"Monet will be there."

"There shall be no excuse, then. He eats quite prodigiously for an artist."

"He is doing something with fog now. He told me that American, that Whistler, has recommended a suite here, at The Savoy, one of the corners, did you know?"

"I am not surprised."

"And so now even Monet comes to you to paint the bridges. These artists love bridges. And this horrible London air: smoke always. It isn't fog at all. Awful. You can't breathe it but you can, apparently, paint it."

The apricots had brought color back into her cheeks. There were others to care for her—friends, family, secretaries, and assistants. She lived with a small army of people, but there were times when she would eat for no one except Escoffier.

"The world now comes to The Savoy," he said and fed her a spoon more.

"But this place can live without you for a fortnight. Rodin comes to Brittany. And this young man, Matisse. He's very talented. He was a lawyer. Did I mention this?"

She had. She had also, repeatedly, mentioned that the Bretons were amazingly medieval. They had very few roads, a very angry sea, and they knew nothing of fashion. The men were long-haired and did not wear trousers but displayed their well-shaped legs in gaiters or rough stockings, their feet shod with buckled shoes. Their women resembled seagulls, although Escoffier had forgotten how exactly an entire race of women wearing bonnets could look like aquatic birds.

"Surely, there is food."

"It is not Paris, but there is food. Lobsters, snails, oysters, clams, sardines—all are pulled from the ocean and dressed simply in olive oil and parsley, salt and pepper, and put into a bowl. That is your lunch. Every day. And Calvados and pink ham. And thin crêpes. And so many ciders."

"Then you will eat?"

"There is no imagination to this food. It moves in your mouth while you eat it. They can't even kill it properly."

"I will send some recipes along with your secretary."

"No. Say you will come." She took a spoonful of cream and brushed it against his lips and then slowly kissed them. "There are octopi on the coast—hundreds of them. Last year we crawled into a cave and it was filled with them. You would like them. Like you, they have very sad eyes."

Escoffier looked at the clock on the mantle. The lateness surprised him. He suddenly felt weary.

"And who is the 'we' of 'We' this year?" Abbéma?"

Sarah had sculpted Louise Abbéma and in turn, Abbéma had painted her and Sarah on a boat ride on the lake in the Bois de Boulogne, for *"le jour anniversaire de leur liaison amoureuse,"* the anniversary of their loving link.

"Of course. Louise. Always."

"She will see that you are fed."

"But you are the ground beneath me."

"And our Dr. Pozzi?"

Even before he'd met the man, Escoffier had seen the photos of the doctor taken by Nadar and the painting by Sargent. He was striking but cunning: much like Damala. An ill-bred angel. Oscar Wilde had just written *Dorian Gray* because of his beauty. Pozzi and Sarah were lovers, of course. They were all Sarah's lovers.

"Pozzi will feed you."

"If you come . . ."

Escoffier took a deep breath and looked out the window. The moon was a thin slice of light. Venus hovered near it, nervous. The rest of the sky was bruised.

"Sarah—"

"Come with me. You are *ma famille.*"

"Sarah—"

"You are my heat, my heart, the walls of my home."

Escoffier took a deep breath. "But you are not mine."

For a moment, Sarah did not seem to understand. She sat back, pulled the covers around her. "Is it that cook?"

"No—"

"I have been told that she spends a great deal of time in the kitchen and in your private quarters."

"Sarah."

"She is the Duke's mistress."

"As you are," he said gently.

"Those black boots she always wears. Mr. Boots, that's what I call her. It makes Bertie laugh. Our Mr. Boots. She is your heart, isn't she?"

"Rosa is a student of French cooking."

"Who needs you as a teacher, of course."

"This is not about Rosa. Please."

"Then let us call her Mr. Boots."

"Please."

"I have a secret about your Mr. Boots." Sarah went into her wardrobe. "Do you see this?" She held up a full-length ermine coat with oversized sleeves and a high collar made of mink dyed black. Escoffier had seen her wear it on many occasions. It was striking. The black fur of the collar made her skin luminescent.

"Queen Victoria's own furrier created this for your Mr. Boots and your old Dear Bertie gave it to me instead. Every time I wear it, I carry its secret. And now every time you see it, you will know its secret, too."

Sarah put the coat on over her naked body. It was June. The night was cool but not cold. She pulled him into her arms.

"Come with me."

"I can't."

"Mr. Boots does not need your cookery more than I do—"

He pulled away slightly. "Please. Don't make this more difficult."

"I cannot live apart from you. Your words are my food, your breath my wine. You are everything to me."

"You are rehearsing for a play. I can hear it in your voice."

"But what if I am not? What if it is true?"

She kissed him, not with passion but with a familiarity that comes with time. The coat fell open. She was still so very beautiful. He buttoned the coat sadly.

"Madame Escoffier is arriving tomorrow."

Sarah didn't seem to hear him at first; she cocked her head to one side.

"Tomorrow," he said again.

"Tomorrow?"

"Yes. The morning train."

"And the children?"

"Paul and Daniel. They are coming, too." And then he said, "To live."

Sarah sat down on the edge of the bed, looking at her hands, not him. She began to rub them together as if they were cold. "How old are they now? The boys. One and five?"

"Nine and five. Sarah—"

"Delphine must be overjoyed to be with you again. Although, Monte Carlo is so beautiful you will have to be very good to her and on your very best behavior to convince her to stay."

"She is with child."

Delphine was as surprised as Escoffier had been. Apparently her sickness and lack of appetite had nothing to do with her dislike of London or missing him.

Sarah's face was unreadable. "Good. Well. Good for you. Things are as they should be again. My dear Escoffier, I need to sleep," she said. "It is late. Can you open the champagne for me?"

Sarah opened the drawer of her nightstand, pulling out a bottle. Escoffier could see the label. "Indicated in insomnia, epilepsy, hysteria, etc."

"The taste is monstrous but I sleep like a child," she said and sat on the marble windowsill and looked out over London. He opened the Moët and poured her a glass. Sat down next to her.

"I am sorry."

"London is not Paris, is it?"

"Delphine's letter arrived while you were at the theater. I didn't know."

"It's beautiful in Paris now. Not too warm yet."

"Paris is always beautiful."

They sat like that for a while, just watching the darkness. The coal clouds lay over the city making the night sky so thick with soot that the stars seemed like gods, hidden and silent. "Pour yourself a glass.

We will toast Madame Escoffier's health and your new child. Let my secretary know what rooms are hers and when she arrives I will send her a proper welcome to the city. Some flowers, perhaps. The British do flowers so very well."

"Sarah—"

She suddenly looked fragile. "Why do you never call me Rosine?" she said softly. "It is my real name and yet you never use it. Why must you always say 'Sarah' as if I am on stage? Are you like them? Another fan? Another beloved monster?"

"Rosine, it is late."

"Join me for one last drink. For a toast," she said. It was more of an order than a suggestion.

"I only brought one glass from the kitchen."

"There's another in the sitting room."

Escoffier went into the next room. It was filled with flowers, as usual, from admirers. Her silk-lined coffin was positioned by the window. He'd never seen her sleep in it. The sight of it made him uneasy. The windows were opened. The damp night air chilled the room and yet the night felt close, gaudy with the fragrance of lilies and roses. It made his heart beat faster; his palms sweat. There didn't seem to be a champagne glass anywhere. There were, however, two velvet boxes that someone had opened and left as if on display at a shop—one held a large diamond necklace, the other matching earrings. Escoffier picked up the card to read who they were from and then reentered her bedroom and that is all that he ever remembered of that night.

That and—mud.

It felt as if he'd suddenly fallen into mud, like in the war, those poor horses that he fed, then killed one by one. Mud again, that cold dark feeling.

The doctor's report would read:

"Bernhardt will live. However, she was found deeply unconscious, showing complete absence of reflexes and only minimal response to pain. Her systolic blood pressure was reduced to 70 mm. Hg, with a pulse of 90 per minute. She was hypothermic (35.2° C.) and the central venous pressure was within normal limits."

The Times would write:

"Finding it impossible to sleep, she determined to take chloral, but by accident took 120 grains, which was an overdose, and the disastrous effects were soon apparent."

The staff at The Savoy had found Escoffier lying prostate outside of her door, weeping, inconsolable. Delphine and the children waited for him at the train station for hours.

"I did not come to London to be embarrassed," she told him, and refused to unpack her bags completely.

A week later, a package was delivered to Escoffier's rooms. It was a full-length ermine coat with oversized sleeves and a high collar made of mink dyed black. Sarah's coat. The card read "From Mr. Boots."

His heart nearly stopped when he saw it.

"And who is this?" Delphine said.

"An associate," he said. "He saw you in the dining room with the children and asked if he could send you a gift. 'Beauty for beauty,' he said. I thought it would be a nice surprise."

"And you are not jealous?"

"Of course not."

"And why not?"

Escoffier hesitated and that was his mistake. And so she answered instead, "Because you no longer love me."

Madame Escoffier.

He wanted to say her name as he had their first night together. He wanted to fill it with that same sense of wonderment, the same shy pleasure; he wanted to take her into his arms, to touch her round belly, to feel their child kick at his hand. He wanted to hold his gangly sons close to him and kiss away their tears. But he had no way of explaining the man he had become. He could not find the words to speak until they arrived back at the train station and he said, "I will become undone without you."

Which, unfortunately, was quite true.

EVEN YEARS HAD GONE BY SINCE HE'D SEEN DELPHINE. No matter. Escoffier had spent the afternoon tasting figs for her at the greengrocers. He'd only come to pick up his "consideration" for the month, the money suppliers paid to him for the privilege, as he liked to think of it, of selling food to The Savoy. But there were so many figs, such abundance, he could not resist. The sight of them lifted his spirits. It was as if he were walking again down the rue du Figuier, the only street in Paris lined completely in ancient fig trees, and taking his fill. His heart was greedy for them; they would be the perfect gift from Mr. Boots.

The beloved Mr. Boots.

While it had begun as a deception born out of panic, through the years weekly shipments to Madame Escoffier from "Mr. Boots" had become a delight for Escoffier. In his letters he was forced to adopt a cheerful formality with his wife, a tone of friendship. But with the shipments of Mr. Boots, he could be an ardent lover.

The fruit alone inspired him. In the heat of summer there were *mirabelles* from Alsace: small and golden cherries, speckled with red.

And *Reine Claude* from Moissac, sweet thin-skinned plums the color of lettuce touched with gold. In August, green hazelnuts and then green walnuts, delicate, milky and fresh. And of course, for just a moment in early fall, *pêches de vigne*, a rare subtle peach so remarkable that a shipment was often priced at a year's wages. And right before winter, *Chasselas de Moissac* grapes: small, pearlescent and so graceful that they grow in Baroque clusters, as if part of a Caravaggio still life.

But that day there were so many figs that he was late for the meeting. He knew Ritz would be cross, but he was often cross, so it made no difference.

When Escoffier finally entered The Savoy's American Bar, Ritz was sitting at the far end waiting in his impeccable black suit. He looked as he always did; he had an unflinching immaculate air about him. He was well shaven, well brushed, the ends of his mustache were perfectly turned upward toward heaven but his hands were clasped together so tightly that his knuckles were white. Over the years, Ritz had become too thin and darkly quiet.

Afternoon tea was in full swing next door in the dining room. Orchestra music floated into the cool dark bar. "To cover the silence which hangs like a pall over an English dining table," as Ritz once said. But at that moment it was merely a nagging reminder of the sacrilege that was going on in the main room.

Afternoon tea was an abomination. No matter how hard Escoffier tried to create the very best of everything, the English wanted only to eat the familiar, wretched and often cloying foods for their teas.

The lemon curd tarts proved to be an endless source of vexation for Escoffier. He knew that the *tarte* should only be made with sweet Menton lemons from Côte d'Azur: it was the only acceptable fruit. The Menton provides a depth of flavor, a mellow tartness with a floral edge, which is remarkable. But the British would not have it. At least three times a week, Escoffier was summoned by one plaid-clad matron or another only to hear the complaint, "This is not like my dear sweet Nan's," to which he replied, *"Je ne parle pas l'anglais"*— even though he had heard the complaint so many times before he knew exactly what they were saying.

And the clotted cream, such trouble. A more refined palate would have demanded *crème chantilly* sweetened with an *eau-de-vie* like Calvados or *eau-de-vie de poire*, because pear is always lovely in the fall. But not the English. Their tea must be the tea they remembered from childhood.

And, of course, there must be seventeen types of tea, although most of the ladies drank champagne and some even went for gin with tonic served in a tall glass with tiny limes. "I feel a touch of scurvy," they would often tell the waiter.

Afternoon tea was a nightmare.

Escoffier took a seat alongside Ritz at the bar, although he would have rather sat at a table. In the dining room, the orchestra swung into a melody from *The Pirates of Penzance* with several ladies singing along to the patter of the "Major-General's Song." He winced. Given the slurry drunken laughter, he assumed that the re-creation of the libretto would probably not be pleasing to the very model of a modern major-general.

"The customer is always right?"

"And usually off key."

"I will never understand the English and their tea. Dinner crowns the day. What more does a tea do except ruin dinner?"

"It fills our pockets and keeps them away from cabbage and sausage."

There were two small cocktail glasses in front of Ritz. One held a drink with a single twist of lemon. The other had an olive. He continually arranged and rearranged the glasses until they sat in a perfect line; the napkins, just so.

"Drink. Opine," he said and handed Escoffier the glass with the lemon. "This is a Martinez from California. Old Tom Gin. Vermouth. Bitters. Maraschino liqueur."

Escoffier took a sniff and handed the glass back by the stem, so as not to warm the drink. "It seems very much like a Manhattan. The juniper of the gin is very nice. Very pronounced. What if you use dry vermouth and eliminate the maraschino?"

Ritz handed him the second glass. "It would be this. Equal parts of gin and Martini e Rossi vermouth. It is called a Martini."

Escoffier sniffed again. "Better."

"Stronger. We will begin with these tonight for the investors' dinner. Money will fly from their pockets."

"Cocktails ruin the palate."

"Cocktails are American, and thereby exotic."

After a time, Escoffier had come to understand that he was not, as Ritz had promised, an ambassador for France at all. He felt very much like the pet chameleon Sarah often wore as a bit of jewelry: decorative, out of his element, and tethered with a gold chain.

He unfolded the menu he'd created for the investors' dinner. Cocktails would most certainly ruin it, but drunken investors were generous investors and the Ritz Hotel Development Company, whose primary partners were Ritz and Escoffier, needed money.

Within the year, they'd planned to open Hôtel Ritz in Paris on the fashionable Place Vendôme and then, the next year, their flagship, the Carlton.

A quick walk from The Savoy, the Carlton would be even more modern, more elegant and more expensive. It would be, frankly, better. And so as soon as it was finished, Ritz said that they would leave their contracts with The Savoy and become as rich as D'Oyly Carte himself.

"Ritz Development hotels will be the greatest in the world."

"And they will not serve afternoon tea?"

"The words *Ritz* and *tea* will never appear in the same sentence again."

Escoffier often dreamt of that day.

And so it became his challenge to construct the menus for the investors' dinners with an eye to extravagance—a particular type of extravagance—one that could be easily charged back to The Savoy, hidden in one account or another.

There was so much at stake that it kept him up at night. The two men were both making more money than the prime minister himself, and Delphine was spending Escoffier's share at an alarming rate— supporting a villa filled with assorted family members was outrageously expensive. If they were to leave The Savoy to open these new ventures, his salary could not falter; there were too many mouths to feed at La Villa Fernand.

Escoffier placed the menu on the bar.

"The wines alone will be one thousand pounds. Excessive?"

"Is that not the point?"

Ritz drank the martini and read aloud.

Caviar frais • Chilled caviar •• *Blinis de Sarrasin* • Buckwheat blinis •• *Oursins de la Méditerranée* • Sea urchins •• *Consommé aux Oeufs de Fauvette* • Consommé with a perfect warbler's egg in honor of the illustrious singer Adelina Patti •• *Velouté Dame-Blanche* • Sweet almond cream soup with star-shaped chicken quenelles •• *Sterlet du Volga à la Moscovite* • Very rare sturgeon that lives between the fresh and salt rivers in the Caspian • • *Barquette de Laitance à la Vénitienne* • Fish roe in pastry boats •• *Chapon fin aux Perles du Périgord* • Capon with truffles from Périgord •• *Cardon épineux à la Toulousaine* • Cardoons poached in veal fat and sauced •• *Selle de Chevreuil aux*

Cerises • Saddle of venison with cherries •• *Suprêmes d'Ecrevisses au Champagne* • Crayfish in a champagne and truffle cream sauce •• *Mandarines Givrées* • Frosted tangerines •• *Terrine de Caille sous la Cendre, aux Raisins* • Terrine of quail with grapes •• *Salade Mignon* • Prawn, artichoke bottoms, black truffle seasoned with mayonnaise sauce •• *Asperges à la Milanaise* • Asparagus prepared in the style of Italy •• *Délices de Foie gras* • *Foie gras* studded with truffles, covered with bacon set in champagne aspic and served very cold with very hot grilled toast •• *Soufflé de Grenade à l'Orientale* • Pomegranate soufflé "oriental style" •• *Biscuit glacé aux Violettes* • Iced cake with violets •• *Fruits de Serre Chaude* • Hothouse fruit

"Echenard supplied the translations. I feel we should go without."

"Investors should know what they are eating."

"Investors should speak French."

"They speak Money. It is the universal language."

The menu was extensive and challenging. The house was filled that night with the main room overbooked. Escoffier looked at his watch. "Bertie and Miss Langtry are still in his suite. His wife and the rest of the Marlborough Set are scheduled to arrive for cocktails at sunset, less than an hour from now."

"Martinis for her, too, then—Prince Edward loves drama."

"And when the future queen appears in the bar with Lillie Langtry's head in her hands, what will the investors think?"

"They will be overjoyed. Investors love to see Royals bicker. It makes them feel important. Money will flow from their hands."

Ritz finished the drink but before he could tap the glass, the barman brought another. He took a sip. Escoffier lowered his voice.

"This dinner tonight. The expense is overwhelming."

"Adelina Patti?"

"She has consented to sing 'Home Sweet Home,' as you requested, but for five thousand pounds. Which account should this be charged to?"

"That is a very good question. How many years of salary is that?"

"For some? A lifetime."

"It will be interesting to see what account you choose, then. House-keeping? That would be amusing. You could say that Prince Edward demanded to sleep on sheets of gold. Of course, he never actually *sleeps*, does he?"

"What would the auditors say to that?"

"They certainly couldn't question him about it."

The auditors had been working for four months at the behest of The Savoy's board of directors. The hotel, its bar and dining rooms were filled every night and yet the half-year accounts showed a drop in net profits from 24 percent in 1895 to just 13 percent.

"Business is always cyclical," Ritz tried to explain. "Consider the tulip. Once only afforded by kings and now nearly a weed."

But the board had been blunt about its displeasure. Behind closed doors it questioned a litany of businesses connected to the hotel that Ritz and Escoffier alone profited from. It carried on at great length about soliciting backing from customers and tradespeople, the practice of accommodating and entertaining family and friends, and were quite incensed that potential partners of the Ritz Hotel Development Company had been allowed to run up large bills that had never been settled. Presents that had nothing to do with The Savoy's business but had been sent to outside parties with the "manager's compliments" annoyed them. Household goods and food charged to the hotel's account that had been delivered to Ritz's new home in Hampstead made D'Oyly Carte feel betrayed.

"This is all standard practice," Ritz said.

"When a hotel is showing a wide profit, yes."

"Thirteen percent is—"

"Not enough. You have been simply using The Savoy as a place to live in, a pied-à-terre, an office, from which to carry on your other schemes and as a lever to float a number of other projects in which the hotel has no interest whatever."

"I am The Savoy."

"You overestimate your worth."

"Perhaps we should ask the Queen or her son."

"I will not be blackmailed."

"I will not be humiliated."

Escoffier was silent. In addition, he'd been accused of setting up his own companies to supply goods to The Savoy, some of which actually belonged to the hotel in the first place, and taking commissions and gifts from tradesmen.

The accusations were obviously ridiculous. While the basic facts were, indeed, accurate there was nothing sinister about these goings on. It was just business. Just *quid pro quo*. The board was acting as if they were criminals.

They were merely "considerations," Escoffier wanted to say. After all, he'd given up so much for The Savoy—his family and France—to bring French culture and cuisine to the English and all he received for his sacrifice was the horrors of afternoon tea and some money, but not nearly enough to maintain two households. He wanted to explain his position, to defend himself, but he said nothing. It would be unseemly to argue. *In a year, I will be gone.*

"Gentlemen, the meeting is over," Ritz said and stood. "Our contracts state that we may pursue other ventures six months of the year. If you are accusing us of wrong-doing, I strongly suggest you offer solid evidence or, as in the case of the general manager before me, I will sue The Savoy and win."

Escoffier followed him out the door.

An army of auditors appeared the next morning. That was four months ago. Escoffier knew they had to be careful. He reviewed the menu again. "This could be seen in a negative light. And Patti— perhaps we should pay her ourselves."

"You named a dish after her, she should just sing."

"If we named the hotel after her, she would still want the money. She now has a parrot she travels with. The only thing it can say is 'Cash! Cash!' "

"What about Melba?"

"She is busy."

"You asked? Did you tell her it was a favor for me?"

"I did. She said she was sorry."

It was true but what she really said was, "I am so sorry that success has turned his head. Ritz is bloated, as are you."

But Escoffier couldn't tell Ritz that. He could barely tell his priest.

"Sorry? If she was actually sorry she could have arranged her schedule."

"That's what she said."

"You should name something awful after her then," Ritz said. "She's getting fat as three pigs."

"Perhaps a diet food. A thin toast to ease her cravings."

"Or The Savoy could feature a suckling pig with a peach in its mouth as the new Peach Melba. It would be quite amusing."

Ritz finished the second martini and listened to the orchestra in the other room for a moment. The music had shifted to Bach's *Minuet in G Major*. Afternoon tea was nearly over. The world as they knew it would soon be restored. "This is a temple of earthly delights, is it not?" The barman brought another drink. Escoffier took it and placed it an arm's length away from Ritz.

"We need to have our wits about us tonight, César."

Ritz leaned over and took the glass from him. "The auditors left today."

"For good?"

"Yes."

"And?"

"And you should meet the investors for cocktails and then excuse yourself and go home. You need to stay away for a day or two while I clear things up. I don't want them taking you into a room for a 'chat,' as the English say, just to see if our stories match. So go home. I'll wire for you."

"I am home."

"To your wife. No one would question your doing that."

Escoffier had not see Delphine since the birth of their daughter, nearly seven years—seven years of shipments from the ardent Mr. Boots—and so he left before cocktails were even served.

T FIRST, DELPHINE COULD STILL REMEMBER THE SCENT of his skin. On Thursdays, curry days, *The English so love their curry,* he told her, Escoffier would come to her bed late at night, the scent of far-off places still lingering on his hands. As the darkness thinned around them, they would make love slowly, quietly, pushing through the exhaustion of work and children and into a world of their own: a world filled with heat and a language that only they could speak.

Once he no longer returned to Monte Carlo, the scent of her husband quickly faded away. The pillows, his old shirts: none of it held the scent of curry, or even the richness of browned onions, nor the depth of braised hens. All she had was her memory of it.

After the first shipment from Mr. Boots arrived at La Villa Fernand—"He seems to follow me everywhere," she wrote Escoffier. "Why?"

He did not answer. And so Delphine began to make brioche.

The cooks of La Villa Fernand stood at the edge of the kitchen and watched as Madame wrapped a clean apron around her silk dress, cut the cake of yeast, just missing the joint of her ring finger, and mixed it with flour, warmed milk and a single fat egg. When she carefully rolled it into a ball and placed it in a large bowl of warm water, they were somewhat reassured that she knew what she was doing, until she spoke.

"Proof is needed," Delphine said. "We must know if the yeast will abandon us." She stood over the bowl, waiting for the ball of dough to expand and then float in the water.

Proof?

The two cooks looked at each other. Proofing is the last stage, the final rise, before the bread goes into the oven. Not the making of a sponge.

Poets, the elder cook thought in disgust, *have no place in a kitchen.*

The two left Delphine alone, that day and every day that she made brioche. They could not bear to tell her that there never is any proof, never a guarantee. At every step, one wrong turn—too much kneading, too warm butter, a momentary cold draft—can ruin brioche. There is no poetry to it, just cool hands and a warm kitchen.

Five eggs. Flour. Salt. Sugar. The recipe from the baker was quite clear. After soft dough is formed, "Crash it against a pastry board. Violently. 100 times exactly."

It seemed ridiculous. *Dough is not a sentient being,* she thought. *It does not know seventy-five slaps from one hundred.*

But it did.

At forty slaps, Delphine began to feel a yielding; the toughness of the dough was starting to break down. Her hands were badly cramped. The baby, Germaine, woke from her nap and was fussing in her crib. The boys wanted chocolate to drink.

"Please, Mama. Please."

Delphine could hear it all, but knew she could not stop "crashing" the dough. If she stopped and fed the baby and made chocolate for the boys, or found one of the servants to do it, by the time she came back to the dough it would be leaden.

"I am writing," she said, although that wasn't what she meant to say, but it seemed somehow true. With each crash of the dough, the poet thought of a trace of a line or the polish for an image. The stars, which she could not see in the sunlight, suddenly shone for her alone and she thought of the possibility of them, the weight of their fire.

After that, "I am writing" is what Delphine always told everyone when she made brioche.

One hundred slaps, and then, even though the dough seemed perfect, round and elastic as it should be, the recipe called for an impossible amount of butter to be gently incorporated. *How is that not like a poem?* When it seemed as if perfection had been reached, there was no depth, no richness.

But butter, spoon after spoon, broke the dough apart. It became stiff in her hands again and greasy. Despair set in. Delphine wanted to stop and add more flour, crash the dough again because that was the part of the process that pleased her.

"Be brave," the baker wrote.

And so even as the dough went slick, she continued to add the butter until, finally, all was incorporated and it held together well enough.

Sometimes "well enough" is all you can hope for.

She covered it with a tea towel and it did rise. And after it rested the second time, it was baked and served warm. It was not perfect—it was thick and dense—but the deep rich taste of it and the wildness of the yeast was enough to bring her to tears.

A cloudburst over Paris / the road alone is darker than I can imagine, she thought.

"Will Monsieur be returning soon?" the cooks asked. Brioche was not everyday bread.

"He is working," she said. "We are all working."

23

THROUGH THE YEARS THERE HAD BEEN LETTERS, OF course. Many. All were addressed to "Georges," as Delphine said they would be, so that he would be reminded that they had become strangers, but he didn't need letters to remind him of that. Every morning he woke up alone, looked out the window into the soot gray morning of London and wondered what had become of his life. He missed the softness of his children, like the scent of dough rising, and Delphine, her warm body, always there, always hungry.

But it was not the reunion he had hoped for.

Delphine did not speak to him upon his arrival. The servants took his bags to the guestroom. The children were outside; no one called them in. For the first time in a very long time, Escoffier had nothing to do. He sat on the small hard bed, a man unaccustomed to napping, and listened to the house around him. It no longer creaked as he'd remembered, or perhaps it did and he no longer heard it. Outside his window, his children played; the sound of their laughter was as foreign as a novel written in a language that one can read but cannot speak.

That evening Delphine had the dining table placed outside along the edge of the cliff overlooking the Mediterranean Sea. She set it herself with the blue Canton porcelain plates from China, fine-cut Bohemian crystal, and a heavy silver service that Escoffier had rescued from the bank sale of Faisan Doré. Down the center of the long table was a series of mismatched silver candelabras, some tall and some squat, which had been used for formal banquets. Set against the coming dusk, the wax flared and spit like dying stars. The children had eaten earlier and had been sent to bed without so much as a kiss from their father.

"I would like to see them," he said.

"Tomorrow."

He did not wish to argue.

Delphine had dressed for dinner that night as if at The Savoy. The sight of her saddened Escoffier. She was wearing the jewelry that he'd sent her for Christmas—teardrop pearl earrings and a matching necklace set with jet and pearls—and the birthday gift of long black kidskin gloves. He'd charged them to The Savoy as a kitchen expense, "for the laying hen"—he wrote. It no longer seemed witty to him.

Her dress was a vivid blue gown. She had others; he'd seen the bills for them. Many of them were twice as expensive as this one. But he and Delphine had bought this dress together. The bodice was low cut and trimmed in lace and it had a large bustle; no one wore those anymore. It barely fit after the birth of their daughter, Germaine, but it still was charming. He chose it for the color alone. It was the same exact shade of the Mediterranean sky and sea, brilliant cobalt, set in silk.

Escoffier, in his black Louis-Philippe dress coat and striped pants, his black mustache freshly waxed, arrived late to the table; no one bothered to call for him. No one waited for him to arrive. Everyone, except Delphine, was already eating when he sat at the table's head. The chair was unsteady, rocked underneath him.

When Delphine finally tucked the children into their beds and arrived at the table, she seemed surprised that Escoffier was seated at the head of the table. She sat in the only empty chair, immediately to his right, and would not look at him but he couldn't stop looking at her. She had grown older in his absence, a bit stooped. Her hair was gray in places. Her fine features were more chiseled by time. He had forgotten how the sun tanned her skin and caused her dark eyes to take on the rich sheen of tempered chocolate.

He wondered how he looked to her. Smaller, perhaps. Certainly gray.

It was a simple supper. There were the langoustines; of course, it was the season. Delphine had made a rich ragout with them using tomato, lemon, herbs and cocoa and set it on a salad of endive, frisee, and red nasturtium blossoms. Even the scent of it was vibrant. The wine was from the country; Escoffier had stopped to visit with an old friend on the way in. There were no sweets at the end of the meal, just baguettes with dry-cured black olives, a light table butter, *beurre d'Isigny*, and a rough farmer's cheese.

When the bread was served, Delphine tore off a chunk. Sniffed. "Too dry."

Escoffier tore off the other end. Bit into it. He didn't take his eyes off her. The chattering table continued on around them and so no one noticed when he took his wife's hand and rubbed it lovingly against his cheek.

She did not look away. "You are sitting in my place," she said.

"And your bread is dry. You are having a very bad day, no?"

"I've not baked in a long time."

"It's a matter of control."

"I'm not interested in control."

"And that's the problem." She stood to walk away but he didn't let go of her hand. "Bread is propelled by yeast. And too much is as bad as too little."

"Much like love."

He stood and spoke quietly, "Much like love. Bread is a simple and yet complicated thing. Yeast, flour and water—very common and yet together magic happens."

"Given the proper environment."

He moved slightly closer. "Heat and patience. It cannot be hurried; it must be earned. Perfect bread is a restrained and calculated seduction."

He leaned in as if to kiss her but did not. The table fell quiet.

"Much like love?" she asked.

"Much like love."

The wolf moon above them was pale and lean.

"It's very late," Delphine said, pulled away, and picked up his plate from the table and handed it to a servant. "Too late, in fact."

That night while everyone else in the great house was asleep, Escoffier opened the door to his wife's room without knocking.

"Come with me."

He was still dressed in his black Louis-Philippe dress coat, cravat and tall platform shoes.

"Why? Because you say so?"

"No. Because I have been baking."

And so, barefoot, in her best lace dressing gown, she followed him. Her hair was undone; the long dark curls, combed with Vaseline, shimmered in the moonlight.

Baking was not what Delphine had expected at all.

Escoffier handed her an apron. She handed it back to him.

"Very well," he said and folded it into a neat square, placed it on the kitchen table and opened the oven. There were two loaves of a golden rye bread, *pain de seigle*. He tapped them quickly, listening for the perfect hollow sound.

"A pan of water in the oven helps retain moisture. If the crumb wall does not stay moist enough, it will crack."

"This is why you came for me? I know how to make bread. I make brioche all the time."

He pulled the bread out of the oven. "Brioche is like pastry. Eggs and butter are more forgiving."

"I make very good brioche."

"And that is very commendable, but bread is what one needs for life. Now watch. You must measure 400g of flour, 280g of water, exactly."

"Or I could leave the measuring to the girl, because I am a poet and not a cook."

His back was to her. All she could see was the line of his elegant jacket, his thinning white hair. *Seven years,* she thought. He stood holding the hot bread in his hand, examining the crust carefully. Calluses made his hands impervious to heat, made them rough. She found that base—and yet still would dream of them.

"And this kitchen needs to be organized," he said. "I could barely find the flour. The rye seemed to be hidden for some reason. Salt should always be left on the counter, that is why it is placed in a cellar, so that the home cook—"

"Remove your shoes."

"My shoes?"

"This is my kitchen. In my kitchen there is no need for your platform shoes to reach my stove because you have no business using my stove. Also there is no need for me to place the salt on the counter. My salt is not your concern. And so, the shoes must go."

"I've brought no others."

"Wait here."

Escoffier took off his shoes, and sat in his stocking feet waiting, uneasy.

"Shoes," she said. They fit perfectly.

"Whose are these?"

"Paul."

"Paul?"

"Your son."

"My son."

"Yes. He is still at home because you have not procured an apprenticeship for him yet. At sixteen, he's now nearly too old to learn a profession."

The shoes suddenly felt too tight. *When did he become a man?*

Escoffier placed the warm bread in the picnic basket along with an uncorked bottle of Bordeaux and a slab of fresh butter wrapped in brown paper. He turned to her and offered his hand, rough and callused—it was the hand of a cook, a laborer.

"Come with me."

Three children. A grand house on the sea filled with all of her family, many of them depending on Escoffier to support them. She now had a life lived in comfort, opulence and influence. A life without him. She hesitated.

"Madame Escoffier?" he said as if it was a question.

Light from the wolf moon slanted through the window. "You can't just come and go in and out of our lives. This is not one of your hotels."

"I understand."

"Fine."

She slipped her hand in his. He kissed it gently.

"Good."

This means nothing, she told herself. Her hand fit perfectly in his, as it always had.

He'd set a tablecloth on the damp grass. The evening air was cool, that kind of wet tropical air that made him miss winter in Monte Carlo. In the ripeness of moonlight, the view was breathtaking: the sharp cliff, the gaslights of the city below them. He poured wine into a fine-cut crystal glass. "For you."

"It will break."

"We never worried about breaking crystal before."

Delphine took the glasses back into the house and replaced them with two clean jelly jars from the cupboard, the ones she always used for the children. She looked out the window at her husband sitting on the edge of the cliff waiting for her return. He was familiar and yet a stranger. She wished he would go away and yet she couldn't imagine her life without the shadow of him.

On the counter there was a bowl of ripe figs that Mr. Boots had had delivered earlier in day. She looked out the window. *Our dear Monsieur Boots.* The morning fog would soon move in; soon the moonlight and Escoffier would disappear. The dark purple skin of the figs reminded her of the night sky. She sliced one in half. The deep red flesh gave off the scent of wild honey. She took a bite. It was like no other fig she had ever eaten, intense and rich.

She placed the other half of the perfect fig on a round white plate, drizzled it with lavender honey. Not too much, just enough to remind Escoffier of a Mediterranean spring, how lush and unbearably sweet it was.

She opened the icebox. Inside there were the leftover langoustines in ragout, her favorite dish. She picked one up and ate it whole; the complexity of the tomato and cocoa was still apparent, still pleasing. "My kitchen," she said and went back out into the night.

"I thought you'd forgotten me," he said and stood.

"I tried, but that proved impossible."

He took the fig from her. "Mr. Boots?"

"He also sent some lovely Italian wine and several Belgian lace tablecloths. He has very good taste."

"He is an ardent lover."

"I wouldn't know."

They sat in the shadow of La Villa Fernand but it felt as if it had suddenly been folded into the darkness.

"I'm going inside. It's too damp," she said.

"The tomatoes. Do you remember them? Days and days of canning tomatoes and putting them into champagne bottles for the winter. How wonderful it was to capture summer in a bottle—in a famous bottle, no less. "

Delphine put the bread and butter back into the picnic hamper and handed him the bottle of wine. "They were for the customers, not us."

"I've kept those bottles, you know," he said. "We could do it again. This summer. This house needs a garden. Right here under this blanket. It's small and rocky but would be good for a kitchen garden. A fine place to grow tomatoes."

"The children do not like tomato sauce."

"They will eat what we tell them to."

"We?"

She did not meet his eye, nor look his way. It was as if he was already back in London, back in his small crowded room looking out into the coal-fired air of the night.

"We were happy then," he said. "Weren't we? Before The Savoy."

"I was happy. But you are Escoffier." Delphine handed him the hamper with his picnic packed away inside of it. "Do not pretend otherwise. It's disingenuous."

She began to walk away but he caught her hand. "Dance with me."

"There's no music."

He pulled her into his arms. "Of course there is," he said. "Listen. Heartbeat. One. Two. Three. One. Two. Three. How is that not like a waltz?"

She held herself away from him. He pulled her closer and whispered, "One. Two. Three. Can you hear it?"

"No."

"Then you aren't trying."

He brushed his lips against her cheek; the softness of his kiss surprised her. Through the maze of hurt and anger, she could indeed feel his heartbeat, their heartbeats. *Quick. Quick. Quick.*

"One. Two. Three."

Quick. Quick. Quick.

"One. Two. Three."

On the edge of the cliff they danced. Small stones gave way beneath their feet, tumbled into the darkness.

"Turn. One. Two. Three. Turn."

Quick. Quick. Quick.

"Madame Escoffier," he said and kissed her with the grace and heat that they had both remembered. The kiss tasted of the langoustines, the ragout, and the undertone of cocoa. "My dear Madame Escoffier."

Quick. Quick Quick.

He slipped her robe away.

Quick. Quick. Quick.

Then her dressing gown.

And when she was pale and naked in the moonlight, he ran his hands along her, memorizing each scar, each turn, each soft part of her. She unbuttoned his shirt, slipped off his jacket.

For a moment she thought of their children, although they were hardly children anymore. The boys would soon have families of their own. Her daughter was eight now and nearly as tall as Escoffier. What would they think if they looked out the window?

"Madame Escoffier."

Delphine looked back at the house, and then at the neighbor's. No lights were on. And so she kissed him and the world fell away around them. All that remained was the wolf moon and the sea and time.

He was so filled with her that he thought his heart would break.

She was silent, her skin cold.

He had fallen asleep and was dreaming when she said, "Don't wake the children when you leave."

"Perhaps I won't leave."

"You don't know how to stay."

He watched as she walked away from him. Her dressing gown and white lace robe made her seem ghostlike. He said nothing; there was nothing to say. He looked over the sea; the wolf moon was sinking; soon it would be morning. He dressed and took the hamper back into the house, replaced the jelly jars with a single crystal glass, and added a wedge from the *Caprice des Dieux*, an intensely rich triple crème that he bought for The Savoy and had the cheesemaker ship to Southsea, Portsmouth, to Escoffier's warehouse, where someone would inspect it, resell it to the hotel at a comfortable profit, and repackage the rest to be placed on the next boat to Monte Carlo for Delphine addressed, of course, from Mr. Boots. He took the figs, too. Then went into the guestroom to pack his suitcase.

Escoffier did not move quickly. He folded each shirt, each sock, with the greatest of care. At every point, he had hoped that Delphine would come out of her room, take his hand, and lead him back to her room, but she did not.

The first train to Paris left the station at sunrise. From there, he would have to catch another to London. The journey was long, longer than the time he'd stayed. Outside of the children's rooms, Escoffier kissed the tips of his fingers and placed each kiss on each door. He didn't want to wake them.

At the station, he boarded the first train to Paris and sat by the window of his compartment: a small proper man in his small proper suit. He watched the sun rise over the Cote d'Azur with its yacht-filled harbors, millionaires' villas and his own grand house, which he might never see again. He opened the food hamper and on the small table before him, set out a white linen napkin, the crystal glass. He angled the perfect slice of cheese and placed the two purple figs next to it. He poured some wine, tore off a chunk of the *pain de seigle* he'd made, and ate as the world sped by his window. He was not sure if he'd ever had such a lovely breakfast before.

When Escoffier finally returned to The Savoy, it was well after midnight. He came in through the alleyway. Everyone had gone, the morning shift had yet to arrive. Without windows, the main kitchen was very dark, lit only by the blue flames of the stoves. He sat on the stairs in the silence and watched the flames burn, unending, as if in their own layer of Hell. There was an odd comfort in it.

How long he'd been asleep was difficult to tell.

"Papa," the boy shook him gently. "Papa, you need to go. Get some rest. We'll take care of this."

He looked at his watch. Five a.m. The kitchen was getting ready for breakfast service. Escoffier gathered his bags and went into the cool gilded lobby and sat for a very long time watching people come and go. There were the disadvantaged royals and fabulous pretenders chatting with the lately rich and the fashionably entitled. There was a New York heiress with a broken leg wheeled in on a rosewood chair with a handful of tiny yapping Pekingese trailing behind her, "the little darlings." There were cardinals and bishops in all their grave glory eyeing the Prince's consorts parading about in respectable clothes. He even saw Mr. Gilbert, without the shadow of Mr. Sullivan, sitting in the American Bar making copious notes.

Eventually, the fight, which began in the kitchen, erupted into the dining room and then spilled into the lobby. The rest of Escoffier's belongings were delivered at his feet and the police escorted him out of The Savoy and into the bitter March day. Once outside the door, they handed him a note of dismissal. It was addressed to both Messrs Ritz and Escoffier, the two primary partners of the Ritz Development

Company, and was quite clear. "'By a resolution passed this morning you have been dismissed from the service of the Hotel for, among other serious reasons, gross negligence and breaches of duty and mismanagement. I am also directed to request that you will be good enough to leave the Hotel at once.'"

"A disagreement has developed," Escoffier wired Delphine.

"The Savoy Hotel Mystery" appeared as an item in *The Star*.

"During the last 24-hours The Savoy has been the scene of disturbances which in a South American Republic would be dignified by the name of revolution. Three managers have been dismissed and 16 fiery French and Swiss cooks (some of them took their long knives and placed themselves in a position of defiance) have been bundled out by the aid of a strong force of Metropolitan police."

More than two hundred telegrams were sent to show support. The Prince of Wales had wired, "Where Ritz goes we follow."

Escoffier had not read a single one.

It was raining in Southsea when he arrived, which made the port town seem even drearier. They were surprised to see him at the warehouse. "I'm afraid there has been a change in the situation," he told Jérôme, the manager.

The man's father and Escoffier had been prisoners of war together. The son had that same look about him; a look that said he was ready for almost anything and sometimes was.

"Divide whatever food and goods are left among the men and sell the building quietly," Escoffier told him.

Jérôme took a bottle of rare bottle of Napoleon cognac from his desk drawer and poured a fistful into perfect Baccarat snifters. Escoffier immediately recognized both as coming from a shipment that he had approved payment for months ago and assumed he'd received. Jérôme could see that on his face. He shrugged and laughed as a young boy would, caught in the act.

What did I expect, Escoffier thought.

"We had a good run, did we not?" Jérôme said and drank the cognac in two gulps.

Escoffier looked at the stone church across the courtyard. Its graveyard overlooked the sea.

"Perhaps *good* is not the word."

He thought again of La Villa Fernand and all the family and extended family who lived there. The monthly bills were staggering.

Jérôme poured himself another. Lifted his glass. "To profit."

Escoffier's remained untouched.

The man slid a package of letters across the desk to him. They were unopened, tied with string. He recognized the handwriting immediately.

"These came for Mr. Boots."

"Of course."

Escoffier put his wife's letters in his satchel. Left without another word.

The Complete Escoffier: A Memoir in Meals

POULARDE ÉMILE ZOLA

Fatted Chicken and Ortolan Presented on a Bed of Foie Gras and Surrounded by Truffle Stuffing

It is important to note that identification is a wildly popular strategy when naming a dish. My *Consommé Georges Sand* was beloved by many who, upon ordering, would sometimes tell the waiter how much they enjoyed reading "Monsieur" Sand's books. Some had even claimed to have met "Monsieur" Sand. One woman, a society matron, had even confessed that she had danced with "him" and found herself slightly in love with "his" keen wit.

As Georges Sand was, and had always been, a woman—the Baroness Dudevant who had passed from this life in 1876—these emphatic declarations initially confused the waiters. However, I instructed them always to agree. And they did. The very best of our staff would often agree so fully that he could, quite convincingly, praise Sand's "manly prose" and "dashing good looks" at great length.

"The customer," as Ritz said, "is always right."

You must always keep in mind that if one is to create a famous dish that the customers will fully embrace, it must be as magnificent as its namesake. I created *Poularde Émile Zola* after the great writer, although it is not something that he would have enjoyed eating. He would have despised it. It is, however, delightful. The sensation of velvety fatted chicken combined with the tiny ortolans is incomparable—like butter. And then, of course, *foie gras*! Who could not eat *foie gras* every day? Well, Zola. He was not fond of it at all. Still, I name this dish "Émile Zola" so that you will eat it in hopes of becoming a brilliant writer and thinker.

Who would not want to be Zola? He was a champion for the underclass of France—he told me this himself. At his funeral, crowds of workers gathered cheering the *cortège* with shouts of "Germinal! Germinal!" after his great masterwork. Who would not want to eat this dish in hopes of attaining such rabid devotion? Of course, those who opposed his political views had murdered him, but in retrospect that is merely a romantic detail and details are the death of art.

I find it most interesting to note that while doing the research for his books, Zola always stayed in a lovely suite of rooms at The Savoy. He would visit the poor during the day and then sleep in silken sheets at night. He also had excellent taste in suits. When I asked about his penchant for luxury, he said, "The scientist need not be a monkey to observe them."

I had heard that in the beginning he was so destitute that he ate sparrows that he trapped on his windowsill. He denied this, but I cannot help but think it was true. Having been a prisoner of war, having been hungry myself, I understand hunger as one understands air. I have what I call a "bone wisdom," it is something that is a part of every step I take in the world. I must believe that this is true of Zola. The bone wisdom in his work is unmistakable.

How he loved food!

Whenever I ventured into the dining room he would always call me to his table and regale me with exquisite recollections of what he had eaten during his travels; his *faiblesses de gourmandise*. Sardines! Oh, how he would speak of sardines! Fresh. Seasoned with salt, pepper, and olive oil—and then grilled over the dying embers of grapevine shoots!

When still moist, they are placed into an earthenware dish that has been rubbed with garlic. The dish is finished with a mixture of fresh parsley and oil from Aix. *Voilà!*

To merely speak of sardines brought tears to Zola's eyes. And cassoulet! How he adored, worshiped, cassoulet prepared *à la Provençale* with tomato, eggplant and zucchini!

Pure rapture.

"When I think of it," he once told me, "the memory of all these country meals brings me back to my childhood spent in Aix-en-Provence."

But peasant food does not sell at The Savoy. It is understandable. Zola himself did not like to be seen eating such foods in public. The few times he did caused Paris to question his aesthetics and to refer to him as a gourmand, which can be, of course, synonymous with the word *glutton*. Since Zola was a man who obviously spent a great deal to cultivate a privileged air, the title profoundly shamed him.

And so I named *Poularde Émile Zola* for him. Originally I created the dish for a maharajah who was surprisingly quite an anglophile. He loved anything English, especially the ladies. "Little birds," he called them. I later discovered that this dish also had a poetic resonance for the Duc d'Orleans, who lived at The Savoy after he was banished for being the rightful pretender to the French throne, a throne that no longer existed. It was a very complicated situation.

However, to me this dish will forever belong to Zola, even though he never ate it. I'm sure that if asked in a moment of weakness, he would instead say that a *boule* of crusty bread made with sweet cream butter and topped with coarse sea salt should forever bear his name.

But he would be wrong. And this is precisely the problem with creating a dish in someone's name. They feel that they should be consulted. They should not. No one cares how they see themselves. It is how the artist sees them that matters.

And so, it is best to create a dish for someone only after they are dead because feelings can, and will, be hurt.

To make *Poularde Émile Zola* carefully clean and peel eight large truffles. They should be as big as a lady's fist. Warm them in butter, season them quickly with salt and pepper, and then add a glass of aged Madeira and leave them to macerate in a clean jar for about ten minutes. While the truffles are soaking, find a good-sized pullet. You must be very careful with the size of the fatted chicken. If it is too large, it is too old, and it is mostly fat and the meat will be tough. It must be a young and supple size. You will know it when you see it. Your heart will leap.

The presentation of this dish will require the maître d'hôtel, three waiters (at the very least), and a portable stovetop. Everything must be done quickly. In the kitchen, stuff the truffles into the chicken and sauté until barely cooked. When it arrives at the table, the maître d'hôtel rapidly slices the breasts from the bone, while a waiter sautés one slice of *foie gras* for each plate. One immaculate slice of pullet is then placed on top of the *foie gras* and surrounded with truffle stuffing.

Seconds behind the presentation of the pullet must be the ortolans. There should be one per guest. The service of this bird is traditionally the provenance of royalty. No matter. Good chefs always find a way to deftly ignore any law. The small creature is the size of your thumb; it is much like a finch. It is to be captured alive, quickly force-fed, and then drowned in Armagnac. Once lifeless, they are sautéed in butter, much like the pullet. At the table, the maître d'hôtel passes the completed plate to a second waiter who tops the chicken with the ortolan and a spoonful of hot meat juice.

At this point timing is critical because it is the practice, since the French Revolution, to eat the bird in its entirety, head, organs, bones and all. While hot.

Each waiter, and the maître d'hôtel, must, with their left hand, simultaneously place the plates in front of each guest and with their right quickly cover the guest's head with a white linen napkin. There can be no compromise. This dish must be served under these exact conditions, as they are necessary to enhance the exotic taste.

The tiny ortolans must be presented on a white plate while the diner's head is covered with a white linen napkin, because this preserves the precious aromas and, of course, hides the diner from France and God.

I have eaten ortolans only once. When the napkin was placed over my head it was as if the world outside had fallen away. I felt weightless. I sat for a long time like this, in that small blank place, until the plate finally came to me. It was so white and, being surrounded by the white linen, all I could see was the tiny bird, so frail and helpless in life and now so beautiful. I felt a profound wave of shame and yet, I also felt desire as I had never before. The intensely rich roasted scent of this poor creature is like something I had never experienced. I was overcome. I could not hold back and bit off the head.

That is never done.

But the taste of the meat was so sweet. I could not stop myself. I had never known such delicacy before. Then, suddenly, there was a rush of the scalding blood. It burned my throat, and yet I would not cry out. I still chewed. I could not stop. The organs were acidic and made the burning of my mouth even more painful. But I was consumed by the experience. Each bone I ground between my teeth both shamed and delighted me. It was like making love to a woman who can never be yours, the sweetness of what is forbidden is in itself worth the fury of Hell.

And so I created this dish. If served properly, each bite of *Poularde Émile Zola* will evoke the starving Zola sitting on his windowsill, sparrow in hand, overcome with guilt and desire, hiding from his own terrible gods and dreaming the dark dreams of lost souls.

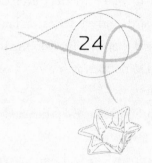

24

ELPHINE'S LETTERS TO MR. BOOTS WERE TIED WITH A
simple bit of twine but that could not hide their beauty.

"A cloudburst over Paris / the road alone is darker than I
can imagine."

They were not so much letters as poems; an exchange of art for food.

"In this thin coat of skin / these silent hands / these clouded eyes /
there is you. / The timbre of my voice rises and falls with thoughts of
you. / In dreams you come to me as my true love, the one who completes. / And then I wake."

Escoffier searched for bits of himself between the lines. He wasn't
sure if he found them or not. He wasn't sure about anything. For the
first time in his life, he had no place to cook and no home to go to.
After the "disagreement" at The Savoy, Delphine made it clear that
he was not welcome at La Villa Fernand.

"Apologize and go back immediately," she wrote. "The household
accounts are too low for such foolishness. I have also noticed that
our Mr. Boots has not made a shipment since this misunderstanding
began. What should I think of that? It wounds me."

It wounds me.

The words burrowed into a small corner of his heart.

It was impossible, of course. *Fini.* The Board of Directors was demanding complete restitution from him—at least two years' wages, a staggering sum. And to make matters even more difficult, Ritz was threatening the Board with a series of lawsuits for wrongful dismissal—and demanded that Escoffier do the same.

"We must be united. Do not betray me."

It all made him sleepless.

Upon his return from Southsea, Escoffier had rented a room in a nondescript hotel as far away from The Savoy as possible. The Ritz Hotel Development Company's new London venture, the Carlton, was still under construction; its opening was more than a year away. When complete, the kitchen would feature a brigade of sixty cooks who could execute a very complicated idea that he'd been thinking of—a menu à la carte. For five hundred. The hotel would be the model of efficiency, but it was still under construction.

If Escoffier wanted to stay in England, he would be forced to engage a suitable set of rooms and that would be expensive. He and Ritz's company had little money to spare. They had other management contracts but until both the Ritz and the Carlton were complete, the company could not match Escoffier's salary from The Savoy, and without The Savoy to help defray fundraising costs, the hotels might never be complete.

The Hôtel Ritz project was not going well. It was scheduled to open in June but cost overruns and delays were threatening to take the Ritz Development Company into bankruptcy. The conversion of the Vendôme and Cambon buildings into one hotel proved to be difficult and more expensive than imagined.

"Let me see what can be done," he told Ritz and promptly left for France. He still kept a *pied-à-terre* from his time at Le Petit Moulin

Rouge. It only made sense that he should return to Paris. He'd managed construction before and hated it. But this was, at least, someplace to go and something to do. The project was small, only fifty rooms.

"A little jewel," Marie Ritz had said.

A little nightmare, Escoffier thought.

He spent his days standing in the cold mud appeasing creditors, builders, tradesman and local politicians. It was exhausting. And, unfortunately, he'd forgotten how small his *pied-à-terre* was. He could barely fit his belongings into it and it had no kitchen. Every night, until the early morning hours, he could be found sitting on top of his tiny bed amidst the chaos of boxes, creating menus he could not cook for a hotel that might or might not get finished at all.

Work, he told himself, *work hard and people will forget The Savoy.*

But he couldn't. He couldn't stop thinking of his kitchen there, the beauty of his staff in motion, the quiet hush of his rooms, and the women, all the beautiful women, who blushed when he kissed their hands.

In the dreary winter of his tiny room, The Savoy seemed as if it were a world scented by roses. And Sarah—Escoffier hadn't seen her since the day he was fired. He'd thought about sending a letter but she'd moved out of the hotel and, according to his friend Renée at the desk, left no forwarding address. He could send it to her home in Paris, but what could he possibly write? "There was a disagreement." While enough of an explanation for Delphine, it would insult Sarah. She was there when it happened.

"She will find me when the moment is right," Escoffier thought, but wasn't sure if he wanted to be found or if she would want to find him.

Whenever he thought of Sarah, he kept thinking of those last moments at The Savoy: the police taking his bags to the street and then coming for him, their hands on his exquisite dress coat. The Board was watching; Richard D'Oyly Carte was in his wheelchair.

The staff was in a state of confusion. The guests were horrified. Some of the men in the kitchen drew knives to defend Escoffier's honor.

In the middle of it all, Sarah appeared, like some sort of hallucination. Her hair wound tornado-like and held in place by an outrageous concoction of bows, she was dressed in a green silk suit with that pet chameleon chained around her neck, hissing. She had just returned from Cross Zoo with her granddaughters. The crying Lysiane kept saying, "Why is he going away? Was he bad? Where are they taking him?" Simone was pale and silent. The chameleon snapped at everyone like a spoilt dragon.

It was all too much. *Much too much.*

Escoffier tried to forget it but couldn't. The look of profound sorrow on Sarah's face was the first thing he thought of when he rose in the morning and the last thing when he went to bed each evening.

After a month in Paris, a letter from Ritz arrived. "Go to Maxim's. Spy. They have extended their menu beyond *pommes frites*, the specialty of the house. Find out what they are planning to serve—but be gracious and do not forget to give the owner Monsieur Cornuché my best wishes. He is a good man, after all."

With a menu of haute cuisine, or any type of cuisine beyond fried potatoes, Maxim's could provide serious competition for the Ritz. It was, after all, the haunt of the most notorious courtesans of the *belle époque*: Jeanne and Anne de Lancy, the twins who tormented suitors by always switching places; Jeanne Derval, who carried her tiny dog in her jeweled chastity belt; and the former *Folies Bergères* dancer Liane de Pougy, who was such a startling beauty and such a bad actress that Sarah Bernhardt once advised her that when she was on stage it would be best if she just kept her "pretty mouth shut."

Maxim's had the potential to become a legend. The café was not that established yet, but its owner, Monsieur Cornuché, was already known as a great restaurateur.

In his letter, Ritz recounted a famous anecdote: "A guest once complained that there was a beetle in his soup and Cornuché picked the bug up and ate it. 'It is merely a raisin,' he announced. It was brilliant!"

And so Escoffier found himself waiting in the seemingly endless line outside of Maxim's. It was just a café. No reservations were accepted, but not everyone was allowed in. The head doorman Gérard, looking very much like a child's nutcracker in his royal blue pants, scarlet hat and gold monocle, was the gatekeeper. He divided guests into two categories, "goodhearts" and "choleras," with most falling in the latter. When he saw Escoffier in the back of the line, he embraced him and called for Cornuché, who, laughing like a child with an unexpected chocolate, said, "You will come to work for us now, then? Savoy's loss will be our gain?"

"Is it true that you have two hundred thousand bottles of wine in your cellar?"

"There are one hundred twelve varieties of champagne alone."

"Then I'd like supper."

"Supper is a very good start. I will consider that a hopeful sign."

It was midnight. Maxim's was filled with the post-theater crowd—those who had attended the last act, as attending only the last act was fashionable and seeing an entire play was not. Cornuché led him through the dining room past many of Escoffier's former customers—some of whom looked away when he passed their tables and some of whom merely looked though him as if he had become invisible. Cornuché took him to a small two-top near the swinging doors that hid the famed "omnibus," the long corridor leading to the bar. The omnibus was not a room, but a tight hallway filled with tables where only the elite of Paris sat, clublike. At Maxim's it was the only place to be. Escoffier was determined that he would not sit anywhere else.

There was nothing wrong with the main dining room, of course. The band was playing a languid song by Reynaldo Hahn, a *mélodie* about infidelity. A charming choice, Escoffier thought, noticing how many of the men in the room were not with their own wives.

Maxim's was a very small place. And very red—the carpet, the curtains, and the hundreds of rose-colored lampshades warming the light that shone upon the rows of tightly packed tables and plush red banquettes. It reminded him of the first-class waiting rooms of rail-road stations with the famous and near famous in their silks and tuxedoes wanting to be seen behaving the way the famous often do—badly.

A pretty young girl with painted cheeks and lips came up to Cornu-ché and whispered something to him. He checked his pocket watch. "Yes. Now. On the front tables," he said and then slipped the girl some bills that she stuck in her *décolletage*. She looked like a drawing of *La Goulue*, "The Glutton," the queen of the Moulin Rouge. She was a close facsimile, but clearly not the real thing.

"That's for both of you," Cornuché said. "Not like the last time."

"But of course."

The girl kissed Cornuché on both cheeks, and then kissed him on the lips. "Here we are scandalous, no?" she said to Escoffier and returned to her table by the window.

Cornuché cleared his throat. "She and her friend will be our sur-prise for the evening."

"She's very beautiful."

"I pay her to be. One must always have beautiful women sit by the window so they can be seen from the sidewalk."

Indeed, along the window, each table was filled with *ces dames*. They were wasp-waisted, their bare shoulders made porcelain with rice powder, and heartbreakingly elegant in their finest gowns, jewels and dream-driven hats.

The women were all so beautiful that Escoffier thought for a moment that he could sit at the offered table. The room was like a

small ornate hothouse, the calla lily chandeliers, the twining flowers of the stained glass roof and of course the large murals of naked
women. And then there were the women themselves—lush, ripe and
waiting.

However, when Cornuché pulled out the chair for Escoffier, the
great chef could not sit. "Perhaps, you should save this table for a couple," he said. "Is there a seat nearer the bar, perhaps?" he said. "Surely
you understand what I am saying?"

Cornuché smiled, slapped Escoffier on the back. "Ah! Of course!
Closer to heaven," he said and swung the doors open, and there
was the omnibus in all its decadent glory. "The spectacle of *grande
galanterie*!"

Escoffier agreed.

He knew many of the players. By the door there were five brothers, all Russian dukes, in full military dress with their companions in
various stages of undress, sitting at a table littered with magnums of
champagne. Next to them, two young girls were sitting on the lap of
Caruso, feeding him oysters. *He'll need those,* Escoffier thought. And
Georges Feydeau, the playwright, was scribbling away in far corner.

Cornuché pointed him out, laughing. "He says it's the finishing
touches on *La Dame de Chez Maxim.* He claims he will make us
famous and finally pay his bill. Given how much he drinks, we need
both of these things to happen."

Each table in the omnibus had a delightful story unfolding and yet
Cornuché walked Escoffier back to the bar itself. "The omnibus is not
for you. I know how much you like the ladies," he said and swung the
doors open. Escoffier could see that the bar was even smaller than the
omnibus and was filled with women only—women in black stockings with hair the color of champagne. Some of them were counting
money; one was recording sums in a ledger. They all stopped talking
when Cornuché led Escoffier into the room.

"Heaven, is it not?"

No, Escoffier thought. *It is not heaven at all.* It was more like an office.

"Would you like some help?" Cornuché whispered. "I can tell you which one is A.F. or R.A.F." Escoffier looked confused. "I make notes," he explained. "R.A.F. *Rien à faire.* You know, 'nothing doing.'"

Escoffier's spy mission to Maxim's was starting to feel like a very large mistake, but then a waiter entered the bar carrying a beautiful chocolate soufflé topped with a bouquet of red roses. "We need the magnum of Moët!" he shouted. "Immediately."

"Miss Bernhardt has arrived?"

Escoffier colored at the mention of her name but Cornuché didn't notice. "You must excuse me, dear Escoffier. There is a ring in the center of those roses that could make the Queen of England blush. One night with divinity apparently costs a great deal these days."

Cornuché held the door open for the bartender and the magnum. Escoffier looked back out into the omnibus. Sarah had just arrived. *In all her glory,* he thought. The Russian dukes were fawning over her. Caruso kissed her hand. She shimmered in the rose-colored light, wearing a dress made entirely of gold silk. Her hat was gold and her neck so filled with jewels that she could hardly move.

"And she's over fifty years old. And a grandmother at that," Cornuché said. "It's amazing what these men will pay for."

Cornuché took the champagne glasses from the waiter, and pushed past him. "Mademoiselle Bernhardt!" he said loudly.

Sarah looked up and saw Escoffier. The man who she was with was some minor Royal, a distant cousin of Prince Edward on the German side. He whispered something in Sarah's ear but she didn't seem to hear him, or even notice that he was there. She was staring at Escoffier—with that horrible sad look. He suddenly couldn't breathe. He pushed past Cornuché and out of the room and into the dining

room where the faux *La Goulue* and her willing friend had begun a
can-can on the tabletops by the window.

When Sarah's letter arrived at his *pied-à-terre* a day later, Escoffier
boarded the next train.

"We can disappear," she wrote and signed it *Rosine Bernardt, veuve
Damala.* Escoffier could not understand why, after nearly a decade
had passed, Sarah still wished to conjure the man's spirit.

Perhaps to remember that even the angels have a dark side.

When Escoffier arrived in Quiberon, he boarded the ferry to *Belle-
Île.* It was empty. The weather was foul, colder than usual. The cross-
ing was brutal. The old boat was buffeted by the sea and followed to
the island by a howling wall of lightning and rain.

Although Sarah had spoken of it often, Escoffier had never been to
this part of Brittany before. When the ferry finally reached the docks,
the storm hesitated a moment and he could see what a painter *en plein
air* would see, what Monet had seen as he desperately held his canvas
so that the insistent wind would not hurl his easel into the sea—the
endless rows of cafés and houses, some pink with blue shutters, some
blue with shutters of green, all set in sharp relief against the bones of
jagged steep cliffs, the gray-green sea and the coal smoke sky. The
colors were so intense, he nearly wept.

"Escoffier!"

There she was—with the storm quickly closing in around her—on
horseback, her wild red hair tangling in the savage wind.

"Get on," she said. "Leave your bags with the harbor master and
he'll deliver them when it's safe."

The wind was now howling down upon them. She held out her
hand to him and he pulled himself up onto the saddle. She kicked the
horse hard; the hail began. Then rain. In a moment, the waves of the
ocean overtook the dock, and then the road, but the horse ran full out.
The ocean, the rain, it was difficult to tell if they were drowning or

not: there was water everywhere but the horse seemed indifferent to the benediction of the storm. He ran through it all, without hesitation, up the steep cliffs through the torrents of rain, the blinding sea-spray and the jagged needles of lightning. He sped along the edge of deep ravines, the swirling rock pools below.

With his arms around her, Escoffier could feel that Sarah was laughing.

"Faster!" she shouted.

"Widow Damala, you are quite mad," he thought, or perhaps actually whispered in her ear; he wasn't sure, but he could feel her laugh even harder.

When they finally arrived, the lights of the harbor at Le Palais were far below them. It was a sheer drop down the cliff into the swirling tide. Sarah's summer home was not a home at all, but an abandoned fort at Pointe des Poulains. Imposing, squat, a square of pink stone and yet when he entered the cool interior, it was so quiet that Escoffier thought he had slipped between this world and that.

After they dried themselves and changed, Sarah said, "Are you hungry?"

No one had ever asked that of Escoffier before. "Do you have food?"

Sarah threw her head back and laughed. "My dear sir, one does not invite Escoffier to her hideaway and not have food."

She was standing in the middle of the kitchen in a mink-lined dressing gown wearing the rough wool socks that were so common to the people of that wild coast but not the sort of thing that Escoffier expected from Bernhardt.

Of course, he was wearing a similar pair, and a red kimono that Sarah swore was designed for men, and which she claimed belonged to her own son, but Escoffier knew that in Japan the color red was always reserved for women and children. Or grandchildren like Sarah's Lysiane and Simone. The robe had that sticky scent that children often have. Still, there was nothing else that fit and his clothes were wringing wet. *A child's robe, what have I come to?* He combed his thinning white hair, brushed his mustache: none of it helped.

"I look like the village idiot."

"If I had slippers and a hunting dog, we'd be the perfect English couple," she said.

He kissed her sweetly. "And so, *veuve Damala*, what is there to eat?"

"There is a *Far Breton*."

The cake was on the kitchen table. He touched it with a finger. It was dense, although it had a tentative spring to it, like flan. *"Clafouti?"*

"Non. It is an entirely different beast."

Sarah put another log on the fire and wiped the dirt from her hands onto her elegant robe and began to pin her unruly wet hair into a topknot. "My dear Escoffier. You have never had *Far Breton?* Cinnamon, vanilla and some plum brandy added to the milk. The prunes and raisins are soaked in Armagnac."

"You baked this? Yourself?"

"Of course. Everyone here can make this. It's very simple."

"I didn't know you could cook."

"I can but never do, but I will tonight. I had the caretaker bring us supplies. Tonight, we shall feast. I shall be your cook."

On the counter there was fish, a John Dory, a bucket of small mussels, a loaf of dense bread, fresh butter and a jug of cider. Escoffier picked up the spiny fish. "A fine specimen," he said.

"From Le Guilvinec."

"Very fine indeed."

The fish was silver and olive green with a series of sharp knifelike fins and a pout-ugly face. Escoffier sniffed it carefully; it still had the scent of the sea. "Today?"

"Earlier this morning. If this were June, he would have brought us a sink full of lobster."

Escoffier began to slice quickly along the sharp dorsal fins.

Sarah took the knife from his hands. "No. Sit."

"There's very little meat. It's very bony. You'll hurt yourself."

"I want to cook. I never cook. Please let me. When my menagerie is here the staff cooks and I cannot help because everyone would be so disappointed that I am mortal."

"But if you cook, what should I do?"

"What do you usually do when someone cooks for you?"

"No one usually cooks for me."

"Well, what would you like to do?"

"Cook."

"Because you don't believe that I can?"

"Because I need to."

She handed him the knife. "Only for you, I give this up."

"Sit by the fire," he said. "Warm yourself."

"Do you know I love you?"

"Only because I can cook."

"That is your charm, yes."

He rolled up the sleeves of the red kimono. "Any cream?"

"Of course. There are also some very fine anchovies in the larder. And potatoes, onions and garlic."

Escoffier opened the door to the pantry and not only were there anchovies but several sausages hanging to dry. "Is this *Andouille de Guémené*?"

"I don't know. More than likely."

He scraped a bit of mold from the sausage and sniffed it. "It is. It has that sweet hay scent. And a Toulouse sausage?"

It was and there was also salted cod, a confit of goose, two pots

of onion-and-black currant jam and a wide variety of dried beans—
mogettes, soissons and *tarbais.*

"This is heaven," he said. "Tomorrow we could make a *cassoulet.*"

"We? You will let me cook?"

"No. Of course not. I was just being polite."

And for the first time in several weeks he laughed and Sarah did,
too.

And so while the storm raged around them, the low pink house
took on the scent of home. It was as if they were the only two people
left in the world. "So you must eat with me," she said.

"I will eat."

"With me?"

"I will eat."

After all this time, nearly twenty-three years, they had never sat
down for a meal together. Escoffier had always served and watched
while she ate.

"If you do not eat with me, I will not eat."

"Then I will sit with you."

"And eat?'

"And eat."

The dining room had large windows that overlooked the cliffs and
the unforgiving night. Instead of fine china and crystal, Sarah set the
rough table as her cook always did with local pottery from Quimper.
The set of plates was naive: roughly octagonal, marigold yellow, with
paintings of the Breton men and women in their native costumes with
the same rough socks. At first, Sarah set both ends of the table, but
then reconsidered and placed the two plates in the center, so that she
and Escoffier could face the storm together.

"Tonight we shall be very much like an old married couple," she
said when she entered the kitchen. She sat and watched him as he

cleaned and then steamed the mussels in the dry cider and garlic, and fried potatoes in duck fat. *"Moules* and *frites,"* he announced when he was finished. He poured her cider into a champagne glass. "For you, madame."

"Merci."

When he took the platter into the dining room and saw the bright yellow table settings, "These plates are—"

"Charming."

"Surprising."

"Not every good meal is served on fine china, my dear Escoffier. Sit." He hesitated. "Sit," she said again.

Outside, the storm pawed at the pink stones of the house. Pushed at the windows. Knocked the shutters off their hinges. They ate together, silently, shyly. Then, quite suddenly, she said, "Be careful of Ritz, my darling. He is too nervous; too self-centered. In the end he could do to you as he did to D'Oyly Carte, the poor man. He's been confined to his bed. Did you know? What a horrible scene in the hotel."

"He's been ill for quite some time."

"Ritz means well but I am afraid he will leave you penniless."

"He is my friend."

"That is why I worry. You are too good to your friends. I know a lawyer who can help."

"There is no need for concern."

"You are too much of an artist, Escoffier. You need to think of the business side of things. Renoir has his brother so that he can paint. Someone must protect you."

This was the last thing Escoffier wanted to talk about. Sarah obviously did not understand what had happened. No one understood. *It was just an overreaction from the Board.*

"Please, Sarah, it is not your worry."

"But you are my friend and so I am making it my worry. I do know a bit about business, you know."

It was true. Through endorsements and investments, Sarah had become one of the world's richest people; her face was on everything from Pears soap to beer bottles. She was the most glamorous woman in the world. But at that moment, she suddenly seemed like a wife—somebody else's wife.

Escoffier looked at her closely. It was as if he'd never really seen her before. The candlelight betrayed her age. Her face had grown wrinkled through the years; her eyes were less filled with fire. Her wild red hair needed to be dyed again; it was streaked with so much gray that he was amazed he had not seen it before. He felt a numbness creep over him. Suddenly she was not perfection or a goddess or a muse but the *veuve Damala*. And at that moment, he was not, as he thought, a great chef, a great artist, not the spirit of France itself, but a man in borrowed clothes—children's clothes, no less.

Nothing more was said. As soon as they were finished eating, Escoffier cleared the plates.

"Are you angry with me?" she said.

"How could I be?"

"I adore César and Marie, too. And their children are such great friends of my little Lysiane and Simone. I just can see that he is not well. He's headed for some sort of breakdown."

Escoffier smiled and patted her hand. "It will be fine."

"Are you attempting to placate me?"

"Of course I am."

"Good. You should always placate me." Sarah stood to follow him into the kitchen, but he kissed her forehead.

"Please," he said. "Let me."

Once the door closed behind him, Escoffier felt that old rush of excitement again. It had been too long since he stood in a kitchen and tried to make sense of what should be called "dinner." He wanted to make a special dish for Sarah, something he could name after her and maybe put on the menu at the Ritz when it opened.

He was at work again. Happy.

Escoffier took the bones of the fish and the head, a bit of minced onion, leek and then thyme, and added to it a glass of white wine and a pint of water.

Sarah came into the kitchen. "How long?"

"Go away."

He tossed a handful of pink peppercorns into the boiling fumet, and then set it to simmer. *Cream for the sauce,* he thought, but was not sure what else. *The reserved fumet enriched with butter, of course. More wine? Champagne? Anchovies?* Each time he found a possible ingredient, he imagined it combined in every possible way; he could taste it without tasting a thing. And with each ingredient, he thought of the Sarah of the stage, not the woman in the next room. The Divine Sarah with her pink lips, pink cheeks, the opulent river of copper hair, and the impossible silver tone, like a flute, of her voice.

Slightly less than half an hour had passed when Escoffier arrived in the dining room with a platter of four perfect pink fillets in a delicate sauce of cream and onion-and-black currant jam.

"For you, madame."

"C'est très magnifique."

"It is magnificent—as you are," he said and served her as if she were dining at The Savoy. He plated the fish and then draped sauce over it. He stood and waited for her to taste it.

"It is as magnificent as the Divine Sarah is," she said. "Rosine Bernardt, *veuve Damala,* is another matter."

She knew him so well.

"Eat," he said.

"And if I eat, tomorrow we will make the *cassoulet*? Together?"

"Together."

"And that is a lie, of course."

"A tender one."

"Are you happy?"

"I am."

"And yet?"

"If only you were not Sarah. Just Rosine. How lovely our lives could be."

"There's never been a lie told so sweetly before."

"Sarah—"

"Here I am known as *Veuve Damala*."

"But this is not the world we live in."

"It is tonight."

And so she took his hand in hers and kissed it gently. "I have always loved you, Cook," she said. "And I will love you until the very day that I die."

Chef, he thought, *not "Cook."*

The Complete Escoffier: A Memoir in Meals

MIGNONETTES D'AGNEAU SAINTE-ALLIANCE
The Circles of Peace

I have given this a great deal of thought and I now believe that Saint Fortunat should depose Saint Laurent from his position as the patron saint of butchers, cooks in general and the *rôtisseur* in particular, although I am not sure whom to speak to about this.

Saint Laurent has always been an imposter in the representation of *gourmandise* for he often was given to fasting and his only culinary experience was that he was broiled to death over a rather large grill. There is no record of his ever cooking anything. Although, according to Saint Ambrose, he apparently did tell his torturers, "This side is done. Turn me over and have a bite." Perhaps that is why he is also the patron saint of comedians.

The feast day of Saint Laurent is August 10 and is always celebrated with cold cuts—how unimaginative. Impossible, in fact. There must be a better representation of cooks in heaven because while I have grilled many types of meat on what the Americans call the "barbecue," including the weenie that was made famous in France after the Great War, I would not want to pray to a weenie for culinary intervention.

Saint Fortunat, however, has always done his very best for me, and

despite the fact that he is now the patron saint of male chefs exclusively,
I am sure he would gladly intervene for the ladies who brave this profession. He did, after all, have many close friendships with females,
the nature of which church writings define as "chaste, pious, delicate
friendships that included the type of charming child's play usually
marking feminine friendship."

I have no idea what the church means exactly by that but Fortunat
was known to deliver baskets of exotic foods to women with personal
poems for their eyes only—and we all know where that sort of behavior leads.

While known for temperance and stability, he was also as competi-
tive as any modern chef. When the sisters of the convent would deliver
their milk and eggs they would sometimes include dainty dishes and
savory meats artistically arranged on plates they had actually made
themselves from clay. Not to be outdone, he would amaze them with
flowers, filling an entire room with lavender and roses, or delicate
glazed chestnuts presented in a sugar basket that he had woven to look
like fine Belgian lace. And he was totally blind. I know many sighted
men who could not do the same. If this is not a miracle, I am not sure
what is.

I also believe it is fair to say that Saint Fortunat created the basis for
the modern menu. Although he could not see, he was a great wanderer
who traveled through Italy and France in search of fine food and drink.
He often paid for his supper with poetry that he wrote in honor of the
meal, praising each dish. Think of it. If a menu is not poetry what is it,
then?

His many excellent poems extolling the virtues of gastronomy,
although unfortunately all in Latin, have been transcribed by Monsieur
Gringoire, the secretary of *La Ligue des Gourmands*, an organization
of the greatest living French chefs in London, which I created and of
which I have served as president. And so, being founder and past presi-

dent, I have announced that upon Saint Fortunat's feast day, the *Ligue des Gourmands* will feast forever more.

There is nothing noble in hunger. During the Great War, twice a week everyone was forced to give up meat and potatoes. To buy meat or chicken, you had to have a coupon. And, perhaps most crushing of all, the government set the price of fish so high that few could afford it and so my supplier would stock very little.

Of course, all adversity presents opportunity.

Venison was exempt, as were eggs, fish, giblets, and bacon. However, the only deer that we could procure was quite old. No matter. With the help of Saint Fortunat and a *daube à la Provençale* featuring a sauce made from anchovy, garlic, capers and a touch of tomato, we served the old meat on a bed of noodles with a chestnut puree. It made for a charming stew. And since we needed at least thirty to forty salmon a week to remain open, we would travel to Scotland and Ireland many times a week, making friends with the fishermen there and buying their catch for a fraction of what it would have been through the distributor. Opportunity was everywhere.

So you see, with the eyes of Saint Fortunat upon you, you can master all setbacks. There was no butter and so I cooked in cocoa butter. There was no fish to be had and so we made do with "fish" of our own creation: finely minced chicken patties dipped in egg and rolled in breadcrumbs. No one knew the difference and so we charged as if they were the real thing. We had no choice. It was our patriotic duty to create a world where there was not a war going on, because to dine at the Carlton made people quite happy and made them feel quite normal. Even when the bombs were crashing all around the city and the sky threatened to become dark with the Zeppelin airships the Carlton could still serve sole on a bed of macaroni *à la Napolitaine*, as if the Germans did not even exist. And so the people came and opened their hearts to us and, luckily, their purses, too.

To feast is to live. Saint Fortunat knew that to be true. And every single time I have invoked him in prayer, he has blessed me with a great success.

Armistice Day. November 11, 1918. 1 p.m. The terrible nightmare was over and I suddenly had 712 reserved for dinner service at the Carlton. Rationing had ravaged my kitchen. I only had six legs of lamb, two small veal haunches, fifteen kilograms of fresh pork and ten chickens. By most standards, this was not enough for a meal for so many but there was such joy in the streets that I could not bear to turn anyone away.

The terrible years were over. Everyone was hungry.

I knew from the Prussian War that if a horse is properly seasoned it can make a fine meal. Along with the limited meat that I had, which I minced together, I had twenty kilograms of canned *pâté de foie gras*, some minced truffles, ten kilograms of bread mixed with sterilized cream and a few moments to run to the cathedral and light a candle in honor of Saint Fortunat.

Never lose your head, even when faced with great difficulty—that must be the motto of every *chef de cuisine*. I prayed to the saint and I could feel him listening to me. On the way back to my kitchen I created in my mind a dish of small *noisettes* and called it *"Mignonettes d'agneau Sainte-Alliance,"* which, despite the fact that it was actually named after a concept offered by Brillat-Savarin in his *Physiology of Taste* as a way to honor the jewels of *haute cuisine—foie gras*, ortolans and truffle—it was translated by my manager as "Mignonettes of Lamb of the Holy Alliance," and suggested to be my brilliant metaphor regarding peace.

Who am I to argue?

And was the dish lamb? It was lamb enough. That is all that can be said.

Even though we were short on supplies, to celebrate peace all one needs to do is to name a few dishes for Allies, such as "Canadian Potatoes" and "Englishwoman's Peas," and serve for the finale something that appeals to the sentimental heart as did my "Bombes of Conviviality" and "Symbols of Peace." Everyone is happy because the war is over and though they don't speak the French language and only recognize a few words, such as "peace" and "English," food always sounds better in French.

This meal eventually brought me great acclaim. The next year, on the anniversary of the day that peace was signed, Mr. Poincaré, President of the French Republic, held a reception in London and much to my surprise presented me with the famed *Chevalier de la Légion d'Honneur*. The award was first given by Napoléon Bonaparte in recognition of excellence and achievement. This memory is engraved on my heart and it is all because of Saint Fortunat and a blessed sleight of hand.

Unfortunately, our dear Saint Fortunat shows us by example that how one speaks of food is more important than what is on the plate. This is incorrect, and perhaps is at the core of why the Vatican will not assign him the role of our patron saint.

Words, you see, are always inadequate.

The moment when you find your baby son sleeping on the kitchen floor, and you pick him up and carry him back to his own bed, and pull the soft worn wool blanket around his neck so that he does not grow cold, does not suffer, and he wakes and says, "God is hiding in my room," and you say, sadly, "He is hiding everywhere" and kiss your small son and taste the salt of his tears—a moment like this cannot be explained because you cannot be certain that these words which engage you will engage someone else in the same way. Even many years later when you find yourself standing by your son's grave, there are no words that can describe that moment, the depth of it.

But a sauce can reflect that moment exactly. Nothing speaks more accurately to the complexity of life than food. Who has not had, let us say, a béarnaise, the child of hollandaise, and has not come away from the taste of it feeling overwhelmed?

At first, it fills the mouth with the softness of butter and then the richness of egg, and before it becomes too rich or too comfortable, the moment shifts and begins to ground itself in darkness with the root of a shallot and the hint of crushed peppercorn. But then, the taste deepens. The memory of rebirth is made manifest with the sacred chervil, sweet and grassy with a note of licorice, whose spring scent is so like myrrh that it recalls the gift of the Wise Men and the holy birth whenever it is tasted. And then, of course, the "King of Herbs," tarragon with its gentle licorice, reminds us not to forget that miracles are possible. And just when we think we understand what we are experiencing, the taste turns again on the tongue, and finishes with shrill vinegar followed by a reduction of wine so that the acid tempers the sauce but never dominates. And, finally, in your mouth, you have the entire experience of father and child that you tried to put into words—from the fleeting comfort to the moment where you finally realize that life is beyond your control and everything needs balance, even faith.

A menu is the orchestration of that experience on a large scale—a world view, as it were.

If I were to create a menu in honor of spring, each and every dish would be some level of green, even the tablecloths would be replaced by soft new grass. To me, the spring is a soft gentle rebirth; it fills the heart with freshness. Even if the diner does not like lima beans, it matters not. A puree of lima beans cannot help but remind one of the fleeting nature of the season.

Unfortunately, and I believe this is because of the reign of Saint Laurent as our patron, many chefs have forgotten the power of a menu. I recently was the guest of honor at a very large dinner in America where they served ice in the water and no wine at supper. The menu was just bits and pieces of things to eat. And so when I was asked to address the group, I reminded them that they needed to do their best to preserve the high standards of French cuisine and not call themselves "cooks" but "*cuisiniers.*"

"A *cuisinier,*" I said, "is a man with professional competence, personal initiative and experienced in his craft: a cook is a man who, too often, has only one tool, a can opener."

A menu, quite frankly, should be how a chef, an artist in his own right, sees the world. Not bits and pieces of things to eat.

While taste conveys the complexity of life, a good chef should keep in mind that food can have a meaning that is often not apparent but affects the palate nonetheless. For example, the "A1 sauce" is now very popular in America. I have tried it. It is very good. What is not understood is that when one takes a bite of a steak that has been smothered in "A1" as the sauce was proclaimed by King George IV, they are eating history. The combination of malt vinegar, dates, mango chutney, apples and orange marmalade all serve as a reminder that the United States was settled by England and will always be England's. The bold combination of malt vinegar and orange marmalade—England's lifeblood—and those flavors of England's conquered—mango from India and apples so strongly identified with America—cannot be ignored.

Food is never as simple as one thinks it is. It is much more dangerous—seducing completely.

If you were to ask what one menu defines me, I would have to say it would be the final dinner that I served Kaiser Wilhelm II upon the *Imperator.* I would also have to say that it also defines my wife, the great poet Delphine Daffis. Perhaps in many ways, it defines her more.

25

THE GIFT SHOULD HAVE BEEN PERFECT FOR SARAH—A rare white truffle from Alba. The story of it was charming. The truffle was scented by Louie, a rather lazy yet prized pink pig, who discovered it by accident. The truffle was found out of season in late December. Highly unusual. The pig had been running loose along the snowy foothills of the Italian Piedmont Mountains. He'd escaped, actually. The farmer thought the pig was gone for good when he came upon the beast snorting with pleasure, and perhaps relief. Louie had been very unlucky that year. He was fleeing his own slaughter.

"I thought the damn beast had gotten too old," the farmer told Escoffier.

"Age is merely a number."

Escoffier was in Paris working on yet another book, this one for housewives, even though he had just published the fourth edition of *Le Guide Culinaire* a few years before. He was also making plans for a celebration of his eightieth birthday—a third trip to America.

"Age has no relevance to productivity."

Sarah was also in Paris, making movies again. One leg. One lung. One kidney. Through the years, she had been losing parts of herself, but it made no difference to her. "As long as I can talk, I can work."

And she loved film. Her first movie, *Le Duel d'Hamlet*, was an early silent shown with an accompanying Edison cylinder. Nearly a dozen films and a decade later, she was 79 years old and starring in talkies. Her house on Boulevard Péreire was to be transformed into a set.

"I will be perched on pillows, with the cameras rolling," she wrote him. "It is in spending oneself that one becomes rich."

"Age makes no difference at all," Escoffier told the farmer. "Work keeps you young."

The white truffle was the size of a hazelnut, firm and velvet to the touch. Escoffier told the farmer to charge it to the Ritz, although he had been retired from the company for many years. *It's the least they can do after all I've done.* The truffle was worth hundreds of francs, so much more than he had. It was so perfect for Sarah, he couldn't help it. *They will not begrudge me this,* he told himself and hoped he was right.

Escoffier wrapped the white truffle in a velvet pouch and the next day appeared at Sarah's door. Her son, Maurice, embraced him, and yet did not let him in.

"Another day, perhaps."

Escoffier was surprised. He had heard that Sarah was ill, but she had been ill all her life. *It will pass,* he thought, it always did, and he wondered when Maurice, the baby that nursed at Sarah's breast, had grown into this sad, elegant graying man.

Escoffier stored the rare truffle in a jar of Arborio rice and placed it in the back of the closet of his small *pied-à-terre*. In the cool darkness, the delicate taste would be somewhat preserved, but he knew that every day the truffle was not eaten it would diminish in its beauty. The rice would slow its decay, but also leach the taste.

Day after day, Escoffier called Maurice to ask if Sarah was able to take visitors. She was not. Escoffier did not move the truffle. He couldn't even look at it.

Time wore away at them both.

The Ritz was not pleased with Escoffier's "purchase." When a young man from accounting appeared at Escoffier's door, the chef let him in, served him tea, and explained the company's options as he saw it.

"I am nearly eighty years old. My name is synonymous with the Ritz. If you wish to garnish my pension, you have that choice. Since the truffle was a gift for Miss Bernhardt, a national treasure, I'm sure the newspapers will be very interested in whatever action you take against me."

Escoffier never heard from the Accounting Department again.

In March, Maurice finally called. Sarah was well enough to begin filming *The Fortune Teller*. She could see him, if only for a moment.

It had been nearly four months since the truffle had been pulled from the ground. Every time Escoffier had opened his closet, he tried not to think of it sitting there, but it was impossible. It was waiting, waning. The idea worried at him. He knew that after all this time, the rice had absorbed whatever taste remained and, perhaps, could not even hold that fleeting beauty in its grains.

Still, when her son finally called, Escoffier gently took the glass jar and placed it in the velvet pouch—*Whatever discovery we make, we make together*—and took the first cab to Sarah's house on Boulevard Pereire.

"She is not well," the son had told him and Maurice looked grave when he arrived, but Escoffier was not prepared for the truth of it. When the door to her sitting room opened, it was filled with serious young people nodding their heads, adjusting lights, arguing, eating, smoking, laughing, and pushing the black beast of a camera back and forth as if it were unwilling to be tamed. In the center of it all was Sarah. Her eyes were dull, her face expressionless. It was as if she were waiting, not for the next shot, but for something darker.

Escoffier's chest began to hurt.

"Quiet!" a man shouted, and the room fell silent.

Later Escoffier would not remember what she had said, what lines she had spoken. All he would remember is that when the filming began her silver bell of a voice, undiminished by time, rang out. Clear, strong. It brought tears to his eyes. *Age matters not.* But when the shot was over, darkness again. The room quickly became undone. He was shaking when Maurice led him to her chaise. He kissed her pink painted cheeks.

"The legend remains victorious in spite of history," she whispered.

"Are you hungry?"

"Aren't you?"

Her son wheeled her into the kitchen and left the two of them alone.

There was a bottle of Moët on ice, chilling. And eggs. Six. Garlic. Cream. Escoffier opened the velvet pouch. "It is very rare," he said. "As you are." But when he poured out the rice, the stench was overwhelming, like old chicken. He sliced the truffle. It had turned clay-orange and brittle.

"*Quand même,*" Sarah said and then she laughed: all bones and fury.

And he laughed, too.

The eggs went uncooked. The champagne was not drunk.

Outside the window, the city of Paris, the city of smoke and silk, was silent.

"I love you, Cook," she said.

"Chef."

Over four thousand times Sarah had died on stage but nothing prepared her for actually dying. It was so quiet. *I was mistaken,* she thought. The next day, the camera caught the shift in her: the slight tug, the slip. The scene was over. Sarah was carried to her bed. Crowds gathered outside of her house for days. Waiting. Maurice issued hourly reports.

"I'll keep them dangling," she said. "They've tortured me all my life, now I'll torture them."

When the bells rang out and all of Paris took to the streets, weeping, Escoffier did not join them. He could not.

It was time to go home.

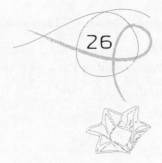

26

THE MAN FROM CUNARD HAD BEEN UNCLEAR. ESCOFFIER was only told that he would be a guest of the cruise line and that his passage to America would be a gift for his eightieth birthday from his former employer. He'd be traveling on the RMS *Berengaria*, the Millionaire's Liner. That was understood. The letter was friendly; it mentioned that the ship was named after Queen Bérengère, who had married Eleanor of Aquitaine's son Richard I.

"The Queen and her Richard lived apart for decades," the Man from Cunard wrote, "but we would not be so cruel as to separate you from your wife the famed poetess Delphine Daffis. It would be our great honor if she could join you on this voyage."

The irony did not escape Escoffier. After sending back a confirmation for one, he promptly lost the letter. He was, after all, back in Paris again. Alone. It was difficult to keep things in order. Retirement at La Villa Fernand had not been going well. *Again.* It was not so much the children and Delphine but the city itself. Monte Carlo had too much of the wrong kind of noise, the fidgeting sounds of everyday life. Paris was where he wanted to be but Delphine refused to leave her home and all the children. And so the chef wrote back saying that Madame Escoffier was too ill to travel and when he found out that she actually was, he was surprised but secretly relieved.

However, that was all the Man from Cunard wrote.

When Escoffier arrived at the dock, the massive ship gave him an uneasy feeling. It was as large as a small city, teeming with thousands of people. It looked very much like the *Titanic*. The Man from Cunard met him on the boarding platform and held his arm as they walked up the long plank.

The man was tall and thin, nondescript, like so many young men of the time. "Happy Birthday," he said when he saw Escoffier and slapped his back as if they were old friends.

The Man from Cunard was American, of course. From "New York," he said and continued talking, barely taking a breath. Escoffier could only understand a few words. Something about "flappers," which made him hope that Josephine Baker was also on board with her *La Révue Nègre* from the *Folies Bergères*. He knew she had taken to the flapper style of costume. And then something about "millionaires." The young man used the word so frequently, and with such zeal, that Escoffier did not have the heart to say to him, *"Je ne parle pas l'anglais,"* even though it was true. After all those years in England and two trips to America, Escoffier was still stubbornly ignorant of English, was still afraid that it would taint his ability to cook. And so he just nodded and smiled, knowing that the young are easily entertained by the sound of their own voice.

"We need to wait for Monsieur Bertrand," Escoffier said.

The directors of the London Cunard Lines had arranged for the chef to travel with the inspector of Cunard Line's restaurants, an old friend.

The Man from Cunard recognized the inspector's name and tapped his watch. "Late," he said.

Escoffier understood. His old friend was always late.

The Man from Cunard grabbed Escoffier's elbow and led him through the crowd. When the ship's captain was introduced, he seemed to be like many captains Escoffier had met before—he was of a comforting age, just gray around the temples, and neatly pressed.

For a moment, Escoffier wondered if that was true of the captain of the *Titanic*. Did he have that cool grace? He couldn't remember. They'd met before the ship left the dock but Escoffier could not remember a single thing about him.

On the other hand, Escoffier remembered his own staff in great detail, and often. The Widow's Fund he'd set up for them was still doing well and for the past fourteen years he'd been able to send yearly checks and notes of encouragement.

It was the very least he could do. He'd been asked to travel along on that voyage, to supervise, but declined. His staff was furious with him. The menus he'd created were too ambitious to cook in a kitchen that rolled with the waves. The last meal aboard the *Titanic* was remarkable. It was a celebration of cuisine that would have impressed the most jaded palate.

There were ten courses in all, beginning with oysters and a choice of *Consommé Olga*, a beef and port wine broth served with glazed vegetables and julienned gherkins, or Cream of Barley Soup. Then there were plate after plate of main courses—Poached Salmon and Cucumbers with *Mousseline* Sauce, a hollandaise enriched with whipped cream; Filet Mignon Lili, steaks fried in butter, then topped with an artichoke bottom, *foie gras* and truffle and served with a *Périgueux* sauce; a sauté of Chicken *Lyonnaise*; Lamb with Mint Sauce; Roast Duckling with Apple Sauce; Roast Squab with Cress and Sirloin of Beef.

There were also a garden's worth of vegetables, prepared both hot and cold. And several potatoes—Château Potatoes, cut to the shape of olives and cooked gently in clarified butter until golden and *Parmentier* Potatoes, a pureed potato mash garnished with crouton and chervil. And, of course, *pâté de foie gras.*

To cleanse the palate, there was a sixth course of *Punch à la Romaine*, dry champagne, simple sugar syrup, the juice of two oranges and two lemons, and a bit of their zest. The mixture was steeped, strained, fortified with rum, frozen, topped with a sweet meringue and served like a sorbet. For dessert there was a choice of Waldorf Pudding, Peaches in Chartreuse Jelly, Chocolate and Vanilla Éclairs and French ice cream. Each course was served with a different wine. The final cheese course was served with fresh fruits and followed by coffee and cigars accompanied by port and, if desired, distilled spirits.

And this was just for first class passengers. Second and third classes were also catered to.

And the ship was sinking.

His staff must have spent their last hours exhausted and cursing him.

"Would you like to see the kitchen?" the Man from Cunard asked.

Escoffier shook his head. The word "kitchen" needed no translation.

As the tour progressed, and the Man from Cunard showed him the parlors and lounges of the vast ship, the velvet upon metal of it, Escoffier found himself thinking of other things. Not his eightieth birthday celebration, nor the elegance of New York, nor the possibility of Miss Baker and her revue performing that evening, but upsetting things, like the lawsuit against Monsieur Delsaut, who kept advertising that he was a student of Escoffier, and the letter Delphine had sent before he left. Yes, it did save him from lying to the Man from Cunard, but it was somewhat alarming: all about her legs and hands, and how they went numb from time to time.

"Neuritis," the doctor called it and even though Delphine had written and said that it wasn't too serious, Escoffier wrote back promising to return to La Villa Fernand for a day or two.

"A holiday. And then back to work."

What work?

He knew Delphine would think that when she received his reply. She had begun to speak of his work as if each new book or article was a faded flag to be used in his surrender from this world, folded over him in death.

"I'm not planning to die," he always told her.

The Man from Cunard took Escoffier back topside and made some sort of joke about the lifeboats, at least Escoffier thought he did. The swinging boats seemed hungry. The Man from Cunard kept pointing at them and laughing; the wit of his comments was lost on the wind.

Escoffier smiled to be polite, but a numbing sensation came over him and part of his vision began to slip away. It was as if a storm cloud covered part of his right eye; there was flashing out of the corner of it and then darkness. In the left, everything had turned mosaic.

The great ship bellowed. A warning. "All aboard," someone shouted. A flurry of people popped champagne and waved goodbye to those on the docks below.

Overhead Escoffier thought he saw a large flock of pure white birds. *Doves?* He squinted to see them, but it was difficult. He was quickly losing his sight.

"*Je suis aveugle*," he said and pointed to his eyes. Blind.

"Blue," the Man from Cunard said and pointed at his own eyes.

The white birds banked again, low this time. Escoffier wondered if anyone else could see them. They passed so closely, if he reached out, he knew he could touch them.

All around him, everyone continued drinking champagne, kissing, laughing, even though the birds flew fast and low through the crowds, weaving in and out. The sight of them made Escoffier's heart beat faster. The sun was sinking into the sea, the sky was streaked with red. The Man from Cunard took two glasses from a passing waiter and held his own high.

"Toast," he said, and then said something about "peace."

How odd, Escoffier thought. *1926. The world is at peace. Isn't it?*

"Could we sit?" the old man asked.

The Man from Cunard cocked his head to one side, confused.

Escoffier pointed at a row of deck chairs filled with passengers, and that seemed to make the man even more confused.

How can these Americans not speak French?

"Sit," Escoffier said again and mimicked sitting in an imaginary chair. "I need to sit down." His eyesight was becoming more and more narrow. Soon the world would become a pinpoint.

The man nodded as if he understood but took Escoffier by the arm past chair after chair, and down below deck.

It wasn't worth arguing over, the old man thought. *I'll finish the tour and then rest in my stateroom.*

They followed the arrows to the pool, obviously a point of pride for the cruise line; the Man from Cunard kept repeating the word "famous," which Escoffier knew, and when the man opened the door to the swimming area, he understood why he had continued to use that word.

The pool was two decks high, Pompeian style. Next to it was a Turkish bath suite, with two hot rooms and parquet floors. It was tiled with small Italian mosaic designs. Escoffier knew it well. The last time he'd seen it, it was filled with Germans, the Kaiser was smiling in the corner, satiated and happy.

The ship itself was famous. Very famous.

"This is the *Imperator,*" Escoffier said.

The Man from Cunard recognized the name of the Kaiser's ship, a near doppelganger to the *Titanic*. He seemed pleased that he was finally being understood. He nodded enthusiastically. "The old girl is called *Berengaria* now," he said slowly, loudly, as if Escoffier were deaf. "Spoils of War!" he was shouting. People turned.

The blindness was now complete.

THE DOCTOR WAS NOT ALARMED. "YOU WORK TOO HARD,
Escoffier. It is only a migraine, although it could have
been a stroke," he said and confined the old man to bed.
"At least for the night. The casino will still be there tomorrow.
Bertrand will come around to check on you in the morning. He
has a full day planned."

Escoffier smiled weakly.

The Man from Cunard looked pale, hovering over him.

"Could you send the young man away," Escoffier said to the doctor.
"With my gratitude, of course."

"Americans," the doctor laughed. "Such a young and earnest people." He put his arm around the nervous man. Whispered something
in his ear. The Man from Cunard turned back to Escoffier, nodded
and quickly left.

"I hope you're hungry," the doctor said. "I sent him for food. I suspect you haven't eaten all day."

It was true.

"The seas should be very still this time of year, but there is always the odd wave," the doctor said. "Try broth at first if you must, but eat. Cunard will make sure that you are fed at least six times a day. It will be their pleasure. They have a very fine kitchen."

"I designed it."

"That's right. I'd forgotten." He shook Escoffier's hand. "Dinner will be here in an hour or so. We make a tart out of snow apples which cannot be missed."

"Snow apples? Very rare."

"Sleep until then."

The doctor turned off the lights and closed the cabin door gently behind him. The boat was already out to sea. Escoffier's stateroom was elaborate with large windows that looked out onto the waters, the hesitant moonlight.

He closed his eyes and tried to remember the taste of snow apples. When he was a child, there was a gnarled tree of them behind his father's blacksmith shop. His mother would always pick them but there were never enough for more than a single tart. Spicy and yet sweet, like McIntosh, but the flesh was so impossibly white, pristine, and the juice was so abundant, that it was like no other apple he had ever tasted.

He fell asleep dreaming of them, the soft flesh against his teeth.

Hours later, Escoffier was deep in sleep when there was a knock at the door of his stateroom. In a moment of confusion, his dream shifted. He suddenly was standing once more in the back of the dining room of the *Imperator*. It was 1913. The world was on the edge of war, although Kaiser Wilhelm swore to all the newspapers, "I am only interested in peace."

Escoffier had believed him. It was impossible not to. Every time he'd see the man, the chef couldn't stop thinking of Dear Old Bertie trying to buy women for the strangely shy boy with the withered hand. Wilhelm may have been the German Emperor, the King of

Prussia, but Escoffier always thought of him as who he had been, Queen Victoria's sad grandson.

After the dinner service was complete, "Stay," the Emperor told Escoffier. "Sit with me. We are friends after all, are we not?"

The ballroom was filled with German dignitaries and military men. After their plates were cleared, an evening of film began. Everything was in German. One film was about lobster fishing and starred a lovely French actress. Escoffier didn't need to know what was being said; the actress was beautiful and so he enjoyed it greatly. The next was roughly edited, badly lit, badly shot, but nonetheless its intent was clear. It was a German intelligence film. The footage explained the submarine maneuvers of the French fleet in Tunis.

The Kaiser was planning to attack France.

Escoffier didn't remember leaving the ballroom. He'd like to think he'd gotten up as soon as he figured out what was happening. He'd like to think he'd climbed into a lifeboat and made his way through the rough seas and back to shore where he called the Palace and demanded to speak to Prince Edward. He'd like to think he did all that.

But he didn't. It was Queen Victoria's grandson, after all. The Emperor. He couldn't cause a scene. His reputation would be called into question and that would be bad for business.

And so Escoffier went to his room and said nothing.

The next morning, the Kaiser requested a meeting with him.

"Do you remember the dinner with Léon Gambetta at Le Petit Moulin Rouge? That Bernhardt creature served us. Do you remember?"

As soon as the meal was mentioned, Escoffier thought of Xavier lying on the floor, his silent head on Sarah's lap. His blood everywhere.

"I remember," he said. Xavier's vineyard in Alsace still belonged to the family of the German officer. They still made the finest wine in the region. He hadn't thought of Xavier in such a long time. "I remember it quite well. I remember every menu I have ever created."

"Gambetta told us of your conversation in the wine cellar. 'Judas,' he called you and meant it kindly. 'You can always trust Escoffier,' he said, 'because he doesn't have the conviction to be Paul. Food is his only God.' "

Escoffier went pale.

The Emperor leaned over and patted his hand. "My friend, do not looked shocked. I only tell you this because I want to say that I have trusted you through the years. We have all trusted you. My grandmother, that horrible Bertie, Gambetta—even Bernhardt, I suspect.

"I only needed to taste the lamb you made that evening, which I sometimes still dream of, to know that you do not care for country, or women, or God. For some that would make you a heathen. For me, that makes you the perfect man. You are untainted by affection or loyalty or love. I admire that. That sort of distance from the heart allows for greatness. It is a trait that I also share."

And then he walked away.

Later that morning, the Emperor's press secretary fed a story to newspapers around the world about the conversation that took place between the two men.

"I am the Emperor of Germany, but you are the Emperor of Chefs."

And so many years later, aboard the former *Imperator*, the door to Escoffier's stateroom opened. Light flooded in. The old man sat up squinting.

"Dinner is served," the Man from Cunard said and rolled a room service table into the stateroom. It was filled with food, so many courses at the same time.

Escoffier was still in his dream.

"Daniel?" he said.

"Dinner," the Man from Cunard corrected.

"God hides everywhere, Daniel."

"Yes, dinner is served."

The Man from Cunard touched Escoffier's shoulder and the dream deflated. The old man looked at the table filled with plates and at the Man from Cunard, who did not look like Daniel at all.

"Dinner," the man said again.

"It will all grow cold, will it not?"

"Oui," the Man from Cunard said, proudly. It was obviously the only French he knew. "And for dessert," he continued and lifted the silver dome off a china plate. "Hot Apple Pie!"

Snow apples.

It was a large golden tart. The old man took his fork and tested the flake of the pastry. Perfect. The fruit was firm and yet when he pressed it with his fork, it was still juicy, and so white. One bite, that was all he needed. The spice of it held its own against the nutmeg and cinnamon. The flavor was so pure and clean. *So innocent,* he thought.

The Man from Cunard waited for the pronouncement.

"Merci," Escoffier said. *"Très bon."*

He took a pen and paper from the bedside stand and wrote a quick note to Monsieur Bertrand, asking if the inspector could have a bushel of snow apples sent to La Villa Fernand. He knew they would not deny him.

"No note required," Escoffier wrote. "Madame will know."

At the banquet in New York for his eightieth birthday, a "brilliant reception at the Ritz Carlton" as the newspapers called it, Escoffier was presented with a golden plaque on which two laurel branches were linked by the medal of the French *Légion d'Honneur.*

He was now an international hero, not just of the Prussian War but also of the Great War. He had been decorated for using French cooking to keep the morale of England high and commended for raising seventy-five thousand francs to distribute among the wives and children of his staff who had been called to the Front. He had also employed the veterans of the world war in his kitchen. And, of course, there was the matter of the loss of his Daniel. That was mentioned, too.

The newspaper noted that he spoke at great length with a "cheerful and paternal tone" and everyone applauded him warmly.

"The art of cooking is that of diplomacy," he would later say. "I have been able to place two thousand French chefs into positions all over the world. Like a grain of wheat sown, they have taken root."

The menu was lovely and unforgettable. And was presented without translation, which pleased Escoffier greatly.

Caviar Frais d'Astrakan
Pain Grillé
Le Rossolnick

• • •

La Mousse de Sole Escortée
du Cardinal des mers à
l'Américaine

• • •

Les Noisettes de Pré-Salé
Favorite
Les Petits Pois à la Française

• • •

Le Perdreaux à la Casserole

• • •

La Salade Coeurs d'Endives
Châtelaine
Les Belles Angevines aux
Fruits d'Or

• • •

Les Mignardises
Café Moka

The Man from Cunard had no idea what he was eating. The applause was deafening.

Two weeks later, Escoffier found himself on the quiet doorstep of La Villa Fernand, finally home, but thinking of the American, the idiotic way the Man from Cunard smiled at everything, and shouted at everything, but how in the evenings he always made sure that Escoffier received his nightcap, the warm milk, raw egg and split of champagne. Escoffier missed the way the man would take him by the arm and carefully lead him through a crowded room. And how neatly the man trimmed all the newspaper articles about his visit and put them in an envelope and mailed them to Madame Escoffier without his asking.

The Man from Cunard did everything that was asked of him, and some things that were not, but whatever he did he did with a great enthusiasm that, eventually, endeared him to the old chef. It was only at the moment when Escoffier reached his villa that he realized two things. First, that the Man from Cunard would be greatly missed. Second, he had forgotten to get his name.

Escoffier knocked on the door of La Villa Fernand, but no one answered. He left his bags on the stoop and let himself in. Delphine had sent the children, grandchildren, great-grandchildren, grand-nieces and grandnephews away, along with the staff. They were alone in the great house together. There was no bell for dinner. No supper on the table.

Delphine, however, had made a small cake for him. It sat in the center of the great table in the dining room.

"We will be like the Russians and eat our cake first."

"And then?"

"More cake."

"Perhaps something more than cake? Supper?"

"There is no supper."

"A bit of fruit? There must be fruit. Aren't apples in season?"

"Yes."

"Apples, then."

"We had apples. Snow apples."

"Very lovely."

"I ate them."

"All of them?"

"They were very lovely. Jeanne and Paul said they were very rare, apparently. Almost impossible to come by."

"And?"

"They were extremely good. I believe they were from Mr. Boots, although I have not heard from him in such a long time. Is he still in Southsea?"

"We've lost touch."

"Really? That's very sad."

"Was there a card?"

"No."

"Perhaps I sent them."

"Why would you send them?"

She raised an eyebrow as if expecting an answer.

"You are right, as always. There is no need to send you gifts of love, as you have my love and I have yours."

"You are very confident. Oh, yes. You are Escoffier. You have every reason to be confident."

"And you are Madame Escoffier."

"And yet, Georges, you do not send me snow apples."

Georges.

"Then let me cook for you, Madame. Let me win your heart again. I will send the girl to town for truffles, *foie gras* and a case of champagne."

"Everyone has left and there is no money."

"There must be something in the house, then. Squab? Venison? Lamb, perhaps. How many stocks do we have? The white, of course. Beef? Fish?"

"There is no stock."

"Jam? Tomatoes? Pickled onions? Honey? Candied lavender? How can there not be food in my kitchen?"

"We have potatoes. Cheese. Butter. Cream. And it is not your kitchen. It is my kitchen."

"And for meats?"

"Your pension check has not arrived yet."

"The cake?"

"The last of the flour."

Escoffier sat back in his chair. "But I would like to cook for you."

"When was the last time you cooked anything?"

That was a very good question. In Paris, he never had to cook. He could always eat at the Ritz or with friends or fellow chefs. "Six years, perhaps. Maybe eight. But it is like swimming. One never forgets how to swim."

She looked wary. "*Aligot*, then."

"I cannot make you mashed potatoes."

"*Aligot* is a meal."

Delphine rose from the table, haltingly. The neuritis, as the doctor called it, was obviously serious and seemed to be progressing. She put her apron around her neck but could not tie it. Her hand went limp.

"Let me," Escoffier said and tied it into a bow, kissed the back of her neck. She picked up a Windsor pan with her good hand, added a fist of butter and placed it on the lowest of heat. "So you are hungry?"

"I am hungry."

"You are always hungry, you old goat."

"It is the one thing you never have complained about."

She took a steamer from the overhead rack, and nearly dropped it.

Escoffier took the pan from her hands and put it on the stove. "Now what do we do? I've never made an *aligot* before."

"That's because goats are not very good cooks. They call themselves chefs, artists, but that is only a deflection from the fact that simple home cooking is too complicated for them. And so it is beneath them."

She went to the pantry and brought back a pail of potatoes and began washing them. "Thirty minutes on the gentlest of temperatures."

"That's a long time."

"You cannot hurry *aligot*."

"It is much like bread?"

"Escoffier, you are a very old goat with very old tricks."

"What type of goat? Breed, Madame."

She looked at him closely. "A *cou blanc*, white-haired with a dark ass."

And so he kissed her and she him. And after a time she pulled away and said, "We are cooking. Please. Control yourself. Peel and dice potatoes and put them in the steamer. Pour hot water over them and then one level dessert-spoon of salt."

"It would be better if we left the jackets on them."

"It would be better if you did it the way it's done."

"White truffles would be lovely with this."

"It would, but there are none. Peel, old man."

Delphine slowly peeled two cloves of garlic. When she tried to stir them into the melted butter, the wooden spoon slipped out of her hand. He came up behind her and put his hand over hers. She said nothing, but leaned against him gently.

When the potatoes were finally soft, she put them in a bowl and covered it with a cloth to absorb the steam. "They have to be dry," she said and when she finally tried to whisk them, again her hand failed.

The future, he thought. *So slowly we unravel into the darkness.*

He took her hand in his. It was smaller, and more brittle than he remembered. Together they slowly whipped the potatoes until the starch began to break down and when it did, she added the butter and garlic, some black pepper and a handful of cheese.

"That's too much cheese," he said. She added a handful more.

"Whisk."

Escoffier continued to whisk despite the fact that the potatoes were now like glue. She continued to add more and more cheese until nearly half a pound was used.

"This has gone to paste."

"You have to believe."

"It is inedible."

"Goats should never be allowed in the kitchen."

She tossed in another handful and the potatoes suddenly clung to the whisk. She added more. "Believe." And more. And Escoffier continued to whisk until the *aligot* became translucent with stiff glossy peaks.

She handed him a fork. "Eat."

He wanted a bowl, but did not ask for one. The *aligot* was hot and the cheese burned his mouth but he ate it and she did, too. They ate from the pan on top of the stove.

"The way they feel in your mouth," he said. "Superb."

"Yes. But now that you mention it, I do think it would have been lovely with white truffles. Much more complex."

And then he kissed her and could taste the salty rich cheese and butter and potato.

And for the first time in a long time they laughed together. *I've so missed you,* he wanted to say but was afraid it would sound untrue.

When the pan of *aligot* was finished, there was still the matter of the cake. It was Belgian chocolate with a glaze of *framboise ganache* and covered in tiny black raspberries. She placed a single wax candle on top, a squat votive from church.

"Is this not how it is done in America?"

"They put one for each year."

"Really? Why?"

"To blow them out."

"They are a very odd people."

"They are enthusiastic."

She did not light the candle. He did not blow it out. She cut the cake and served two small pieces. The crumb was beautiful; he picked at it with his fork.

"Duck eggs," she said. "The extra fat makes the difference. And they are quite convenient. There are ducks everywhere and they are indiscriminate in their mating habits."

"Very nice."

He did not eat the cake. Nor did she. The taste of *aligot* was still on their lips.

"And the voyage?" she said.

"The RMS *Berengaria* was named after an abandoned queen."

"Was it a nice boat?"

"It was the *Imperator*."

The moment felt airless. She took his hand in hers.

They sat for a while listening to the sounds of the evening. The whitecaps, gray with night, were hushed and nearly forgotten but the rumble of a distant train, the honk and squeal of automobiles and, underneath it all, the music of the cafés, each melody distinct—an accordion riff as ripe as Paris, an abandoned singer with the rain of Pissarro darkening every phrase, a battered hound of piano—and each whisper, each shout, was a story that did not need words, just beauty and gravity.

In eighty years so much had changed around La Villa Fernand and so very little.

He looked out the window into the garden. "I'm glad you planted that."

"Happiness is our best revenge."

He kissed her tenderly, with the last lushness of autumn. And even though she was not a woman given to blushing, her face flushed.

"Madame Escoffier, I have always loved you."

It no longer mattered if she believed him. Tomorrow Escoffier would go again to Paris. But that night, they held each for a long time, just listening to their hearts, their own private waltz: listening in three-quarter time.

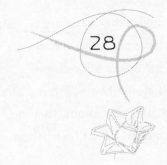

F ALL PASSED AND WINTER WAS UPON LA VILLA FERNAND, but even the seasons no longer mattered.

"Does God dream?" Delphine asked but only Escoffier could hear her. It was nearly 2 a.m. Sabine was in the kitchen warming the milk for his nightcap. Everyone in the house was asleep; they had said their goodbyes to Delphine once more, perhaps for the last time, and the children, grandchildren, great-grandchildren, grandnieces and grandnephews fell exhausted into their beds.

Escoffier was asleep, too. He had been confined to his room; the doctor told him his heart was leaking again. He had become unsteady, always dizzy and unwilling to eat. Time had lost its meaning, past and present slipped through his mind without a destination.

"What would He dream of?" she asked. Her voice was so clear it was as if she were in the room with him.

"What contains King Edward potatoes, garlic, butter, Cantal cheese and pepper?"

"*Aligot?*"

"Yes."

"And our Mr. Boots, what does he dream of?"

"I have no idea."

"Of course you do."

She knew, of course. She always knew.

He wanted to laugh but could not find the heart for it. "Are you afraid?" he asked.

"No. I'm thinking of *aligot*."

"I would think God dreams of it."

"It's all I can think about now."

"I love you, Madame Escoffier."

"There were times when you had forgotten this."

He said nothing. It was true and they both knew it.

"To be forgotten is the saddest thing of all," she said.

Escoffier held his hands up to the wall. If Sabine had opened the door to his room, he would have appeared to be holding it up, but it was the other way around. It was, through the power of Delphine's voice, holding him to the earth.

"Am I awake?" he asked.

"Does it matter?"

And she said nothing more.

Escoffier fell back into his own dreams again. Mud was everywhere. *War.* It was cold against his feet; it was in the bowl of broth he was given for his meal, and in the water he cleaned himself with. It was in the hollow sucking sound of his boots as he was marched though the field filled with bones of the dead picked clean by dogs and the desperate. And there was that smell again, he could not escape it— the sweet green yellow mist of mustard gas. It was difficult to forget how it sometimes reminded him of stone mustard and sometimes of garlic and how even when the fog of it had rolled away, the bodies still reeked from it.

"Monsieur Escoffier?"

He awoke in a cold sweat. "Sarah?"

Sabine sat down on the edge of the bed. "Your milk will get cold, Monsieur."

"Your leg is better?"

"Still gone."

Sabine had grown accustomed to the confusion. At this moment, he was, obviously, back in the time of the Great War. Sarah's leg had been amputated right before it began. She'd taken a fall off the stage and it never quite recovered, and so she was carried to the front on a chaise longue to entertain the troops.

"Drink your milk," she said, but he would not.

He lectured her at great length about her safety at the Front and ended with "You must be careful. What would I do without you, Rosine?"

"Cook," she said. "It's what you always do."

"True."

He'd fallen asleep in the middle of his writings. The bed was littered with pages; ink stained the sheets. Sabine picked up the work and began to read as he spoke about the Kaiser, Dear Bertie, and then, suddenly, Mussolini.

"His father was a blacksmith, as was mine. He is very small, too. Why are we so alike? What does this mean?"

He was panicked again. Talk of war always did that to him now. Sabine sat on the side of his bed, holding the pages of his memoir. "This work is very good. You are quite correct. There are too many patron saints. Saint Fortunat, I agree with you. Only male cooks, why? In most professional kitchens, women need to be prayed for."

"I am awake?"

"Of course."

She handed him the mug of milk; it was now cold. A thick skin had formed on the top. There was no money anymore for his nightly split of champagne but he didn't seem to notice.

"This is a very good chapter, but there's no recipe in it."

"What do you mean?"

"The other chapters had recipes. The other ones that you wrote."

Escoffier looked at the pages. His eyes were red-rimmed and glossy. He slipped from this world to that. She took the pages from him.

"Tomorrow," she said. "We will add a recipe tomorrow." She turned to leave and he caught her by the hand.

"Sabine?"

"Yes?"

"Do you know how to make *aligot*?"

"*Non.*"

"Ask Bobo to show you."

"I will," she said, but did not. Madame's death soon covered everything like fine gray soot.

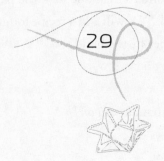

29

THE NEXT MORNING, ESCOFFIER SEEMED HEALTHIER, AS if released from some horrible burden. Happy even. His face had a ruddy look to it. The children, grandchildren and grandnieces and grandnephews tried not to notice. He asked for both breakfast and lunch and ate them.

"It's obscene," the nurse told the doctor. "The wife dies and the old man is reborn."

"Do you understand what we're saying, Papa?" Paul asked gently. "About Mother."

"Yes. Of course," Escoffier said. "What should we have for supper? Sabine, did Mr. Boots deliver a package recently?"

"Is there something you'd like?"

The old man handed her a list. At first it looked like gibberish, the handwriting was so shaky, but it clearly was a grocery list. She read it aloud to make sure. "Eggs, white truffles, caviar—"

"Truffles, caviar?" Paul said. "Is that really appropriate?"

"Of course."

Paul took the blankets and covered his father's shaking hands. "Sabine, leave us."

"I'll be in the kitchen."

Bobo was waiting for her there.

"And?"

"He's happy."

She handed him the stack of pages that Escoffier had been working on. "There's nothing here, though. Just stories, mostly. The recipe for fried chicken looks very good." Then she handed him the shopping list.

"White truffles?"

She shrugged.

"What time?"

"19:00."

"Will that be enough time?"

"It will have to be."

Overhead, the grandchildren, great-grandchildren, grandnieces and grandnephews ran down the hallway, then down the front stairway.

She shook his hand. "Thank you, chef."

"And you, chef."

And he was gone.

Paul sat at the foot of the bed and watched his father tumble in and out of sleep. The thin winter light made Escoffier seem grayer than he should be, smaller than he should be. He looked like a stranger, which, in so many ways, he was.

"Does Jeanne have the *Petite Mignonne?*" he asked when he finally woke.

"Peaches?"

The question took Paul back to his own small kitchen, his wife,

Jeanne, and Escoffier, long retired, sweating joyously together creating pots of exotic jams and jellies. Each new fruit—Italian elderberries, white raspberries from the Alps, and Queen Victoria's favorite, the Purple Mangosteen from Indonesia—created a new puzzle that could only be solved by sugar and more sugar and high heat and laughter.

"We are schemers," Escoffier said to his daughter-in-law. "Are we not?"

Jeanne would kiss him sweetly. "You are the schemer. I am merely the schemer's apprentice."

"My magicians," Paul would call them both and they shyly, ruddy-faced and pleased, would smile.

We come to love so late, Paul thought.

"I need them for your mother," Escoffier said.

She is gone, he thought. *Please remember.* "It is not peach season. June, I think."

"But Jeanne was to go to the market. Did she not? Are the children ill?"

"They are fine."

"But the peaches?"

"When you are better."

"No. Jeanne knows. The Royal George and *Gross Mignonne*, fat and obscene, are everywhere but the *Petite Mignonne* is so remarkable: white-skinned and small as a flat stone. It is so rich and filled with juice, that mingling of wild rose and honey, that you finally know heaven. And such a surprise they are—so complex. When you pick them if they are in the branches that are shaded, they are merely a blush of yellow. However, if you pick them in the full light, they are bright red. It is amazing."

"We will get peaches."

"No. Not just any peaches. *Petite Mignonne*. I must insist. Tell

Jeanne. They are like small hearts hiding from the sun, ripe only when broken. A beautiful metaphor. Your mother will be quite pleased."

Paul turned away. He didn't want Escoffier to see him crying. The old man reached out and took his son's hand in his and kissed it. His lips were so cold.

"What is wrong, Paul?"

"You are confused, Papa."

"I am not."

Paul could not turn to face his father. He looked out the window. After a time he said, "She is gone, you know."

"Jeanne? Where would she go?"

"Maman est morte."

"She is only waiting."

Paul could not stop weeping. Escoffier kissed his hand again, leaned into him and whispered, "Hearts, both large and small, always hide from the sun and only show their true nature when broken. Is that not true?"

"It's just fruit."

"But not to a poet like your mother. To your mother, a peach is the impossible beauty of God."

Paul embraced his father—the small frail body—and could feel his heart beating, and then his own heart like an echo. He could feel them both leaking; both breaking, both lush and ripe and filled with the memory of sunlight. He held his father in his arms so gently, the old man fell into a deep dreamless sleep.

TWO WEEKS LATER, LA VILLA FERNAND WAS NEARLY
empty, hollowed out by grief. "Papa wants to be alone," Paul
told everyone, although he did not like the idea of leaving
him with strangers. He was eighty-nine, after all. And not well. But
the old man insisted.

"Just for a few days," he said.

Escoffier also ordered Sabine to clean the kitchen. "Package everything that is not needed. Label it. Place it in the cellar."

"And your bottles?"

"Break them."

"All of them?"

"All of them."

And so late that night, one by one, Sabine and Bobo threw the bottles
into the calm azure sea. The ships of the navy, *La Royale*, were dark, the
harbor hushed. Each bottle bobbed in the waves for several moments,
awaiting reprieve, then took on water and spun into the depths.

"Are you crying?" he asked.

"Are you hungry?"

At 2 a.m., when Sabine delivered his nightcap, Escoffier was not in bed, but waiting for her at his desk. He was dressed in his Louis-Philippe dress coat and striped trousers. "For you," he said. *"Le Guide Culinaire."* He opened to a page and began to read.

"The expression 'boiling hot' is unsuitable. Fat never boils. It burns first. This is true of all fat. To fry, oil should only be moderately hot."

"What are we frying?"

He handed her the book. "Joy, my dear. Do not forget joy." And then walked down the hallway, unsteady, to Madame Escoffier's bedroom and closed the door behind him.

Sabine was unsure of what to do. She sat on the floor outside Madame's room for a long time, listening. She was afraid to leave him alone. When she finally gathered her courage, she opened the door. The room still smelled of Madame Escoffier, of lavender and talc.

The curtains were pulled back, the lights of the city and the harbor below looked like so many fallen stars. Escoffier was asleep on top of the white lace sheets, still dressed in his Louis-Philippe dress coat and striped trousers. He seemed peaceful; she didn't want to wake him and so she gently closed the door behind her.

The next morning, Sabine laid out the food that Bobo had brought from the Grand. "I think these are the last truffles in the region," he told her. "We should stay with him."

"He wants to be alone for a while."

"He could burn the house down. Or cut himself. Or become disoriented."

"Or find joy."

When Escoffier finally came down to the kitchen that morning, he sat for a long time in the quiet. The smell of bleach, the silence—they seemed the same to him. Both had erased all traces of life from the room. Instead of rows of copper pans polished and waiting, there were only two pans—a Windsor and *pôele*, the "fraying-pan."

The warmth of the sun shining through the window made him sleepy but there was still so much work to do.

It is, after all, a terrible thing to be forgotten; he had never thought of it that way before.

A wire basket of eggs awaited: some were green, some the palest of pink. Some were speckled brown and others, blue and green. There were a few tiny gull eggs, a smattering of quail and two fat duck eggs. The farmer gave every egg he had to Bobo for Escoffier. Each one was beautiful in its own right.

Escoffier chose six of the brown. He'd not cooked by himself for years. The shells were tougher then he remembered. He had to tap them with a knife several times before they cracked; yolks broke, bits of shell fell into the bowl. He beat them gently and placed a clove of garlic on the end of the knife, a knob of butter in the *pôele* and closed his eyes.

The smell of sweet cream. The edge of garlic. His leaking heart.

At sunset, Bobo and Sabine arrived at the house with the rest of the food on Escoffier's list. They managed to get nearly everything including Russian caviar and angry lobsters but the Grand Hôtel could no longer get *foie gras*. There was talk of rationing; plans were already being drawn up.

Escoffier had changed into his chef's whites and was seated at the kitchen table surrounded by colored inks, a drawing pad, and dozens of old menus. He wore a single medal, the Rosette of an Officer of the Legion, which had been conferred upon him in 1928. Surprisingly Wilhelm II, the former Emperor, King and Commander-in-Chief, was there at the ceremony and said a few words.

"Of course, I came," he told him later. "We're friends after all, aren't we?"

After all.

After war, after Daniel, after it all—there he was. Queen Victoria's grandson. The war broke him. Germany had abandoned him. Escoffier had heard that he'd been living in exile in Holland, longing for English tea. And that he'd become afraid of barbers. That looked to be true. His hair had turned white and hung down his back. Untrimmed, his mustache grew wild around his lips.

He'd renounced the war. "It was nothing that I ever wanted," he told anyone who listened but few did. It was not just that he had been the enemy, but accusations of homosexuality had made him an outcast.

"Have you forgotten me, old friend?"

He had. The last time Escoffier even thought of Wilhelm was the night he retuned home to La Villa Fernand after his voyage on the RMS *Berengaria*. That was the last night Madame Escoffier had been well; the last night she had actually cooked for him with her own hands.

"We are friends after all," Escoffier reassured him. And the battered man kissed him as a brother would. Embraced him, weeping.

To be forgotten is the saddest thing. The Rosette of an Officer of the Legion now served as a reminder of that.

"Where do we begin?" Bobo asked.

"Bones," Escoffier said. "They hold memory in their marrow; they are the essence of a life lived."

"And so we begin with stock?"

"Sabine, the small Canton bowls, please. One ladle. Then taste. Truly taste it. In silence. In reverence. Then ask yourself what you are tasting. And then add another ladle, this time with thin slices of truffle, enough to cover the top. Using too little truffle is wasteful. You need an opulent amount for full impact. Let the heat from the soup warm it. Then again, taste it. In silence."

The old man handed Bobo a recipe. "*Oeufs Brouillés à la Bohémienne,* Bohemian Scrambled Eggs. It has truffles and is served in a brioche. Lovely."

"For Madame?"

"*Non.* For Bobo, our *'Bohémiene.'* "

"And for Madame?" Sabine asked.

Escoffier put his arm around Bobo. "Do you know how to make an *aligot*?"

"I know of it, of course. I've never made one. Potatoes and cheese. Whipped for a very long time. Very simple."

"It only seems simple. Make it for Sabine. Madame Escoffier would like that."

Escoffier put his arm around Sabine, too, and held them both for a moment. They could feel his thin bones rattle with each breath.

"And the dish for Madame?" Sabine asked.

He walked away without another word.

"He just needs some sleep," she said.

"Or help. What would it hurt if we made a menu and said it was his? Who would know?"

Sabine unpacked the baskets. "Champagne. Caviar. Eggs. Lobster. Tarragon. Crème fraîche. White truffles. Peas and pigeons."

"The makings of a romantic meal."

"What of the *aligot*? There is cheese and potatoes."

"*Bourgeois.* This is the wife of Escoffier."

Sabine put the veal stock in the Windsor pan to heat. When it was ready, she measured one ladle of stock into each blue bowl. They sat in the stark kitchen, in silence, in reverence. One spoon after the other— the stock was dark, primal. Roasting the bones added a surprising richness and depth. "You were right," he said. "But then you knew that."

She took the white truffle from the basket. "Let's not," he said. "We'll save it for tomorrow. Papa can join us."

"Then this," she said and picked up the two lobsters and set them on the table near the bowl. They smelled of the ocean. "Now close your eyes and taste again."

The stock was scented with lobster, as if the creatures were already part of the meal.

"Clever girl."

"Lobster, *crème fraîche,* tarragon and shallot?"

"Lobster with tarragon cream?"

"And veal stock. The preparation? Not boiled, too common. Broiled dries."

"Fricassée d'Homard à la Crème d'Estragon."

"Fricassee, yes. And named à la Madame Delphine Daffis Escoffier?"

"It would sell many covers." He took ink and paper and began to write.

"Very good," she said. "Write this, too—'When it comes to the act of preparing lobsters, one must first open a bottle of the very best champagne that one can find. I am quite fond of the Moët.' "

Sabine poured the champagne they had brought into a glass bowl and without hesitation plunged the struggling lobsters into it head first. "Hold the lobster until he is sedated and a peaceful death can be assumed."

"An entire bottle?"

"He told me this himself."

They watched as the lobsters began to slow. Sabine turned the oven on high and continued to dictate.

"Now you must ask yourself an essential question. Are you a sensitive person or a beast like me? If you are a beast, you should simply cut the lobsters cleanly down the middle without a second thought."

"That's ridiculous. How else can you fricassee if not to cut them in two?"

"You can put them in a hot oven until they stop moving."

"No one's going to do that."

She tossed the lobsters into the oven. Slammed the door shut.

"They'll overcook."

"They'll be fine."

Bobo poured some Moët from the bowl into the two jelly jars. "To Papa."

"The tears of lobsters."

Sabine checked her watch; it was well past supper. She hadn't eaten. She wanted a cigarette, but not now. Not in the kitchen.

"The rest of it should be simple," Bobo said. "Chop tarragon, shallot. Add butter to a *pôele*. Sauté. Add shelled lobster tail and then *crème fraîche*. Cover. 10 minutes."

"Even a housewife could do it?"

"Even you. It can be on the menu next week. *Un Dîner d'Amoureux from Escoffier to Escoffier.* We will begin with scrambled eggs served in their shell with wild osetra caviar and follow with a casserole of pigeon and peas. Pigeon would be an amusing addition. *Le Pigeon aux Petits Pois en Cocotte.* Then finish simply with wild strawberries served with Brie that has been drizzled with candied lavender and honey. A refreshing finale, not heavy. This way the lovers will still have energy for each other."

Sabine took the lobsters out of the oven. Split them in half. Chopped the herbs. Bobo poured her another glass of champagne from the bowl.

"He could deny he wrote this," she said.

"We'll insist."

"If he didn't want to create a dish for his wife, perhaps it was for private reasons."

Bobo took a long sip from his glass. "It is a romantic story that he created one last menu for his wife of sixty-odd years, is it not?"

"But it is just a story."

"The story is everything."

Upstairs in his room, Escoffier was still working. His hands shook so badly that the ink stained his hands, his desk and the cuffs of his neatly pressed shirt. He could barely read what he'd written, but he wrote furiously,

"This is a difficult dish; do not allow the seemingly simple ingredients to deceive you. Potatoes. Butter. Cream. Each ingredient must be put together in a particular fashion and in the prescribed manner. Every choice you make, every step you alter, affects your ability to change the ordinary into the extraordinary. You must be brave. You cannot falter. This is a dish of quiet miracles. You must believe in them."

He wrote so quickly that his hand began to cramp. He had to hurry to finish. After all, Madame Escoffier was waiting.

The Complete Escoffier: A Memoir in Meals

CHERRIES JUBILEE

Always name a successor to manage your kitchen. Groom him well and keep him at all costs. The fire at the Carlton made me realize this. Even though I was at the age of retirement, I was unwilling to accept it.

The fire came up through the kitchen elevator and reached the fourth and fifth floors of the hotel within minutes. There are various versions as to how it started. I was not in the kitchen at the time, but upstairs in my rooms meeting with a publisher. Many of the hotel guests were changing for dinner and were in various stages of undress. Some were in their baths.

When the fire made its way up the elevator shaft, the floor beneath me caught fire and began to smoke. When the doors opened, I ran into the hallway and all I could see was smoke. I could hear screaming and praying. Smoke was everywhere and the elevator I had just been standing in burst into flames.

"Come with me!" I shouted and continued to shout. "Follow me!" I knew where the fire escape was. "Take my hand. Take my hand."

And they did. I took the hand of the woman next to me and she took the next person's hand and one by one we formed a chain, some of us dressed, some of us naked, but all of us holding on to each other. We raced the flames. As we ran I threw open every door, screaming, "Follow me. Follow my voice."

And then suddenly I thought, *Where is Finney?*

The Broadway actor Jameson Lee Finney was an agreeable sort of man. He'd come to Europe for a vacation and was departing within the week to rejoin his new bride in America. He often held court in the dining room and was always complimentary to me about the fish: the sole in particular. How he loved it.

Americans can be very enthusiastic about many things, including fish.

"Monsieur Finney?"

He did not answer although I had seen him go to his room to dress for dinner just moments before I entered the elevator.

When I finally pushed through the door of the fire escape, the cold night air pushed the smoke back. I could not see Jameson anywhere. The hallway was black with smoke, and dark, but I knew where his room was; three doors from mine. I took a deep breath and ran back for him. His door was unlocked. I ran in.

"Finney?!"

Nothing. Fire suddenly wrapped itself around the doorway. "Monsieur Finney?!" No answer. My lungs were closing down. I pulled the blanket from the bed.

I saw the bathroom door.

I remember thinking that I should open it. But the fire was suddenly moving through the room. I wrapped the blanket around me, and ran into the hall. The blanket was burning. Fire slid down walls as if water.

"Finney?!"

I ran. I ran as fast as I could and at the end of the hallway, I dropped the blanket, and threw myself through the open door of the fire escape.

The guests were all still standing on the roof. Trapped. The fire had burned the two floors below us. I looked over the edge; there was a naked woman hanging from a balcony. One floor below her, a man in a towel was getting ready to jump to the street below.

Our only salvation was to leap across to the next building, His Majesty's Theater, and then make our way down that fire escape and out into the street.

"Jump!" I said. "Everyone jump!"

It was only two or three feet at the most, but no one moved.

On the street below, people were screaming. "Jump."

No one moved.

"Follow me."

I took off my shoes and jumped across to the building, then opened my arms. "I'll catch you," I said. "Follow me."

One by one, the guests leapt across into the night, into my arms and into safety. I often staggered back, nearly toppled by the weight of them, but no matter. We were all safe.

In the sinister glow of the flames, we applauded. Joyous. Relieved.

I tried to keep Finney out of my mind. *He is safe. Safe.*

The moment was so moving and so tragic that I have never forgotten it.

"Follow me."

Two hundred fifty firemen and twenty-five engines soon arrived on the scene. My kitchen was flooded, although the dining room was untouched. While the firemen worked above us putting out the flames, my staff found their way to the kitchen. At 1 a.m. the press found us working to salvage whatever we could. There was at least two million francs worth of damage.

Apparently, I was asked what I thought about the fire. I don't remember being asked anything at all.

"What do you expect?" I was quoted as saying, "I have roasted so many millions of chickens in the twelve years I have been at this hotel that perhaps they wanted to take their revenge and roast me in turn. But they have only succeeded in singeing my feathers."

I remember that we were all standing in the kitchen laughing. But I try not to think about that.

Despite the damage, we reopened within the week. Our first menu included *Soles Coquelin,* Jameson Lee Finney's favorite dish. He so loved fish. When they found him he was in the bathroom, naked. His body was burned beyond recognition.

I often think of him paralyzed by fear, waiting to be saved.

It was time to relinquish my post.

And so, I groomed Ba. Nguyễn Sinh Cung was his proper name. "The Accomplished," he said it meant in Vietnamese, although everyone called him "Ba." He was a frail young man, kindhearted, intelligent and polite. He cared for the poor, as I did. The first time he came to my attention was when he was a dishwasher. He would often send large uneaten pieces of meat back to the kitchen to be trimmed and saved.

When I asked him why he did this, he said, "These things shouldn't be thrown away. You could give them to the poor."

He did not yet know of our decades-long arrangement with the Sisters, our Quail Pilaf à la Little Sisters of the Poor and their Gala Nights.

Ba had a chef's heart, although most chefs would have just trimmed the meat, put it back on the plate and served it to another diner.

"My dear young friend, please listen to me," I said. "Leave your revolutionary ideas aside for now, and I will teach you the art of cooking, which will bring you a lot of money. Do you agree?"

He stayed with me four years. I thought he would remain forever.

His French was beautiful. He was such a loyalist that he and his fiancée, a dressmaker, Marie Brière, wrote impassioned articles criticizing the use of English words by French sportswriters. They demanded Prime Minister Raymond Poincaré outlaw such Franglish as *"le manager," "le round,"* and *"le knock-out."* I agreed entirely.

We spent many a pleasant afternoon perfecting the art of *pâte brisée.* Pastry was a passion of his. More butter, less butter; one kind of flour or the other—he had the mind of a chemist and would cheerfully spend hours working to create the perfect crust. He was a very careful man.

I now believe that the fire would not have happened if Ba had been there. And if it did, he would have opened that bathroom door. Despite his frailness, Ba had a fearless air about him.

Unfortunately, one evening after the kitchen had closed Ba came into my office and resigned. The French had overthrown the Emperor of Vietnam, Duy Tan. I felt as if I had betrayed Ba myself.

"It is time, my friend," he said. *"Adieu, mon ami."* He kissed me on both cheeks. "I hope that someday my people will call me 'Hồ Chí Minh,' 'Bringer of Light.'"

I did not know what to say.

The night Ba walked out of my kitchen, I had the same feeling that I had the night of the fire, the same helplessness.

"Follow me," I said but he was already out the door and could not hear.

Later, I was told that Ba changed his name to Nguyễn Ái Quốc, Nguyen the Patriot, and had been held in prison until he'd died of tuberculosis.

Although the information was from a low-ranking French government official, and therefore suspect, the thought still pains me. If this is true, this good, kind man died without becoming the "Bringer of Light," without leaving a legacy in the world.

"Follow me."

If only he had heard me. Not everyone can make a mark on this world, but Ba could have. He had that quality. He was a leader. But now he will be sadly forgotten.

There is so much forgetting in this world. My Cherries Jubilee is a very good example of this.

While everyone who eats this dish will always think of the great Queen Victoria, her Jubilee, and remember that cherries were her favorite food, the recipe does not contain ice cream. It never did. If there had been ice cream, the dish would not have been so embraced by the Queen as representative of her spirit as a monarch. It was the lushness of the cherries, the dark sweetness that she enjoyed. They are by design an erotic fruit—does a cherry not remind one of a woman's own dark fruit? This fact did not escape the Queen. She ate it greedily. She was a complicated woman.

And so, it is important that one understand the recipe correctly. It is as follows:

Simmer stoned cherries in sugar syrup. Drain. Place them in a golden bowl, which must be at least fourteen-carat weight, and reduce the syrup, thickening it with cornstarch or arrowroot diluted with cold water. Combine the syrup with a tablespoon of warmed kirsch and pour over the cherries. Step back. Set aflame.

As you can see, ice cream would be an insult. Unfortunately, some publishers print the ice cream version as the "real" recipe, and in some extreme cases, they even forget to mention my name.

This is why it is difficult to leave a legacy behind. Even when I write these pages, I think that if this book does not go to the publisher before I die, it will fall into the hands of others who will take my thoughts and change them. Maybe even this very chapter will, in the end, not include Ba. Or maybe it will mention Ba but not Cherries Jubilee because the editor will be embarrassed to have insight into the secret life of a queen. Or, maybe, he will just forget to put this chapter in.

Forgetting. Everyone is now forgetting.

Again, the Germans.

The only way to combat forgetting is to cook. A well-prepared dish adds beauty, depth and complexity to life. Food is a thing of enchantment and to believe in enchantment, and to weave its spell, is a radical and necessary act.

And so. Silently. Cook.

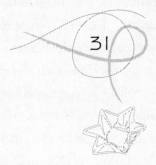

31

ESS THAN TWO WEEKS AFTER THE DEATH OF HIS WIFE, Delphine Daffis, a French poetess of distinction and officer of the Academy, Escoffier's heart gave out.

At 2 a.m. Sabine found him. His mouth was slightly open, as if hungry. She sat with him until the authorities came. "He shouldn't be alone," she told them.

"You're an odd girl," the man said.

After they took his body away, Sabine walked through the streets of Monte Carlo until she came to the long thin house overlooking the Grand Hôtel.

Bobo held her for a long time, until she stopped crying. Until he did, too.

"He was released," his doctor told the newspaper and explained about Madame's long illness and peaceful death. "They had a great love," he said, although he hardly knew them.

On February 14, 1935, the story ran around the world. And on that day, the celebration of the Feast of the blessed Saint Valentine, *Un Dîner d'Amoureux from Escoffier to Escoffier* featuring *Fricassée d'Homard à la Crème d'Estragon à la Madame Delphine Daffis Escoffier* was scheduled to make its debut at the Grand Hôtel.

It did not.

On the feast day, Auguste Escoffier, *Officier de la Légion d'Honneur*, was taken from La Villa Fernand to the village of his birth, Villeneuve-Loubert, to an ancient cemetery filled with rows of Escoffiers, as well as those who had married into the family, the Blancs and the Bernodins. The entire line extended back to the eighteenth century, slab after slab of marble overlooking the tiny village whose rows of red-tiled roofs lined the hillside. At the south edge of the ancient cemetery, there was a mausoleum with elegant wrought iron gates and a small vault with three marble plaques, side by side, "Delphine," "Daniel," now "Auguste."

The funeral was by invitation only. Sabine was left behind to pack up the rest of La Villa Fernand. The bank called the notes on the house and the manager himself delivered the papers to Paul, who did not know his father's financial problems were that extreme but was not entirely surprised. Sabine was told to inventory and organize the remaining belongings of Escoffier so that the family could sort through the things they wished to keep and the things that they wished to sell to museums and libraries after the war. They knew there would be a demand for such things. He was, after all, Escoffier.

Bobo had not been invited, either. He arrived at La Villa Fernand later that night carrying a large hamper of food. Inside there were only two things: a salad of carrots, baby zucchini and spinach dressed in lemon and olive oil and a small baked pumpkin, hollowed out and filled with a stuffing of leftover lamb, cream, farmer's cheese and green olives. It was beautiful. The skin was shiny; the small lid was cocked to one side.

"Housewife cooking as you requested," he said and opened the bottle of red wine that he had brought. "Is there anything left in the cellar?"

"Just a Moët. I found it on the last rack, in the back. I think it was forgotten."

Bobo put another log on the fire in the dining room. The pumpkin was still warm. Sabine sliced into it and picked up a bit with her fingers. It was soft, savory and only slightly sweet. The room filled with the scent of garlic and roasted lamb. They sat at the dining room table, next to each other, knees touching. Bobo handed her a glass of wine.

"It's odd without him," he said and his voice echoed.

She raised her glass to the heavens, and so did he.

"This pumpkin is very good," she said.

"From Provence. My pastry chef wrote it down for me."

"Unfair." She took another forkful. " 'Tell me what you eat and I will tell you who you are?' How will I know you?"

"Mystery is good."

Bobo gave her a copy of the menu that they had created together. "A keepsake," he said. The *Dîner d'Amoureux from Escoffier to Escoffier* was printed on a deep red parchment, with each course embossed in burnished gold leaf.

She ran her fingers over the lettering. "Elegant and yet savage. Just like the heart of a chef."

"People would have eventually found out it was just our imaginings of Papa's heart, and not the real thing."

"We could have said it was ours, in honor of them."

"People get funny about the dead. Who are we to honor a master?"

"It's too beautiful to waste."

"True. It did everything a fine meal should. It told a story. It made me imagine what my own heart would be like after all those years of marriage. The subtleness of the eggs and caviar; the richness of the lobster—it all made me think. I even had it printed in a way that was regal and slightly tarnished but still, hopefully, beautiful. As I think my heart would be."

Above them, the floor creaked. For a moment it seemed as if Escoffier were in his room again. Writing.

"Old houses," Bobo said.

Sabine handed him the paper that she had found on the floor next to Escoffier's bed. He read it carefully.

"Mashed potato with white truffles?"

"It's like an *aligot* because it's whipped so long, but it seems unique, does it not?"

"It speaks of magic but it is just mashed potatoes."

"But it is for Madame."

"And no one can ever know. The great Escoffier could not wish mashed potatoes, even with truffles, as the only dish that he dedicated to his wife."

Bobo poured a bit more wine into their glasses. "Where will you go now?"

"My father wants me to come back to Paris. Tomorrow."

"And tonight?"

"I have a few boxes to put away."

"I could leave the kitchen light on for you at the house."

He said this so shyly, at first Sabine wasn't sure what he meant but then he shrugged. His face was indeed beautiful, his blue eyes tired. His hair was going gray in fits and starts although there was a calmness to him that she hadn't noticed before. *Heaven is a lonely place.*

"People will talk."

"If they do, we could do something about it. Eventually. If you like."

"Or we could do nothing and enrage my father."

"If you like."

Bobo kissed her. Just once. No more. "It feels like he's watching."

"He is."

And yet the very timbers of the house, the floors, the ceilings, all felt bloodless, like bones, drying, the marrow worn away by life itself.

Bobo packed the remains of their dinner. Sabine watched as he walked past the garden and out into the street.

She picked up the dishes and put them in the sink. *Let the banker wash them,* she thought, and put on the last clean apron and weighed out a pound and a half of small yellow potatoes. She placed them in the Windsor pan with just enough water to cover as they boiled, about four inches. While the potatoes cooked, she took a survey of what was left in the house.

The furniture had been covered with white sheets and pushed to one side to await the van to take it. Whatever was deemed trash had already been burned in the garden. In Delphine's room, the old Victorian coat lay across the bed where Sabine had left it. It still shed, still smelled musty. Paul told her to pack it away. "We'll tell the auction house it belonged to the Queen."

Sabine couldn't. It was beautiful. Floor-length with oversized sleeves and a high collar made from some sort of dyed mink. And Papa did create the recipe and so it was rightfully hers.

She put it on and went into the kitchen.

"One cup of warm heavy cream, ten tablespoons of unsalted butter—emulsify this on the lowest possible heat. Every action you take makes a small impact on the final product. You must cook the potatoes in their jackets and with the least amount of water, or else they will not properly absorb it. You must emulsify the butter and cream in a continuous motion, or else it will separate.

"How much attention you pay to something so simple, so basic, like love, is crucial."

The last bottle of champagne was chilled. Sabine opened it and poured herself a glass. Took off the apron. She did not remove the old fur coat. She did, however, twist her long hair into a topknot, as her father had told her to do when she first came.

She worked as if she were a ghost.

With the wooden spoon, she beat the potatoes over low heat to dry them and then bit by bit added the cream and butter emulsification. She did exactly what the recipe said but it didn't seem to work. The potatoes became stiff and formed a small round ball around the spoon. She lowered the heat, splashed champagne into the pan. Tried again. It still didn't work.

She boiled more potatoes, cut the last of the butter and started again. After a time, the potatoes slowly, gently, became puree. The recipe required that half the mixture then be placed in a buttered baking dish, covered with a thick layer of thinly sliced white truffles and a layer of Parmigiano-Reggiano cheese, and dotted with butter. "Repeat until all the potatoes are used. Then place in a very hot oven for 10 to 15 minutes until a brown crust is formed."

The baking dishes were all packed away and so she used the cast iron "fraying pan." It was not pretty but it worked. The crust turned golden brown and filled the house with the rich perfume of white truffles and warm cheese.

Sabine took her glass of champagne and the pan of potatoes into the dining room and sat at the table. The last log in the fireplace was nearly cinders. She took the recipe and tossed it into the fire. It flamed for a moment, snapped and then caught. Glorious and burning.

Bobo was right. It was, after all, only mashed potatoes. Time consuming. Difficult to make. Not a legacy at all.

It was nearly dawn. Like a swimmer short of air, the sun was pushing its way up through the blinding noise of blue that was the sea. The sky surrounding La Villa Fernand was bleeding color and light.

That fur, that hair, that divine face, ghost after ghost. This life. Or that.

And then she took a spoonful.

"Joy."

NOTES

This novel is based on the bones of facts. Auguste Escoffier pioneered the modern dining experience. He was the first to coin the word *deliciousness*, which translates to "umami." He was separated from his wife for decades and yet retired with her. He died shortly after she did. He also won her in a pool game. The Savoy fired him over accusations of extortion and theft. He did send packages to a Mr. Boots in Southsea, England, who disappeared without a trace after Escoffier left The Savoy's employ. He also was a practicing Catholic and a philanthropist who was linked to both Sarah Bernhardt and Rosa Lewis. There was a fire. He was a hero. His mentorship of Hồ Chí Minh is disputed, but has never been disproved, so the former President of the Democratic Republic of Vietnam does indeed make an appearance in these pages.

After spending two years on this project, that's about all I know for sure.

In my research, I used a wide variety of sources including Kenneth James's biography, *Escoffier: The King of Chefs*; *My Double Life: The Memoirs of Sarah Bernhardt*; *Blue Trout and Black Truffles:*

The Peregrinations of an Epicure by Joseph Wechsberg; *The Gourmet's Guide to London* (1914) by Nathaniel Newnham-Davis; *In the Courts of Memory, 1858–1875: From Contemporary Letters* by Lillie de Hegermann-Lindencrone (1912), in addition to articles from several newspapers and Wikipedia. While delightful, many of these works were wildly contradictory and some were completely incorrect.

Luckily, this is a work of fiction.

The list of facts, and alleged facts, go on and on but what is left unsaid is often the most interesting part of any life. That is where this book begins.

Escoffier's cookbooks, memoir, letters and the articles about him created the voice of this character but we all know that I did not write about the real man. The elegant savage found in these pages is who we all are when we address the plate. The magician, the priest, the dreamer, the artist—it is our most hungry self.

That is the only fact that truly matters.